Nina Milne has always dreamed of writing for Mills & Boon Romance—ever since she played libraries with her mother's stacks of Mills & Boon romances as a child. On her way to this dream Nina acquired an English degree, a hero of her own, three gorgeous children and—somehow!—an accountancy qualification. She lives in Brighton and has filled her house with stacks of books—her very own *real* library.

Christine Rimmer came to her profession the long way around. She tried everything from acting to teaching to telephone sales. Now she's finally found work that suits her perfectly. She insists she never had a problem keeping a job—she was merely gaining "life experience" for her future as a novelist. Christine lives with her family in Oregon. Visit her at www.christinerimmer.com.

MAROONED WITH THE MILLIONAIRE

NINA MILNE

THE NANNY'S DOUBLE TROUBLE

CHRISTINE RIMMER

MILLS & BOON

First Published in Great Britain 2018
by Mills & Boon, an imprint of HarperCollinsPublishers,
1 London Bridge Street, London, SE1 9GF

Marooned With the Millionaire © 2018 Nina Milne
The Nanny's Double Trouble © 2018 Christine Rimmer

ISBN: 978-0-263-26493-7

38-0518

MIX
Paper from
responsible sources
FSC C007454
FSC
www.fsc.org

This book is produced from independently certified FSC™ paper to ensure responsible forest management.

For more information visit: www.harpercollins.co.uk/green

Printed and bound in Spain
by CPI, Barcelona

MAROONED WITH THE MILLIONAIRE

NINA MILNE

To one of my very best friends,
who has proved the healing power of love.

CHAPTER ONE

MARCUS ALRIKSON LEANED back in the ergonomic comfort of the luxurious leather chair—his one extravagance in an office he spent way too much of his time in. But needs must when the devil drove. Even when the devil was his own personal demon—the one that ensured he never lost sight of the need to succeed.

Right now his focus was on ensuring that the royal wedding was a success. It could be argued that as Chief Advisor to the Prince of Lycander his remit didn't include wedding planning— and in truth the bride's dress and the groom's choice of tie didn't interest him in the slightest. The security of the royal nuptials, however, was very much his responsibility—after all alongside his role of Chief Advisor he also headed up Alrikson Security, a byword in security provision services across Europe.

There was also the fact that he had a great deal of respect for Prince Frederick—the Prince was a good man, a ruler with a vision for the future of Lycander. A vision shared by Marcus.

He focused on the screen and studied his plan. His formidable brain assessed the risks, considered the most acute of angles, searched for the tiniest of chinks in the armour of defence and protocol that surrounded the upcoming wedding extravaganza.

In mere weeks Prince Frederick of Lycander would marry Sunita Bashwani-Greenberg, an ex-supermodel and mother of his two-year-old son Amil.

The union was a love-match that the people of Lycander had mixed feelings about. Frederick's ascent to the throne had been shrouded in tragedy and scandal, and it had taken him two years of fair and just rule even to begin the process of bringing the Lycandrian people round. And the throne still wobbled—Frederick had many enemies who would happily overthrow him and end Lycander's monarchy, enemies who would sabotage the wedding.

Not on Marcus's watch. It was crucial that this wedding went without a hitch.

His frown intensified as he glared at the screen, looking up only when he heard a knock on the door.

'Come in.'

A rare smile touched his lips as his sister entered the room. 'Elvira.'

'Hey, big bro.'

'What can I do for you?'

As always he felt a profound relief when he saw his little sister, and a sense of gratitude that her life had worked out—that she seemed to have adjusted after her shaky start. Now twenty-two, she was content and successful and in her final year of studying law at university.

Speaking of which… His smile vanished. 'Shouldn't you be at lectures?'

'Relax. I'm free of lectures this morning. My tutor's ill, so I thought I'd drop in.'

He should have known Elvira wouldn't skip a lecture; for all his big-brother crackdown he knew that his sister took her studies seriously, and truly appreciated the opportunities life had granted her.

No, not life. Those opportunities had come courtesy of death—the death of their criminal, alcoholic, violent parents in a fire. The same fire that a twelve-year-old Marcus had rescued his younger sister from, the identical inferno he had failed to rescue his parents from. Jonny and Alicia Brockley had perished.

Marcus and Elvira had been adopted, and their lives had dramatically altered course. For the better. The knowledge was a permanent biting ache of guilt.

Marcus shook his head—now was not the moment for a trip down the ravaged and torturous twists of memory lane.

'Anything in particular on your mind?' he asked as he gestured for Elvira to sit, and waited as she curled up in the comfy chair he'd sequestered from one of the many rooms of the Lycander Palace. His office was a mishmash taken from the mounds of furniture stockpiled by previous royal incumbents.

'April Fotherington turned up at uni today…for "a chat".'

Marcus drummed his fingers on the desk in an irritated tattoo. April Fotherington was a writer for a popular up-market celebrity magazine, and she was in the process of writing a feel-good article on the Lycander wedding. With an emphasis on *feel-good*. That had been the deal Marcus had made with the magazine's editor-in-chief. In person. Emphatically.

So a question begged. 'Why would April need to have a chat with you? You don't know Frederick or Sunita.'

'She wasn't asking about them. She was asking about Axel. About the night of his death and his relationship with Frederick.'

Damn it to hell.

Axel. He had been Marcus's best friend, Frederick's older brother, tragically killed in a car crash two years before. 'Do you think she knows anything?'

Elvira shrugged. 'I don't think she *knows* anything. But I think she suspects something is a bit off—which is a problem. April Fotherington is good at what she does and she may well pursue this angle.'

'Did you give anything away?'

Elvira narrowed her eyes. 'Of course I didn't. Give me *some* credit, Marcus.'

'Sorry—and I'm sorry you were put in this position.'

Frustrated anger welled inside him—the type that in his early years would have had him punching a wall. Now he had learnt to convert it into cold, hard determination.

'I'll deal with it. April won't bother you again.'

'Whoa—hold on.' Elvira frowned. 'Don't go overboard—all she did was ask a few questions, and I may be completely wrong to think she suspects anything. She was perfectly nice about it as well.'

'I get that. But I—'

'You hate that your little sister is involved in this. But it's not your fault. *Or* hers.'

Yet somehow it felt that way to him.

'Thank you, Elvi.' Marcus rose to his feet.

Elvira's brow creased into deeper grooves. 'Where are you going?'

He grabbed his leather jacket from the back of the chair and shrugged into it.

'I'm going to give you a lift to wherever you want to go, and then I am going to do my job and close April Fotherington down.'

April glanced down at her notebook, then up and around at her hotel room. Situated on the outskirts of Lycander's town centre, it was pleasant enough, though not extravagant—well within her editor's budgetary requirements. The room's impersonal anonymity suited her, being reminiscent of her own small London flat.

Chewing the end of her pencil, she stared down at the words she had written.

Fact One: Two years ago Axel, heir to the throne of Lycander, died in a fatal car crash after attending an official state function.

Fact Two: At said function Axel claimed that his younger brother Frederick had originally been asked to attend, and Axel had demanded to take his place.

Fact Three: Prince Frederick, then known as the Playboy Prince, instead attended a celebrity-packed party aboard a yacht.

Fact Four: In the here and now I have interviewed a political activist called Brian Sewell, who claims that, 'Axel should never have been there. Frederick bailed out at the last moment to attend some jet-setting party and Axel stepped up—just like he always did. Frederick didn't give a sh— Pardon me. He didn't give a damn about Lycander; he only cared about himself and his hedonistic lifestyle. He should have died in that car crash, not Axel. Axel didn't want to attend that function—he had other plans.'

April's gaze lingered on the words *died* and *car crash* and black despair threatened, jabbing at every nerve-end, twisting her brain with jagged flashes of memory.

Her baby son's face, his milky smell, the down of his hair as a newborn, the first gummy smile, the first toddling step... And then nothing. There would be no more firsts. No more anything.

Because Edward had died in a car crash.

Her fault—the knowledge throbbed and pulsed her brain.

Fact One: I was planning on leaving my husband, Edwards's father—Dean Stanworth.

Fact Two: Dean discovered my plans and arrived

*home in a drunken violent fury, snatched Edward
and drove off.*

*Fact Three: He crashed, and both he and Ed-
ward perished.*

Breathe, focus. She used all the tricks of the grief trade,
so carefully learned, and tried to numb the pain. One last
exhale and she was able to regard her notebook again, read
the facts about Axel with structured dispassion. Able to
block away the grief that clamoured behind the barricades.

The question now was: what next? Speak with Prince
Frederick about it? No. Too soon. She needed further veri-
fication—after all, there was every chance her source was
unreliable… Brian Sewell was a known anti-monarchist.
Yet the intuition born of three years of dedication to her
job—countless interviews—told her this was the truth.

Damn it.

She liked Frederick, she liked Sunita, and her commis-
sion was to write a happy piece—a feel-good fairy tale
article that indicated belief in a happy-ever-after. April
might not have achieved a happy-ever-after of her own,
once the glitter had blown away her own personal fairy
tale had decayed into a dark story of misery-ever-after.
But that didn't mean she begrudged happiness to others.
However—and there always seemed to *be* a 'however'—
she believed in the truth.

If *she* had faced up to the truth earlier, tragedy might
have been averted.

Relief swathed her as the phone rang, distracting her
from another visit to the past. It was imperative she kept
herself on track. Picking up the receiver, she identified
herself.

'Good morning, Ms Fotherington.' The hotel receptionist's professional bell-like tone was clear. 'Marcus Alrikson is here for your meeting.'

Marcus Alrikson? Meeting?

April's mind slalomed, raced, whirred as she considered the words. For a start she did not *have* a meeting scheduled with Lycander's millionaire Chief Advisor, because he had made it crystal-clear that he didn't see any need for one.

April hadn't taken it personally—Marcus Alrikson hadn't given a single press interview in the past two years. He was a man who wielded massive influence and acted behind the scenes. Of course she knew about him. A self-made millionaire by the age of twenty-five, thanks to his start-up company, Alrikson Security, and from a privileged background. He'd attended a prestigious school where he'd met Prince Axel of Lycander, and after Axel's death he'd been appointed Chief Advisor to Prince Frederick.

She'd *seen* him before too, of course, but only from a distance or in a photo, or in the very briefest of video clips as he strode through packs of reporters. Enough for her to garner the sense of a man who radiated an aura of tightly self-contained power, and to register the fact that he had the looks and build to wow the public, if he so wished.

Yet that desire was quite clearly *not* on the man's wish list—his expression always neutral with a veer towards grim.

So what was he doing here?

Clearly her meeting with his sister Elvira had rattled his cage.

Excellent.

'I'll be right down.'

Grabbing her oversized bag, she spared one glance at her reflection as she headed to the door. Good thing she always dressed 'business casual', and her wardrobe choices were simple. Today she'd opted for slim-leg trousers, a tucked-in shirt and a blazer. Sensible flat shoes. There was no need to do anything to her dark auburn hair; her chosen style was short, sleek and easy to maintain.

So she was ready to face whatever Marcus might throw at her—and she had no doubt there would be something. Marcus Alrikson was anti-press, and if he was here that meant his feathers had been seriously ruffled.

The lift took her down to the marble lobby, and she crossed to the curved reception desk and nearly screeched to halt. The man standing there was...*gorgeous*.

Those glimpses of him, those images, couldn't have prepared her for the reality of Marcus Alrikson in the flesh. Or for her visceral reaction to him. Her tummy twisted and her hormones fizzed out of their deep hibernation mode with a suddenness that had her brain at panic stations. Shock slowed her steps further.

April didn't *do* attraction; her hormones hadn't so much as whispered in the past years. In fact forget hibernation— she'd been pretty sure her hormones were stone-cold dead. And that had been fine by her. The fuse of attraction could set off a chain reaction that ended in misery—that was a life lesson she'd learnt. So *this* fuse was being doused right now.

Marcus's eyebrows rose and he raised his hand in salute. *Get a grip and get moving!*

As she headed towards him she reminded herself that she'd interviewed princes and billionaires, Hollywood A-listers and models. But, dammit, this man had a presence that had nothing to do with his undeniable wealth, status, or even his equally undeniable good-looks: dark unruly hair, a shade overlong, midnight-blue eyes, a firm jaw, and a strong nose that looked as if it might have broken at some point.

OK. So he was good-looking. But that wasn't the point. The point was the story—and she'd clearly provoked concern at the very least or he wouldn't be here. Yet he didn't look remotely worried, or angry, though there was a sense of taut energy in his stance—an energy she sensed was his perpetual state, a part of who he was.

'Mr Alrikson.'

There was a moment, a fleeting instant, when his expression registered the tiniest glimmer of surprise. Surprise and something else—his dark gaze had rested on her face, something had flickered and her treacherous body had responded, craving to move nearer to him.

Staunchly she kept her feet planted on the floor. 'This is unexpected.'

'Yes, it is.' He frowned, as if the words had escaped of their own volition. Then, 'Please, call me Marcus.'

She inclined her head, knowing that common courtesy indicated a need to shake hands. But she didn't want to. Stupid, she knew, but her body's reaction to him had caught her utterly off guard, wrong-footed her enough that it was a relief not to be in heels.

This was ridiculous. Her distrust of good-looking men was based on experience of the bitter kind. Handsome men had a different perspective on life—a belief that they were God's gift, and an easy arrogance that could lead to less than desirable character traits.

Never judge a book by its cover was a saying she believed in wholeheartedly.

'Marcus. I wasn't aware that we'd scheduled a meeting. In fact I am certain we didn't, because you made it very clear that you felt there was no need to meet me. Instead you very kindly had your office give me this scintillating quote: "I wish the couple every happiness".'

Easy does it, April.

She really did have to get a grasp of events. If she could pull off an interview with Marcus it would be a journalistic coup. So antagonising him was a rookie error she could ill afford. Blaming Marcus for throwing her into a loop-the-loop was foolish in the extreme.

'Yup. That about covers it.' Any initial response to her was clearly under control now, and his voice was an easy, deep drawl.

'So why are you here?'

'Because I thought you had been commissioned to write a feel-good article on the Lycander wedding—with an exclusive focus on the happy couple.'

'Yes. That's correct.'

'So why did you feel the need to accost my sister?'

'"Accost" is a strong word. I simply spoke with her.'

'Accost is an entirely *accurate* word. You accosted her at her university campus without any attempt to schedule a meeting.'

'I thought she might be helpful in shedding light on an…an angle I have come across.'

'I find that hard to believe. Elvira is barely acquainted with either the Prince *or* Sunita.'

'As I said, it's a different angle.'

'So I gather—and I look forward to hearing exactly what that angle is.'

April's mind weighed and discarded options. Her intuition that Elvira had been hiding something seemed vindicated now that here in front of her was a main player. But perhaps the most sensible option would be to decline to cross swords with a man who was undoubtedly a master fencer. Instead she should take this as tacit confirmation that there was some truth to her suspicions and pursue her investigation.

'I'm afraid I'm not ready to share yet.'

'I'm afraid that isn't acceptable.'

Now it was her turn to raise her eyebrows. 'Is that a threat?'

'Of course not. It's an observation. I have a deal with your magazine—if you are in the process of reneging on that deal then I have the right to know. Both the Prince and

Sunita have more than co-operated with you thus far, as have various palace officials. That co-operation will cease.'

A part of her knew she should be jubilant—he *must* be rattled. Yet he didn't look it—instead he looked utterly at ease…a man who believed he was in control of the situation.

'Sounds like a threat to me.'

'Not at all. Consider it a negotiation. Why don't I buy you a coffee and we can discuss terms?'

A sudden jolt of anticipation shot a frisson of awareness through her. On some stupid level she *wanted* this skirmish, and she knew the reasons why were more complex than her pursuit of an angle to a story. She had the horrible feeling it had something to do with the insidious tug of awareness her brain was desperately trying to shut down.

'Let's go,' she said.

CHAPTER TWO

MARCUS FORCED HIS expression to remain neutral. No way did he want to project any of the disquiet that had surfaced inside him. April had a reputation as being a writer with integrity; her articles never gossiped—or if they did the gossip was fact not rumour or speculation. Which was exactly why anyone with a secret to hide hoped to slip under her radar.

Unfortunately the Prince of Lycander *did* have a secret, and it looked as though April Fotherington's radar was abuzz. The angle she was in hot pursuit of was exactly the slope he *didn't* want her to climb. Because at the summit lay political disaster.

That was what he needed to focus on…shame his body had other ideas. One look at April and *va-va-voom*—he'd been worried his eyeballs would pop out on cartoon springs. Her beauty was undeniable, and yet he couldn't quite identify what it was about her that had caused such an intense tug of desire. Especially when she represented a danger to everything he had worked for over the past few years.

Perhaps it was best not to analyse the situation, or he might give in to the desire to study her at greater length, absorb her natural grace as she walked slightly ahead of him, check out the length of her legs, the slender span of her waist, the dark auburn of her hair that tapered onto the delicate nape of her neck…

Whoa. What was wrong with him? Right now April classed as the enemy, and his focus needed to be on shutting down this story—not ogling the opposition.

And so he continued through the lobby, eyes focused firmly above her head as they entered the hotel restaurant now nigh on empty in the post-breakfast pre-lunch lull. Scanning the room, he picked the optimum table—one that granted privacy and the opportunity to check the room for potential eavesdroppers.

He strode across the plush carpeted floor to a corner table, flanked by walls and potted greenery. A waiter materialised, pulled out chairs and proffered a menu, which Marcus waved away.

'I'll have a double espresso.'

'Latte for me, please,' April supplied.

He allowed himself to study her for a moment, telling himself it was a simple assessment to enable him to read her better. And if it unsettled her a little—well, all the better.

Dark auburn hair framed a heart-shaped face. Vivid green eyes of a colour he had never seen before—darker and softer than emerald—brought to mind forests and elven folklore. Her face held an allure that she seemed genuinely unaware of—there was no attempt at being coy, nor any overt flirtatiousness in her body language. And yet he could sense a simmer of awareness—the type of awareness that made his gaze linger a little too long on her generous lips, on the graceful tilt of her neck…

Stop. Get with the plan.

The point was to unsettle April, not himself. This situation was dangerous, and he needed to keep focused on what was important. April Fotherington's lips definitively did *not* come under that category.

'So...' he said.

'So?' she returned.

'Why don't you tell me what your angle is?'

Tipping her head slightly to one side, she contemplated him. No doubt wondering how little she could disclose and get away with.

Seeing the waiter approach, he raised a hand. 'Hang on. Our coffee's here.'

They both waited in silence as their drinks were carefully deposited in front of them, and then for a few more beats until the waiter was out of earshot.

'Go ahead,' he said.

She blew out an exaggerated puff of air. 'Telling you is a non-starter. Once I tell you, you'll try and kill the story.'

'Yes. We both know that. But if you *don't* tell me you'll lose all access to the Prince and his bride and we'll call in a different magazine.'

A frown creased her forehead. 'Isn't this overkill? All I've done is have a chat to your sister.'

'Not true, April, and we both know it. You also met with Brian Sewell.'

The anger he'd felt at that discovery resurfaced, and he forced his body to remain relaxed, his voice almost casual.

Her whole body stilled, but other than that she gave no indication of guilt. 'Yes, I did.'

'Did you approach him?'

'No. He approached me. I understand he is a great proponent of democracy and I wanted a different perspective to put into the article. I won't apologise for that.'

'I'm not asking for an apology. I'm asking you not to pursue whatever line he has cast.'

Green eyes met his with cool aplomb. 'I can't do that. If there is a story there I need to follow it.'

'Even if it isn't the story you have been commissioned to write?'

'Maybe it's a better story.'

'And that's all you care about, isn't it? The story? Circulation? Your reputation? And never mind the collateral damage.'

'No!' Her eyes flashed sparks at him as she pushed her cup away and leant across the table. 'I care about the truth. And if this story is true then clearly all *you* care about is covering up the truth.'

'I will tell you exactly what I care about. I care about Lycander. I care about my country and its people.'

'Then surely you believe that "your" people deserve the truth? That is all I want to discover. The truth.'

The fervour with which she spoke was quiet but absolute, and for a second it caused him to pause.

'Then perhaps you should choose your sources more carefully.'

'Meaning…?'

'Meaning Brian Sewell is not exactly a credible source. Plus, as I heard it, he was pretty plastered at your lunch yesterday—I'm not sure his drunken ramblings will stand up to scrutiny.'

Her green eyes narrowed and her entire body vibrated with outrage. 'Are you *spying* on me?'

'No. But I *am* keeping tabs on Brian Sewell. He is a dissident of the worst type.'

'There is no crime in being a dissident.'

'No, but there *is* a crime in organising and encouraging violent rallies—mobs made up of people who simply want an excuse to legitimise violence and mayhem.'

'Then why haven't you arrested him?'

Because the man was more slippery than a jellied eel. He played the part of a concerned citizen who simply wished to advocate a voice for democracy to perfection, but in reality he was no more than the leader of a criminal gang of nutters.

'Nothing would give me greater pleasure, believe me, and as soon as I have a watertight case against him Sewell *will* be behind bars.'

'Well, I believe a man is innocent until proved guilty, and right now Brian Sewell looks perfectly credible to me.'

'Brian Sewell is dangerous and manipulative.'

She snorted—there was no other word for it.

'Please give me *some* credit. I am not an idiot and I have no intention of being manipulated. If his claims don't stack up I won't publish them—or even refer to them in any form.'

'By then it may be too late—Sewell has spun you a web of dirt, and dirt sticks. To investigate you will have to ask questions, and then the story will gain momentum—the type of momentum that people like Sewell will harness. Then it won't matter whether it is true or not—the ramifications for Frederick will be huge, as well as casting a blight over his wedding.'

She shook her head. 'This still doesn't make sense. I get that you may be worried—but *this* worried? You must have to deal with stuff like this all the time. There must be plenty of people opposed to the monarchy, and I am quite sure you are more than capable of dealing with them and their stories. You've got your tightie-whities in a knot over this one because you think I may have something explosive—something *true*.'

There was a pause—then horror etched her face, along with a tinge of disbelief, and despite the seriousness of the conversation a smile tipped his lips.

'Lucky for me, I don't wear tightie-whities.'

The flush deepened and he knew with crystal clarity that she was wondering exactly what he *did* wear… And suddenly he couldn't help but wonder the same about her. Her gaze meshed with his and awareness swirled the air.

Then she shook her head. 'I don't think your choice

of underwear is salient right now. Or ever will be,' she added hurriedly.

She was so very right. Irritation sloughed over his skin. What the *hell* was he doing?

'The bottom line is that if Brian Sewell is telling the truth then I have a duty to disclose that truth.' She looked at him. 'But I'll tell you what I can offer.' She leant forward. 'Why don't you put your money where your mouth is? I'll interview *you*. You can comment on Brian Sewell's claims. If they aren't true then tell me flat-out that he's lying.' Her eyes were intent now. 'I am not after dirt. I don't want to blacken anyone's name or cause unnecessary harm or distress with salacious rumour. That's not what I do. I want the truth. So let me question *you* on the record about Brian Sewell's comments.'

For an insane moment he was tempted—to explain the truth and trust April to see that decisions that had been made on the back of guilt, misery and tragedy had been made for the greater good. Decisions had been made to cover up the truth not because anyone had done anything wrong, but because the truth might have resulted in the overthrow of the monarchy.

Prince Frederick *should* have been at that state function, and he *had* bailed out at the last minute because he'd wanted to attend a party to celebrate pulling off an amazing business coup. Axel had agreed to attend in his place and had decided to pretend that *he* had instigated the swap in order to show Frederick in a more favourable light.

Then had come the tragedy—on leaving the dinner Axel had been involved in a fatal car crash. If the people of Lycander had discovered that it should have been Frederick in that car they might have lynched him, and the monarchy might well have been overthrown. So there *had* been a cover-up. He had no idea how Sewell had got hold of the information, but he had. Maybe he had simply hazarded a lucky guess…but there it was—the less than shining truth.

He squashed the crazy, inexplicable temptation to share it. Surely he was too experienced to be hoodwinked by a pair of intense green eyes? How could he trust her? He barely knew her. Yes, perhaps she would reveal the truth in a sympathetic way, but it was too big a risk to take. Marcus would not throw everything and everyone he held dear to wolves and vermin like Sewell.

Prince Frederick of Lycander cared about his land and his people, and he was slowly but surely bringing Lycander back to a place of prosperity and fairness for all. The truth was not an option. Equally, though, there was no way he would lie—he'd be a fool thrice over to lie to a writer of April's calibre.

So, neither the truth nor a lie…

'No can do,' he said easily. 'I don't do interviews—under *any* circumstances. I won't make an exception to that rule, but I *will* show you why I think you should drop this story.'

Her brow creased in puzzlement. 'Show me?'

He rose to his feet, hitched his wallet from his jacket pocket and put some money on the table. 'Come with me. I'm going to take you on a tour.'

Her brow creased. 'A tour?'

'Yup.'

Her eyes narrowed in clear suspicion. 'Why? I don't get it. You're a busy man. Wouldn't it be easier to just answer some questions?'

'No. The minute I go on record this story gains publicity and credibility. You know it. I know it. So I'd rather do this differently.'

'What happened to the threats?'

'I'd prefer to try the civilised way first.' Because, whatever she was, she wasn't a run-of-the-mill writer or a gossip columnist. 'What do you say?'

Head tilted to one side, she considered, then nodded. 'OK. I'm intrigued. Let's go.'

A couple of phone calls later they exited the hotel lobby. What else could she have said? April mused as she pushed through the revolving door. No writer would have turned down the opportunity of a surprise tour from Marcus Alrikson. Problem was, she had a sneaking suspicion that no *woman* would turn it down either, and she had misgivings as to whether it was the writer or the woman in her that had acquiesced.

The writer, of course. It couldn't be any other way. The very *idea* of being attracted to Marcus Alrikson—to any man—made her shiver in repudiation. Never again. That side of her life had been laid waste and would remain desolate through her own choice. If her hormones were foolish enough to try for resurrection she would mow them down without hesitation.

'Where are we going?' she enquired as they walked along increasingly tourist-thronged pavements towards the city centre.

Marcus gestured around. 'What do you see?'

'A shopping mecca for those who love fashion.'

Designer names abounded—clothes most people could only dream of called out to those with money to burn or credit cards to burden.

His dark blue eyes scanned her outfit, swept her body from top to toe, and to her own irritation she blushed. Then his gaze returned to hers and a funny little thrill shot through her veins at the expression in his eyes—a smoulder that she knew she hadn't imagined.

'It sounds like you aren't one of their number.'

Sounds or *looks*? For an instant a stupid part of her bridled at his judgement, even though it was spot-on.

'No. I'm not.'

Once she had been intent on always looking good, because Dean had insisted on it. He'd wanted his wife to be 'a credit' to him—wanted every man in the room to envy him.

Standing there in the heat of the Lycandrian sun April froze...could almost hear Dean's rich Southern drawl. At the time she had taken his words as a sign of his pride in her, too smitten to see the truth—that to Dean she'd been a trophy, a prize and nothing more. So she'd made sure her clothes were the latest fashion, the most expensive and exclusive brands, had spent hours in the hairdressers, at the gym, putting on make-up. But now...

'I try to be professional, but that's as far as it goes. As part of my job I do keep up with the latest trends. Readers like details on what people are wearing.' She waved a hand around. 'Whilst I'm not a shopper, I appreciate the appeal to the rich.'

'And a big part of Lycander's economy relies on attracting the rich and the glamorous to our shores. We *want* designer names—we *want* the tourists and the parties. But we can't *only* cater for the celebrity crowd. We need to look after our own people. So now I want to show you a different side of Lycander.'

A sleek black chauffeured car pulled up to the kerb and April climbed in first, forcing herself not to scrunch up as close to the window as possible to lessen their proximity. *Daft.* This had to stop—right now she needed to concentrate, to determine whether or not this was some complicated political manoeuvre to persuade her to abandon her pursuit of the truth.

The truth—that was what was important. Ever since the tragedy in which she'd lost Edward, after she'd clawed her way out of the pit of despair, she'd vowed never to side-step the truth.

She watched the Lycander landscape flash by, saw the busy, prosperous streets recede and slowly morph into roads on a sliding scale of prosperity that eventually spiralled downwards, until a sense of squalor gradually pervaded. Buildings became less well maintained, shops became smaller and dingier, walls were scratched with the bright slash of graffiti. And as the miles were swallowed up soon the designer-laden city centre seemed like a bubble, an impossible dream.

Aware of his watchful gaze, she turned her head and saw the intensity of his expression. His face was suddenly harder, shadowed with grimness, his blue eyes dark with purpose.

'When you think of Lycander, what images come to mind?' he asked. 'Other than that of a designer paradise, with yachts and jet-setters.'

'Exports. Olives, wine and lemons. Beaches. Casinos. Wealth.'

'Yes. All that exists. And under Prince Alphonse the casinos and rich celebrity hordes thrived. But he took the money they generated and instead of spending it on the country spent it on himself. He taxed the olives, the lemons, the vineyards, and he squandered the money on his lavish lifestyle. He squandered his people's future.'

'But…but surely someone could have stopped him?'

'No. In Lycander, the ruler's word is law.'

'Then Brian Sewell has a point. The monarchy sucks.'

'It depends on the ruler. Obviously Lycander's fortunes are linked to the ruler's morality and capabilities. History shows that overall the good times have outweighed the bad—most rulers have truly cared and ruled with justice.'

'But Alphonse didn't?'

'No. But Axel would have, and Frederick does. Or at

least he is trying to.' He shrugged. 'Perhaps one day democracy *will* be the right way forward—perhaps Frederick himself will decide to make those changes. But now is not the time. Lycander is not ready.'

'What gives *you* the right to decide that?'

'Nothing. It is not my decision—it is my *belief*. And I will fight for that belief.'

'Then maybe you should let Brian Sewell fight for his.'

'Through inciting violence and riots? Through a campaign of rumour and mire?'

'OK. Not Brian Sewell. But those who believe that a ruler should be elected…shouldn't be given such immense power simply through birth and blood.'

'Lycander has had a monarchy for centuries, and on the whole it has worked. Right now it *is* working. But there is an enormous amount of work to do, and Frederick is the man to do it.'

'Frederick—or you?' The words came unbidden, ignited by the sheer determination in his voice.

'Frederick is the Prince and he has a vision that I share. It is my honour to be of help to him.'

'And if you and he disagree on policy? What happens then?'

Marcus shook his head. 'This isn't an interview, April.'

'I know that. This is off the record.'

Marcus snorted. 'But if you quote that "a leading figure in Frederick's council" privately said blah-blah-blah, I'm sure people will join the dots.'

'I won't quote anything you don't want to be quoted.'

'That's what you say now, but if our relationship goes downhill you may change your mind. For the record, I don't want to be quoted. Period. What I *do* want is for you to drop the story.'

'You still haven't shown me why.'

'*This* is why.'

He gestured out of the window and April turned her head.

Now they were in a different place all together. The streets were grubby, poverty was pervasive. Shops were shuttered, broken windows and rusted corrugated iron denoted a desolation that was a world away from lemons, olives and wine.

'This is the result of Alphonse's rule, and this is what Frederick wants to turn around. But to do that we need time—time that can't be taken by a democratic, political fund-sucking fight.'

He leant forward and murmured to the driver, and two minutes later the car pulled to a stop.

'I want to show you what we're trying to do.'

CHAPTER THREE

MARCUS ALIGHTED FROM the car and April scooted across the seat after him, emerged and looked around.

This area was different again—not like the plush wealth of the city, nor the high glitz of Lycander's high life, but it had an air of hope, shown by the green of a park, the few small cafés and shops that weren't boarded up. One large building had a fresh coat of paint and boxes of flowers on the windowsills. The sound of music came from inside and the front doors were wide open. Groups of youths chatted outside, clustered in the sunshine.

'This is a newly founded community centre. We opened it seven months ago, with funds from Lycander's coffers and overseas help from the Caversham Foundation.'

April nodded. 'Set up and run by Ethan and Ruby Caversham.'

'I read your interview with them.'

'They are incredible people.'

They truly were—April had warmed to the couple and their genuine belief in the foundation they ran for troubled teenagers.

'Yes, and they helped us with money and, equally importantly, with advice.' Marcus shrugged. 'It takes more than money to get something like this to work. Teenagers have to *want* to come here, and they need to come here not to fight and continue gang warfare but because they want to help implement change.'

Before she could respond a group of five teenagers headed towards them, with more than a hint of swagger, and April stepped a little closer to Marcus. Big mistake. Strength emanated from him, and the sheer solidity of him, the scent of leather and a woodsy overtone, almost made her mewl.

Without subtlety she leapt sideways—she'd take her chances with the youths, who she could now see didn't actually seem any threat. In fact she'd swear their studied nonchalance disguised pleasure.

'Hey, Marcus.'

'Blake.' Marcus stepped forward and the two exchanged some sort of complicated handshake.

'You here to train?'

'Not today.' Marcus shook his head. 'I'm here to show April around—she's a writer. April, this is Blake and Gemma, Jacob, Aurelie and Isaac.'

'Why'd you bring *her* here?' The suspicion in Gemma's voice would have curdled milk. 'She's a gossip columnist. She won't be interested in the likes of us.'

'I'm a writer,' April interjected. 'I'm interested in all aspects of Lycander.'

'Not just this ridiculous, showy waste of money royal wedding?' Blake said. 'And the so-called perfection of the Prince and his bride? My family can't afford food whilst *they* squander millions on fireworks.'

Gemma shook her head emphatically, her bright blonde hair swishing in disagreement. 'You need to look at the bigger picture, Blake. Sure, they're spending a whole heap of money—but solely on Lycandrian goods, which will bring in loads of revenue to Lycander. Revenue that Frederick will put back into the system to benefit the people, so that your family and mine won't have to rely on food banks.'

'Charity.' There was no disguise for the bitterness in Blake's voice as he kicked at the kerbside. 'People say that we're layabouts and criminals, but what are we *supposed* to do?'

Isaac weighed in. 'Accept the benefits on offer. Frederick has set up free courses. My dad has enrolled on a mechanics programme. Once he qualifies, maybe he'll be given a chance at a better life.'

'That's one man out of thousands.'

'No one said change can happen overnight. It's a start.'

The debate continued and April glanced at Marcus, who had taken no part in the discussion. He simply leant against a wall and watched with interest, respect and definite pride. He caught her gaze and for a long moment held it, his dark blue eyes intent. She gave a near shiver—not of fear, but of sheer attraction.

Pushing off the wall, he asked, 'So what do you all think of having a democracy?'

Gemma shrugged. 'If you'd asked me two years ago when Axel died I'd have said yes.'

At the mention of Axel, April sensed a small movement next to her and turned her head, caught the flash of pain fleeting across Marcus's dark blue eyes, the shadow of grief and loss. Not obvious, but evident to her. Hell, she could smell grief a mile off—sniff it out with the bitter sense of personal experience.

Without thought she moved a little closer to him, in an instinctive desire to offer sympathy as they listened to Gemma.

'Because I believed Frederick would be a repeat of Alphonse—a playboy rather than a tyrant, a ruler who wouldn't care about Lycander. But he promised that he would follow Axel's policies, and so far he has. So right now I'm happy to give him a chance. But only if he is the real deal—if it turns out this is all a con, a ploy, a lie, then I'll be on the streets in protest.'

'So,' April asked, 'who here and now would vote for a democracy?'

By now more people had gathered, and there was a hum as the question circulated.

'Those for?'

Hands were raised, but nowhere near as many as April would have expected.

'Those against?' Now there was a sea of hands, including Blake's.

The discussion continued, and it was clear the group had forgotten that April was even there.

She turned to Marcus. 'Interesting.'

'Sure is. Because if you had seen a lot of these teens a few months ago they wouldn't have cared. That's part of the problem—sheer apathy or a mindless belief of the kind Brian Sewell encourages. He takes people's rightful dissatisfaction with the system and turns it into hatred and violence.'

'Whereas here you encourage people to think about it. And that is interesting too.'

'In what way?'

'It's *you*, isn't it? This is *your* project, your input. I saw how those kids looked at you—they care about your opinion and I saw how proud you are of them.'

There was a pause and she couldn't help it—she grinned.

'You're blushing.'

'I am not blushing.'

'Yes, you are.' Without thought she reached up. 'Right there.'

Lord knew she meant to point at his cheek, but somehow along the line the wires got crossed between her brain and her fingers and instead she brushed her hand down the angle of his cheekbone, along the firm line of his jaw tinged with early-afternoon shadow.

Her breath caught in her throat and for too long—*way* too long—her hand remained against his skin. Until finally her brain caught up with events and panic descended, sending the order to snatch her fingers away.

Unfortunately the panic also took a stranglehold on her vocal cords and no words, no excuses, no witty quip came to her lips.

'Now I think it's *you* who may be blushing.'

His deep voice caressed her skin and then he lifted a hand and oh-so-gently trailed a finger down her own cheek. Her tummy clenched at the hot flash of desire that shot through her.

'Right there.'

It was a good thing he didn't know that right now he'd be hard put to find a part of her body that *wasn't* flushed with heat. An image of his finger continuing its trail streamed through her brain and she closed her eyes and summoned up the power of common sense.

Hadn't she learnt her lesson? Learnt how attraction could deceive and twist and lead her astray? *Enough.* This man had a goal—to keep her from her story—and maybe his intent now was to distract her from her purpose.

Moving backwards, she summoned a rictus smile. But as she forced herself to look at him she saw his expression was full of horror as her own, and she knew that whatever had just happened Marcus's surprise equalled her own.

That hadn't been a strategic move by Lycander's Chief Advisor—in fact he looked as flummoxed as she felt. He, however, was recovering considerably quicker.

'Right. We seem to have got distracted by a blushing

contest. I declare it a draw. Now, why don't I show you around the inside of the centre?'

He nodded towards the group of teens, who were still deep in conversation.

'For the record, these kids are Lycander's future, and I want them to have a future that doesn't include seeing the inside of a prison. They deserve a lot more than that.'

His words pulled her into reality, brought her focus back. She nodded, deciding that the best way to go was to expel the whole memory of the past few minutes and erase it from her timeline. Hard, though, when her skin still tingled. She tried to concentrate solely on her surroundings, creating a memory of the image because she knew that this was a place she would like to write about.

April could see the thought that had been put into the interior of the centre, the efforts to make it look less institutional and more 'homelike'. No doubt a lot of the youths here didn't have the best home life, and so would appreciate the comfy sofas and recliner chairs and bean bags, the television and the well-stocked bookshelves, the up-to-date magazines stacked on tables.

There was a gym, a room with a pool table, a ping-pong table and then, after going down a corridor, they entered a room that contained a boxing ring.

'Boxing?' April tried to keep the disapproval from her voice.

'Yes. Training is a great way to let off steam. There's a whole lot of illegal boxing that goes on in the streets—the kind that can actually kill. I want this to be somewhere kids can come and pursue boxing safely.'

'But it's dangerous and violent and…'

'It's a sport. One that requires discipline and dedication. Danger and violence is on the streets.'

'So, do *you* box?'

'Yes.'

Heaven help her—because April certainly couldn't help herself. An image of him stripped down, training with a punch bag, his muscles a testimony to discipline and dedication, shot across her mind.

'Why?' she managed, her reporter's instincts coming to her rescue. 'What's the appeal?'

'I started in my teens.'

His tone was less than forthcoming, and it wasn't really an answer.

'In fact it was boxing that started this place off. I set up a fight, offered to take anyone on in a one-on-one. I thought it would give them an incentive to come here.'

April stared at him. 'And the best incentive you could come up with was to offer yourself up as a target?' Horror touched her. 'Couldn't you have brought someone else in?'

'I could've—but it wouldn't have been as effective. I wanted to get their attention, show them that I'm more than some flash millionaire politician trying to rule over them. So, yes, I put myself on the line.'

He smiled suddenly and April blinked—the smile transformed his face, lit his dark blue eyes with a glint of amusement, and her toes twitched in her sensible flat navy shoes.

'Don't look so aghast. I'm actually pretty good.'

'Yes, but you were up against fighters who might bend the rules. You could have been seriously hurt.'

She knew they were talking about teenagers, here, but she was pretty sure that a lot of the youths on the streets might be short on years but would be long on experience.

'It was worth the risk. It got people here. A huge crowd, in fact, who stayed when it was over and listened to what I had to say about what was going to be on offer here. You heard Blake—these people are poor, but they have their pride. Most of them don't want hand-outs. They wouldn't have come here otherwise.'

'What happened?'

'I won. It was bloody, but the fights were fair. All but one, where the kid pulled a knife and got turfed out—not by me, but by the crowd. Three fights, and at the end they were willing to listen. The next day some of them came back, the day after a few more, and slowly… I think it's working.'

His voice, the sheer force of his belief and zeal, held her mesmerised. As she looked around the ring she could picture the scene, hear the drip of blood on the canvas, the silence and the cheers of the crowds, the aura of grit and the focus of the fighters. Most of all she could see Marcus—a man willing quite literally to fight for his beliefs, to endure pain in order to win victory for others.

The idea took her breath away, made her feel a little light-headed even as she wondered why. What drove him to this? Grief over his best friend? A need to propel Axel's vision into reality? Perhaps, but she thought there must be more to it. Whatever it was, she was damn sure he wouldn't tell *her*.

'I think it's working too,' she agreed. 'Those kids are all thinking, and they all care one way or another. And they are all here.'

She followed him down another long corridor towards the unmistakable scent of food and the sizzle of onions and chips.

'I'll show you the canteen and then we'll be on our way,' Marcus said.

They entered a spacious room, complete with wooden tables and benches, one of which was being polished by a young girl April reckoned couldn't be much older than seventeen.

'Hey, Mia.'

Marcus's voice was gentle, and the girl looked up and gave him a shy smile.

'Hi.' She straightened up.

'Getting ready for the hordes to arrive for lunch?'

She nodded.

April walked forward with Marcus and smiled.

'Mia, this is April. She's a writer. April, this is Mia. And this…'

Mia had bent over, and too late April spotted the pram next to the bench. Mia scooped an infant out.

'This is Charlie,' Mia said softly, her face alight with pride.

April froze, caught wrong-footed, and desperately tried to remember all the defence mechanisms she'd learnt—how to shield herself when it was impossible to avoid a baby.

Marcus stepped forward and the baby gave an impossibly sweet gummy grin of excitement.

'Charlie loves Marcus,' Mia said as Charlie tumbled forward, clearly desperate for Marcus to take him.

Even through the descent of grief April registered that Marcus seemed very comfortable with the baby, holding him with the impression of ease and making quacking noises that elicited a stream of giggles from Charlie.

The sound twisted April's heart. She could feel the room begin to spin and desperately tried to distance herself, to shut down her emotions before they became too hard to hold. It would usually be fine, but this had taken her by surprise—and, worse, Charlie had a real look of Edward about him. The same colour hair, tufted up into little spikes, the same gurgle in his laugh, the same chubby legs…

If she held very still she could almost allow herself to imagine for one wonderful moment that it *was* Edward.

Nearly as soon as it had come the illusion vanished, leaving behind tears of sadness. Somehow she held it together. 'He is gorgeous.' The tremble in her voice would hopefully pass without comment—and yet she was aware that Marcus's forehead had creased into a watchful expression.

'Thank you,' Mia said as she took Charlie back from Marcus. 'I need to go and check on the menu. It was nice to meet you. Wave to Marcus, Charlie.'

Relief flooded April as Mia walked away. Time to pull herself together. A few years ago that would have been impossible. But now she could do it—she *would* do it.

Her family had helped her put herself back together in the dark aftermath of Edward's death, and she would not let them or herself down by returning to that black pit of despair. Instead she would focus on her life, her job, her future. The existence she had mapped out for herself, in which she had found a level of peace.

'Are you OK?'

Marcus's voice was gruff with a concern that both warmed her and made more tears threaten.

'I'm fine.'

His frown deepened. 'Are you sure? You looked as though you'd been sucker-punched straight in the chest and left down for the count.'

An apt description—not that she would admit it.

'I'm not in the boxing ring, Marcus, and last I looked there wasn't anyone throwing their fists around. It must have been a trick of the light. I'm completely fine.' She glanced at her watch. 'Now, I'm afraid I need to get back. I can get a cab. Thank you for the tour—I really appreciate it. It's given me a lot to think about.'

'Whoa. Hang on.'

Dark blue eyes studied her face and she forced herself to hold his gaze. The grief was under control now, but harder to leash was her awareness of him, of the fact that his gaze seemed to heat her skin.

'I'm glad you're OK, and I'm glad you enjoyed the tour. Can I take it that you'll drop the story?'

Her eyes narrowed. 'No, you can't. I said you've given me a lot to think about—that implies I need to go away and *think*.'

For a second she thought he'd argue; instead he nodded, though she could see reluctance etched on his face.

'Fair enough. Then let's meet tomorrow. Would lunch-time suit you? Say twelve-thirty?'

There it was again—that silly, stupid thrill of anticipation at the thought of seeing Marcus again. Madness. But no matter. After tomorrow there would be no need to see him again. Whatever decision she came to.

'That's fine.'

CHAPTER FOUR

MARCUS REREAD THE paragraph outlining fiscal policy for the third time, uttered a curse, and shoved the bound folder across his desk, oblivious to the dappled rays of golden Lycandrian morning sunshine or the sweet smell of mimosa that wafted in from outside.

If only he was as immune to images of April Fotherington. Yet her image intruded with persistence, flitting across his brain and pushing out the facts in the report.

Foolish! She wasn't even his type. Insofar as he even *had* a type. Sure, she was attractive, but he had met plenty of attractive women in his time and none had had the ability to distract him from work. He had a work ethic that had driven him from the moment of his adoption—an iron determination to make something of his life. To atone for the night of the fire, and to make a difference in the world.

He'd figured out that to do that he needed money, so he'd built up his business and attained millionaire status. Now he was determined to help Frederick bring about change to Lycander—and he would *not* let an attraction stand in the way of that.

Perhaps it wasn't an attraction…

Hah, Marcus—really?

Maybe, his brain persisted, his subconscious was trying

to warn him that this woman was a threat, an adversary he needed to defeat rather than a woman he wanted to…

Wanted to what? Have a relationship with? He didn't *do* relationships. Sleep with? Not happening. April was not his sort of woman…not an anonymous, discreet ship passing in the night, the type of woman who would never expect more than the very little he could offer: a brief interlude, physical release, and then moving on without regret.

There was a vulnerability about April, and despite her denial the previous day he sensed that she had demons that could vie with his own. And that meant she was so far off-limits she might as well be in a different stratosphere.

Pulling the report back towards him, he tackled paragraph three again, glaring the words into submission. Sheer will-power propelled him through the report, two meetings and a visit to the head office of Alrikson Security. But images of April filtered the net of his determination for the duration, and en route to pick her up he felt a strange, fizzy thread of anticipation run through his gut, followed by a bubbling doubt.

Why had he asked her to lunch? Yes, he needed to see her, but he could have done that in his office. Why make it a lunch date? Date? No. *Meeting*—that was the word.

Oh, God. It was time to get a grip. April represented a threat to Lycander he needed to eliminate. End of. He would do whatever it took to ensure his country was given the chance to return to prosperity. It was inconceivable that something as petty as physical attraction should get in the way of that.

Yet as the car pulled up outside the hotel with its bright awning and gilded doors, and he spotted April outside, clad in dark tailored trousers and a dove-grey short-sleeved blouse, his body tensed. His nerves went on alert in recognition of the kind of primal magnetic pull no amount of will-power could eradicate—a tug as far from petty as it was possible to be.

Fine. If he couldn't eliminate it he would ignore it, conceal it, fight it…

A frown etching his forehead, he climbed out of the car and moved round to open the door for her. 'Hi,' he managed.

'Hi.'

For a moment, he would have sworn he'd glimpsed a hint of shyness as she gestured downward.

'I hope I'm dressed OK? I wasn't sure where we're going.'

A sensation suspiciously akin to panic roiled in his gut. Why on earth had this seemed a good idea?

'For a picnic,' he muttered. *Muttered?* 'A picnic,' he repeated firmly. 'I thought that would be more private.'

Her expression registered a panic that no doubt mirrored his own. 'Private?'

'So that no one will be able to overhear our conversation,' he added hurriedly. 'Plus, yesterday you saw a lot of urban Lycander. I thought you might like to see somewhere more tranquil.'

In addition, he'd hoped a sylvan setting would influence her, that his words would be more persuasive in a less official ambiance.

'We're going to eat in the royal forest. I've arranged for the food to be delivered. It was a bit short notice, so it won't be anything fancy, I'm afraid, but…'

As silence greeted this, it belatedly occurred to Marcus that the idea that had seemed brilliant in the confines of his office that morning no longer seemed quite so stellar.

Perhaps he should have wined and dined her in style? Perhaps a charm offensive would have dazzled her and impressed her into compliance? Unfortunately charm wasn't his bag—was not a tool of his trade.

Even as a child he'd lacked charm. Charm would have got him nowhere with his parents—would have made no difference to their levels of violence or indifference, depending on their alcohol consumption or their reaction to the drug of the day. Charm certainly wouldn't have helped him on the tough streets of his childhood, where sheer brute strength and the ability to fight dirty had been the only currency worth a dime. And by the time of his adoption it had all been too late—charm had quite simply never come into play. So it was unrealistic to expect it to come to his aid now. As for the picnic... He must have been running mad.

'Of course if you would prefer we could simply divert to my office and...'

But then she smiled and his words dried up.

'No. Sorry, you took me by surprise. A picnic sounds lovely, and it does seem the best way to make sure our conversation remains between us.'

'OK. Great.'

The car pulled into the small car park, and as they climbed out Marcus's phone rang.

'Hi, Marcus. I've got the picnic and I've brought it to Umbrella Copse.'

'Thank you, Gloria. We'll be right there.'

Perhaps this would work out after all. He could see April's appreciation as she tipped her head upwards to catch the dappled rays of the sun that filtered through the luxuriant trees, flecking the vibrant greens with droplets of gold. For an instant his gaze lingered on the elegant length of her neck, then moved over the beauty of her face, the smattering of freckles on the bridge of her nose, the...

Stop and focus.

The point was that the lazy drone of bees, the call of the black kites, all seemed to indicate the need for tranquility and concord. Which would hopefully aid him in his quest—the reason he was here. To ensure that April dropped her story.

Then they reached the glade and Marcus came to an abrupt halt as he took in the scene before him.

For a long moment words failed him.

A wooden slatted picnic table was covered in a snow-white tablecloth, and laid with gleaming silver cutlery, fluted crystal glasses and bone china plates. A bottle of Lycander's best Sauvignon Blanc nestled in a state-of-the-art cooler. A wicker picnic basket was on the bench, and Gloria was busy unpacking an array of delicacies onto large china platters.

She turned and beamed at him. 'Perfect timing,' she declared.

Marcus attempted to regroup as he mentally replayed his earlier conversation with Gloria in his head.

'Hi Gloria. Could I ask a favour? Would you be able to rustle up a picnic for two—nothing fancy?'

Now he said, 'Gloria—this is…amazing. But you shouldn't have gone to so much trouble. I wasn't expecting anything like this.'

'It is no trouble.' The dark-haired woman turned to April. 'In all the time I have worked with him not once has he asked for a picnic, and not once has he asked us to create a meal for him and a lady—so we decided to make this special.'

Marcus opened his mouth to explain that this was a strictly business lunch and then closed it again. Gloria had gone to a great deal of trouble and, however low on charm he was, he wouldn't hurt her feelings.

'It's fabulous, Gloria. Thank you—and please thank everyone in the kitchens as well.'

'Of course.' Gloria arranged a centrepiece posy of freshly picked flowers—a glorious burst of red, orange and yellow blooms—and smiled with satisfaction. 'Enjoy.'

'Please add my thanks as well,' April said, and her voice was full of appreciation but underlaid with a tinge of panic he recognised all too well.

'You're very welcome. Enjoy.' A beaming smile, a nod, and Gloria was gone.

Swallowing the urge to call her back—after all that would be cowardly in the extreme—Marcus looked at April, then at the picnic, and then back at April.

'Um…'

Forget charm—even the art of conversation had deserted him, and a miasma of awkwardness descended. It seemed clear that April had been thrown a curve ball too—her cool self-containment looked more than a little fragmented.

And then, to his surprise, she gave a small chuckle—a sound that seemed to surprise her as much as it did him.

'Your face!' she said. 'You looked absolutely horrified. Though I have to admit you covered it beautifully.'

He couldn't help it; her smile transformed her face, lightened it in a way he couldn't fully explain, and the sight caused his own lips to upturn. 'I really am sorry. I didn't want to make you feel awkward. It didn't cross my mind Gloria would think this was a date.'

'Because you don't *ever* date?'

'I really don't.'

Not his thing. The closeness, the questions, the intimacy of a date was not to his liking. Every so often there was a woman—he didn't embrace celibacy—but if pushed to describe his relationships the adjectives that came to mind were 'brief', 'clean' and 'functional'. 'Relationship' was too deep a word—they were more like understandings, interludes, soon over and forgotten, conducted discreetly and anonymously, outside of Lycander.

'I can't really see the point.'

Her eyebrows arched. 'Most people would disagree.

It's a chance to get to know someone, work out if you're compatible…'

'I don't need to have dinner with someone to work out compatibility.'

Pink tinged her cheeks and suddenly awareness swept in on the summer breeze, heightening his senses, illuminating the green of the leaves, the glitter of the cutlery in the sunshine, and urging him to step forward and show her exactly how well matched he knew *they* would be.

She hauled in an audible breath. 'I wasn't talking about physical compatibility. I meant…overall compatibility—whether you actually *like* the other person, have something in common with them.'

'Nope—still not relevant.'

'So you are only interested in the physical side of things?'

'Yes.'

'At least you're honest.'

Was it his imagination or did she actually look intrigued rather than critical or outraged? Belatedly his radar kicked in. April was a reporter—of *course* she was intrigued. She was probably converting his words into some sort of headline right now. *Lycander's Lothario says, 'Let's get physical!'*

Note to whatever brain cells he had left: *this woman is an adversary.*

'Yes.' He gestured to the table. 'Anyway, we seem to be off track. Now we've established that this isn't a date I think we should get started.'

'Agreed.'

But to his escalating annoyance it wasn't as easy as all that. Even as he busied himself with the pouring of wine, the choice of food, he knew the simple movements were overhung with an insidious curiosity as to what it would be like if this *were* a date. Would they clink their glasses in a toast to each other? Accidentally entangle their feet under the table? Pop morsels of food into each other's mouths?

For an instant his gaze lingered on the lushness of her lips and he wondered if he was losing his grasp on sanity. Not once in his life had he felt the temptation to feed a woman a morsel of pâté on sourdough bread, and he sure as heck wasn't starting now.

Time to get back on track and recall that this was emphatically *not* a date, or anything resembling it. It was a negotiation table. 'So. To business. I'll keep it simple. Will you drop the story?'

Her body tensed as if in acknowledgment of the fact that they were now down to brass tacks—that the interlude, whatever it had meant, was over.

'It's not that straightforward.'

'Yes, it is. Frederick is a good ruler and he needs time— he needs to be given a chance, exactly as the majority of those teenagers you met yesterday believe.'

'They also said they would only believe in the monarchy if it wasn't founded on a lie.' April shook her head, looked down at her plate and spread more pâté onto a slice of bread, as if to distract herself. 'But if what Brian Sewell told me is true then Frederick's ascent to the throne *is* based on a lie. So I have a solution. I'll tell you what he said, and if you tell me he is lying I'll drop the story.'

April sipped her wine and then met his gaze full-on. Her directness brooked no quarter.

'Frederick should have been in the car the night Axel died. He bailed out from that function to go and party and Axel took his place—even though Axel pretended it was all his idea.'

She paused as she studied his face, and he focused on maintaining an expression of calm interest.

'Is that true?'

'I'll take the Fifth.'

'So it *is* true?'

'I didn't say that. But what I *will* say is that even if it were true, hypothetically speaking, it wouldn't matter.'

'The truth *always* matters.' Her voice was absolute in its conviction. 'The bottom line is that Frederick chose pleasure over duty and his brother paid with his life. The people deserve to know that.'

'Why?'

'Because if he lied to them once he could lie to them again.'

Time to change tack. 'For a start, the truth isn't that black and white, cut and dried—whatever cliché you like. Frederick *did* attend a party the night of Axel's death. But it was a business function to celebrate a business deal—not some wild celebrity shindig. Frederick founded Freddy Petrelli's Olive Oil, and the deal took his company into the global arena. *Axel* was heir to the throne—Frederick had no interest in politics at the time. So I'm not sure your "pleasure over duty" theme will hold water.'

'Then what is all the fuss about? Why would it have been covered up in the first place?'

'Because Axel was Lycander's hope for the future—the Golden Prince who would take Lycander back to prosperity and fairness. At the time Frederick was pretty unpopular—he was seen as being like his father because of his party lifestyle. Bottom line is that the people would have *preferred* Frederick to have been in that car, and they loathed the idea that *he* was now heir to the throne. The throne was already rocking; if they had known he should have been in the car the monarchy could have been overturned.'

'So, hypothetically speaking, you agree that a cover-up was the right way to go?'

'It is what Axel would have wanted. Whatever it took for his vision of Lycander to be achieved and for the monarchy he believed in to remain stable.'

That was what had driven Marcus to step forward to offer Frederick his support, even when his own grief was at its height.

'He believed in Frederick.'

'That isn't the point. The point is that by concealing the truth Frederick may have changed history—changed people's lives.'

'For the better.'

'Maybe, but maybe not. And maybe not long-term. And—'

'You can play alternative endings until you're rainbow-coloured, but at the end of the day you make the decision you make on the day.'

'And what if it turns out to be the wrong one?'

'Then you have to live with the consequences.'

The words came out way too harsh as memory stirred, pulling him back to eighteen years before, and the decision he'd made then. He'd rescued Elvira from the fire and had made the decision not to go back in for his parents.

Little matter that, given the state of the fire, he would most likely not have survived. Little matter that he had been restrained by his neighbours. He knew that if Elvira had still been inside somehow he would have broken free and tried to save her—would have perished in the attempt. But he hadn't done so for his parents. A decision made that he had to live with. And God have mercy on his soul.

He pulled his mind from his own thoughts and flinched at the expression on April's face. The colour had leeched from her face and despite her best efforts to cover it up her hand shook as she placed her glass down. Wine slopped over the side and spread a puddle on the white of the tablecloth.

'April…?' In that second he knew with bone-deep certainty that whatever demons haunted April, whatever decisions she rued in her life, they rivalled his own. 'I'm sorry.'

'No. *I'm* sorry.' She reached for a napkin, fumbled, and hauled in an audible breath. 'I'm fine.'

'No. You aren't.'

He could sense the pain that emanated from her and wanted to soothe it. Lord knew he could empathise with the whip of guilt and pain. Without thought he reached out and covered her hand in his, and felt sensation jolt his veins and heat his blood. Her green eyes widened, as if her reaction to his touch had jerked her from the edge of pain.

'Then I *will* be fine.'

Her gaze lingered on his hand and gently she pulled her own out from under it, retrieved the napkin and scrubbed at the wine stain.

'But there is something I want to know. You told me how the *people* felt about Frederick and Axel. What about *you*? Axel was your best friend. How did *you* feel?'

Marcus closed his eyes in an attempt to ward the question off; this was something he had spoken to no one about—not even Elvira. But suddenly here and now, as he opened his eyes, met her gaze and saw the genuine compassion in them, for a moment he wanted to share the grief.

Axel had been like a brother to him—the one person he had let a little close. They had been best friends as boys, had run and played together, argued politics and crafted Lycander's future together. But...

'My feelings are irrelevant. It is Lycander that matters. Nothing can bring Axel back. His death was a tragedy, but maybe his legacy can live on.'

April nodded, her green eyes wide with empathy as well as sympathy. 'I am sorry for your loss,' she said simply, 'and I appreciate how strongly you believe that Frederick is the right person to rule Lycander now. And I do understand why you want me to drop the story.'

'Will you?'

'I don't know. I'm not sure it is up to me to make a decision of such enormity with such huge possible repercussions. I need to think.'

'Understood.'

There would be no point in pushing her and in truth he understood her stance.

'So, right now why don't you have some of Gloria's chocolate and apple torte, famed throughout the region? And then I'll drop you back to your hotel.'

She nodded slowly. 'Thank you.'

But as they ate the sumptuously decadent dessert conversation dwindled, both of them caught up in their own thoughts, both of them with decisions to make.

Marcus glanced at the serious intent on April's face as she dabbed up the last flakes of pastry with one finger. He didn't know which way her choice would fall—he suspected neither did she.

A sylvan picnic hadn't cut the mustard, nor even the Lycander tomato chutney, so he needed to move to Plan B.

CHAPTER FIVE

APRIL OPENED HER eyes and puffed out a sigh. She might as well face it—sleep had left the hotel room and it wasn't coming back. Unless her fitful, restless swivel round the sheets counted.

Every time she closed her eyes Marcus Alrikson—drat the man—insisted on an invasion of her dreams. As she lay there, gazing wide-eyed at the ceiling, irritation and a dollop of sheer guilt swathed her already heated skin and she pushed the duvet off with more force than necessary.

This was unacceptable. This unwanted attraction had caused her to lose the thing she valued most—her objectivity. She couldn't see her way forward—couldn't work out what to do about the story she almost wished she'd never discovered. Part of her wanted to drop it. Problem was, she couldn't be sure of her motivation. Had she allowed her attraction for him to cloud her judgement and make her want to do what he said?

Her entire being revolted against the very concept that she would be foolish enough to do that again. Attraction had rendered her unable to see Dean as he truly was—had propelled her into a foolish, disastrous and tragic marriage.

April wanted to pull the duvet over her head and go into hibernation mode... *No way.* That way lay the path back to depression. Right now she needed to kill this attraction off, shut her hormones down and focus on a return to her safe, even-keeled life—the one she had worked so hard to construct, brick by painstaking brick.

The buzz of her phone provided a welcome relief from her thoughts.

'Hey, Kathy.' Her editor, who could perhaps help with this dilemma. Except she wasn't sure she wanted the decision taken out of her hands...

'April. Glad I caught you. I've just spoken with Marcus Alrikson and it sounds like you've ruffled some feathers.'

For a moment words deserted her as the sheer gall of the man blasted her. But it wasn't only anger—there was a sense of betrayal as well. He'd gone over her head to her editor.

'I really don't know what you were *thinking*, April. We were very lucky to get this exclusive coverage of the Lycander Royal wedding, and we agreed to write a feel-good article on the lifestyle of the royal couple—not to dig up a political scandal. You have single-handedly nearly screwed that up.'

The tone of the other woman's voice twanged a nerve— a reminder of the numerous occasions on which Dean and his family had explained to April why she didn't measure up. As a wife, a mother, a person... The memory kept her vocal cords in stranglehold, conveying an almost hypnotic belief that, yes, she *was* wrong, stupid...

April dug her nails into the palm of her hand to wake herself up. Tragedy had reformed her and she was no longer that woman. 'Kathy,' she broke in, 'this is not just a scandal. It's a political story that could have huge ramifications if it's true.'

'Perhaps, but it is not the sort of story our readers would be interested in. Marcus Alrikson has made it plain that if we don't back off they back *out*—and the wedding coverage will go to *What's Up?* instead. I will not lose this to our biggest competitor. So drop the story.'

'But—' April began, feeling conflicting emotions tear at her. Relief that the decision had been taken out of her hands versus her principles, which told her that the decision was hers to make, and had to be made on different grounds than readership numbers.

'No buts. Drop the story. I had an agreement with Marcus Alrikson—I intend to keep it.'

Five minutes later April flung her phone onto the bed. In record time she shed her tartan PJs, tugged on jeans and a dark blue T-shirt, grabbed her bag and blazer and left her hotel room. How *dared* he? Of all the arrogant, idiotic—

Her mental invective halted as she strode through the lobby, out through the revolving doors and glared around for a taxi.

Once at Marcus's offices she didn't even pause—she stormed inside with no more than a perfunctory glance at the historic grandeur of the building. Right now she didn't care if he was in Fort bloody Knox—she'd find him. And if he wasn't in she'd wait for as long as it took.

Attempting to summon a polite smile, she approached the semi-circular reception desk. 'Is Marcus Alrikson available?'

'Ah, you must be April. I'm Karen. Marcus asked me to take you straight up when you arrived.'

'He did?' A tiny puff of wind left her sails of fury, but April soon remedied that as adrenalin pulsed through her. If he was willing to fight, then bring it on. 'Excellent.'

She followed the petite blonde receptionist down a maze of corridors and up a flight of oak-banister stairs—the building appeared to have been haphazardly converted from royal residence to office complex.

'Is Marcus expecting me at a certain time?'

The woman nodded. 'He said somewhere between nine-thirty and ten-thirty.'

So she was *that* predictable, was she?

April caught a glimpse of her reflection in a gilded mirror. Her eyes had squinted to slits and her expression defined the word *glower*, so she couldn't blame Karen for her apprehensive glance.

Finally they reached a door where a discreet plaque showed they'd reached their destination. A perfunctory knock, then Karen announced April's name in a relieved murmur and scurried back down the corridor.

Marcus rose from behind a teak desk that screeched antiquity. 'April. I'm guessing you've spoken with Kathy.'

'Yes, I have, and I am here to tell you that you are *despicable*. You went over my head and behind my back to my editor. I could have been sacked.'

'Rubbish!' But a tinge of discomfort climbed his cheeks. 'I explained that you had strayed from the brief, but I also made it crystal-clear that you were doing a fantastic job on the wedding article and that I categorically wanted you to continue with that.'

April could hear the hiss of metaphorical steam from her ears. 'So now you want my *thanks*?'

'No.' All signs of unease had vanished. 'I simply want you to get on with the agreed article.'

'I am. But I have come across a separate story about Axel and I have told you I need time to consider what to do about it.'

'And that's what you now have. Time. Write the article on the wedding. At the end of that, if you want to pursue the other story you can. There will be nothing I can do about it. But I want to make sure you do really consider the consequences.' He moved away from the desk, his frustration evident in each stride. 'I am not asking you to cover up a crime. Even if Brian Sewell is telling the truth, Frederick did nothing wrong; the events of that night were simply a tragedy. One we all have to live with and make the best of.'

The words smote her—extinguished her anger in an ice-cold deluge. She knew oh-so-well how a few minutes could change your entire world. How one decision could have a domino effect you had never intended. But did that make you any less guilty…? April didn't think so. In which case Frederick should have to face up to what he'd done.

Yet *she* hadn't, had she? What jury had judged *her*? What punishment had *she* received apart from the life sentence of having to live each and every day without Edward, imagining how it might have been? He would have been six years old. Six years and few months. He'd be at school… He'd…

Stop. That way led nowhere. The clock couldn't be turned back. Perhaps Frederick wished it could be.

Think.

Hard to do that when once again her body was hyper-alert to the man now standing so tantalisingly close to her. For a moment of insanity she wanted to close the gap between them and throw herself at the bulk of him, lose herself, submerge these roiling thoughts in desire. After all, he had said it himself—his only interest in women was on a physical level. And for years and years April hadn't felt so much as a semi-spark, a micro-spark of desire for any man.

Get. A. Grip. Think. Objectively.

Marcus met her gaze full-on. 'I believe it is in Lycander's best interests for this story not to be pursued. You also have my personal word that Frederick has done nothing wrong.'

'Your "personal word" is simply an expression of your personal opinion. Many others may not agree. Plus, it's hard to put much stock in your word.'

Now anger flashed across his face and instinctively she stepped back; fear could still surface after all these years.

His expression morphed into a frown at her involuntary reaction and she forced herself to continue. 'Going to Kathy was hardly above-board.'

'I did what I needed to do.'

There was no compromise in his tone, and again she braced herself, waiting for the tide of anger, the bluster, the threats.

Instead he said, 'I won't apologise for that. But I *am* sorry if there was negative fallout for you. I did my best to minimise that.'

For a second she had the feeling that he had surprised himself. Dammit, she almost felt *grateful*—and that made her even more furious. True, he could have requested she be kicked off the story altogether, but she had still been manipulated and she hated it—it was too reminiscent of her time with Dean, and she would not take it.

But what could she do? Tell Marcus to stuff it? Resign from the wedding article and pursue the other story? The problem with that was that it smacked of cutting her nose off to spite her face. For a start it would be professional idiocy and, truth be told, she still wasn't sure she even wanted to pursue the story.

What to do? What to do?

Objectivity still eluded her. Not even a particle of it was to be found as she tried to think. Her story had the power to be the catalyst to topple a throne—and she *did* need time to decide what to do with it. But, dammit, she wouldn't just sit back and be manipulated.

'So you've guaranteed that I take time to consider? Fine. But I need something more than time.'

'Such as?'

Suspicion tinged his voice and her anger resurfaced as he assumed the reason.

'I won't be blackmailed.'

The anger swelled, rolled words off her tongue. 'If you

want me to take your word for it that pursuing this story is the morally wrong thing to do, then prove it. Let me shadow you—let me see what Lycander is all about. Show me what Frederick is doing. More than the community centre.'

She took a deep breath. She'd show him *blackmail*.

'And I want an exclusive article with *you*. We could call it *The Real Marcus Alrikson*. On the record.'

Even as she said the words she felt an unholy glee at the knowledge that this would be his worst nightmare.

For a second, sheer horror etched his face. 'Forget it. I told you—I won't be blackmailed.'

'It's not blackmail. It's a means to help me make a decision and a way for me to retrieve my reputation with Kathy.'

There was a long silence as he gazed past her, clearly deep in thought. His fingers drummed the desk in an impatient tattoo and then ceased as he looked at her.

For an instant she thought he'd call her bluff, but then he nodded. 'OK. But I get to vet the finished product.'

'We can *discuss* the finished product,' she conceded even as she frowned. Had that been too easy? Why on earth had he capitulated? 'But that doesn't mean you get to rewrite it, and when I interview you it will be *on* the record. You get that, right?'

'Sure,' he said easily—and as she looked into those dark eyes she knew damn well that he had no intent of letting her anywhere *near* the real him. Well, they would see…

Curiosity, determination and a funny little thrill shot through her. 'So, when do we start?'

'No time like the present. I have meetings scheduled this morning on education, on overseas aid, and a general security briefing. I'll need to talk to Frederick and get this cleared. Then, tonight, we'll attend a charity ball.'

'A charity ball?'

Insidious panic touched her. The entire concept of attendance at any glitterati function as a guest filled her with acute anxiety. Too overwhelming—too much. Since Edward's death she had avoided social occasions as if they truly could give her the plague—the thought of making conversation was too much.

'Yes. It's an annual event, hosted by Rafael Martinez and his wife—'

'Cora Derwent,' April completed. 'Lady Kaitlin Derwent's twin sister. The same Lady Kaitlin who was once linked with Prince Frederick.'

'That's the one.' Marcus picked up his phone. 'I'll call now and explain that I'll be taking up my plus one option.'

'I... I don't have anything to wear.'

His look indicated that he felt she might have lost the plot. 'You are in a shopper's paradise, April. That won't be a problem.'

'Of course.' Seeing his look of puzzlement, she forced a smile. 'I'll hit the shops at lunchtime.'

For heaven's sake, she should be *pleased*—she would be attending a function where celebrities would abound, and most importantly she'd won an exclusive scoop—the chance to shadow Marcus Alrikson for four days.

The words encircled her brain. *Shadow Marcus Alrikson for four days.*

Suddenly the sense of victory was hollow in her tummy. What on earth had made her believe this was a good idea?

'Why is this a good idea?'

Prince Frederick sat behind the ornate antique desk in the Lycander throne room, a look of genuine bewilderment on his face.

Marcus sat opposite him and did his best to maintain an expression of being totally in control of the situation.

'Let me get this straight,' Frederick continued, one

blond eyebrow raised in question. 'You have agreed to let April Fotherington shadow you for four days, including council meetings, and she is going to write an article on "the real Marcus Alrikson" as well as the wedding article?'

'Yes.'

'I don't get it.' Frederick shook his head. 'I mean, I understand you don't want April to pursue the other story, but this doesn't sound like the usual ruthless Alrikson approach.'

'Sometimes the ruthless approach isn't the best option.' Even to himself the words sounded lame. 'I decided this was the best way to head off the threat.'

Yup. More and more lame.

The royal eyebrow rose further. 'But at the end of the four days April might still pursue the story?'

Marcus nodded, wondering how to explain something he didn't understand himself. 'I realise that. But...'

Somehow he wanted April to *choose* to drop the story. He resisted the urge to close his eyes in sheer frustration with himself, and gathered himself together.

'In the next four days I will close Brian Sewell down. We are close to getting the evidence we need to nail him. Once he is discredited, her story will have no foundation. I'll also uncover any other potential sources.'

Frederick frowned, his blue eyes shadowed. 'Perhaps she's right. Perhaps I *should* simply tell the truth.'

'It isn't that easy,' Marcus said. 'And we both know the time isn't right.'

Frederick exhaled a sigh and bowed his head in acknowledgment before his lips turned up in a sudden impish smile. 'Well, I will look forward to reading all about "the real Marcus Alrikson".' He shrugged. 'Though I still haven't grasped why you agreed to that either.'

Who knew? Unfortunately Marcus had a sneaking suspicion that it was to do with his impulsive regret that he'd gone over April's head to her editor—got her into trouble, betrayed her. Still…

'I have no intention of giving her any interesting material, so I doubt the article will see the light of day.'

Frederick's smile increased in size to accommodate his patent disbelief, but to Marcus's relief he refrained from comment.

'Keep me posted,' was all he said.

Marcus nodded. 'I'll see you later at the council meeting.' *With a certain reporter in tow…*

Two and a half hours and two meetings later Marcus watched as his colleagues filed out of the room, then turned to look at April.

Although he had forced himself to focus on the agenda, he'd found his gaze inexorably pulled towards her, where she'd sat quietly, her expression intent as she unobtrusively took copious notes.

'What did you think?' he asked.

'It was fascinating. I've never had the opportunity to be part of something like this. I loved it. And I was impressed—Frederick does really care, and so do you. About education and about how Lycander can play a part in the world.'

'Education is central to the future, and we also owe a debt to the children who grew up in Alphonse's reign, who have been let down by the system for years. Those teenagers, young adults, adults who didn't get any education, who learnt their life lessons on the streets. I don't want them to be forgotten.' *The people he and Elvira could have become.* 'I want them to be given choices and opportunities.'

'Do you think it's too late for some of them?'

'I don't know. But I know we have to try. Some of those people are the next generation; we need the teens of today to believe that the system that let them down has changed.

That's why we must crack down on crime and apathy and poverty. The whole sorry cycle.' He shrugged. 'I'm sorry. You've had three hours of policy. I won't bore you further.'

'I'm not bored at all. How can something so important be tedious?'

Her expression showed genuine sincerity, and when he remembered her true interest in the community centre he couldn't help but ask, 'Have you never thought of moving on from celebrity interviews to more serious articles?'

It was as if he'd pulled a plug—his words doused her light of enthusiasm utterly.

'No. I've found my niche and I'm happy there.'

'Why?'

'I enjoy what I do and I don't want the hassle of starting again. I was lucky to get this job and I'm in a good place. I don't want to rock the boat.'

Ever. He could almost hear the unspoken word. 'So you want your life to remain exactly as it is?'

'Yes.' April tilted her chin in a gesture that stated defiance, yet he noted she'd folded her arms as if in self-defence. 'What's wrong with that?'

'You're not even thirty. Surely you have career aspirations? And presumably one day you want a family?'

'Nope.' The word held an almost bleak finality, and as if she'd realised she hurried on. 'I've met all my aspirations. I don't need any more. My life is where I need it to be. I don't ask for or want more.' She closed her notebook with an emphatic *thunk*. 'Right. I'm off to the shops.'

The topic of her future was clearly closed and padlocked, but that didn't stop the questions in Marcus's head. April was young, beautiful, intelligent, and interested in way more than celebrity chit-chat—so why on earth didn't she want more? And had she really vetoed having a family? That didn't make sense.

Or maybe it did. After all, he was thirty and he'd done exactly that.

Not, he reminded himself, that April's life goals mattered to *him*. Except in so far as an understanding of them might make it easier for him to persuade her to drop the story about the night of Axel's death. He just didn't like to see her sell herself short...

Not your business.

'Actually, I can help out there,' he said. 'Sunita has recommended a boutique.' He glanced at his watch. 'I'll take you there now.'

An expression he couldn't interpret crossed her face.

'Is that a problem?'

'I'm quite capable of shopping by myself. There is no need to come with me.'

'I couldn't agree more, but Sunita asked me to—apparently people have taken to going into boutiques pretending they have been sent by her in the hope of getting a discount. I need to come along to vouch for you.'

'Oh.'

Marcus frowned. He couldn't help but wonder what train her thoughts had climbed aboard.

'Then...um...thank you.'

'No problem. Let's go. We can walk from here. It's called Fashion Plate.'

The short journey was achieved in silence. Marcus could sense the discomfort emanating from April, as if she were heading out to do something she found almost distasteful. It seemed clear that her claim to dislike shopping was genuine.

Though she *did* stop as they approached the shop in order to study the window display—four mannequins of different race, hair colour, height and build had been posed as if they were marching around a plate-shaped display of accessories—shoes, bags and even tiaras.

As they pushed the shop door open to the sound of a small discreet chime, a woman headed straight for them. Svelte and elegant, she epitomised *chic*, and her smile was the perfect blend of welcome and discretion.

'Welcome to Fashion Plate.' Her eyes widened slightly as she looked at Marcus. 'I am Gabrielle. *You* are Marcus Alrikson and this must be April. Your PA contacted me, and of course we are most happy to help.' Her eyes swept over April and she nodded. 'We have set aside some time for a fitting, and of course to discuss what you are looking for. I understand you need a dress for the Martinez Charity Ball?'

'Yes.'

April had tensed beside him, her expression less than enthused, though her tone was polite.

'But there is absolutely no need for a fitting as I am pushed for time. I am quite happy to simply browse and find a dress myself.'

Gabrielle looked horrified. 'No, no. I wouldn't hear of it.' Her expert eye travelled over April again. 'You and Mr Alrikson will be given refreshments in our private room, and I will find a selection of dresses for you to look at. You are a friend of Sunita and I insist.'

'Um…' April hesitated and then, with a fulminating stare at Marcus—for all the world as though this were *his* fault—followed Gabrielle through the shop.

Minutes later they had been seated in a small but cleverly furnished boudoir-like room. The walls held a selection of black and white photographs from different eras of fashion, as well as large mirrors that created a feeling of space. Another assistant served them tea in exquisite china cups, along with a plate of melt-in-the-mouth biscuits.

April waited until the assistant had left, and then glared at Marcus. 'Well, thanks for the help.'

'What did you expect me to do? Acquiescence seemed

to be the quickest way forward.' He smiled. 'You're lucky *I* came with you and not Sunita—believe me, she would have insisted you go the whole nine yards with the fitting. The only reason she didn't come is that Amil isn't very well, and whilst Sunita may love clothes she loves Amil more.'

For a second he thought April flinched, and in a movement so swift he barely noticed she squeezed her hand into a fist, almost as if she were pushing her nails into her palm, and then she relaxed her hand again.

'As she should—he is her son. But you're right. This *would* have been even worse if she were here. Sunita and I have a differing view on clothes. For her, they are a vocation. She is a mine of knowledge and expertise on all aspects—the design, the feel, the material, the costs, the labour. She feels real passion for clothes.'

'And for you?'

'They are functional.' Picking up a biscuit, she took a small bite and huffed out a sigh. 'Anyway, whilst we are stuck in here we may as well use the time. What's *your* take on clothes?'

'Same as yours. They are functional.'

April waited, then made a 'come on' gesture with her hands. 'Could you expand on that?'

'Not really. There isn't much else to say.'

'Let's try it a different way. This morning you got up and at some point changed out of your PJs into your clothes.'

'Actually, I don't wear pyjamas.'

April closed her eyes, a tantalising hint of pink climbing her cheekbones, and Marcus couldn't help himself.

'Not even so much as a pair of tightie-whities. The technical term I think is "commando". In other words stark boll—'

Her eyes sprang open. 'I get it. Thank you. Vividly. I'm sure my readers will appreciate the detail,' she added.

Damn. That victory had been short-lived—the idea of Lycander's population imagining the Prince's Chief Advisor going commando did *not* fill him with joy.

'*Touché,*' he acknowledged.

'So you dressed in jeans and a T-shirt. Why?'

'Comfort. We decided a couple of years ago to drop the need for suits or formal clothing during council meetings. We knew the meetings could be time-consuming and sometimes stressful. Comfort seemed a priority.'

'Was it your idea?'

'Yes.'

April surveyed him for a moment, her head tilted to one side. 'But there was another reason, wasn't there?'

Damn, she was good at reading people. 'Of course not.'

With a sigh, she put down her pen. 'Off the record?'

'OK. Fine. I suggested it because I thought it would give Frederick *more* authority rather than less. I thought it would make him more human and indicate to the council that he was open to new ideas and not an autocrat like his father.'

'So you believe that clothes can be useful?'

'Yes.'

In his childhood, clothes had been a sorry affair—unwashed, ill-fitting and scruffy. Until that magical day when his parents had inadvertently let him see a stash of goods 'off the back of a lorry' and he had taken a pair of designer trainers. They had been livid, but he hadn't cared. Those trainers had shown him the power that could be wielded by clothes—the kudos he'd gained from street kids who wouldn't usually look at him had been an eye-opener.

'People judge you by your clothes, and you can use that to your own advantage. You shouldn't judge a book by its cover, but most people do.'

'That can be a monumental mistake.'

'It's still a fact. Clothes send a message, and as such they are a tool to be used.'

'Is that what you do? You personally? Do you dress for other people?'

'No. I dress for myself. But if an expensive suit will prove a point to whoever I am sitting across a negotiating table from then I may choose to wear it. The image you project can matter in some situations.'

Before she could respond, there was a knock on the door and Gabrielle entered with three dresses draped over her arm. In a deft movement she hung two up on a rail by the door and held up the remaining one.

'I think this is the one.'

Marcus glanced at the dress. His knowledge of fashion wasn't up to much, but he registered an impression of red, stripes and lace. Turning to see April's reaction, he clocked her panic before she shook her head in a firm rejection.

'It's beautiful, Gabrielle, but it isn't me. It's too obvious. I'm a writer—an observer. I don't want to be noticed.'

The words made a level of sense—indeed, they echoed the view he had just put forward about the importance of clothes—so perhaps he had misinterpreted the panic. And yet...

'Surely tonight it doesn't matter? After all I am your subject and I know you're observing me already, so please don't hold back on my account.'

Perhaps his motivation was selfish—he knew she would look incredible in the dress and he wanted to see her in it.

'I would still prefer to be less visible rather than more. This event will be star-studded—I'd like to observe the guests without being noticed.'

Gabrielle waved away the objection. 'At an event like this one you will stand out if you do *not* wear something like this. There will be nothing that will mark you out more clearly as an observer than wearing a dull black dress that conceals your assets rather than showcasing them.'

Her gaze swept again over April's current outfit of jeans, T-shirt and blazer, and although she was way too professional to shudder, Marcus felt it was a close-run thing.

It was clear that Gabrielle's argument had temporarily stymied April, and Marcus settled back on the small spindle-legged chair to observe the action.

Gabrielle continued with enthusiasm. 'Take this opportunity. Tonight you will be noticed no matter what; you will arrive on the arm of Marcus Alrikson, and no matter what capacity that is in people will be looking at you. So...this dress...it is a necessity.'

April paled, and now there could be no mistake—for some reason Gabrielle's words had left her stricken, and without thought Marcus rose to his feet, his amusement routed by concern and an instinct to protect her. For some unfathomable reason the idea of wearing this dress clearly had April in a state...

'We appreciate all the help. But I think it would be best if you could find April a simple black dress, or whatever it is April wants. After all Sunita always tells me it is important that a person feels comfortable in her skin as well as in her dress.'

The mention of Sunita did the trick. 'Of course.' Gabrielle hesitated, then turned to April. 'I apologise if I overstepped—but you are a beautiful woman and it is my instinct to want to show that to the world.'

April managed a smile. 'Thank you. That is a generous thing to say—and please don't feel you've overstepped. I am just not very good with clothes.'

Once Gabrielle had left she turned to Marcus.

'Thank you.'

'No problem.' He gestured towards the dresses. 'If you

don't like them then you don't like them. That's your pre-
rogative. You should wear whatever you want to wear.'

'And it doesn't bother you?'

Her question held an element of timidity that seemed
totally out of character.

'No. Why should it?'

'Because… Well, it's occurred to me that Gabrielle is
right. All eyes are going to be on us. You never take a plus-
one to events like this, and you don't ever give interviews.'

He shrugged. 'I have no problem with people looking at us.'

'And you have no problem with me wearing whatever I
choose to wear?'

'No.' He had absolutely zip idea where she was going
with this.

For a long moment she studied his expression, and a
small sweet smile tipped her lips. 'You mean that, don't
you?'

'Of course I do.' Marcus frowned. 'Are you worried
about what *I* choose to wear?'

'Of course not. You can come in your pyjamas for all I
care—' She broke off, a ludicrous look of dismay on her
face. 'If you had any, I mean…though… I mean… Well…
obviously I'd prefer you to be wearing *something*.' Suddenly she giggled. 'Though if you weren't I guess at least
no one would be looking at *me*. Whatever I wear.'

Her laughter was clear, melodious and infectious, and
he couldn't help but join in. Then somehow the whole
conversation, her sheer beauty, and their shared laughter prompted a change in the atmosphere and their mirth
subsided.

They stared at each other and then he stepped forward,
reducing the gap between them. She followed suit. Now
they were so close he could count the smattering of faint
freckles on the bridge of her nose.

'April...?'

But before she could answer there was a knock on the door. April jumped backwards and turned away from him as Gabrielle re-entered.

She looked from one to the other but said nothing. 'I have found this,' she announced, holding up a long black dress, her nose slightly wrinkled in disapproval.

'Thank you. I'll try it on.' Without looking at Marcus, April said, 'Do you mind waiting outside?'

'No problem.'

Right now fresh air was exactly what he needed—that or a long cold shower, or a brisk run.

Ten minutes later April emerged from the shop, a bag held loosely in her hand.

'Successful?' he asked.

She glanced down at the bag and then back to him. 'Time will tell.'

CHAPTER SIX

APRIL SURVEYED HER reflection in the hotel room's mirror and wondered if she had perhaps run a little mad, even lifting a hand to her forehead to check her temperature.

What had possessed her? What *still* possessed her?

She had no idea.

But as she'd stood in that room with Gabrielle she had looked at the black dress and then at the other one.

Gabrielle had given a small Gallic shrug. 'It matters not which dress you wear. He will not take his eyes from you. That is plain.'

April shook her head. 'It's not like that. I am writing an article on him. That's all.'

Gabrielle had given her a look of polite disbelief but said nothing as April had continued to look at both dresses.

Then, 'Perhaps I *will* try it on. The first one.'

'*Bon!* Good!'

Gabrielle had ushered her into the fitting room and minutes later April had stared at her reflection. The same reflection she stared at now. Of a woman she barely recognised. With the emphasis on 'barely'. The dress was strapless, showing off her shoulders and arms, discreetly tantalising with a hint of cleavage. The nude underlay was covered by a layer of red lace and a bold swathe of red stripes that swept to the floor. The whole concoction magically hinted at sensuality.

What had she been thinking?

She knew the answer to that. In a moment of insanity she had wanted to make absolutely sure that Marcus had eyes for no other woman than her—had wanted to wear a dress that would dazzle him and court his admiration, would summon that dark appreciation and desire to his eyes.

But now caution blew a cold cloud over the idea. Last time she had dressed to dazzle it had been for Dean. But Marcus wasn't Dean. He might be good-looking—OK, gorgeous—and he might be charismatic, but he wasn't controlling and he had no interest whatsoever in a trophy date. Not a jot. And yet she had chosen this dress in all its tantalising glory.

Now, as she looked at her reflection, regret began to trickle in. Because whilst the dress lived up to all Gabrielle had promised it was *more* than the dress. Her eyes sparkled with luminosity and her whole bearing seemed...different. There was no escaping the fact that her hormones had kidnapped her common sense. But only up to a point. Yes, she wanted appreciation, but it would go no further than that.

As she headed from her room, down in the lift and along the corridor to the lobby, anticipation built and scrambled inside her. When she saw Marcus her breath caught in her throat. Forget gorgeous—he looked stratospherically scrumptious. The tuxedo gave him a devil-may-care aura, and the shower-damp hair, the breadth of his shoulders and most of all the fire of approval that lit his dark eyes made her dizzy.

His gaze raked over her, caused heat to flood her veins. 'You look stunning.'

He took a step closer and her heart hopped, jumped and skipped. Threw in a somersault for good measure.

'But I knew you would look beautiful in whatever you wore.'

Now her heart cartwheeled, and she didn't know what to say except a whispered, 'Thank you. But really it's the dress...not me.'

Silence fell and she sought to fill it before she threw caution to the wind, grabbed the lapels of his tux, kissed him and dragged him straight upstairs.

No, no, no! Say something. Anything, however idiotic, will do.

'I'm hoping it will give me confidence. I don't usually attend events like this—I tend to interview people one on one—very civilised and arranged in advance, in a situation where the interviewees want to talk about themselves. To be honest I'm not very social, so I'm a bit nervous.'

It wasn't working. He was too close—so close she wanted to lean forward and sniff him, to try and identify the scent that seemed to be sending her hormones into overdrive.

Don't do it!

'You can always talk to me,' he pointed out, and his smile was so wicked that she suspected he knew damn well exactly what she wanted to do.

She needed to get a grip—of something other than him.

Stepping back, she nodded. 'I plan to. After all, that's what I'm being paid to do.' The reminder was as much to herself as to him. 'We'd better go.'

The brief car journey whizzed by, and as she looked out at the dusky grey skies, inhaled the warm evening breeze tinged with mimosa and orange blossom, sensations were tumultuous within her. Everything seemed heightened—her skin was super-sensitive, her whole being attuned to every sound and scent. But most of all she was aware of Marcus.

Then they arrived, and as she stepped out next to him

somehow her nerves were quietened by his sheer presence and the reassurance provided by the effortless strength he exuded.

The building itself was sufficient to catch her attention; the sandstone of the embassy gleamed in the moonlight, the turrets and pillars of a bygone era somehow adding to the fairy tale surrealness of the whole evening.

The inside was no less splendid.

'It's magnificent,' she said. 'A pocket of history.'

Without preamble she fumbled in her clutch bag and pulled out her notebook, scribbling down some key words so she could do the setting justice when she wrote the article. The familiarity of writing was a comfort, a nose-thumb at her hormones.

See—I'm here to work, not to relish in physical allure. Ha!

As she returned the book to her bag she looked up to see a familiar couple heading towards them: Rafael Martinez and Cora Derwent, the evening's hosts. Rafael, as ever, looked brooding, whilst Cora smiled in recognition—a smile that held radiance as her red hair glittered under the light of the chandeliers.

'Marcus. Good to see you.' Rafael held his hand out.

Cora kissed April. 'And April as well. I saw you'd been added to the guest list and thought how lovely it was that the two of you had got together.'

April felt tell-tale heat flush her face. Cora's voice held genuine approval and she knew the words had been meant in all sincerity.

'Actually,' she said, irritated that her voice held too much squeak, 'I'm writing an article on Marcus.'

Cora glanced quickly from April to Marcus and then nodded. 'How exciting! That is even more of a coup—and if you do as good a job as you did with Kaitlin and Daniel's wedding then Marcus is in safe hands. And, talking of weddings, how is the royal one going?'

'A security nightmare, I'd imagine?' Rafael interpolated.

'I've had easier assignments,' Marcus said. 'But, more importantly, both Frederick and Sunita told me to convey their congratulations.'

In that instant April realised the reason for Cora's radiance, the glow that lit her from within. Cora's hand went instinctively to curve over the swell of her belly and Rafael's face broke into a smile so broad and awe-filled that tears prickled at the back of April's eyes.

Instinct and a learnt ability to deal with situations like this came to her rescue. She knew that Cora and Rafael deserved the happiness of parenthood, and she truly did wish them all the joy in the world. But still, this glimpse into that serenity could not help but be a reminder of all she had lost.

It was a loss that she could never come to terms with, even while she had had to accept that life went on. That whilst *her* world had collapsed, everyone else's kept on spinning.

'Congratulations from me as well,' she said, suddenly all too aware of Marcus's intent gaze.

'Thank you. We are beyond ecstatic. If you would like to write a lifestyle article on *us* at any point you're more than welcome. After all, we have a lot to thank you for.'

'You do?' The turn in the conversation was a gift—as long as she could think of Cora as a subject, the current of emotion would be easier to control.

'Yup. Your article on Sunita meant that Frederick found love, and that made Kaitlin very happy.'

'Happy enough to forgive me? I was a thorn in her side when she was with Frederick.'

'You were—but that's because you were after the truth.

You knew something wasn't quite right, and now… Now all the Derwents have achieved what we thought to be impossible—a happy-ever-after. And Rafael and I are lucky enough to be having a baby.'

This time April was prepared, and she didn't so much as flinch. Cora glanced round. 'Now, if there's anyone else you have your eye on for an interview I'm happy to introduce you!'

For an insane moment April wanted to refuse, to remain near Marcus. The idea of socialising sent a shiver of anxiety over her skin. During her ill-fated marriage there had been parties aplenty, and she'd grown to loathe them. Dean's critical, watchful gaze had made her clumsy by default, filched all possible enjoyment from the event.

But she wasn't here with Dean, and once, in the dim and distant past before him, April had *loved* parties—had revelled in being in good company, exchanging ideas, dancing, talking, having fun. That April seemed like a stranger now—someone it was truly impossible for her to believe had been herself. Perhaps tonight she could find an echo of that carefree girl…

Squaring her shoulders, she nodded. 'Thank you, Cora. I'd like that.'

Marcus's gaze lingered on the graceful sway of April's walk, on the natural poise that nonetheless held a hint of trepidation. How he knew that, he wasn't sure—but he did, and for a moment the urge to follow her nearly overcame his common sense.

'You like her.' Rafael's words were not a question, and Marcus turned to face him.

'She is a writer, on a mission to interview the "real" Marcus Alrikson. You know how I feel about the press.'

'Yet you like her. You should act on it, my friend.'

Marcus shook his head. 'Just because *you* have succumbed to wedded bliss, don't try and pull the rest of us in.'

Rafael smiled. 'Once that is how I felt. Then somehow Cora…she changed my mind and I have no regrets. And now with the baby… I feel truly blessed.'

A twinge of something perilously close to envy pinched a nerve, and Marcus blinked in irritated recognition of the emotion. This was nuts. No way did he want a family—he knew his own limitations and was more than happy to abide by them.

Rafael was shaking his head, almost as if he were questioning his own good fortune. 'Who would have thought it? Not me a couple of years ago—I can tell you that. So, my advice to you? If you like her, at least admit it to *yourself*.'

'It's not a question of liking her or not.' Now he sounded defensive. 'In three days' time she will go her way and I will go mine. End of.'

Rafael raised one dark brow but forbore from comment.

As if to prove his point Marcus made sure to circulate the room—though it took more effort than seemed strictly necessary not to check on April's whereabouts. But he forced himself to succeed, and it was only when a gong was struck to announce dinner that he glimpsed her again as she headed to their table.

Once they were seated, waiters circled with unobtrusive discretion so that it seemed as if wine and food appeared almost magically. A starter that combined baby artichokes with figs and huge tasty almonds was followed by a traditional paella that glistened with saffron-coated rice, embedded with enormous clams and bright red peppers.

Marcus was soon monopolised by a man with decided views on Lycander's overseas policies, but even as he focused on keeping his temper he felt a sudden tension still April's body, and realised she was no longer a participant in the general hum and chatter of the table.

Fragments of conversation drifted towards him.

'We just can't decide whether to have another baby or not...'

'How many are you on?'

'Three, but they are all so adorable and they seem to get better as they grow older.'

'Mind you, I sometimes think teenagers are more work than toddlers...'

'So amazing to watch them grow into people, if you know what I mean...'

And then, 'April, I am *so* sorry—you must be bored stupid. Unless, of course, you have children?'

Her leg clenched next to his, so tightly his own muscles ached in sympathy, and surely the silence stretched just a little too long before she answered.

'No, I don't. But, truly, don't stop on account of me. I'm a lifestyle writer, after all, so it's interesting for me to hear how all of you mix motherhood, your jobs and celebrity.'

The words were casual, and yet instinct prompted him to lean in. 'I can see a way to combine our conversations. I'd be very interested to hear your views on education...'

And from there the conversation flowed around a plethora of topics, from school reminiscences to weddings.

Throughout, April deflected all attempts to elicit any personal information about her life, whilst garnering plentiful knowledge about others. So by the time the last decadent spoonful of dessert had been scooped up, and Rafael had risen to his feet to make a speech, Marcus knew no more about April than he had before.

Not that it mattered, he reminded himself—after all, her life story was hardly relevant. Instead he focused on Rafael.

'As you know, each year this dinner honours a different charity. This year, with respect and remembrance of Prince Axel, our donation is to Drive for Life. DFL is a charity that pioneers safe driving and helps the victims and survivors of car accidents, including those who are left behind. The parents, children, families and friends of those whose lives have been snatched without notice.'

Although Marcus had known about the chosen charity—a charity he supported wholeheartedly on a personal level—the words touched him with renewed grief as Rafael spoke of those who had suffered through accidents such as the one that had taken Axel.

He wasn't surprised to sense April's reaction—to hear her small intake of breath and feel the tension that stilled her body—Rafael's words were emotive. What he *hadn't* expected was for her to leave… But that was exactly what she did.

A murmured, 'Excuse me,' an additional apology and she was gone.

OK… It could be that she quite simply needed a bathroom break, but that was an unlikely scenario. To leave at this point in Rafael's speech was…if not rude, then close to it. Perhaps the food had disagreed with her and she'd had no choice but to exit.

The minutes ticked on. Rafael sat down to a round of applause and Marcus turned his head towards the door. No sign of her. He could sit here and wonder, or he could follow her.

He headed towards the restrooms as a first port of call and halted outside the Ladies'. Obviously he couldn't go in there, but as he leant back against the wall it soon became clear that no one was handily going to come out and answer his query as to whether April was inside.

So with a quick glance down the corridor he opened the door and entered. Silence. No cry of outrage greeted him, so he called out, 'April?'

Further silence—and then he heard the slightest of shuffles.

Feeling like a first-class idiot, he tried not to think of the ramifications if it *wasn't* April in there... *Lycander's Chief Advisor caught peering under cubicle door in the Ladies'.*

'April? If that is you, please say so now as I'm less than comfortable in here.'

There was a small sigh redolent of tears and his chest squeezed in the sure knowledge she'd been crying. 'Then maybe you shouldn't have followed me. There *is* such a thing as privacy.'

'Are you OK?'

Another silence. Then, 'Not really. I just need five minutes and I'll be back at the table. Please go before we draw attention to our joint absence.'

Marcus hesitated, then realised he really couldn't linger in here, nor force her out. 'OK...'

April pressed her hands against her eyes. *No more tears... please no, more tears.* But Rafael's speech had plumbed the depths of her soul, forced a replay of her past.

Vivid images had flickered in her brain.

Standing in front of Edward's cot, trying to protect him from Dean's rage. The sound of thunder in the background—a prelude to the storm and the tragedy to come. The dense grey pounding rain and the lash of wind against the windows. The pungent smell of alcohol and hatred that had emanated from her husband. The pain when he'd punched her out of the way and the deadly, deadly fear when he'd snatched Edward up. Her desperate pleas as she'd tried to stop him, reaching up from the floor in supplication...

Somehow she'd dragged herself after him, heard the roar of his sports car as he had gunned it away from the kerb. And then a few hours later the police had been on the doorstep, deluged by the rain...

So in the here and now she'd left the table, knowing she

was about to break down, and had made it to the sanctuary of this cubicle, where she had allowed herself to weep silently. She'd swallowed down tears when Marcus had entered and pulled herself together. Now she needed to keep herself together—no more unravelling.

She pushed the cubicle door open and headed to the basin, staring at her reflection in the ornate gilt mirror as she washed her hands and inhaled the scent of rose petals that permeated the air.

It seemed ludicrous now that at the start of the evening she'd almost had a sense of anticipation—had held a small bubble of optimism that it might even be a tad enjoyable. How could it be? Social events invariably brought about conversation that evoked poignant memories—a minefield that she had to prepare herself for. Worse, they prompted the need to dissemble, to erase years of her life, her marriage and her son. Quite simply to pretend her beautiful baby hadn't existed.

Stop. Before Marcus returns to find you.

Somehow the thought of Marcus steadied her, and with one last glance in the gilded mirror she turned and headed for the door. Pulling it open, she screeched to a halt as Marcus pushed himself off the adjacent wall in one lithe movement.

'What on earth are you doing here?'

'Waiting for you.'

'I told you to go back to the table.'

He raised an eyebrow. 'No one told me you were in charge,' he murmured, and the small smile on his lips goose-bumped a little shiver over her skin.

Right now the attraction was a welcome distraction from her grief. For a second she wondered if he somehow knew that.

'So what do you want to do now?' he asked. 'If you like I can drive you back to the hotel.'

For a second temptation beckoned, but she knocked it back. This was a work assignment and she would see it through.

'I appreciate your concern but I am fine. Really. I want to go back in.'

'Then that is what we will do.'

Grateful for his acceptance of her decision, she followed him back down the corridor, re-entering the ballroom as Rafael announced that the dancing would now commence.

'Shall we?' Marcus asked.

For a second she gaped at him. 'Shall we what?'

'Dance?'

Refusal would be the sensible option—she knew that— yet the simple word *No* refused to materialise on her lips.

'I'm sure your readers will be interested in how I acquit myself on the dance floor.'

He had a point, but deep down she knew that wasn't the true motivation for her desire to dance with him. Right now the pull of attraction was moving her away from the cusp of despair. She wanted to be held in his arms...wanted to be up close and cocooned by his strength and powerful aura.

Dammit. When there was so much heartache in the world, so much tragedy and grief, right here and now it felt important to acknowledge the sheer life-giving force of physical attraction.

'You're right.'

What harm could there be in one dance? Especially when she could kid herself it was for research purposes...

But from the second he placed an arm around her waist and they stepped onto the dance floor research went out of the window. It seemed nonsensical that his touch could burn though the lacy material of her dress, ridiculous that desire should strum her body with a riff causing a fever of combustible proportions.

Her head spun as if she had gone through a portal into

a more rarefied atmosphere—a world where she could somehow manage to shut out everything but the here and now. Memories, guilt and despair were all still out there, but they couldn't get into this insulated bubble where all she could be aware of was Marcus.

The beat of his heart under her fingers, the strength of his chest, the feel of his arm around her waist, his clasp light yet firm and somehow full of promise, the smell of him, his proximity...

She looked up at him, fascinated by every molecule of his skin. Instinct dared her to move her hand and brush the nape of his neck. She heard his intake of breath as he pulled her closer—so close she knew he was as aroused as she...

Then memory sheared through her insulation, superimposed an image of the past...ten years before...a college dance...a different time, a different man. A man who had seemed to empower her but in fact had enslaved her, had somehow made her dance to his every tune. *Dean*. She had fallen for him, sucked in by his looks, his charisma, by the arrogance that she had mistaken for confidence. In that dance, that evening, she had believed herself to be on top of the world—whereas in reality she had been on the brink of ruin.

Never again would she let desire shut out all else.

Somehow she managed not to wrest herself from Marcus's grasp. Instead she dropped her hand from his neck to his shoulder and unglued her body from his—there was no other word for it. Shame swathed her. Somehow she focused on a point over his shoulder and tried to suppress the seething sensation inside her.

'April...?'

His voice tested her resolve but didn't break it. All she had to do was conjure up a vision of Dean—not the Dean she'd first danced with, but the man he'd turned out to be and the horrific chain of events that dance had precipitated.

'You OK?'

'Yes. Actually, no.' To her horror, she could hear the anger in her voice, the frustration and the sheer emotion. 'This attraction is wrong. Unless, of course, I'm imagining it?'

Right now she would almost prefer the humiliation of being told it was all one-sided.

'You aren't imagining it and it isn't wrong. It's just unfortunate.'

Unfortunate? Ouch.

Totally perversely, hurt was added to the anger that swirled inside her.

'It's too complicated, given our situation—given that you're researching an article on the "real" Marcus Alrikson.'

April frowned. She got why this attraction sucked from *her* viewpoint, but from his...? Then the penny dropped.

'You think I'll kiss and tell?'

'It's a possibility I have to consider.'

Now her anger upped its ante and turned into rage. Common sense attempted to indicate that he had a point, but she lasered it down. He should know that she would *never* do anything so grubby.

Curbing the urge to really give him something to consider—like a knee straight where it hurt most—she narrowed her eyes. 'I assure you there will be no "tell", because there will be no "kiss".'

He opened his mouth and then closed it again, and she wondered what he had been going to say. Whatever it was he'd clearly decided against it. Instead he gave a small nod and said, 'That works for me.'

April wasn't sure how she got through the rest of the evening, but spurred on by pure anger she forced herself to circulate, to talk to as many people as possible about their opinion on Marcus Alrikson.

She gritted her teeth as she heard the words 'dedicated,' 'committed', 'drop-dead gorgeous' and 'unapproachable'—that from a woman who had once tried to ask him out. There was also 'ruthless', 'arrogant', 'fair'...

Finally the orchestra played its penultimate dance. Then Cora Derwent took the stage, thanked everyone for their generous donations and announced that there would be one final speech before the last dance—from Marcus Alrikson.

April blinked and sudden guilt touched her. This event had been in memory of Axel. In her own grief she hadn't really thought about how Marcus must be feeling.

He climbed to the podium and stood, at ease, confident that everyone would listen to his words.

'First, don't worry—I'll keep it brief. Second, don't worry—I'm not after any more of the contents of your wallets. I want to take this opportunity to say thank you for your generosity tonight, and I want to say a few words about Prince Axel. And I am not speaking to you now as Chief Advisor to the Prince, but as Axel's best friend.

'Axel was a good man—and I mean that in all senses. He had a sense of honour and he truly cared about Lycander and all its people. He had a vision, and it is a true tragedy that he never had a chance to turn that vision into reality. But that aside, what grieves me most is the knowledge that his life ended way too soon. I grieve because I will never hear his laugh again, never have another beer after a game of squash.

'Axel lost his chance to grow older, to marry and to have children, to feel the Lycandrian sun on his face. For that I grieve. But I promise, Axel, my old friend, that your memory will live on; I miss you as a friend as well as a ruler I would have been proud to serve.' He lifted his glass. 'To Axel.'

April blinked back tears, wishing with a familiar fierceness that somehow she could change her past. Those words echoed her own grief—that Edward would never grow older, play football, attend school…

Applause broke out as everyone in the room lifted their glasses, and then the orchestra started to play the last tune of the night and people began to congregate on the dance floor.

April headed straight to Marcus. 'I'm sorry,' she said.

'For what?'

'For not realising this evening must be hard for you, too. Because of Axel.'

His gaze sharpened, and too late she realised her slip: the addition of the word 'too' had been a tacit admission of her own state.

'Yes, it is. But I know that charities like DFL work hard to prevent similar tragedies. Axel would have approved of that.'

'I get that, but it's still hard.'

'Yes.'

April took a deep breath. 'Can we forget about earlier?'

'Yes. I'm sorry, too. I shouldn't have been so tactless.'

There was a small silence and then April looked up at him. 'Can I ask you something? Off the record?'

'You can *ask*.'

'How do you deal with the grief?'

Marcus hesitated. Then, 'I'll show you.'

CHAPTER SEVEN

As they climbed into the chauffeur-driven car Marcus wondered if this was a good idea. Then again, were *any* of his ideas with regard to April good ones? Somehow he thought not. That dance? *Very* bad idea; his body still hadn't got over it. His agreement to her writing an article on 'the real Marcus Alrikson'? Also not one of his better moments.

And now he had chosen to prolong their time together. But he could sense her pain, her grief, and like it or not he wanted to help in some way.

'Alrikson Security, please, Roberto.'

As the vehicle made its smooth way through mostly deserted roads Marcus leant back against the leather seat.

'When Axel died, at first I quite simply didn't believe it. It didn't seem possible that a man I had spoken to mere hours before could be gone. The sheer surrealness of it stunned me. It seemed impossible that I couldn't do something to change fate's decree. That I couldn't turn the clock back.'

Just as he hadn't been able to after the fire—hadn't been able to alter the moment when he hadn't gone back in.

'When I finally accepted he was gone, I raged.'

He had contemplated drowning his grief in a bottle; he'd known from observation that alcohol could numb everything, wipe it all out. But he'd also known that that way lay addiction and misery—his genes might point to that option, but he would never make the choices his parents had made.

'What did you do?'

The car pulled up outside the sleek headquarters of his company and they alighted. Marcus keyed them in and led the way to the lifts, pressing the button for the basement. Minutes later they were in the underground gym he'd had installed.

'I took it out on a punch bag. For hours.' Until sheer exhaustion had temporarily anaesthetised his pain. 'Day after day.' A pause. 'Do you want to try it?'

'Me? Punch a bag? I couldn't.'

'Why not?'

'Because it's… I'd feel stupid. I'm hardly fighting fit—I doubt I'd make much of an impact. I can't remember the last time I went to the gym.'

'It's not a competition or a test. It's a way to unleash all those feelings. The anger, the grief, the rage…'

She shook her head. 'I'd rather not feel them at all.'

'At the end of a workout you'll be too numbed by exhaustion to feel *anything*.'

He could see that the idea appealed. But, 'I couldn't do it anyway. Not in this dress.'

'You can borrow some of my workout clothes. It's up to you. If you don't feel comfortable, don't do it. But don't worry about looking stupid or being weak. You're neither. It's a way to stay in control. You control the feelings; they don't control you.'

April stared at the punch bag and then nodded. 'OK. Thank you. I'd like to give it a try.'

'Changing rooms are this way.'

April looked at the T-shirt and, succumbing to temptation, held it to her face. It smelt freshly laundered—not even the faintest Marcus scent discernible. Yet the idea that this material had once touched his skin added a frisson to the emotional whirlpool that already twisted inside her as she tugged the soft cotton garment over her head.

She closed her eyes. What was *wrong* with her? Had she completely lost the plot?

That was a no-brainer. The plot had been left behind long ago that day—possibly in Gabrielle's boutique. Now she appeared to be winging it without a script.

She tried to picture herself actually aiming a punch, and to her own surprise felt a strange thrill course through her body at the prospect. Because right now she was all over the place and she loathed it. If she really could rid herself of the intensity of these sensations then it was a win-win situation. Because once they were gone she would make damn sure they didn't come back.

The thought propelled her into the oversized shorts. Tugging at the cord, she cinched them round her waist, and a couple of expert rolls of the waistband rendered them acceptable. The movement was a reminder of those carefree school days when she and her friends had hitched their school skirts to madly short lengths the moment they were out of parental sight. Days so long ago, when her life had stretched before her full of glorious possibility.

And then Dean had entered it…

Emotions swirled again, and she left the changing room and headed back to the gym, where she halted on the threshold, frozen into immobility.

Just great!

Marcus, too, had changed—into tracksuit bottoms and a T-shirt that seemed moulded to his upper torso. Honed muscles were on display, and suddenly her mouth was dry and her lungs seemed to have forgotten their function.

'Hey.'

He smiled at her and she forced herself not to close her eyes.

'I thought it would be easier if I show you the best way to do this, as well as explain it. There are some things you need to know before I can let you loose.'

His common-sense tone was exactly what she needed to make this whole situation less surreal, and she listened as he explained, his deep voice full of reassurance as he reiterated the importance of not tensing up and maintaining balance.

'So now I'll show you...'

April tried to treat it as a lesson, tried to focus only on the technical aspects, but it quite simply wasn't possible. Not when the sheer glory of his sculpted body was on display and his grace, agility and clean movement as he jabbed the punch bag caused havoc with her insides.

'You ready?' he asked.

'Yes.'

With an effort she calmed her breathing, tried to pretend this was all research for an article, but for once her brain let her down, left her unable to formulate sentences.

'I'll tape your hands to protect them, and don't forget—'

'To keep my wrists straight,' she finished.

However hard she tried, she couldn't disguise the tremble in her fingers as she held out her hands—couldn't hold back the audible intake of breath as he wrapped the tape around them. Every movement felt like a caress.

'OK. You're good to go. Remember—not too forceful the first time.'

She pulled back and hit the bag, jarred her hand.

'Keep it easy. Imagine getting rid of the anger, the grief, but remember *you're* the one in control—you're in charge.'

The deep timbre of his voice washed over her, calling to something inside her. The punch bag came into sharp focus, and somewhere inside her feelings began to bur-

geon. Grief rolled out its black carpet alongside anger...
rage that life had inflicted such tragedy on her, fury with
herself for her own culpable part in it.

The punch bag seemed to swirl with images—images
she wanted to destroy, to pound into oblivion. Again and
again.

Then suddenly she was being held back, contained.
'Whoa. Time to stop, April.'

The images faded and she blinked the sweat from her
eyes, pulling herself back into the present, where Marcus
held her in a loose grip.

'Sorry,' she said.

'No need to apologise. I only stopped you because I was
worried you were overdoing it. I don't want you to damage your wrists. How are you feeling now?'

He released her and stepped back as she turned to face
him, tried to assess how she felt.

'Drained.'

The anger and grief had gone. She knew they'd be back,
but for now they had released their hold.

Meeting his gaze, she ventured a small smile. 'Better, I think.'

His lips turned up in answer. 'Good. I think you may
be a natural.'

Was it his smile, or his proximity, or the fact that she
had just exposed something of herself? Who knew? All she
did know was that awareness had started to swirl around
them.

Realisation dawned that she might have punched out
her anger, but her desire hadn't got the message and had
clearly manacled itself inside her. And now it burgeoned
into the knowledge that all it would take was one step and
their bodies would touch. One movement and she could
rest her hand on his chest, feel the wall of muscle through
the thin material of his T-shirt.

Bad idea.

But she didn't care.

One step—that was all it took.

Marcus's gaze didn't waver from hers, and his dark eyes burnt with a desire that matched her own. Without a word he reached for her. His hands curved round her waist in a possessive grip that thrilled her as he tugged her even closer. He lowered his head and his lips met hers, their touch so new, so wonderful, it pierced her very soul. At first it was feather-light, and then, as she parted her lips in a small moan, he deepened the kiss and backed her against the wall. April slid her hands under his T-shirt. Her head spun in the sheer soar and swoop of desire.

'April...'

His voice was ragged now, and she stared at him wide-eyed, bereft because his lips had left hers.

'You said earlier that you didn't want this. If you still feel the same way, now is the time to say so.' He hauled in a breath. 'Before stopping this becomes even harder than it is right now.'

The words took a while to permeate the fog of desire and her emotions warred. How did he have the control to stop? Yet she had to appreciate the fact that he had—that he hadn't taken advantage of the situation and was giving her a choice. A choice she didn't know how to make.

'I—'

At that instant the buzz of his phone saved her, and she watched as he tugged the phone from his pocket, glanced at the screen and answered it. He moved away, and she wondered if he had taken the call simply to give them both some space.

April closed her eyes and felt a sudden hit of mortification—she had behaved like some idiot adolescent, had got carried away by lust in a basement gym, for heaven's sake.

He ended the call and headed back to her.

'I'm sorry,' April said. 'That was a mistake.'

'Yes.'

Hurt twanged as he stepped closer.

'If we decide to act on this attraction I want us both to be happy with the idea and understand the parameters—and I'd rather the setting was not here.'

Oh.

Her heart pounded her ribcage as she pondered his words. 'So you don't think it's a mistake in principle?'

'I don't know.' His mouth twisted ruefully. 'What I *do* know is that it's not just going to vanish, and we need to work out a way to deal with it. But not here and now.'

'No.' It occurred to April how late it was. 'Shall I meet you at the office tomorrow morning?'

'Actually, there's been a change of plan. That's what the call was about. Frederick and Sunita are considering possible honeymoon locations and I'm vetting them for security purposes. Tomorrow we'll go and check out one of them.'

Great! A trip to a honeymoon resort—*exactly* what they needed. But maybe it was. After all, there would be plenty of people there—staff, guests, chaperones galore. How hard could it be?

'OK. That sounds good. Where is it?' Somehow her attempt at normal conversation had induced a false sense of calm within her, allowing her to pretend the kiss hadn't happened.

'In the middle of the ocean. Eden Island, to be precise. It's about four hours from Lycander. Apparently the island was originally owned by a Greek tycoon—he built a single dwelling on it for his wife, who was an artist, and she would go there to paint. He died a few years ago and she died recently. The heir is some distant relative who can't decide whether to sell it or turn it into a resort. In the meantime he has offered it to Frederick and Sunita.'

Single dwelling? So much for the hoped-for staff, chaperones and guests.

April gave a sideways glance at the punch bag. Perhaps she should ask Marcus if they could bring it with them.

CHAPTER EIGHT

MARCUS WAITED FOR April to settle herself into the helicopter cockpit, watching as she glanced around with a visible hint of trepidation. She was clearly in strict writer mode: notebook in hand, pencil tucked endearingly behind one ear, looking slightly uncomfortable in a black and white sun dress rather than the inevitable trousers, T-shirt and blazer combo.

Sidetracked, he couldn't help but comment, 'Nice dress. Another one?'

The hint of a blush touched her cheek even as she glared at him. 'Thank you. Courtesy of Sunita. It was hand-delivered to my hotel room this morning. During our interviews we've discussed clothes and my wardrobe—or lack of it—a lot. Her note said that she was pretty sure that I wouldn't have a dress suitable for a tropical island. So…' She gestured downwards. 'Anyway, I didn't expect a helicopter.'

'I promise I'm a fully qualified and experienced pilot.'

'I'm sure you are. It's just that in my head we were going by boat.'

'This is faster. We should get there early afternoon, have a few hours on the island, then be back late evening.'

'I've read that storms are predicted. Though it's hard to imagine that now.' Outside the heat shimmered with a glaring intensity.

Marcus nodded. 'They are—but not for a couple of days.'

Once airborne, as always, Marcus entered a zone of his own—one in which the power of the aircraft and the sheer magic that enabled him to control its flight through the air took over.

To his relief April was the perfect companion, making no effort to attempt any form of conversation, given the noise levels, and seemingly content to look out of the window, headphones in place. Every so often she would scribble down some notes.

Within two hours they approached Eden Island, the aerial view a panoramic vista. Marcus brought the helicopter to land on the helipad, his sense of achievement at a smooth, perfect landing always a boost.

'I really enjoyed that.' April turned to him, and her smile twisted something in his chest. 'You fly beautifully.'

'Thank you.'

'When did you start?'

'As soon as I could afford it. I'd always dreamed of being able to fly.'

The reason was ludicrous—stemming from the one time he'd believed his father to be sharing something genuine with him. For a minute the memory was so real he could visualise it...

He could see the six-year-old boy he had once been... remember that rare occasion when his father had seemed to feel affection towards his son. The tendril of pride and happiness he'd felt that he was at his father's feet.

'Son, right now it's like I'm soaring over peaks and mountains and it feels *so* damned good.'

Then his own voice: 'I wish I could do that. Will you teach me how?'

There had been the raucous sound of his mother's laughter. 'Let him try some.'

But his father had shaken his head. 'You never know—

maybe there'll be a chance for him to fly in a different way.'

That evening had soon dissolved into misery, but still Marcus treasured that memory, had given it significance because it had been one of the only kindnesses his father had ever shown him—not putting his son on the path to addiction at such a tender age.

'Marcus?'

April's voice tugged him back to the present and he blinked, focused on her face, freshly aware of the beauty of her features.

'Sorry. Yes. Flying was a childhood dream, and when I set up Alrikson Security I decided to make it reality. Now you could say it's a bit of a hobby.'

'An expensive hobby!'

'Sure. But one I can afford.'

She nodded in acknowledgement. 'I know. It's common knowledge that you made your first million well before you were twenty-five.' She paused. 'Does it ever bother you?'

'What?'

'That you have so much when others have so little? Kids like Gemma and Blake?' She raised a hand. 'Don't get me wrong—I know you've earned your money fair and square, that you set up Alrikson Security and made it a global success, but you also had the benefit of a privileged upbringing.'

Also common knowledge. He'd been educated at a prestigious school, had hobnobbed with royalty, no less. Her words tapped into his reservoir of guilt, took him back to the questions that had always dominated his life.

If a fire hadn't ended his parents' life, where would he be? If he'd gone back into the flames and rescued them, would he still have achieved success? Or would he be in prison? Would he have learnt to fly only in his mind, with the aid of drugs?

'Yes, it does bother me. But it wouldn't really benefit Gemma and Blake if I handed my entire fortune over to them. What will help them is change—social change, governmental change—but also I want to give them *choice*. Because there is always choice in life—an instant where you make a decision. An opportunity when you can say yes or no.'

'What if you make the wrong choice?'

Her question was quiet, and he sensed it held a wealth of meaning—regret, wistfulness, despair—and somehow he knew that at some time she, too, had made a decision that caused demons to eat away at her soul.

'Then you have to live with it, and live your life to the very best of your ability.' As he had done for Elvira's sake—his need to make his sister's life worthwhile had always ruled his actions.

Her head tipped to one side as she considered the words, and he wondered what thoughts were crossing her mind. Whatever they were, it seemed she had no intention of sharing them.

Instead she pulled out the notebook. 'Any other hobbies?' she asked.

'I don't really have time for much more than boxing and flying. What about you?'

'No.' As if realising the paucity of the syllable she continued, 'I used to play tennis and the guitar.'

'Did you sing?'

'A little.' She made it sound as if it was so far back in a dim and distant past that she couldn't really remember it. 'But I'm meant to be interviewing *you*, remember?'

And he was here to assess this potential honeymoon location's security risk.

With a nod of acknowledgement he unclasped the seatbelts and they clambered out onto the Tarmac helipad. The heat hit him, enveloped him in a sultry blanket, and next to him April caught her breath.

'It's…incredible. It's every stereotypical island paradise rolled into one. It's got the works—white sand, turquoise waves, palm trees and glorious sunshine.'

Marcus nodded, but in reality all he could see as he stared at the swathes of sun-baked sand broken up by clusters of palm trees were the potential security risks. Frederick's plan was to bypass security altogether—which was clearly not viable. There was nothing to prevent any would-be assassin from simply tooling up in a boat. As for the admittedly less dangerous threat of paparazzi—he might as well put up a welcome banner and serve refreshments.

He glanced around, suddenly uneasy… The heat was almost too oppressive—a reminder of the possibility of an impending storm.

'Let's go and check out the house.'

As far as he was concerned there would need to be a minimum of three security officers patrolling the helipad and any place where a boat could dock. Plus they'd have to rig up some extra temporary accommodation.

April looked at him with curiosity. 'You look distinctly grumpy. Surely when you see a place like this it makes you feel appreciative of its sheer tranquillity?'

'Not right now. Right now all I see is a potential security risk and a forthcoming argument with Frederick. He wants no security, and that is not possible.'

'Well, you can hardly blame him for wanting privacy on his honeymoon.'

'Unfortunately privacy and royalty rarely go hand in hand.'

They reached the house—an idyllic beach villa on stilts, with whitewashed stone walls, a thatched roof and vast windows.

They stepped inside and April gazed around. 'Wow!'

She had a point, and he wasn't surprised that she had her notebook out and was scribbling notes at breakneck speed.

Marcus had known what to expect, but even so the interior impressed him. The front door opened onto a spacious lounge area that led out to a covered veranda, where a woven hammock stretched invitingly next to a two-seater wicker swing chair. The furniture was simple, but solid, and it oozed comfort.

The lounge led into a corridor, from where one door led to a well-equipped white-walled kitchen. As he circled the room he noted that there was egress from this room as well as the front door. He checked the locks and sighed at their simplicity, then opened a door to a huge and well-stocked larder before leading the way back to the corridor and through another door.

The bedroom. They both halted. There was little point in trying to avert his gaze from the four-poster bed that dominated the room—it was a glorious, decadent piece of furniture. White lacy gauze hung from the top and sumptuous pillows beckoned. The whole damn thing positively screamed, *Use me, please!*

They both stood as if transfixed, and he felt awkwardness engulf him.

Really, Marcus?

He was thirty years old and embarrassed by a bed simply because he was with a woman.

He needed to get a grip, but it took an immense effort to step into the room, open the wardrobe doors, then exit onto the outside veranda—yet another security headache. And all made worse by the fact that when he went back inside April was actually inspecting the damn bed. As he watched she ran her fingers over the covers, leant forward to inspect the headboard. The black and white dress moulded to her body and desire leapt inside him, clenching his gut even as he reminded himself of the impossibility of acting on it.

She stood up straight, saw him, and jumped backwards from the bed, pulling the pen from behind her ear and starting to scribble once more.

'I'll need to vet those notes.'

'Why?'

'Because if they *do* honeymoon here the last thing I need from a security point of view is a detailed description of the honeymoon location.'

'OK.'

'No argument?'

To his chagrin he realised he *wanted* an argument. *For real, Marcus?* Was he actually looking to pick a fight out of sheer frustration? Because here and now, in this cosy, intimate honeymoon setting, it seemed important to remember that April and he were closer to adversaries than friends, let alone anything more?

'Of course not. I like Frederick and Sunita—I don't want to compromise their security.'

'If you like them so much, how can you contemplate contributing to toppling their life?'

'Because this isn't personal. It's about whether or not the people of Lycander have a right to know the truth about their ruler.'

He shook his head, suddenly sure that it was more than that. 'I think it *is* personal. This is about you and your belief that Frederick should pay for the decision he made, regardless of his motivations for making it.'

'That makes me sound punitive—as if I am setting myself up to be judge and jury.' Her voice shook with pure anger.

'Aren't you?'

Suddenly he was no longer angry; instead he was wondering why she felt such a need for the absolute truth.

'And if you are, then perhaps you need to consider the mitigating circumstances. If Brian Sewell's claims are true, all Frederick did was go along with a white lie—originally told by Axel himself—in order to prevent a possible revolt which would have overturned everything Axel believed in and would have been disastrous for Lycander. From a personal viewpoint, Frederick was perfectly happy with the life he had—he didn't want to rule. But now he is doing everything in his power to be a good ruler, to turn his country around. If you choose to make him pay for that, then that is your choice to make. Just be sure you can live with it.'

April stared at him, eyes wide, and he wasn't sure which emotion was uppermost in her mind—anger or perhaps shock. And still desire urged him to kiss her. *Stupid.*

It was time to go. He turned to close the door to the balcony, and paused to glance up at the sky. Late afternoon and nary a cloud—and yet there was an oppressive feel to the heat.

'We need to go.'

Perhaps the storm was more imminent than expected—but even so Lycander was only a four-hour flight away. It wouldn't break before then.

'Fine.'

There was both anger and hurt in the word, but Marcus refused to react. He'd called it as he'd seen it.

They crossed the beach to the helipad and climbed aboard in silence. Marcus carried out the routine checks, forcing himself to be thorough even as his instinct told him to make haste. It was an instinct honed in childhood to alert him to incipient danger—either on the streets, where gang warfare had been rife, or in his home where his parents' actions had been rendered unpredictable by their addictions.

Once en route he relaxed slightly—only to realise that relaxation had been premature. The helicopter suddenly jolted—almost as though it had encountered some form of resistance in the clear, cloud-free sky…almost as though something had hit the rotor blade. Another jolt. And another.

Next to him, April gave a small gasp but otherwise remained still. Marcus weighed the options—there was clearly a problem but he wasn't sure what it was. That meant… 'I'm turning back. When I land, get down as fast as you can safely and run.'

It seemed unlikely that the aircraft would go up in flames, but he was taking no chances.

She nodded, and admiration touched him at her calmness. Then all his focus was on the helicopter, on getting April to safety. And so, within a scant ninety minutes of leaving, they returned to Eden Island.

April scrambled out of the helicopter and headed away from the helipad at a run. Marcus was right behind her. Once a safe distance away, they stopped and turned to look at the aircraft.

'What happened?' she asked breathlessly, her mind scrambling to catch up with events.

'I'm not sure. My gut reaction is that for some reason the helicopter reacted to the atmosphere in some way—something to do with the incoming storm. That, or it's malfunctioning for other reasons. Either way, it's not safe to fly.'

'So what do we do now?'

'We're stuck here until someone can come out to get us—and that's obviously not advisable until the storm has come and gone.'

April looked at him, horror-struck, her lips slightly parted, her green eyes wide. 'So we're…we're stranded here? In a storm?'

Fear touched her along with the deep visceral sadness and pain that storms evoked in her. The association of storm and tragedy was interwoven into her very soul;

the sound of thunder a portent of remembered doom that brought her a cascade of memories of the day of Edward's death.

'There must be something you can do!'

'Such as what?'

'Maybe someone could come and get us in a boat?'

Because right now an imminent storm didn't seem possible—the early evening heat was still intense, the sand baking through the soles of her flip-flops, although the dusky sky did hold a faint scent of rain.

'There is no way I am risking getting someone out here just because you and I can't deal with being stuck here together.'

April closed her eyes. Marcus didn't know about her fear of storms, or the reason why, and she wanted to keep it that way. But it wasn't only the idea of a potential storm that bothered her right now. It was also his words of earlier. They had hit a whole plethora of nerves, and even now they fizzed around her neural network, evoking anger and hurt and horrible uncertainty.

Had she lost her objectivity? Was she *really* a writer motivated by her own personal experiences, made bitter and judgemental by her own horrific mistakes? The idea was so uncomfortable she was almost squirming in the sand.

'Right now,' Marcus continued, 'we'd best focus on battening down the hatches in the house before the storm strikes.'

He was right. She was behaving like an idiot when it was time to act like a professional. 'Sorry. You're right. Let's get back to the villa. How long do you think we'll be stranded here? And how bad do you think it will get?'

'It depends on when the storm hits and how badly. Best to be prepared for the worst-case scenario.'

'In that case I'll check food and supplies. Will the power short out, do you think?'

'It's probable, but I think there's a box of candles in the wardrobe in the bedroom.'

'I'll check there first, then sort out food.'

'Good. I'll go and make sure the windows and doors are safe.'

As she headed to the bedroom she kept her eyes resolutely away from the bed; that was one item of furniture she would *not* be using during her enforced sojourn here.

Opening the wardrobe door, she grabbed the box of candles and carried it through to the kitchen. A quick inspection showed a well-stocked freezer and larder, alongside plenty of bottled water. The kitchen boasted a top-of-the-range oven and an all-singing, all-dancing microwave.

Panic began to surface—she was marooned with a man she was insanely attracted to and a storm was about to break. OK… The best thing to do was to keep busy—so what else could she do?

Well, if they were stuck here for more than a night or two without power they would need food…

April considered the options and then set to work, determined to show Marcus that she was a competent, objective, *together* person.

'That smells good.'

She looked up as the kitchen door opened.

'You sound surprised,' April observed.

'I thought you were checking supplies, not cooking them.'

'I figured if the power goes off we won't be able to heat anything up, and whilst I know we can survive on tinned food I thought it would be a good idea to cook up some food we can eat cold. I'm doing marinated chicken wings, and a rice salad, and I'm cooking up some chickpeas and couscous as well. There's also caviar and crackers, and some very exotic-looking tinned fruit.' She paused. 'How is our security?'

'This place is thankfully pretty sturdy. I'm a little worried about the windows, but if it comes to it we can move into the larder—it's contained, and I suspect was made with the idea of a storm shelter in mind. We'll be all right.'

His air of calm authority gave her some much-needed reassurance.

He gestured to the stove. 'Can I help? It really does smell amazing.'

'No. I'm good.' Cooking was providing her with a semblance of normality. Here in the windowless kitchen it was possible to pretend there was no storm out there. 'Though, to be honest, it's a while since I've cooked from scratch, so odds are the food may not be that good.'

A small frown creased his brow and she hurried on.

'Do you cook?' A deft basting of the chicken wings and she popped them in the oven. 'I may as well interview you whilst I have the chance.' *Professionally.* 'In a typical day, what do you eat?'

'Are you sure anyone will be interested in this?'

'Of course they will. It makes you more human.'

'OK. In the mornings I have a cup of coffee at home. I get to work and maybe have a brioche or a pastry at my desk. At lunch, it depends where I am—if I'm in the office I'll make myself a sandwich or a salad; if I'm out I'll grab something on the run. Then in the evening I have to admit it's usually a takeaway or a ready meal or something pretty basic. Pasta or an omelette. I snack in between on fruit and nuts, and every year I make a resolution to learn how to cook.'

As if uncomfortable with sharing even that much information with the public, he leant back with a small shake of the head.

'What about you? Where did you learn to cook like this?'

'My parents both loved cooking and they made it a family thing. Right from when my sisters and I were little we cooked. The kitchen was the hub of the house and we all loved it.'

Memories came of Rosa, Lauren and herself, all giggling at her father's daft jokes while her mother was stirring a sauce, of her parents' amicable bickering over which herb would work best, the well-thumbed recipe books, the scent of garlic sauteing... Happy memories. Memories she'd once wanted to recreate with her own family and now never would.

Stop. Focus.

'What about your parents? Did they like cooking with you and Elvira?'

'Cooking was never their forte.'

His voice was casual enough, but she sensed a reserve, a careful vetting of his words.

'So you didn't bake with your mum or barbecue with your dad or vice versa?'

'Nope.'

April waited, but that appeared to be it.

'So, give me a day in your life. You get up, go to work, come home?'

'Yup. That may sound dull, but because my work is so diverse it really isn't.'

'So you don't get lonely?'

'Nope.'

'And you've never been tempted to share your life with a partner?'

'Nope.'

April narrowed her eyes, checked the chicken and regrouped. It had been a while since she'd interviewed someone who quite simply didn't want to be interviewed. Truth be told she'd *never* interviewed anyone so reluctant. Perhaps she needed a more open-ended approach.

'Hypothetically speaking, what sort of woman would tempt you to change your stance?'

'That woman doesn't exist—in reality or in La-La Land.'

'How about you pretend that your life depends upon it and describe your ideal woman?'

'I can't. I'm not trying to be difficult—'

'Much…' April muttered.

'But I can't describe someone I can't imagine. I like my own company. I don't have a template for an "ideal woman". In truth, I can't imagine living with anyone, sharing my space…' A small shudder rippled through his body. 'I told you—I can barely make it through a dinner date.'

'You must be able to come up with *something*.'

'It's not that easy. *You* try it—do you have an ideal man? A tick list of attributes?'

The question took her by surprise; none of her interviewees had ever showed any interest in *her*. 'This isn't about me.'

'I know that, but you want me to do something that is a lot harder than you make it sound.'

'No. Because I know you are quite capable of coming up with an ideal woman template. Isn't that what you did for Frederick? Before he met Sunita you believed that Lady Kaitlin Derwent was the ideal woman for Frederick, and presumably you believed that they could make a go of marriage.'

Ha! Her turn to wrong-foot him. But not for long.

He smiled in acknowledgement. 'The Prince's relationships are his own concern.'

'But it *is* true, isn't it, that you believed he should make an alliance based on politics, not love?'

'I agreed with the Prince that as ruler of Lycander he

should get married, but I didn't dictate his choice of bride. The choice has always been Frederick's to make, as it is he who will be travelling to the altar with her. Though of course in my role as advisor I can offer advice on the political ramifications of his marriage.'

'And Frederick has chosen to marry Sunita, the woman he loves, rather than a princess or an aristocrat or someone with good connections.'

'Yes, he has.'

'If you were Lycander's ruler would you do the same? Marry for love? Or would you marry for duty?'

'Well, seeing as I am not in love, and see little prospect of that, I would take the latter course.'

'You would sacrifice your single life for the sake of duty?'

'Yes. I suppose I would. But I would make an attempt to minimise the sacrifice—I'd marry someone I liked, who hopefully liked me, and I'd make sure we both had our own space—perhaps even separate houses—and—'

'Good to know romance isn't dead.'

'I'm not romantic.'

'What about love? Do you believe in love?'

'Of course. I just don't believe in it for *me*. That doesn't mean I don't wish happiness for other people. Look at Frederick and Sunita. You interviewed Frederick before he was reunited with Sunita.'

'Yes, back then he was…shut down, cold, reserved. And now…'

'Now he is a man transformed by love. For his fiancée and his son. And of course I wish him happiness.'

'Then why don't you want that happiness for yourself?' It didn't make sense.

'Because it wouldn't work for me. My route to happiness is different. In the same way that some people like to play the ukulele and other people wouldn't know which way up to hold one.'

'You're comparing love to playing the ukulele?'

'Why not? There are people who get a huge amount of joy and happiness from the ukulele, or any other musical instrument, and people like me who have the musical ability and innate talent of a non-performing flea.'

'You can't compare the two.' April frowned. 'Musical skill is a talent, but the ability to love is universal.'

'No. Some people find love comes easily to them. For others it is something that, however hard they practice, they simply can't do. That's why there are so many break-ups and the divorce rate is on the up. I'd rather accept my own limitations and be happy with them. Love is not for me.'

'Why not?' She still didn't get it—and wasn't sure she really bought his spiel.

'Because I don't have any innate ability for it. I'm not a romantic person—which is exactly why I am not on the market for a relationship. Never have been, never will be.'

'Never?'

'Nope. Feel free to check out my romantic history. My slate is clean.'

'So in thirty years you've never been in love, never had a relationship, never been out with anyone?'

'Well, it depends if you count Rita Gillam when I was fifteen—I went out with her for about three weeks and then she dumped me because I wasn't "suitable boyfriend material". By which she meant I didn't spend my money on chocolates or roses and I preferred to spend most of my spare time poring over motorbike magazines. Then there was Laura Hollsworth—I think we lasted four weeks before she figured I didn't come up to scratch. If memory serves me right, I wanted to go and see an action film and she wanted to see a girlie weepie. I suggested we toss a coin to decide and that was it—I was toast.

'Since then there has been a similar theme—the general consensus is that I'm not a good long-term bet. And I think that's fair enough. I love my job, I love my life, and I don't have the time or inclination or *anything* to offer a woman except very short term physical gratification. My current arrangements work. Low-maintenance, mutual pleasure, no risk.'

'No family?'

The words came with an effort and she knew they were infused with a bleakness she had not meant to transmit. They were a reminder of all her own one-time hopes and aspirations. Yet it was a question she had to ask—part of the interview process.

'What about kids?' she persisted.

For a moment an image of Edward crowded her brain, and she wondered how Marcus could willingly forgo the joy of having a child.

'I've accepted that isn't my path. I don't want a relationship, and that means I can't have children. It wouldn't be fair on anyone—most importantly the child.'

His voice was matter-of-fact and yet she was convinced there was a strand of wistfulness in it, an elusive something she couldn't put her finger on. *Daft*—she must be imagining it.

The oven beeped, and she definitely didn't imagine the relief on Marcus's face.

'Excellent,' he said as he sprang to his feet. 'I'm looking forward to this.'

'Really—don't get your hopes up too high. I haven't cooked in a while—cordon bleu it *won't* be.'

A faint frown creased his brow again. 'I'll set the table.'

CHAPTER NINE

MARCUS WATCHED AS April busied herself serving the food. She had completely put him through the wringer with her attempts to extract information he'd rather not have divulged. He could see the quote now: *All the real Marcus Alrikson can offer a woman is short-term physical gratification!* Disastrous.

But right now that wasn't what bothered him most; he felt a sense of injustice. Somehow April had gleaned a whole load of information about him, yet managed to vouchsafe absolutely nothing about herself. Article or not, that didn't seem fair.

'So,' he said. 'What about you?'

'What *about* me?'

'I know you said you don't want a family, but what's your take on relationships?'

'I don't *have* a take—because I'm not interested in a relationship of any sort.' She walked over to the table and placed the platter of food in the middle.

'So you don't date at all?'

'Why is that such a surprise to a man who loathes dates?'

'Because I may not date but, as we've ascertained, I do still enter short-term affairs.'

'Well, I don't.' Gesturing at the food, she added, 'Help yourself.'

Without further ado he sampled the chicken and closed his eyes. 'April, this is truly wonderful.'

She cut a sliver of chicken and tasted it, her brow creased as she concentrated. 'Perhaps a bit too much lemon—or maybe I could have cooked it a little less time—'

'Stop.' Marcus realised what else had been bugging him. 'Every time I say something nice about you, you reject the compliment. It's as if you're waiting for the "but". This food is delicious. Period.'

April stared at him for a long moment. 'Maybe I'm modest.'

'Maybe—but it seems to me that you don't actually believe the compliments. You can't see that the food is lovely, that you looked beautiful in that dress last night.'

'I... I...' She paused, looked down at her plate.

'You need to believe in yourself. That's what I tell Gemma and Blake and all those teenagers. They have to believe in themselves and their own unique talents.'

It was one of the most important skills that he wanted to teach those teenagers in Lycander's poverty stricken areas.

'I *do* believe in myself.' Her voice sounded hesitant, but then she frowned, as though annoyed with herself. 'And I believe in my chicken.'

'Good! Because it is delicious.'

'Thank you. And thank you for pointing out that I can be a bit over-critical of myself. It's a bad habit I thought I'd got rid of.'

Genuine self-annoyance was etched on her face and he knew he'd hit a nerve. 'Any reason for it?'

April hesitated, and then shrugged as if there was no harm in sharing the information. 'A super-critical ex. Everything I cooked, Dean would find some fault with it. It was always a bit burnt, or had a pinch too much salt, or

I'd underdone the beef or overcooked the steak… It got to the point where I got so nervous I made more mistakes, and then I suppose the criticism became justified… I used to believe my cooking reflected my emotions—the stews became a little more bitter day by day, the chili con carne a little less spicy, the lemons a bit more sour.'

Her attempt at casualness fell flat—instead sadness permeated her voice now, and he wanted to reach out, hold her, tell her that Dean wasn't worth it.

But before he could do anything a loud crash had him on his feet as a curse dropped from his lips.

Hell. He'd taken his eye off the weather, so intent on his conversation with April that in truth he'd almost forgotten the storm outside. Insulated in the windowless room, it had been easy to forget the reason they were there—easy to forget everything except the woman opposite him.

Fool.

'Wait here.'

'No way. I'm coming with you.'

'No.'

'Yes.' Her mouth set in a line of determination. 'I don't need you to play the hero, Marcus.'

'I'm not playing the hero. I'm being sensible. I don't know how much damage has been done out there. One of us needs to check.'

'Fine.'

He opened the kitchen door and slipped out, banging it shut behind him. He moved down the corridor and into the lounge, where he saw the window had cracked from the impact of an uprooted tree that the gale had slammed against it.

Swiftly Marcus closed the door and returned to the kitchen, where April had already cleared the table, packing the remaining food into containers. Her face was pale and he noticed her knuckles had whitened where she grasped the table-edge.

'What happened? How bad is it?'

'The window in the lounge has cracked, but not completely shattered as yet. The storm is really going for it now. My plan is to barricade the lounge door in the hope that we can contain the damage to that room. But in case the storm breaks through we need to hole up in the larder.'

'I'll help with the barricade.'

'You don't have to. I can handle it. If you'd feel safer in the larder that's—'

'No. I want to help and I'd rather be doing something constructive—it will stop my imagination from going into an overdrive of scenarios.'

'OK.'

Admiration touched him at her attitude. Her body language showed her fear as they walked towards the lounge—the clench of her hands, the pallor of her face—but her step did not falter. And once in the lounge, after one glance at the expanse of cracked window, where wind and rain now flung themselves at the glass in a grey lashing of force, she set to work.

It was almost as if her reaction wasn't fear of the storm itself *per se*.

Working quickly, they emptied the room of furniture and then piled it up against the door.

'That's the best we can do,' Marcus said. 'Let's grab some cushions and blankets from the bedroom and then get ourselves into the larder. There's enough room for us to sleep in there if need be.'

To his annoyance there was the smallest of tremors in his voice. *Unbelievable, Alrikson.* A storm was raging out there, and he was thinking about his libido!

'Let's go.'

It didn't take long for Marcus to realise that his libido

would be difficult to exclude from the party. The larder, whilst it was spacious for storage, was not really designed to accommodate two adults, let alone allow a sizeable chunk of space between them.

It was an aspect of the larder that had clearly occurred to April as well.

'Well, this is cosy,' she said, and then looked aghast both at the words and the utterly false breeziness she'd uttered them with. 'And *safe*. That's the most important thing, isn't it?'

'Yes, it is.'

Her face creased with worry. 'How bad do you think it will be for Lycander?'

'Hard to say. We put up flood walls recently, but the winds and rains will still cause a lot of damage.'

Frustration suddenly flooded him. He should be there. Helping.

'You *can't* be there,' she said. 'However much you want to be.'

Marcus blinked, wondered since when he'd been so easy to read. Since never.

'I know that. Nonetheless, I could make a difference back there.'

'You've made a difference here. If you hadn't turned the helicopter back we could have died. We could have been caught in this—could have crashed into the sea, could have been blown away... That was your call and you made it. So, yes, we *are* stuck here. But there are emergency services in Lycander. And I'll bet you and Prince Frederick have overhauled them. I bet you've put procedures in place to deal with this. And those procedures will save lives. That is the most important thing—*life*. Anything else can be replaced. So right now this larder is the safest place for you to be.'

Her voice grew serious.

'All we can do is hunker down and hope the storm doesn't get in. We just need to work out a way to pass the time…'

And there was his libido again. The words that she'd meant in all innocence took on a double meaning and silence spread an awkward blanket over them.

April looked around, as if in search of an activity, a distraction. 'How about a game of I Spy? That's what my parents always suggested on long car journeys.'

'I've never played it,' Marcus said.

It would never have occurred to his birth parents to play *anything* with their children. And, once adopted, Marcus had done his best to stay out of the way, not to intrude on his new family.

He'd known that Louise and Bill Alrikson had adopted him as an add-on—for Elvira's sake. Elvira had been the child they'd craved; they'd certainly not set out to take on a damaged twelve-year-old. And who could blame them? Certainly not Marcus. It had made perfect sense.

So he'd tried to make himself invisible, so that they and Elvira could get on with forging a bond, being a family.

'Marcus?' April's voice tugged him back to the present.

'I Spy it is,' he said.

April looked around the room, her green eyes skittering over all the items on the shelves. 'I spy with my little eye something beginning with C.'

'Coriander.' Marcus was absolutely sure he was right. Her gaze had rested on the herb section for a few extra seconds.

'Nope.'

'How do I know that you aren't changing your mind? Shouldn't you write it down somewhere?'

A roll of her eyes indicated disbelief. 'For a start, C isn't for "cheat". Second—surely we can trust each other to play a kids' game?'

Humph. 'China…cake mix…coffee…cafetière…'

April kept on shaking her head. Sitting there hugging her knees she looked absurdly youthful, and more than a little gleeful at his continued failure.

'There is nothing else in here that begins with a C. Come on, admit it—you're stringing me along.' He'd known trust was overrated.

'Nope. Do you give up?'

Reluctantly, after a final scan of the shelves, he nodded. 'OK. I give up.'

She gave a small crow of laughter and pointed upwards. 'Ceiling.'

'I cannot *believe* I didn't get that.'

'Hey, it's your first game—cut yourself some slack! My turn again.'

Many games later, Marcus shook his head. 'You are clearly an expert in this. You must have gone on a *lot* of car journeys in your childhood.'

'A fair few—and my sisters and I were all fiercely competitive so I had to be good! Especially as I'm the youngest.'

'It sounds like you were close when you were young.'

'We were. I was lucky to have such a lovely childhood—and my parents are still as in love now as they were then. They gave us the right balance of love and care and boundaries. There was lots of laughter and fun, but we were also encouraged to do well and reach our potential.'

'And you're still close now?'

'Yes. We are.'

'So surely you must want to recreate that kind of family life yourself? Yet you told me that you want your life to remain exactly as it is. And if your parents encouraged you to reach your potential, surely you want to advance your career? Move on to more serious journalism…?'

There was so much about April that he didn't understand, and he wanted to.

'It doesn't work like that. My upbringing was fantastic, but that doesn't mean I can magically recreate it. It's not like copying a painting. My life is fine as it is.'

'So this is what you want? To be a celebrity lifestyle writer? To be single? That's all you want for the rest of your days?'

'Yes. Why is that so hard to believe? Don't *you* want to remain single for the rest of your days?'

'Yes, but I haven't signed up to a life of celibacy. And I have goals. I want to learn how to fly a plane and do stunt flying. I want to build more community centres. I want to help take Lycander into the future. Expand my security business.' He shrugged. 'It's important to have dreams.'

April closed her eyes for a moment and then opened them again. 'I appreciate the concern, but why does it matter to you so much?'

'Because you only get one life—and, like you said earlier, that is the most important thing. *Life.* So don't waste the one you have. Make the choice to go for what you want.'

'I *have* made that choice.' Her words held finality. 'My life is how I want it to be.'

As he opened his mouth to argue the overhead light went out, plunging them into darkness, and she gasped. On instinct he reached out and found her hand, clasped it firmly in his.

'I'm OK,' she said. 'It just gave me a shock. Reminded me of what's going on out there and the havoc a storm can wreak.'

They both waited in silence, straining their ears to see if they could hear the noise of the storm.

'Loss of power isn't unusual,' he said.

'I know. It sounds mad, but I almost forgot the storm

is out there. Now…now I can almost hear the howl of the gale.' She took in a deep breath and shifted slightly closer to him in the darkness. 'Sorry. I just hate storms. *Hate* the destruction and tragedy that is going on out there.'

He could hear the raw emotion in her voice and knew that for reasons he wasn't sure of April was hurting. He wanted to offer comfort.

'I know, but we can't control events out there. We have done all we can do, and I don't believe the storm will get in. My earlier checks indicated that the roof has been constructed with storm proofing in mind. Also, the fact the lounge window didn't break is a positive. But, worst-case scenario, if the house starts to break up we stick close together. Protect ourselves with mattresses, rugs and blankets, take cover under the table or the bench. OK?'

Maintaining his grasp on her hand, he reached for the torch with his other and clicked it on.

'We need to conserve the batteries, but let's find the candles now and then maybe you can teach me a few more games to while away the time. I'm sure I spotted a pack of cards somewhere.'

'OK. I'll get the candles. If I'm going to die, I'm damned if I'll die in the dark.'

'You are *not* going to die. Not on my watch.'

'You can't promise that, Marcus.' Her voice was fierce and without compromise. 'I know you will do everything in your power to keep us safe, but you don't have power over life and death.'

Releasing his hand, she rose to her feet, pulled out a couple of candles and positioned them carefully on the floor. Once they were lit he switched the torch off and they both gazed at the flickering flames as a light vanilla and rose petal scent tinged the air.

'You're right,' he said quietly. 'I don't. But I will do my damnedest to keep you safe.'

Never again would he allow anyone to die if he could prevent it.

'I know you will—and of course I hope we survive,' she said quietly. 'But if we don't, do you have any regrets? Anything you wish you'd done?'

'I have plenty of regrets, but there is nothing I can do about any of them.'

There was no hope of redemption when it came to the fire and its aftermath. Yet a sudden image of his adoptive parents came to his mind. Louise and Bill—he'd never once called them Mum and Dad. They had wanted him to but he hadn't been able to. To have done so would have meant forgetting his birth parents, and he hadn't been able to do that—had felt he owed them some allegiance after all.

Yet Louise and Bill had been there for him—perhaps not as April's parents had, but as much as he'd let them.

'Except… I do wish I'd thanked my parents for everything they did for me.' When they got back to Lycander he would do that. Not with money, but with words. 'What about you? Any regrets?'

'Yes. But the actions and choices I regret are unchangeable.'

For a while there was silence, broken only by the sputter of the candles, and then she turned to him, her face set, her green eyes glittering with intensity.

'There is one regret I would have if I were to die.'

The softness of her voice fluttered over his skin. 'What's that?'

'You.' Her gaze didn't waver. 'In all the years since Dean I haven't felt even a spark of attraction for any man. Until you. So if this is my last night on this earth then I want to act on the attraction.'

His breath caught in his throat, the direct honesty of her statement catching him on the raw, and every fibre of his being wanted to enfold her in his arms. But he didn't.

'And what if this *isn't* your last night on earth?'

'Then…' She shifted closer to him. 'So be it. I will have no regrets in the morning. I *want* this, Marcus. I want *you*. On your terms. What did you say you could offer? Short-term physical gratification? That sounds good to me.'

'Are you sure?'

'Yes.' Leaning forward, she oh-so-gently ran her fingers over the crease in his brow. 'I *am* sure. I want exactly what you described. Something purely physical and at the end we walk away. I don't want to die, whether it is now or in fifty years, wishing I'd taken this opportunity to…to *feel* something. All bases are covered, I promise. No regrets.'

'No regrets,' he echoed as he finally allowed his desire out from under the iron control he'd exerted for so long now.

He turned and pulled her into his arms, the relief so intense he almost ached with it. A tremor shuddered through her body, and at the realisation that her need matched his own all words fled his brain.

Instinct took over, and their movements were made clumsy by urgency as together they pulled at the cushions and blankets, making a makeshift bed on the stone floor.

For a fleeting second he considered the irony of that decadent four-poster bed.

As if she could read his mind, April shook her head. 'It doesn't matter. All that matters is *this*.'

She stood on tiptoe and pressed her lips against his and he realised she was right. Nothing mattered except the sensual sweetness of her lips, her touch on the nape of his neck, the silken strands of her hair under his fingers, the press of her body against his. All that mattered was April.

She gave a small moan as he deepened the kiss, and her fingers slid under his T-shirt and over his chest. His groan mingled with hers and he gently tumbled her down onto the makeshift bed.

And then all was lost.

The danger of the storm was forgotten, though their awareness of the fragility of life burned with an intensity that somehow meshed with desire and strengthened their visceral, primitive need to meld together, to give and receive pleasure...

CHAPTER TEN

APRIL AWOKE AND tried to remember where the hell she was as she inhaled the lingering aroma of vanilla mixed with the scent of cold stone and herbs and spices. The events of the previous day…the previous night—who knew?—flooded back, and for a moment she wondered if they had been a dream. No! It had all been real: the passion, the shared soft laughter and the swoop and soar of joy.

But now…now it was over.

No regrets, she reminded herself. Those hours in his arms couldn't be rued—or repeated.

Opening her eyes, she realised it had been Marcus who had awoken her. Marcus who was standing up, already dressed in jeans. She felt heat tinge her face at the sheer glory of his body. He smiled down at her, a genuine up-turn of his lips, but it held a hint of wariness matched by the expression in his dark blue eyes.

'Morning,' he said.

'Good morning.' *Deep breath.* 'What now?'

For a second she hoped he would lie down again, so that they could resume where they'd left off. But that wasn't the agreement and, more to the point…

'Do you think the storm is over?'

'I'm hoping so. I haven't heard any sounds in the past few hours to indicate that it made its way in, but either way I think it's time to check.'

It occurred to her that he hadn't slept; she felt incredulity that *she* had. But she had. Exhausted, sated, and most embarrassingly *safe*, she'd fallen asleep in his arms.

'Good plan. I'll get ready.'

By which she meant somehow transform herself from fully unclothed to fully dressed. Given the fact that the storm might have caused untold havoc, and given what they had done just hours before, April knew it was ridiculous to feel a sense of awkwardness. But, like it or not, she did.

As if he sensed the problem, he gathered up her clothes without comment or any trace of discomfort and handed them to her, then turned away as she wriggled around under the blankets. Perversely, his tact twanged a nerve— he could at least cast a furtive look in her direction, try to sneak a final glance. Only Marcus didn't work like that. It was physical satisfaction followed by a walk away without a backward glance.

'Ready?' he asked, as if he couldn't wait to take those first steps.

'Ready.'

As they both reached the door he halted. 'April. About last night…'

She shook her head. 'I told you I agreed to your terms. Hell, I *wanted* your terms. Now it's time for the walking away part. We can't walk away from each other quite yet, but we can walk away from what happened. With no regrets. At all.'

'Good. Let's go and see what's happened.'

Trepidation filled her as he pushed the larder door open and they stepped out. The kitchen was untouched, their barricade still against the door. Swiftly they moved forward, shifted the table and stepped into the corridor.

'Oh.'

April bit her lip at the sight of the chaos—the walls

were drenched and the lounge barricades hadn't held up. Debris and splintered wood daubed the floor. The lounge was wrecked—the windows completely shattered, everything a sodden broken mess—and the bedroom had fared little better, though the heavy bed remained intact.

For a second sadness pierced her that the idyllic single dwelling a man had made for the woman he loved had come to this.

Yet as she gazed outside it seemed almost impossible to believe. The blue sky was studded with white clouds and the newly risen sun promised a day of heat and balmy breezes.

'Listen.'

A sound drifted in through the glassless window space: the unmistakable drone of a helicopter.

'Come on.'

April followed Marcus as he strode across the sand towards the helipad, where a craft bearing the royal crown was coming into land.

A pilot waved and soon alighted. 'Are you OK?'

'We're fine. How bad is the damage?'

'Bad. The Prince and Princess-to-be are out with the emergency services, but His Highness ordered me to come out here as soon as it was safe to fly, in case you were in trouble.'

'We're fine, but we need to get back so this is much appreciated. We're ready to go.'

'Um…' April hesitated. 'I know it's important to get back fast, but could we check to see if the food is salvageable? Obviously the food in the freezer will have defrosted, and there is a lot of it. If we took it back we could hand it out…'

Perhaps it was foolish—with Marcus's wealth he could afford to buy the contents of the freezer a hundred times over. But somehow the idea of leaving food to decay in the heat seemed wrong.

Half an hour later they were airborne. April looked down on the island where she'd experienced so much and a jolt of wonder shot through her. So many emotions had come into play—so many sensations she'd thought she'd never feel again. Even now her skin still hummed with the afterglow of pleasure, even as she braced herself for the aftermath of the storm.

Marcus dropped his phone onto the seat beside him. 'The community centre got hit—it stood up to the storm, but...'

April felt her blood run cold. 'Was anyone hurt?'

'Yes. Mia and Charlie. Gemma and Blake rescued them; they realised they hadn't been evacuated and went back in. The kitchen wasn't properly secured; a window had been left open and the gale had shot in and swept things off the shelves. Mia got hit and was knocked out, and Charlie, left to his own devices, crawled off.'

Rubbing her hands up and down her arms, April shivered despite the glare of the sun through the chopper windows. 'Are they all right?'

'Yes. Still in hospital for observation, but there is no cause for concern—thanks to Gemma and Blake.'

'That was brave of them—to go back in.'

'Yes, it was.'

April frowned—there was pride in his tone and in his stance, but there was something else as well. Pain and bleakness and a flash of self-loathing. Which didn't make sense unless...

'If you had been there *you* would have gone in, but you couldn't be there.'

'I know.'

April frowned. He clearly wasn't beating himself up over his absence. So what *was* he beating himself up for?

A few phone calls later he said, 'We'll go to the community centre first, then visit the hospital, and then we'll go wherever we're most needed.'

'It's a plan.'

A good plan, that would keep them busy. Already Eden Island had begun to take on a dreamlike quality against the backdrop of how the storm had affected Lycander.

Once they'd arrived at the centre Marcus strode from the chauffeured car and then slowed. For a moment they watched, unobserved.

The building gave off an aura of business and purpose. Groups of teens were busy at restoration tasks, someone had set up some music, and it seemed clear that the community had come together to restore the centre.

'Marcus!' A teen dressed in overalls headed at speed towards him, her blonde ponytail swinging. She launched herself against his chest and hugged him. 'We were worried about you. When you didn't turn up here we thought...'

'I'm fine, Gemma. Are *you* all right? I heard what you and Blake did—you are both incredible.'

'Thank you. We figured it's what you would have done.'

April saw his quickly camouflaged wince, but Gemma continued blithely on.

'If you'd been here. Where *were* you?'

'Stranded on an island,' he explained. 'But right now it looks like there's work to do.'

Gemma nodded. 'Blake and I and some of the others have set up the centre as a makeshift shelter for those whose homes have been destroyed, but obviously we have to make sure it's safe. We're also really missing Mia in the kitchen, because people need food. So many of the buildings here didn't stand up to the storm—there are lots of people who have lost everything.'

Marcus nodded. 'You're doing a fabulous job, Gemma.'

'Thank you. But I'm glad you're here.'

'Thanks to April we have some provisions with us, and—'

'If you like I can take over kitchen duty until Mia gets back.'

The words had come out before April had even realised she would utter them. For a second she wanted to call them back, her instincts telling her not to get involved. She *observed* life—she didn't participate.

Yet Marcus's words echoed in her brain. *'You have to live your life to the best of your ability.'*

'Really?' Gemma's face lit up. 'Can you cook?'

'Yes. I can. I'm happy to try and sort out the food donations and then work out what we need and ways to pass excess stuff on before it goes out of date. I'll talk to Mia as well. If you could give me some helpers, I'll get the food we do have stored safely and get started.'

'And I'll organise an official safety check,' Marcus said.

April nodded and headed towards the kitchen, rolled up her sleeves and got stuck in, directing the four youths allocated to her by Gemma.

It was a good couple of hours before Marcus entered the kitchen, his face dirt-streaked, his dark hair unkempt—he looked utterly gorgeous and her idiotic heart did a funny little leap.

'If you're ready, we could go to the hospital now?'

'Perfect. Thank you, everyone. I'll be back tomorrow at about six a.m.'

There was some good-natured moaning, but all four teenagers promised to turn up to help.

Once in the car, Marcus glanced sideways at her. 'This is good of you, but it's nothing to do with your actual job. How will you manage the time?'

'Kathy will understand that my deadlines need to be flexible.' In truth, oddly enough, she didn't care if her editor *didn't* understand. 'I can rearrange anything in my diary. This is more important.'

Five years before a storm had played its part in the wreckage of her life. Without the torrential rain it was possible that, despite his intoxicated state, Dean wouldn't have crashed the car. Now she was in a position to help, in however small a way. Help others whose lives had been devastated. She wanted to do that.

'It's the least I can do. Some of those teens have lost so much, and yet they are still thinking about others. How bad is it elsewhere?'

'I've spoken with Frederick. He's in the lower district, helping the emergency services evacuate a building with about twenty trapped in it. And Sunita's set up a nursery/childcare centre at the palace.'

The car soon pulled up at the hospital, and they entered the slightly dilapidated building. But April noted that whilst the décor might lack style it was scrupulously clean, and the staff had an energised, competent air that signalled reassurance.

A nurse directed them to Mia's ward and ushered them to her bed. She was sitting up, with Charlie next to her, and April's step faltered, despite the fact that she should have been prepared for this.

'Marcus.' Mia's face lit up, and so too did her son's.

Charlie scrambled across the bed and Marcus stepped forward to scoop him up. 'Hey, little fella. I hear you've had a bit of an adventure since I saw you last.'

Charlie beamed and promptly grabbed a chunk of Marcus's hair.

'How are you, Mia?'

'I am fine, and more importantly so is Charlie—thanks to Gemma and Blake. I don't know how to thank them.'

April pulled herself together, took a seat by the bed and

soon engaged Mia in conversation about the kitchen and how she could best help.

But all the while she was oh-so-aware of Marcus as he sat on the floor with Charlie. Her heart twisted as she watched them, and sheer relief that Charlie had survived collided with her grief that Edward hadn't. Both events had been brought about by what seemed like chance—a collision of the planets, a string of circumstances that had resulted in joy and tragedy respectively. A child had lived and a child had died.

A child.

As she gazed at Charlie, so reminding her of Edward, somewhere in the deep recesses of her brain a warning bell began to toll.

Last night they hadn't used anything...

She pushed the thought away, unable even to contemplate its enormity. Panic circulated in her veins like some deadly virus, and she forced her vocal cords to work, needing spoken words to drown out the reality that buzzed in her brain.

'So there are more provisions in the cellar?' she asked.

Mia cast her a curious look. 'Yes, but I want to tell you about the oven—it is a little temperamental, but all you have to remember is...'

Focus.

But without thought April moved her hand to touch her tummy. Too late, she saw that Marcus was watching her, his dark eyes thoughtful, and she snatched her hand away.

CHAPTER ELEVEN

ONE SIMPLE GESTURE and the world had crashed around his head. How could he have been so *stupid*? Why had protection not so much as occurred to him?

Frantically he cast his mind back.

'I don't want to die, whether it is now or in fifty years, wishing I'd taken this opportunity to...to feel something. All bases are covered, I promise. No regrets.'

Had he been fool enough to take 'all bases are covered'—that ambiguous phrase—as an assertion that she had contraception covered? Why had he not asked...considered...*thought*? He had no answer—not a one—because back then, cocooned from the storm, all that had mattered was the moment.

Worse than an adolescent.

Panic waved tumultuously in his gut as he tried to assimilate the possibility that April might be pregnant.

Chill out.

There was a chance that he had completely misinterpreted her gesture. He looked at April, noted the pallor of her skin, the twist of her hands in her lap.

Charlie gave a gurgle of protest and Marcus realised he had allowed himself to be distracted from the tower-building game they were involved in. Carefully he balanced the final brick, and with a huge beam Charlie swatted the tower over.

'Craaaaaaash!' Marcus said, and was rewarded by another smile.

Before they could embark on a repeat performance, an older woman entered the room. 'Hi, Mama,' Mia said from the bed.

'Hi, sweetheart.' The woman looked tired, but her smile was full of love. 'Sorry I took so long. I needed to give Mrs Martini a hand back from the shops.'

'No problem. Charlie is having a whale of a time.'

Marcus rose to his feet, scooping Charlie up with him. 'Good to see you again, Mrs Hernandez.'

'And you.' She took her grandson, who tumbled happily into her arms.

'This is April,' Mia said. 'She's going to help out at the centre until I'm better.'

Marcus watched as April came forward and engaged in polite conversation, studying her every feature, the silhouette of her slender body, and he wondered…wondered… wondered.

There was only one way to find out.

Stepping towards the bed, he smiled down at Mia. 'You take care. I'll be back to visit soon.'

Minutes later they exited the hospital and April nigh on scurried ahead.

'I'll get a taxi back to my hotel and head to the centre first thing in the morning.' A deep breath. 'I think, given the circumstances, we can call it a day now. I have plenty for the article and—'

'Given the circumstances, we need to talk.'

'Really, we don't. Are you worried that I'll write about last night? Of course I won't—that was between us.'

'We need to talk. If you want to have this conversation on the street, here and now, fine. Or we can go back to my place.'

For a moment he thought she would make a run for it, and then she shrugged. 'Fine. We'll go back to your place.'

There was nothing further to say. The idea of small talk—of *any* talk apart from the question that burnt his lips—was impossible.

They climbed into the car and Marcus directed his driver to take them home, ignoring the expression of surprise on Roberto's usually impassive features. After all it was understandable—he had never before taken a woman back to his home, unless you counted Elvira.

As they pulled up outside the luxury penthouse building that he had spent so much money on and so little time in, he realised that it wasn't really a home—it was a place to stay. A place that represented proof of his wealth and status, showed him how far he had come from the slums of outer Lycander. It was a symbol, a bachelor pad—not a place where anyone would have a child.

Whoa. Hold your horses, Alrikson.

It could be that he had this all wrong and had totally misinterpreted that single gesture.

Yet as they entered his uncluttered lounge, with its vast windowed wall that led out onto a rooftop terrace overlooking Lycander, giving a view of the palace's spires and the city's historic landmarks, and he could ask the question, suddenly he no longer wanted to.

Instead... 'What would you like to eat?'

'I'm not hungry.'

'You must be hungry. By my reckoning, neither of us have eaten properly since yesterday. And you need to eat.'

After all she might be eating for two.

The idea wrenched his gut with an emotion he couldn't catch hold of. Fear, panic, and through all that a silver strand of irrational awe.

'Why?' Suspicion curdled her voice.

'Tomorrow will be a full-on day. I'll rustle up something.'

'I thought you couldn't cook.'

'I can't—but I can boil pasta and heat up a sauce.'

As if recognising that he wouldn't take no for an answer, she nodded. 'OK. Thank you.'

He gestured to the enormous glass dining table and watched as she perched on a chair and stared out over the rooftops, her gaze averted from his. 'I won't be long.'

Half an hour later she looked up from her empty plate. 'You were right. I *did* need that.'

Now he knew he could wait no longer. 'Is there a chance that you are pregnant?'

Her hesitation said it all, and was followed by, 'I'm sorry, Marcus. I can't believe I didn't think...didn't...'

He could see her agitation as she twisted her hands together and he pushed his plate away, reached out to cover her hands. His heart-rate had accelerated in sheer reaction, he felt disembodied, giddy...

'You don't need to apologise. I am as much to blame as you. How likely is it that you're pregnant?'

'It's definitely a possibility, but I just don't know. My period isn't always reliable, but I'm due in about a week or so. All I can do is wait.' Extracting her hands, she rose. 'I'll let you know one way or the other, but I expect nothing from you. Last night was my idea and my responsibility.'

'If you are pregnant the baby is *our* responsibility.'

The word *baby* seemed to rock her backwards, her arms wrapped around her midriff. He rose and walked around the table, pulling her resistant body against his, and held her. Despite her rigidity she didn't push him away, so he stroked his hand down her back, uttering soothing noises.

'If you *are* pregnant we'll work it out. You're not alone in this, April.'

Words which had had the intent of reassurance instead caused her to stand back and utter a low cry of, 'No!'

'What do you mean?'

She hauled in a deep breath and dropped her hands to her sides. 'I mean *we* won't be working anything out. If I *am* pregnant any decision about the…the baby…is mine to make. Alone.'

'Absolutely not. If you are pregnant we would have made that baby together. You and me. So any decision is *ours*.' Fear gripped him. 'If you are planning to have a termination then—'

'I'm not!' Her voice broke. 'I'm not going to do that. Not because I don't believe a woman has a right to make exactly that choice, but because that is not what I'd want to do. If I am pregnant then I will not have a termination— you have my word on that.'

Anger obscured his hurt. 'So you are basically saying that it will be *your* decision whether or not I can be part of the baby's life?'

'Yes, I am.'

This was daft. 'Why don't we save this conversation until a week's time, when we know whether we even need to have it?'

'OK.' Her relief was palpable. 'Good plan. I'll quickly use the bathroom and then call a taxi to take me to the hotel.'

'Roberto can take you.'

'Thank you.'

April stared at her reflection in the bathroom mirror, at the smudges of exhaustion and the green sheen of panic that clouded her eyes. Disbelief at her own stupidity dizzied her.

Oh, God… What was she going to do?

Well, what she was *not* going to do was break down. For

a start, she might not be pregnant. But if she was, she knew the way forward—there was no way she could have a baby. The idea sent a surge of terror, anxiety and pain straight through her. No baby deserved a mother who had demonstrated such irresponsibility in her first shot at parenthood.

She had loved Edward with every fibre of her being, and yet her actions had set off a chain reaction that had resulted in his death. The thought of taking on the responsibility of motherhood again was impossible. Yet she had also meant every word she'd said to Marcus; she would not terminate a pregnancy.

Which left only one option.

Steeling herself, she returned to the sleek lounge. 'OK. I'll let you know what the test result is in a week.'

'Whoa. Not so fast. I've been thinking.'

Great. Just what she needed.

'I want you to spend the week with me.'

'That's nuts. Why on earth would I do that?' The very idea was enough to add the fizz of anxiety to her already overwrought nerves.

'Because if you *are* pregnant then I want to be part of the baby's life. According to you, that is your decision to make—so why not stay here and get to know me better? Plus, this is going to be a stressful week of waiting for us both, so it makes sense for us to spend it together. And...' For a second he looked almost embarrassed. 'And if you *are* pregnant then I want to be part of it. I want to keep an eye on you, make sure you eat properly...'

Warmth touched her at the idea of being looked after— a warmth she doused instantly in a cold stream of reality.

'There is really no need.' Steeling herself, she dug her nails into the palms of her hands and forced herself to meet his gaze. 'Because I know exactly what I will do if I am pregnant—my decision is already made. If I am pregnant I will be giving the baby up for adoption.'

There was silence. His face registered shock, disbelief, and worst of all disappointment. In *her*. And that hurt.

'Why?'

'It doesn't matter why.'

It didn't matter that the idea of giving up a baby half killed her. Bottom line: she knew any baby deserved so much more than she could give. She was too empty, too devastated, too guilty. Another baby would be a shadow, a substitute for Edward, and that was wrong. If there was a baby he deserved a family that felt joyful to have him, the way she had felt about Edward.

'It matters to me.'

'I told you—I don't want my life to change. I have a job and a lifestyle that won't fit a baby. I'd rather my baby had a stable, secure family.'

The words sounded hollow—however hard she tried she couldn't infuse them with even a semblance of truth, and she saw the frown descend on his brow.

'Let's say that's the truth. What about *me*? Do you really, *morally*, believe that it is OK to give *my* baby up?'

She closed her eyes. Why couldn't Marcus be the sort of man who didn't care? In fact, indignation touched her. 'You said yourself that you don't want to be a dad.'

His lips tightened. 'No, I didn't. I said that it wouldn't be fair for me to have a child when I have no wish to be in a long-term relationship, when I can't offer a child the stability of a family unit, and when my work hours are so erratic.'

'Exactly. Adoption would offer a child everything that you've just said you can't give. Parents in a long-term relationship who can offer stability and security. Parents who desperately want a child—who aren't merely doing their duty.'

He shook his head. 'It wouldn't feel right for my own flesh and blood to know I had rejected him or her because

I couldn't be bothered to change my lifestyle to accommodate him.'

The words stung—she couldn't hide the flinch—and his frown deepened.

Before he could say anything, she jumped in. 'So you don't agree with adoption?'

'I didn't say that.'

He paused, clearly weighing up the words he would speak, and there was a sudden ironic tilt to his voice she couldn't compute.

'Sometimes adoption is the best option for a child—circumstances in which the natural parents are truly unfit... alcoholics, drug addicts, violent hardened criminals who would have no idea how to keep a baby safe and loved. Then, of *course* adoption is in the child's best interests. But your motivation is different; you would voluntarily be giving up a baby because motherhood doesn't gel with your lifestyle.'

Condemnation hardened his tone.

'That is your choice. But I don't choose it. I want to be part of this baby's life, if it exists, and I will fight for that right if need be. Or you can make it simple: let me have custody.'

For a second April stared at him, dizzy with emotions. But the one that seared her soul was guilt. How could she contemplate this? Could she truly give her baby up? She quelled the doubt in a torrent of facts. True, she was neither an addict nor a violent criminal—but she had already proved herself unfit for motherhood. Any baby she had would grow up in the shadow of his lost brother, would have to live with a mother who had been emptied of joy, who might slide back into the pit of depression. Her baby deserved the best—and that wasn't April. Could it be Marcus?

She shook her head, the sheer enormity of that question too much. 'I can't do that. I don't know you.'

And God knew her judgement of men was hardly top-notch. Her misjudgement of Dean had led to tragedy. She could not allow herself a replay.

'How can I judge your capacity to be a father? I have no right to judge anyone but myself.'

Big mistake.

An arrested look entered his dark eyes and the anger dimmed. 'Is that what you've done? Judged yourself to be unfit?'

'Marcus. My mind is made up. If I am pregnant I am giving the baby up for adoption. I will inform social services or the adoption agency of your wishes and they can make the call.' She took a deep calming breath. 'Now I am leaving. I'll be in touch in a week.'

'No.'

His voice was firm, and yet thoughtful—she could almost hear the whir of the cogs and wheels of his brain.

'My earlier comments stand. You can stay here. Right now I have nothing but your word that you will contact me or keep me in the loop. You say you can't judge me…you say you don't know me. We can at least remedy the latter. Get to know me. The *real* Marcus Alrikson. I'll prove to you that I am good father material.'

'I can't do that.'

The idea made her tummy swirl, caused nausea to threaten. This was all too much; she wanted to sink into a bed somewhere and wake up when it was all over.

'Because what if I get it wrong, like I did before?'

'I don't understand.'

'I am not a good character judge. I've proved that in the past.'

'With the super-critical ex? Dean?'

'Yes. I married him when I was twenty years old and

our marriage lasted four years. In those four years he made me feel worthless. He sapped my confidence, made me feel stupid, ugly, clumsy... Name a negative and I felt it. But at the outset I thought he was wonderful—the ideal man, perfect husband and father material.'

Bitterness coated her tongue, painted her words with vinegar, and her voice broke.

'I was wrong. So I will not—*cannot*—trust my judgement on this. Because if I get it wrong again the baby will suffer, and I won't have that.'

'OK. I understand.'

His face was inscrutable but she could sense his struggle to contain anger—though she suspected the anger was directed at Dean.

'I am truly sorry that he put you through that. More sorry than I can say. All I can do is swear to you that I am not like that and ask you to give me a chance. Ask you to stay with me for this week. Until you can take the test. It's going to be a difficult week. Let's face it together.'

Weariness touched her, along with a desire to cry. Because there was compassion in his eyes, and how could she refuse a man who was merely asking for the chance to prove himself? What right had she to judge that he wasn't a good man? He had done nothing to indicate anything but decency in his love for his country, his compassion for those teenagers...

'OK,' she said softly.

'Thank you. I'll make up the bed in the spare room.'

To her sheer disbelief her hormones—which must have been on vacation for the past twenty-four hours and had not yet caught up with the action—gave a sharp burst of protest. Cue a mental rolling of her eyes and the sudden desire to burst into tears on his broad chest.

Get real April.

'Thank you,' she said.

* * *

Marcus sat at his bedroom window and stared out as dawn crept over the city, turning the sky from grey to golden. Sleep had proved elusive, with his whole body preternaturally aware of April only a few doors away.

Stupid that desire still flared for a woman who planned to give up her baby so she could pursue her lifestyle. But desire wasn't the only emotion in the mix—and when he remembered her explanation of her marriage his hands clenched into fists. An urge to comfort her, just hold her, had vied with an urge to find Dean and use him as a punch bag.

Damn it.

It did not add up. Every instinct he owned told him that April was talking through her hat, her shoes and every other accessory. For a start, he didn't get the impression that she loved her lifestyle. Second, he knew with a bone-deep certainty that she would be a wonderful mother—that the best thing for this hypothetical baby would be April.

So why couldn't she see that? There hadn't been even a hint of indecision in the steel of her voice as she'd stated her intent. But her eyes had told a different story—of misery and despair.

It did not add up. Somewhere the equation was flawed. He had every intention of discovering what was going on, and if April were to be pregnant he would do his best to persuade her to keep the baby. Which, a small voice pointed out, would also be very convenient for him. That way he could be part of the baby's life.

Selfish? Maybe.

Realistic? Absolutely.

Best for the baby? He believed so.

If it proved to be necessary in a week's time, that was what he would fight for. But first, of course, there was a week to get through—a week with April in his home, his sanctuary, his space.

A noise caught his attention and he deduced that his house guest was also awake. Moments later he entered the kitchen, where April was opening a cupboard.

'Sorry. I didn't mean to wake you. I wanted some water before I head off to the centre.'

'Hang on. First you need breakfast.'

'I thought you didn't do breakfast?'

'I don't usually have breakfast at home,' he agreed. 'But I don't usually have guests. I'm sure I can rustle up something. Scrambled eggs on toast?'

April shook her head. 'I'd rather avoid scrambled eggs, just in case...' Her voice trailed off. 'Pregnant women are advised to avoid undercooked eggs. So eggs are fine, but they need to be thoroughly cooked.'

'OK. How about an omelette? Or I have some cereal... I'll go shopping at some point today if you make a list.'

'Cereal is fine. And why don't I shop and cook this week? I really don't mind.'

'OK.'

The domesticity of their conversation was surreal—as was assembling two bowls, a selection of cereal, making coffee for two, and eating at the table rather than standing up at the kitchen counter.

'I've been thinking,' April said as she poured milk onto chocolate flavour cereal stars. 'I'd like to meet your family.'

The request caught him on the hop, and without thought his lips opened to voice emphatic refusal. 'No.'

'Why not?'

'Because they don't need to be involved at this stage. I've never taken a woman home to meet my family and I don't want them to get the wrong impression.'

Or the right one, for that matter.

'I understand that—but we could say it's for the article. I did ask you if I could meet them at the outset.'

'And I said no. I don't like the idea of my family being interviewed about me.'

'Well, it isn't about *your* likes or dislikes. If you are serious about applying for sole custody of a baby, then your family are an integral part of the set-up. I need to meet them.'

'I understand that, and if we discover you are pregnant then you can.'

Even if the thought sent a shiver of discomfort down his spine. Not because he thought Louise and Bill would disgrace him, but because he didn't want April to see how much of an outsider he was in his own family. He had no doubt they would welcome a baby—would love a baby— but that wouldn't change the fundamental distance between him and his adoptive parents.

April shook her head. 'I need to meet them *now*—see what they are like now, when they have no stake in being anything other than what they are. At the end of this week if I *am* pregnant I can't stay here—can't meet your family knowing they'll be judging me for my decision. But I want to meet them—want to know that if there is a baby, and if he ends up with you, he has a good family. Grandparents who will support you and love him. I want to meet them.'

There was anguish in her voice now, and his chest banded in sympathy even as he tried to understand why she would make a decision like this.

'OK. I'll set it up.' Marcus pushed his bowl away in an abrupt movement of sheer frustration. 'But I wish you'd tell me why you're doing this, April. I don't get it.'

'You don't have to.' Weariness slumped her shoulders for a moment, and then she rose to her feet. 'Thank you for agreeing. I promise I'll be discreet. Now, I'd better go.'

CHAPTER TWELVE

 APRIL GLANCED DOWN at the message on her phone.

Meeting arranged. Dinner tonight at family house. M

A flutter of nerves touched her but she quelled them; there was no need for her to worry about the impression she made. This was about her having some information in case she was pregnant. With the key words being 'in case'.

Somehow over the course of the day, as she had cooked and scrubbed, sorted out food donations and thrown herself into helping the hundreds of displaced and hungry people who'd come to the centre, her own worries had receded and some perspective had returned. It hadn't helped that careful calculation of her cycle indicated that it was definitely possible that a baby was on the cards, but the sheer business of the day had meant there was no time to dwell on it.

With a final scrub of the counters and a quick check that everything was prepared for the next day, she exited the centre—then turned as she heard her name being called.

'Hi, Gemma. Is everything OK?'

'Yes. I just wanted to say thank you. Everyone has told us how fantastic you've been—with the food, and the way you've really listened to people and helped them.'

'There is no need to thank me. I have been bowled over

by how brave all these people are. God knows I wish I could do more.'

'I think you can. That's what I wanted to ask you. If you'd write about it all—about the centre, about all these people... I know the Prince is doing his best, and I know Marcus is too. But if more awareness could be raised maybe we could fundraise more—maybe we could make the world see that even places like Lycander, where the rich and famous hob-nob, have a darker side.'

For a second April's mind buzzed with the idea and she considered taking it on, getting involved... And then cold, hard sanity screeched in and put a stop to such a nonsensical idea. Getting involved was exactly what had pitchforked her into the horrendous entanglement she was in now.

Ever since she had met Marcus something had happened to her. Willy-nilly, she'd taken a step away from the bubble-like, insulated existence she had created. Prompted by the unfurling of unwanted, unbidden feelings and desires, she'd been stupid enough to expose herself—and it needed to stop now. Before, her life had been the way she wanted it and, dammit, one way or another she had to get back into that bubble.

'I'm sorry, Gemma. I'm a celebrity lifestyle writer. I wouldn't be able to do the story the justice it deserves.'

The disappointment on Gemma's face pierced her, but she forced herself to stand by her words. In six days, no matter what, she would leave Lycander—leave all this behind her.

'You could do it if you wanted to,' Gemma said simply. 'You're choosing not to.'

April tried to think of a response, but knew anything she said would sound like an excuse. How could she explain to Gemma that she might be pregnant, that even if she wasn't she had to get away? The world outside her safe, calm bubble was too bright, too overwhelming, too scary.

'I'm sorry,' was the best she could come up with.

'Don't worry about it. And thank you again for all your help at the centre.'

Swivelling on her heel, Gemma turned back towards the community centre and April tamped down the guilt and headed for the sleek black car that had pulled up at the kerb.

Marcus emerged and opened the door for her, then waited as she slid in before climbing in after her.

'Is everything OK?'

'Fine. It went well today. But it's sad to see all those people who have lost so much. I am impressed with how efficient and well organised the services are—and Frederick has promised temporary accommodation to all who need it and he seems to be making good on that promise.'

She glanced at him.

'That can't be easy to get sorted, and I'm guessing that you have spent a large part of your day on it.' He looked tired, with dark smudges under his eyes, and she wondered when he'd last actually slept.

'It's not only that. It's about how to sort out the housing issue. This can't happen again, so that means new houses will have to be constructed properly. And that means continued upheaval and, of course, a need for revenue.' He shook his head. 'Anyway, that isn't your problem.'

'Are you sure you want to see your parents tonight? I didn't mean it had to be instantly.'

'That's fine—at least we won't have to cook. I've said that you have a dairy allergy. That way you can avoid eggs and unpasteurised cheese or milk without having to explain why.'

Warmth touched her that somewhere in his day Marcus

had found time to research the foods that pregnant women needed to avoid.

'Thank you.'

'There is something I need to tell you. It's not a big deal, but it may come up. Elvira and I are adopted.'

It was impossible to read his expression. His features were silhouetted against the dusky Lycander evening. Her brain whirred as she processed the information and its meaning, and guilt smote her anew. Her decision to choose adoption if she was pregnant must have resonated with him on such a deep level.

'I... I don't know what to say.'

'There is no need to say anything.' His voice was flat. 'And please don't jump to any conclusions. Adoption was the very best option for Elvira and for me, and I have nothing but gratitude that we were taken in.'

A glance out of the window and he nodded.

'We're here.'

April blinked, realising he had timed this in such a way that she would have no opportunity to ask questions. In truth, her brain was too abuzz for her even to be able to formulate any. Why hadn't Marcus told her?

Hurt touched her but she focused on her surroundings, wanting to imprint them on her mind so that if it came to it one day she would be able to picture her child here.

She followed Marcus across a gravelled courtyard, saw the sprawl of a beautiful terracotta-hued villa lit by an alluring twinkle of artful fairy lights. The door opened and an elegant woman with ash-blonde hair opened the door.

'Marcus. It is so lovely to see you.' She turned to April, a look of wariness and curiosity in her bright blue eyes. 'And you must be April. I'm Louise. I've read so many of your articles; you have a wonderful turn of phrase.'

'Thank you. It's very kind of you to invite me to dinner.'

'Our pleasure. Come in.'

April followed Louise into a spacious living room, aware of the quiet elegance of its furnishings that created a homely, comfortable atmosphere. A dark-haired man stood in front of a mantelpiece—a man who, oddly enough, reminded her of Marcus. Of course now she knew that the resemblance couldn't be hereditary—so what was it? Perhaps it was the man's stance, his posture of confidence and authority. The smile he gave his wife softened his face, and she could see an unspoken communication pass between them.

'Good evening, April. I'm Bill Alrikson. Can I offer you a drink?'

'I'd love a soft drink—I'm working tonight and I have a busy day tomorrow, so I'd best avoid alcohol.'

Too much information, April.

Louise turned in an abrupt movement and April did her best to look as bland as possible, realising she had taken a step closer to Marcus—a move Louise had also clocked.

Relief swathed her as the door opened and Elvira burst in.

'Big Bro!' she exclaimed, and headed straight for Marcus, giving him a hug. Then, 'Mama… Pops.' Two more hugs and then she turned to April, a smile on her face but wariness rather than welcome in her dark blue eyes.

'So,' Louise said, 'I understand you're writing about "the real Marcus Alrikson". How can we help?'

Straight to the chase.

Belatedly it occurred to April that she should have prepared some questions—she could hardly come out with, *Do you think he'd make a good dad?* Or, *What sort of grandparents would you be?*

'Could you maybe tell me a bit about his childhood?'

Further mistake.

She had no idea when Marcus had been adopted—didn't

even know whether he and Elvira were from the same birth family or not.

But Louise didn't bat an eyelid. 'Of course. Marcus was a very serious child, and that's why some of my very favourite memories are of when he laughed or even smiled.' She turned to her husband. 'Do you remember the bicycle?'

'Yes.' Bill stepped forward and handed April a mocktail. 'It was a birthday gift. Marcus never asked for anything, but we were sure he'd love a bike. I still remember his face when he saw it. It lit up.' Bill handed Marcus a whisky. 'And then he offered to pay us back for it.'

'Obviously we refused,' Louise interpolated, with a quick glance at her husband. 'And then he took the bike and disappeared for hours. He came back with cuts and bruises but with another smile on his face because he could ride it. It was a two-smile day!'

'Then there was the time he ran away from boarding school,' Bill said.

Louise shook her head. 'Elvira had just started school, and Marcus took it into his head that he needed to be here to make sure she didn't get bullied.'

The image of a teenage Marcus arriving home to protect his little sister was so vivid in April's head that she blinked to clear it.

'Did it work?' she asked, turning to Elvira, who was watching her with suspicion still evident in her gaze. It occurred to April that the protective instinct worked two ways.

'Of course,' Elvira said, throwing a quick affectionate smile at her brother. 'Mum and Dad let him stay at home and take me to and from school—it set me up for years. All my friends thought he was the coolest thing ever. They all hero-worshipped him and everyone wanted to come to my house in case he was there.'

'Then I guess I made the right call,' Marcus said.

'Well, that's what *we* thought,' Louise said. 'Which is why we squared it with your *very* irate head of house.'

'I didn't know you did that.'

Marcus looked surprised, and Louise smiled at him—a smile that April sensed held an undercurrent of sadness.

Then, as if she'd felt April's gaze, Louise stood up. 'If we're ready, let's head in to dinner.'

Dinner was amazing—the food melt-in-the-mouth incredible. Conversation flowed, orchestrated by Louise and Bill. Topics ranged from politics to business to the nitty-gritty of Elvira's university course.

Marcus played his part—and yet there was something April couldn't put her finger on. It was almost as if Marcus was effacing himself from the conversation.

'This is an amazing house,' April said. 'Did you grow up here?'

'No,' Elvira chipped in. 'We grew up in town—it's where I live now. We converted it into a student house when Mum and Dad moved here a couple of years ago. Marcus gave them this house.'

Marcus frowned, and April knew he hadn't wanted his sister to divulge that fact.

'Time for dessert,' Louise said.

'Can I help?' April offered.

'That would be lovely,' the older woman agreed.

Marcus's frown deepened into a scowl.

April couldn't help it—she grinned down at him as they left. 'Don't look so grumpy, Marcus. I'm sure Louise has nothing but good things to share about you.'

Before he could answer she hotfooted it after Louise into a typical country kitchen where she felt instantly at home. Louise opened the fridge and pulled out the most decadent chocolate cake April had ever seen.

'Vegan—so it's dairy-free,' Louise said.

'Thank you.' A pang of guilt shot through April. 'I am *so* sorry to put you to so much trouble.'

'It's no trouble.'

Louise extracted a bowl of raspberries and closed the fridge door.

'We didn't want to accept the house,' she said suddenly. 'We knew it was Marcus's way of paying us back and we didn't want that. We never wanted him to feel in our debt, but I know he did. In the end we agreed to take it because it meant so much to him that we did. And because he chose a house he knew I'd always loved. Goodness knows how he persuaded the previous owner to sell, or how much he had to pay for it...' She shrugged. 'I guess I wanted you to know that we aren't after his money.'

'I wouldn't have thought that.'

'Good. So, is there anything else you want to ask me? I can tell you exactly how proud we are of Marcus—of his achievements and his sheer courage and grit. He worked so very hard to catch up on his education—didn't give up even when he realised how far behind he was. And the way he was with Elvira...it was heartbreaking. He looked after her with a gentleness and a love I can't describe. He was and is an amazing brother.'

Louise handed April a stack of plates.

April wanted to ask so much more but restrained herself—she knew that Marcus would loathe the idea that they were discussing him, and yet this was her opportunity to discover more about the man she might have made a baby with. The temptation was great but before she could say another word the door opened and Marcus came in.

'Sorry to interrupt—'

'No, you aren't,' Louise said. 'But don't worry, Marcus, I haven't said anything you wouldn't like. And now it's time for dessert.'

Two pieces of cake and a cup of tea later, April thanked Louise and Bill for the meal.

'I'm glad it was all right. I was surprised at how many of my usual dishes include dairy. I'd love it if you could share some dairy-free recipes with me.'

April blinked. Her mind was a complete blank; not a single dairy-free idea could she come up with. Did pasta contain milk?

'Of course. I'll get your email address from Marcus.'

'Thank you.'

But there was a small frown on Louise's face as she turned to Marcus to say goodbye.

'Take care, both of you.'

'We will. Thank you again.'

April felt a ridiculous pang as she walked towards the car; in all probability she would never see Louise and Bill again. For an insane moment, as the car glided through the midnight-blue darkness, an absurd fantasy filled her mind and she drifted between waking and sleep. Her and Marcus…a couple…herself with a baby in her arms… Louise and Bill looking on… In-laws who liked her…believed in her… Marcus with his arm around her as he gazed down at the tiny precious bundle in her arms.

And then the image faded and changed, and instead she saw herself with Edward as he took his first tottering step…fast-forwarded to weeks later and the police on the doorstep, telling her that Edward was dead…gone… at rest for ever.

April sat bolt-upright with a small cry and instantly Marcus scooted across the seat, his warm bulk next to hers.

'April?'

She blinked. 'I'm fine.'

Oddly enough, she was—after all, those half-dreams had shown her that her decision was right. Tragedy had touched her life irrevocably and she would be tainted for ever. Another baby was an impossible mirage.

'I liked your parents.'

His face was slightly averted, and for a moment he said nothing. Then, 'I'm glad. They are good people.'

'They are clearly very proud of you.'

More silence, though she would swear he had puffed out the smallest *'pah'*.

'Why do I get the impression you don't believe that?'

'I don't know.'

Relief vibrated from him as the car pulled to a stop outside his apartment, but her eyes narrowed in determination—he was *not* going to escape that easily. Louise and Bill *were* proud of him.

Once inside the lounge, she resumed. 'You do *know* they are proud of you, right?'

Discomfort etched his features as he thrust his hands into his pockets. 'April, drop this, OK? I know Louise and Bill are pleased I've done well in life.'

'But that's different from knowing they're proud of you—not because you've made lots of money but because you're the person you are.'

'And I owe them a huge debt. One I will do my best to pay back.'

'How? With *money*?'

'How else? They paid for my education, fed me, clothed me, gave me the means to make my wealth.'

'They are your *parents*—they love you; they don't want your money.' She put her hands on her hips. 'Is this the type of parent you plan to be? Will you be keeping track of every penny you spend and expecting it to be paid back with interest?'

'No! Of course not. That's different.'

'How?'

'I was twelve when Elvira and I were adopted. Elvira

was only four. Louise and Bill had never planned to adopt an older child—they wanted a little one. They fell for Elvira and decided out of the goodness of their hearts to take me as well. For Elvira's sake. The social workers couldn't believe it—and neither could I. As I told you, they're good people. So, yes, I do owe them a debt.'

For a moment April wondered how it must have felt to that twelve-year-old boy—to have been taken in out of charity rather than love. And then she remembered Louise's expression when she'd described the bond between Marcus and his sister.

'Perhaps they didn't intend to adopt an older child, but that doesn't mean they took you just for Elvira's sake. Maybe they took you for both your sakes. Whatever their motivation, they grew to love you.'

'You don't have to try to make me feel good about this, April. Love doesn't come into it—their charitable action allowed me to be part of Elvira's life. I didn't expect anything more from them.'

'Didn't expect or *couldn't* accept?' The question fell from her lips without permission from her brain, and his brows pulled together in a glower.

'Meaning…?'

'Meaning that they love you and you seem to be having difficulty accepting that.'

'Spare me, please. You've spent a few hours over a dinner table with them—that does *not* endow you with the ability to judge their emotional state. Eighteen years ago I was a street kid. I was illiterate, foul-mouthed, and my greatest talent was my ability to fight dirty. Really, I was *not* loveable, and no one in their right mind would have taken me in.'

'But you turned yourself around—surely you see how amazing that is?'

Only he didn't—she could see that in the stubborn jut

of his jaw, in the darkness of his expression as he looked back into the past and saw something that she couldn't.

Without thought she moved closer to him, wanting to make him listen to her, force him to acquiesce to what was so obvious to her.

'Marcus...'

'Drop it, April. You got what you wanted. To meet Louise and Bill. There is absolutely no need for your pseudo-psychology.'

April halted in her tracks; the words made her flinch.

'Or if you do feel the need perhaps you should aim the spotlight at yourself. *You* are the one who wants to give up a baby—your own flesh and blood. Maybe you need me to fall in with all this for yourself, so that you can believe all adoption stories have a happy ending.'

For a moment her feet wanted to move backwards, but she forced herself to remain where she was. Because despite the harshness of his words she recognised that he had a right to say them—that they weren't the kind of put-down that Dean had delighted in. They were the barbs of a man in pain himself.

'You are entitled to that opinion,' she said quietly. 'But it isn't pseudo-psychology to recognise genuine love. You can deny it as much as you like, but your parents love you because you deserve to be loved. And, whether you believe me or not, if I am pregnant I will love this baby more than you can imagine.'

He raised his hand as if to reach out for her, and now she did step backwards.

'I'm heading to bed. I'll see you tomorrow.'

CHAPTER THIRTEEN

EVER SINCE THEIR catastrophic conversation following the disastrous dinner April had avoided him. They met briefly over breakfast and dinner, when they uttered inane civilities, but she remained aloof, hidden behind a veneer of politeness and cool indifference—and Marcus couldn't blame her. He'd behaved like the proverbial horse's backside. Worse, he was too much of a coward even to apologise, in case it sparked another catastrophic conversation.

But things couldn't go on like this. The week was very nearly over and April looked exhausted—so he'd decided today would be different.

Marcus looked at the breakfast he had laid out on the table and waited as he heard April's footsteps approach. She pushed the door open and then checked on the threshold, looking from him to the table. Surprise raised her brows.

'What's this?'

'Pancakes,' he said with a touch of pride. 'Admittedly the second batch—the first ones were a disaster. I wasn't sure what you would want with them, so I thought I'd give you a choice. Bacon, maple syrup, lemon juice, sugar, blueberries—and there's chocolate ice cream in the freezer.'

'You've gone to a lot of trouble.'

Her expression was a near comical mix of wariness and innate politeness, and he grinned.

'It's OK. You don't have to be polite. Just sit down and tuck in.'

Another hesitation and then she shrugged. 'OK.'

Half an hour later satisfaction touched him as she polished off pancake number four.

'I'll tidy up, then I need go,' she said.

'Not so fast. There's been a change of plan.'

'What do you mean?'

'Frederick has ordered us to take a day off, and I've decided to obey the royal command.'

'Well, I haven't. They're expecting me at the community centre and...'

Bracing himself, Marcus shook his head. 'Actually, they aren't. Mia is back now, and I've asked Mrs Hernandez to help out today.'

Her green eyes narrowed and her fingers twitched in a clear desire to pick up her empty plate and hurl it at his head.

'Well, I'm going in anyway.'

'Then at least let me tell you what I have planned for the day. First I am going to spend at least ten minutes apologising for my behaviour the other night. Then I want to take you for a day in the Lycander countryside and a picnic lunch. You've worked yourself into the ground in the past week and you deserve a day of rest. If you really can't stand to go with me I could ask Elvira to go with you—or Gloria, or anyone else you want.'

April stared at him for a long moment. 'Let's start with the apology and go from there.'

Reaching out, he covered her hand with his. 'I'm truly sorry, April. I shouldn't have said what I did. I don't understand why you would give a baby up, because I truly believe you would make a wonderful mother. But I need to trust that you have your reasons—not try to make you feel bad about the decision. Because I do totally believe in your love for a baby.'

Tears sheened her green eyes. 'Thank you.' Her fingers tightened around his. 'I owe you an apology as well. I overstepped. Your relationship with Louise and Bill is your business, and you're right. You lived your whole childhood with them; I spent a few hours with them around a dinner table. That doesn't give me the right to judge.'

It didn't, and yet he hadn't been able to forget her words—had wondered if perhaps he had got it all wrong. *Could* Louise and Bill have grown to love him? The idea didn't seem possible—after all, if that were so wouldn't they have told him?

'Also, I realise now that for you the idea of me giving a baby up for adoption must be even more complicated than it would be for anyone else, and I am truly sorry for that.'

Marcus shook his head; he couldn't let her beat herself up any further. 'I appreciate that—and, yes. of course my circumstances play a part in my reaction. But I *do* believe in adoption in the right circumstances. In our case our birth parents died and we were very lucky to be taken in by Louise and Bill.'

'Marcus, I am so sorry. It must have been devastating to lose your parents. I thought—' She broke off, looking confused.

'You thought I'd been taken away from my birth parents?'

It was fair enough—after all, he'd told her that he'd been an illiterate, foul-mouthed, unloveable street fighter at the time of his adoption.

'I wasn't—though maybe I should have been.' It was another question he tussled with. 'My birth parents were alcoholics, drug addicts, criminals. But—'

'But they were still the only parents you had?'

'Yes.' And as such of course he'd loved them. For all the good it had done him.

With the benefit of hindsight, he understood that the path of addiction his parents had ended up on had distorted their ability to feel, to parent, to love. Their need for the next drink, the next hit, had outweighed anything else. But he also knew they had felt *something* for him, however insubstantial.

'It was complex,' he agreed now, as he pushed thoughts of the past away. He wanted today to be a happy day—to create *good* memories. 'But we've been sidetracked. I don't want today to be about the past, or the future. Let's live in the moment.'

She hesitated, her green eyes wide as they rested on his face, and then she nodded, smiled a smile that lit her face. 'It's a plan.'

'So...a picnic in the countryside?'

'I think that sounds lovely. I'll change into something more suitable for a picnic and then let's go.'

Twenty minutes later she re-entered the kitchen, a tentative smile on her lips and a sliver of doubt in her eyes.

'What do you think?' she asked. 'I literally grabbed it off a clothes stall a couple of days ago, because I knew I was running low on clean clothes and might not have time to do a wash.'

'I think it's beautiful. I think *you're* beautiful.'

The words were out before he could stop them—because they were true. The simple sun dress, a swirl of turquoise and sea-green, accentuated her slender curves and the length of her legs. But it was more than that; her features were relaxed, and her green eyes sparkled with a luminosity they had lacked for the past days.

'Thank you.' She smiled suddenly. 'And please note my gracious acceptance of the compliment. Now, shall I rustle up a picnic?'

'No need. I've done it. Well, I went to the supermarket and bought some stuff.'

To his considerable relief the very kind lady behind the deli counter had taken pity on him and put together a selection she had promised him would be perfect for a countryside picnic.

'Let's go. I've given Roberto the day off, so it's just you and me.'

Just you and me.

The words seemed to echo in the air, reverberating with promise and anticipation, and Marcus threw caution to the wind and reached out for her hand. Hands clasped, they headed for the car.

As he drove along he could sense April relax as she absorbed the beauty of the Lycandrian countryside—the variety and shades of green hedgerows and leaves, the golden fields and the sun-kissed breeze tinged with the scent of lemons.

'It's so peaceful,' she said. 'It's almost impossible to believe that we're only hours away from the city. Where are we going?'

'A meadow with a river running through it and a weeping willow where we can sit in the shade and have our picnic. And I've brought a kite.' For a moment he felt like an absolute idiot, and glanced sideways at her to see if she was laughing at him.

But her face was illuminated with a smile that made him catch his breath.

'That sounds idyllic. I haven't flown a kite in years.'

'Neither have I. Louise and Bill brought Elvira here to teach her how and she asked me to come too, so I did.'

For a moment he revisited the memory, and it occurred to him that that wasn't exactly how it had happened. First Bill and Louise had asked *him* and he'd refused—sure that he would be in the way, that he had been asked out of duty. He frowned as he wondered if perhaps…just perhaps… April had a point.

'We're here.'

They alighted from the car and he led the way across the fields to the meadow, and somehow once again it seemed the most natural thing in the world to take her hand. They reached the weeping willow and spread the blanket out under the sweep of its branches, then unpacked an array of delicacies from the wicker basket.

'This is amazing. Thank you.' She bit into a parmesan and gruyere cheese straw and rested back against the tree trunk with a contented sigh. 'One day we should hire a mini-bus and bring the teens out here. Gemma and Blake and Mia…everyone.'

'We will. Lord knows they deserve some peace and quiet…a break.'

'It will be a long time before life goes back to normal for them and their families, won't it?' Her voice sounded sad.

'Yes. But I promise you that the new "normal" will be a lot better than the old one. Frederick and I have been in consultation with city planners and architects, surveyors and construction firms, and it's all coming together. Safe, proper housing is a priority.'

'I know you will make it happen. And that brings me to something I want to tell you. I've decided to drop the story about Axel and Frederick and the night of the tragedy.'

Relief caused him to smile, even as curiosity prompted him to ask, 'Why?'

'Because if there is one thing I've learnt from this tragedy it's that Frederick cares about Lycander and every one of his people, and for me to start a sequence of events that might topple him at a time when Lycander needs him would be wrong.'

'What about the truth?'

'I still believe in the truth, and I still believe that the people deserve that truth. I spoke with Frederick.'

'You did?'

'Yes. Briefly. I told him that I knew but I wouldn't pursue it—and he promised me that one day he will tell the truth, when the time is right. When he's had a chance to prove to everyone that he is not the Playboy Prince they once despised. If Frederick did wrong, he's doing his best to do right now. That's what you told me once, isn't it? That if you have done wrong then sometimes all you can do is live as good a life as you can to redeem yourself. So I'll drop the story.'

'I'm glad,' he said simply.

'There is also the fact that Brian Sewell is scum. I caught him at the community centre the other day, trying to convince everyone that their poor-quality housing was Frederick's fault and they should take to the streets in protest instead of setting up shelters!'

'What happened?'

'I gave him a piece of my mind and Blake and Isaac threw him out. Clearly all that boxing training paid off; he went like a lamb.'

The sheer indignation in her voice showed. 'You really care, don't you?' he said.

The words caused her to pause, an arrested look in her green eyes.

'Why don't you stay?'

'Stay?'

'Yes. In Lycander. For a while. You can base yourself anywhere as a writer, and you could stay on at the centre for a while if you wanted. I know how much help you are there. Perhaps you could even write a piece on the centre...'

His voice trailed off as he wondered what exactly he was asking.

Clearly she was wondering the same. 'Would you want me to stay regardless of whether or not I'm pregnant?'

Yes. The word exploded in his mind and he shook his head. Of course he didn't want April to stay. Obviously he wouldn't mind, because it would make no difference to him. *Could* make no difference to him.

'That would be up to you,' he said evenly. 'But maybe we should wait and see what the test says before we decide anything.' He rose to his feet. 'Now, let's fly that kite.'

As he unpacked the multi-coloured kite he was tantalisingly aware of her proximity: the light scent of orange blossom, the soft silk of her auburn hair so close as they bent over the kite.

'Would you like to go first?'

'Absolutely.'

Soon they were racing across the meadow, both of them whooping with joy as after a few false starts the breeze caught the kite and it swooped ever upward. April reeled out the string with an expert flick of her wrist. It bobbed high overhead with a jaunty dance and they came to a halt, breathless with laughter.

'That's how life should be,' he said. 'Like the flight of a kite, with the freedom to swoop and soar at will.'

'Only it isn't at will, is it?' she returned. 'It's at the whim of the wind or the person who pulls the string.'

'So you think it's better to be in a cage of your own making?'

'Yes. At least that way you can minimise the risk of plummeting down to your destruction, or getting tangled in a tree, or quite simply being abandoned by the string-puller.'

'Or you can learn to ride the wind to the best of your ability and live your life with all the highs and the lows.'

April sighed. 'OK. We're not really talking about the kite any more, are we?'

'No. We're talking about *you*. You say you want your life to remain as it is, but that way you shut out the possibility of so much—so many opportunities. The chance to write more serious articles, the chance to change other people's lives, perhaps the chance to love and have a family.'

'I told you. I don't want that. You of all people should understand that. You've ruled it out for yourself.'

'That's different. You did want it once, or you would never have married Dean in the first place. You did believe in love and happy-ever-after, and I don't want one man to ruin that dream for you. I don't want you to be caged in by his actions, to give up on the future you deserve.'

'I appreciate that. I do. But that happy-ever-after—it's not for me.'

'I'm sorry, April. I shouldn't have said anything. I don't want to ruin the day.' He could see sadness in her green eyes, an ache that made him want to hold her in his arms and somehow make the pain go away.

'You haven't ruined it. Not at all.'

Green eyes wide, she edged closer to him, frowned and then swiftly tied the kite string to the branch of a small sapling. Facing him, her head tipped up to meet his gaze full-on, she placed her hands on his shoulders.

'I promise. It's been an incredible day, Marcus, and one I will always remember.'

Standing on tiptoe, she kissed his cheek. A tendril of her hair whispered against his cheek, her scent tilted his senses—and he couldn't help himself. Gently he cupped her jaw and lowered his lips over hers in a kiss so sweetly sensual his head spun in sheer giddiness.

He didn't know how long they stood there, lips locked in the flower-strewn meadow, surrounded by the gentle balm of the breeze and the gentle call of the birds, the kite still dancing above them in the cerulean sky. But finally she broke away.

'The perfect end to a perfect day,' she said, with a smile that caught at his chest.

April paced the lounge, unable to sleep, unable to do anything. That kiss *had* been the perfect end to a perfect day. But now the day was over and night had fallen and soon—oh-so-soon—she would know the answer to the question that had pounded her brain for days. The darkness outside, the deep midnight-black sky with its twinkle of stars did nothing to soothe her.

How she wished she could stare at those stars and they could tell her the future.

The click of the door alerted her and she turned to see Marcus silhouetted in the doorway.

'Sorry, I didn't want to wake you. That's why I came in here. To pace.'

'I wasn't asleep; the waiting is getting to me too.'

He came to stand beside her, by the enormous bay window.

April hesitated. 'I bought a pregnancy test. One you can do early.'

'How early?'

'I could do it now. I'm just too chicken.'

'I think you should do it. We need to know—one way or the other it's always better to know.'

He was right: better to face up to the truth rather than hide away from it. She *knew* that. Yet cold panic cascaded in a clammy sheen over her skin as she faltered out, 'OK…'

She took in a deep breath, needing to tell him something.

'But first… If I am pregnant, and if you still want custody when the baby is born, you can have it.'

She had come to realise that in this case she could trust

her judgement. Marcus was not like Dean. He was a truly good man—a man with flaws, for sure, but his flaws would never permit him to hurt or demean anyone else. He could admit it when he was wrong, he could be strong, and he could be gentle. She knew with all her heart that he would keep their baby safe.

His face was pale in the light that suddenly flooded the room as the moon pulled out from behind a cloud.

'I… Thank you, April. I swear I will be the best dad I can be.' He tried a smile. 'Now, why don't you go off and then we'll find out whether there will be any need for me to be one?'

'Wish me luck.'

With a ghost of a smile she headed for the bathroom, her heart slamming her ribcage in panic-stricken beats.

The agonising wait seemed eternal, but once the time was up April hesitated, unable to look. The tension was so taut in her tummy that she thought she might buckle with cramp.

Come on, April.

She had to know. She couldn't skulk in Marcus's bathroom for ever. It wouldn't be practical.

And so, with a near-hysterical deep breath, she looked.

CHAPTER FOURTEEN

MARCUS WAS STANDING by the window when she returned to the lounge. The light was still off, the room lit only by the pale moonbeams and star-glow from without. He spun round as she entered, his hands clenched into fists by his sides, the question in his eyes almost anguished.

'I'm not pregnant.'

She said the words clearly, woodenly, her emotions numbed, but not so frozen that she didn't see it—disappointment, zigzagging over his expression in a flash, before he stepped forward with a smile that didn't reach his eyes.

'That's a relief.'

But he couldn't pull it off.

'You don't mean that,' she said, her voice half-question, half-statement.

Three strides took him to the drinks cabinet in the corner of the room, where he pulled out a whisky bottle.

'You're right. I don't mean it.' He gestured at the bottle. 'Drink?'

'No, thank you. I don't understand. Why aren't you relieved?'

'I don't know.' He sank onto the state-of-the-art sofa, drink in hand. 'I guess this was my shot. My one chance to be a dad.' He shook his head as if in disbelief at his own words.

'It doesn't have to be. If you want a child you could adopt.'

'No. I've told you already that wouldn't be fair. There are plenty of couples like Louise and Bill out there, who can offer a child way more than I can. It would be selfish of me, unfair to them and to any child to take one. What I had to offer *this* baby was my blood; he or she would have been a baby I could have felt would be better off with me.'

'You have plenty to offer. You will be a wonderful dad. I can see that from the way you are with Charlie, the way you are with Gemma and Blake and Mia. I can see it, full-stop. More than that, you told me not to limit myself—neither should you. Try to meet a woman. Maybe the next time you opt for "physical gratification", don't walk away. Try a date instead. Give it a shot.'

Yet even as she said it emotion squeezed her gut at the idea of Marcus with another woman—Marcus holding another woman's baby.

'I can't.'

'Why not?'

'Because I'm not cut out to be a family man.'

Bitterness infused his tone as he placed the crystal tumbler on the table with a *thunk*.

'I told you my parents died—I didn't tell you how. They died in a fire. They got high and must have decided to light candles, or cook something. I woke up to the smell of smoke. I rushed to find Elvira but she wasn't there. My parents must have taken her out of her cot. I legged it into the lounge. The flames were awful. I found Elvira but I couldn't wake my parents up. I got Elvira out and then... I didn't go back in. Our neighbours held me back, said it was too dangerous.'

April released the breath she hadn't even realised she held. 'Then you *couldn't* have gone back in.'

He picked the glass up, cradled it in one hand. 'That's a matter of opinion. Maybe I could have fought harder—maybe I *should* have fought harder. Nothing would have stopped me going back in if Elvira had still been in there. I hesitated for just a minute, and in that minute the roof caved in.'

'Where were the emergency services?'

'On their way. They were too late.'

April didn't know what else to say. She could picture the scene in vivid detail: the choking, gagging fog of smoke, the intensity of heat from the red-orange flames shooting up into the dark Lycander sky...the same sky she could see right now. And the twelve-year-old boy watching, knowing that inside the building his parents lay, unable to help themselves.

'You *cannot* blame yourself.'

'Who would you suggest I blame?'

'Anyone but yourself. What happened was a tragedy, but it was brought about by a chain of circumstances and choices that were not your fault.'

'*One* of those choices was mine.'

'You didn't make a choice—you hesitated for a moment. That is not the same thing at all. Plus, your neighbours were right—you might well have died if you'd gone in.'

He raised a hand. 'Enough. I appreciate you're trying to make me feel better, but you can't. That moment of hesitation changed everything, and whilst I can't go back and change it I can at least learn from it.'

But what had he learnt? Not to love or be loved. No wonder he had never been able to let Louise and Bill in. She could only imagine the immense guilt he must feel about accepting love from a different set of parents.

No wonder he felt he was unworthy of love—he believed he had contributed to his parents' death. Just as *she* believed she had contributed to Edward's. So if she couldn't make him feel better, perhaps she could at least let him know she understood.

'You're right. I can't make you feel better. But I do understand.'

She moved closer to the sofa, wanting him to see her face.

'There's something I haven't told you. Dean and I had a baby. A little boy called Edward.'

His hand jerked and whisky slopped over the side of the glass he had picked up once again. He deposited it on a table as he rose to stand beside her.

But she stepped away.

'Don't—please. I don't want to break down. I just want to say it. I told you about the disaster that was my marriage…how Dean made me feel like nothing. But somewhere, somehow I found the courage to leave him. I had it all planned. But the plans went wrong. Because, you see, I made a stupid decision—tried to be too clever. I should have walked straight out. Instead I decided to pack. Dean found me, guessed what I intended and went nuts. Snatched Edward. I couldn't stop him. He swatted me aside as though I truly was nothing. He ran off with our son, put him in the car and drove off. He'd been drinking, he didn't secure Edward properly, and there was a storm—rain pouring down, visibility atrocious. There was an accident and they both died.'

Marcus opened his mouth but she shook her head.

'There is nothing you can say. Nothing anyone can say. When I lost Edward I lost everything. I fell apart, sank into a pit of despair. The only reason I climbed out was because of my family—they cared for me, looked after me, and I pulled myself out, created a new life for myself. A life that I can manage. A cage, if you like, but it's better than the pit. I still know how it feels to look back and see that line in the sand—the before and after, the moment when if you could go back you could change history.'

Now he stepped forward and took her in his arms, held her tight, so close that she could feel the strength of his compassion, his sympathy, his empathy, the extent of how much he cared. She wrapped her arms around him and returned the pressure.

When he spoke it was over her head, his voice raw with emotion. 'I wish with all my heart that I could turn back the clock for you—that I could somehow protect you from the loss and pain you have endured.'

'Thank you.'

Eventually they pulled apart and he looked at her, his dark eyes intense. 'Stay,' he said, the one word filled with meaning.

'I don't understand.'

'In the meadow I asked you to stay in Lycander. I'm asking again. Stay. Here. With me. For a week, a month, a few days.'

For a stupid, wonderful instant she wanted to say yes, to stay for a while—but then she shook her head. 'It wouldn't work. Right now you're feeling sorry for me, and that is no basis for any sort of relationship.'

'This isn't to do with pity.'

'Then what *is* it to do with?'

'I want to spend more time with you. Isn't that what you suggested I do? Go on a date? Try for more than short-term physical gratification?'

'I did. But not with me.' Tears prickled the back of her eyes and she blinked hard, refusing to allow them exit.

He reached out and took both her hands in his, his grasp gentle and yet full of strength and reassurance. '*Yes*, with you,' he said. 'Why don't we spend some time together because we *want* to? See where it could go. No expectations, no promises...'

'I can't do that.' The very idea caused panic, a visceral fear, to judder through her. 'And you deserve a woman who can—a woman there's the possibility of a future with. I have nothing left to give. I can only maintain my cage—my insulated bubble, as I prefer to think of it. These past weeks I've ventured out—with you. I've had a taste of the world outside my bubble. I've experienced joy and happiness and anger, and I've witnessed pain and suffering. Now I need to go back into my bubble.'

Hurt flashed across his face, followed by acceptance, and in that instant she knew exactly what he was thinking. That he wasn't enough—wasn't enough to make her want to stay out of her cage. That what he had to offer was insufficient.

'It's not you.' How could she make those clichéd words real? 'Don't you see? I can't do it. It's too much, too scary.' And he deserved so much more than her.

'It's OK.'

His deep voice soothed her.

'I understand—and you're right. It was a stupid idea. Not because of you, but because of me. I hope that one day someone will come along and entice you out of that bubble.'

Helplessness assailed her, along with an absurd desire either to pummel his chest with her fists or throw herself against him and burst into tears.

Could she agree? Could she stay with him? See what happened?

No. Because she knew what would happen. She would fall for him...plummet into an abyss of emotion that she could not deal with. So all she could do was get out. But the thought of leaving—right here and now like this, when they had both shared so much—seemed impossible. Seemed wrong.

'That won't happen,' she heard herself say. 'But I hope that one day *you* will find happiness and love and have the chance to be a dad. I know you'll make a great one.'

And still she couldn't bring herself to leave…couldn't pull her hands from his. Realisation hit her like lead. It was too late—she had already fallen. She loved him, and was already mid-tumble into a mire of sensation and feelings.

No. She punched the knowledge aside in sheer repudiation. This wasn't love—it was confusion…a need to say goodbye properly.

She looked up at him. 'Marcus?'

The word was half-question, half-entreaty.

'Could we…could we have one more night?'

There was no need for further words. He pulled her into his arms and relief, gratitude and desire enmeshed her. A small moan escaped her lips, and then all else was forgotten in their bittersweet embrace as he swept her up into his arms and carried her from the room.

Marcus opened his eyes and knew that April was gone. His whole being was bereft, even as he felt some grim satisfaction that he had kept the promise she had extracted from him in the early hours of the morning.

'Please let me say goodbye now.'

Her hair had been tickling his chin and his arms had been wrapped around her. He hadn't wanted her to say goodbye at all. But he'd respected her wishes and agreed.

Of course he'd known when she'd woken—had forced himself to remain still as she'd slipped from the bed, quietly picked up her clothes and dropped a feather-light kiss on his cheek before she'd tiptoed out of the room. And out of his life. Because shortly after that he'd heard the door click shut and had known that April was gone.

He needed to get on with his life—there could have been no future with April. He had been a fool even to contemplate any deviation from his path.

April had been through so much—had worked out a way to live her life despite the tragedy she had experienced. He could offer her nothing, really, except perhaps medium-term gratification. For a mad moment he'd been allowed a glimpse of a different future—had had a vision of himself as a dad—but he knew now it had been nothing but an illusion. April had been sensible enough to see that and to reject the insubstantial offer he had made her.

He closed his eyes and allowed himself the memory of the past few hours—hours of such bittersweet joy that his gut wrenched at the knowledge they would never be repeated. He'd never hold April in his arms again, never caress her skin, hear her laugh or…

Enough.

He'd survived for years without April and he'd survive now. There was work to be done and plenty of it.

Swinging himself out of bed, he headed for the bathroom, closing his senses to the elusive drift of April's perfume—the delicate rose that hitched his breath in his chest. Avoiding the kitchen, he left the house as soon as possible.

Yet everywhere seemed to hold a memory, and by evening his head pounded with the effort of not thinking.

A knock on the office door elicited a sigh and a terse, 'Come in.' Surprise raised his brows as Louise entered, a tentative smile on her face. He couldn't remember either Louise or Bill ever coming to his office without prior arrangement.

Maybe because you made it plain they weren't welcome.

He could almost hear April's voice and now infused his own with defensive cheer. 'Louise! How lovely to see you. I was going to call later to thank you and Bill for everything you've done. Sunita said you've been fantastic in the nursery.'

'I was glad to help. Those poor parents needed somewhere they knew their children would be safe and fed and looked after whilst they tried to put their lives back together. But that's not why I'm here. I got a thank-you message from April, but I understand that she has now left Lycander?'

'Yes.'

'I'm sorry. I saw the way you looked at each other last week and I thought... I hoped that maybe you two were together.'

'No.'

'Do you have feelings for her?'

Marcus blinked at her, feeling a touch flummoxed. He and Louise quite simply did not have conversations like this.

'I...'

Louise continued almost chattily. 'I think you do. Maybe you even love her.'

The words seemed to come from a long way away, and then they exploded in a sonic boom around him. *Love*. He *loved* April. The idea was so ginormous, so huge, so terrifying he couldn't even summon the ability to deny it.

'I...it doesn't matter if I do. I asked her to stay and she didn't.'

Louise looked at him as if he were missing a few brain cells. 'Did you tell her how you feel or did you just let her go?'

'I let her go. You can't *make* people love you.'

'No, you can't. But you *can* try to persuade them. I know I'm biased, but what's not to love? You are kind, generous, strong, brave and loyal.'

His body flinched in automatic rejection of the words and Louise leant forward, placed her hands on his desk.

'Marcus. There are things that I should have said before. Things I didn't say because you never wished to speak of them and I thought it best not to. Perhaps I was simply too much of a coward. That fire was not your fault and neither was the death of your parents. It was a tragedy brought about by the choices your parents made. The choices you have made in *your* life have been principled and honourable. You were twelve years old but you saved Elvira—at great risk to yourself.'

'But I didn't save *them*.'

'No. You didn't. And no one expected you to. You would have died if you had gone back into that building and that would have been an even bigger tragedy. You are a *good* person, Marcus, and I am proud that you are my son. Now believe in yourself. If you love April tell her so. Don't leave it too late, like I have with you.'

'It's not too late.'

Marcus moved around the desk and without thought took this wonderful woman into his arms. 'I love you too, and when I get back we'll talk. You and me and Dad.'

'It's a deal.' Louise made a shooing motion. 'Now, *go*.'

And with that she left.

Before he could even begin to think about their conversation there was another knock on the door and Frederick entered.

Marcus rose to his feet.

'I have come to grant you leave of absence so you can go and find April,' said Frederick.

Marcus blinked. 'I wasn't aware I'd taken out a social media advert proclaiming my emotional state.'

'I am not an idiot. Plus I recognise the signs. It's not so long ago that you told me to go after the woman I loved. I am here to return the favour. Go. But before you do—your father is waiting to see you.'

Marcus guessed he shouldn't be surprised.

Frederick left and Bill entered, for all the world as if this were some Broadway show: *Exit the Prince, stage left. Enter the father, stage right.*

Stepping forward he shook hands with Bill, who looked at him apologetically.

'I know Louise has just been here, but I wanted to wish you luck and echo what she said. I'm proud of you, and I couldn't have wished for a better son.' His adoptive dad grinned slightly awkwardly. 'And I hope we can spend a bit more time together in the future.'

'I'd like that.' And he meant every word.

Bill held out a hand. 'Good luck with April. Take a tip from me and don't give up. I didn't have it easy with Louise, you know. She had some damn fool idea in her head that because she couldn't have kids I wouldn't want her. I told her that all I wanted in the world was her, and it was true. And then we were blessed with you and Elvira, so we did good. So will you.'

If only it could be that easy. He knew everyone meant well, but they seemed to believe that April would just fall into his arms, and Marcus knew damn well that it wouldn't be that simple. The odds of her loving him back seemed remote. Perhaps she would elect to keep walking away and not look back.

His stomach clenched and then he thumped the desk. *No.* He would not think like that. He was a fighter and, so help him, he would fight for April like he had never fought before.

April stared out of the window at the London drizzle. It suited her mood—grey, miserable, dull—and she was missing Marcus with an ache she didn't want to acknowledge. Her desolation was deep, poignant...as though a part of her was missing.

And it wasn't only Marcus—she missed Lycander, the

community centre, the people, even Roberto the chauffeur, whom she had bonded with over their mutual love of chocolate.

She gave another sigh—one she tried to swallow as her father walked in. She summoned a smile, though from Alex Fotherington's expression he wasn't fooled for an instant.

'Come on, petal. Why don't you tell me what's wrong?'

'Me. I'm just all *wrong*—befuddled and confused and—'

'I'm glad.'

April stared at him. 'Glad? Well, gee, thanks a bunch, Dad.'

'I *am* glad. Because you're feeling *something*.'

'I don't *want* to feel anything.' Talk about throwing her toys out of the pram… 'Last time I felt miserable it was—'

'Was over a tragedy you could have done nothing about. That was flat-out misery of the type I hope you never have to feel again. This is a different misery, and I suspect it's one you can choose to do something about.'

'How?'

'I think you've woken up, and I think all the emotions you've kept caged are surfacing and you're starting to live life again. I'd further guess that your befuddled confusion has something to do with love. If it does, don't reject it, April. Love is too precious.'

Love? The word rebounded around the room like a cannonball and she could feel the reverberations through her whole body She *loved* Marcus! What an idiot she was. A fool thrice over.

'I *have* to reject it!' she yelled suddenly, aghast with herself at the volume of her voice. 'Look where love landed me last time.'

'"Last time" was a long time ago, and a lot of people

were taken in by Dean. But Dean was *one* person. You made *one* mistake in love.'

'And it cost my son his *life*.'

'No, sweetheart. Your belief in love did *not* cost Edward his life. Dean's actions and some very bad luck cost Edward his life, and that does not mean you should never love or trust again. I don't believe you ever loved Dean. You were young and you got carried away. If life had worked out I think you would have realised that mistake without the tragedy that unfolded. Love did not cost Edward his life—love made the short time he had on this earth a happy time. Love is a precious commodity, and if you're lucky enough to love and be loved I hope you embrace it rather than shut it out.'

April stared at her dad's much-loved face and then rose to her feet and hugged him. 'Thank you. I still feel befuddled and confused, but I also feel better.'

'You're very welcome, sweetheart. I wish you luck with your decision.'

April sank down by the window again and wondered what to do…

Two days later

April sat by the graveside, ran her fingers over the headstone. She touched the items she'd placed so lovingly around the site. The windmill that turned in the breeze—Edward had been fascinated by the whirr and swirl of the colours as a baby. A tall vase filled with bright flowers—a standing order with the local florist still honoured. Edward's headstone.

She wasn't sure how long she'd been sitting there, gazing at the stone.

'Edward, I love you, oh-so-much, and I am so very sorry I couldn't protect you.'

Hugging her knees, she looked out over the cemetery and thought about her chosen course of action. And although there was panic in the mix of her feelings, there was also a sense of rightness. She did love Marcus, and—

She tensed at the sound of approaching footsteps, praying it wasn't a member of Dean's family…

She rose, turned, and froze in disbelief, sure she must be in the grip of hallucination. But there was something too real about the solid bulk, the aura, the pent-up energy of Marcus Alrikson that brooked no denial.

'I'm sorry to come here…to intrude…but I didn't want to risk the chance of missing you. Would you prefer it if I wait somewhere else? Or we could arrange to meet later? Or—?'

'No.' She shook her head. 'I'm glad you're here. It sounds a little nuts, but I came here to tell Edward something important—to clear my head and make my peace… I'm not sure—' She broke off, aware that she wasn't making sense. 'How did you find me?' The question was more curious than angry.

'Your parents told me where you were.'

'They did?'

'I persuaded them that it was a desperate case.'

A horrible thought entered her head. 'If it's about the article, I'll send you a copy to approve first—'

'The article? Of *course* it's not about the article. You can write what you like. Hell, I'll pose for a centrefold in a pair of tightie-whities, if you like.'

April stared at him. He sounded…agitated. Marcus Alrikson? Agitated?

Suddenly, to her own surprise, she laughed, knowing that if Edward's spirit could hear he wouldn't mind.

'That won't be necessary. So what's so desperate?' A sudden lurch of hope jumped around in her tummy.

'I should never have kept that promise,' he said. 'To let

you say goodbye. Because I don't want you to walk away. Not then, not now, not ever.'

'Why not?' The words were a whisper.

'Because I love you.'

There was a silence and then he smiled, as if by saying the words he had released magic into the air. And perhaps he had, because tendrils of potential happiness seemed to be unfurling inside her.

Yet how could this be possible?

She shook her head. 'It doesn't make sense. You said yourself that you didn't want love, or a relationship—that you *couldn't* love.'

'That is what I thought. What I have believed for too many years. It took you to show me that I was wrong. On all counts. You see, I grew up with no understanding of what real love meant. Until Elvira was born. When my parents brought her home I knew that I would do anything for her. But then the fire happened and something inside me froze. I still loved Elvira—but I couldn't love anyone else. Couldn't acknowledge love because I was so mixed up. But somehow you melted that freeze. Over the past weeks you've changed me, unlocked something inside me. You made me want to reach out—made me question my perspective on the past and my upbringing. But most of all you made me love you. I accept that this may all be too much, that you don't love *me*, but I want a chance to persuade you to do just that.'

April smiled suddenly as she reached down for her bag. 'Look.' She delved inside and pulled out an envelope, handed it to him. 'Open it.'

He did so. 'A ticket to Lycander? You were coming back?'

'Yes. To find you. To tell you that I love you. That I have fallen for you hook, line and sinker. That I can't go back into my insulated bubble, my cage, and I don't want to. I'd prefer to be free to love you, because love is too precious to waste. I *love* you, Marcus. I love your honour and your integrity. I love the way you make me feel—the way you have pulled me back into the sunshine. I love that you make me feel safe and exasperated and downright annoyed. I love how much you care about people and making the world a better place. I love you. And I want to spend all my days and nights with you.'

His smile lit his face, lit her world, made her glow inside and out.

'There's something else as well. I still haven't got my period. I don't know what, if anything, that means. I still might not be pregnant, given the test we did was negative, but it's made me think. Either way, I would love to have a baby with you. I know it will be an emotional journey, but...'

With Marcus by her side it was a journey she knew she could take—one she wanted to take.

'Edward will always have a place in my heart, but my love for him is different from the love I will have for another baby.'

'And because of my love for you Edward will always have a place in *my* heart too.'

She heard the sincerity in his voice, knew that he meant every word, and stepped forward into the warmth of his embrace, resting her head on his chest and knowing with all her heart that this man was her soul mate.

'You opened my eyes, April. To the possibility of a future I thought I could never have. A future filled with love and happiness.'

She smiled up at him, secure in the knowledge that it was a future they would walk into together, with no regrets at all.

EPILOGUE

Ten months later

APRIL LOOKED UP as her husband—her *husband*...the word still filled her with love, awe and a near-disbelief at her own luck that this wonderful man loved her—entered the room on tiptoe.

'She's asleep,' April whispered as Marcus approached the cot where their beautiful daughter Eleanor lay, her tiny hands curled into fists by her head, which was covered with wisps of dark curls.

'Nearly as beautiful as her mother,' Marcus said, and April grinned up at him.

'Very diplomatic—but I know perfectly well that this little one already has you twisted round her little finger.' She gazed tenderly down at her daughter. 'And I don't blame you one little bit. I still can't believe how blessed we are.'

It was true—from the moment they had discovered that she was, in fact, pregnant Marcus had been her rock. His joy and his pride and his understanding had been further proof, if she had needed it, that this man was truly amazing.

The past months had been a wonderful journey they had made together. Each day had cemented their love further, laid down a foundation she knew would endure for the rest of their lives. Together they had chosen and bought a beautiful house in Lycander; together they had prepared a nursery for their baby—painted the walls, stencilled drawings in their spare time.

April continued to work at the community centre, and had written a series of articles on the plight of the poor and disadvantaged in Lycander, and Marcus continued to help forge change in the country he loved. And through it all their love for each other and their unborn baby had grown.

Of course there had been difficult moments—moments when poignant memories of Edward had caused her sadness—but always Marcus had been there, with his love, and together they had created new and happy memories in the present.

'I know. We are truly blessed. I have no idea what I did to deserve this much happiness.'

Marcus put his arm around her, held her close, and she felt his love as warm as a blanket surrounding her.

'I love you, April. Now and for ever.'

'Now and for ever,' she echoed, meaning it with every fibre of her body and soul.

* * * * *

THE NANNY'S
DOUBLE TROUBLE

CHRISTINE RIMMER

For Marie Campbell,
friend and fellow book lover,
whose totally adorable basset hounds,
Fancy, Luke, Beau, Moses, Rachel,
Clementine and Sampson,
are the inspiration for Daniel Bravo's basset,
sweet Maisey Fae.

Chapter One

When Keely Ostergard entered the upstairs playroom, she found Daniel Bravo lying on the floor. His eighteen-month-old daughter, Frannie, sat beside him, rhythmically tapping his broad chest with a giant plastic spoon.

"Boom, Da-Da," Frannie said. "Boom, boom, boom."

Meanwhile, Jake, Frannie's twin, stood at Daniel's head on plump toddler legs, little hands over his eyes in a beginner's attempt at peekaboo.

Watching them, Keely couldn't help thinking that for a man who'd never wanted children of his own, Daniel sure was a dream with them. The guy rarely smiled, yet he lavished his kids with attention and affection.

"Boo!" cried Jake, followed by a delighted toddler belly laugh that had him toppling head over heels toward his father's face. Daniel caught him easily and started to tickle him, bringing more happy chortling from Jake.

Frannie spotted Keely first. "Keewee!" She dropped her spoon, lurched to her feet and toddled across the floor with her little arms wide.

Keely scooped her up. She smelled so sweet, like vanilla and apples. "How's my girl?"

Frannie's reply was almost in English. "I goo."

Daniel sat up, Jake still in his arms. "Keely." He looked a little worried at the sight of her. She came by often to see the kids, but she'd always called first. Not this time. He asked, "Everything okay?"

"Absolutely." She kissed Frannie's plump cheek. "Sorry, I know I should have called." But if she'd called and said she would like to speak with him, he would have asked what was going on, and she didn't want to get into that until they were face-to-face. He could too easily blow her off over the phone.

Grace, Daniel's youngest sister, who had answered the door at Keely's knock, entered the playroom right then. "Keely needs to talk to you, Daniel."

"Sure—down you go, big fella." He set the giggling Jake on his feet.

"Come on, you two." Grace took Frannie from Keely and held out her hand for Jake. "Bath time." She set off, carrying Frannie and pulling Jake along, on her way to the big bathroom down the hall.

Daniel stood still in the middle of the floor, watching her. "How 'bout a drink?"

"Sounds good."

Downstairs in the kitchen, he poured them each two fingers of very old scotch, neat. Keely wasn't much of a drinker, and scotch wasn't her favorite. But she had an offer to make, and she wanted him to say yes to it. Sharing a drink first might loosen him up a little.

She raised her glass and took a small sip. It burned going down, and she tried not to shudder. "Strong stuff."

He looked at her sideways and grumbled, "Why didn't you just say you hate scotch?"

"No. Really. It's very good."

He stared at her doubtfully for a couple of awkward seconds and then, with a shrug, he looked out the window. It was after seven on a cool Friday night in March, and already dark out. Beyond the glass, garden lights glowed golden through the thickening fog. Behind her, somewhere far out in the bay, down the tree-covered hill from the front of the house, a foghorn sounded.

Keely rested her hand on the cool, smooth soapstone counter. It was a beautiful kitchen. Her cousin, Lillie, had redone it with meticulous, loving care. It had lustrous heated wood floors in a herringbone pattern, a giant farm-style sink, twinkly glass backsplashes and chef-grade appliances.

Lillie.

Keely's throat got tight just thinking of her. She'd died eighteen months ago, leaving behind two adorable newborn babies—and one very grim husband. For the last fifteen years or so, Daniel had hardly been what Keely would call a happy guy anyway, but since they lost Lillie, the man rarely cracked a smile.

She took another sip and inched up on the reason she'd stopped by. "So then, what will you do for childcare now?"

He shifted his gaze back to her. "What *can* I do? Guess I'll try the nanny service again."

Keely almost laughed, though it wasn't all that funny. "Will you ask for the one with the alcohol problem or the one who gets sick all the time? Or maybe the one who's in love with you?" Daniel was a Viking of a man, big and buff and really good-looking in his too-serious, borderline-broody way. It wasn't the least surprising that one of the endless string of nannies and babysitters had decided she was meant to become a second mother to his children and show him how to heal his wounded heart.

He pinched the bridge of his manly nose as though he might be getting a headache. "Something will come up." His eyes—of a rather eerie pale blue—had circles under them. Clearly, he hadn't been sleeping well lately.

Keely felt kind of guilty for teasing him. Okay, she harbored some animosity toward him for what had gone down between him and her cousin in the last months of Lillie's life. But that was private stuff, husband-and-wife stuff, stuff Lillie had shared with Keely in strictest confidence.

Daniel wasn't a bad guy. He'd just had to shoulder too much, too soon. On the plus side, he was a man you could count on—and pretty much everyone did. Keely needed to remember his good qualities whenever she felt tempted to blame him for making Lillie unhappy.

He was doing the best he could, and he did have a real problem. President and CEO of Valentine Logging, Daniel worked long hours. He needed reliable childcare for the twins. Yet the nannies came and went. And Daniel's mother-in-law, Keely's aunt Gretchen, had always been his nanny of last resort, stepping up to take care of the kids every time another caregiver bit the dust.

Then two days ago Gretchen tripped and fell—over Jake. The little boy was fine, but Gretchen had four broken bones in her right foot. At seventy and now on crutches, Keely's aunt was no longer in any condition to be chasing after little ones. Daniel needed another nanny, and he needed one now.

And that was where Keely came in.

She knocked back the rest of her scotch. It seared a bracing path down her throat as she plunked her glass on the counter. "Okay, so here's the thing…"

Daniel gazed at her almost prayerfully. "Tell me you know a real-life Mary Poppins. Someone with excellent references who can't wait to move in here and take care of my kids."

"'Can't wait' might be a little strong, and Mary Poppins I'm not. But as for references, your mother-in-law will vouch for me. In fact, Aunt Gretchen has asked me to take over with the kids for a while, and I've said yes."

Daniel's mouth went slack. "You? You're kidding."

Should she be insulted? She answered tartly, "I am completely serious. The kids know me, I love them dearly and I'm happy to step in."

He pinned her with that too-pale stare. "It's just not right."

"Of course it's right. Lillie was my sister in all the ways that matter. Jake and Frannie need me right now. I know you and I aren't best friends, but you've got to have someone you can depend on. That would be me."

"You make it sound like I've got something against you, Keely. I don't."

She didn't believe him. But how he felt about her wasn't the point. Jake and Frannie were what mattered. Yes, he could probably hire yet another nanny from the service he used. But the kids deserved consistency and someone who loved them.

"Great." She plastered on a giant smile. "Daniel, It's

going to be fine, I promise you. Better me than yet another stranger."

His brow wrinkled to match the turned-down corners of his mouth. "You're busy. You've got that gallery to run and those quilt things you make."

Quilt things? Seriously?

Keely was a successful fabric artist as well as the proud owner of her own gallery, Sand & Sea, down in the historic district of their small Oregon town of Valentine Bay. And whatever Daniel chose to call textile arts, he did have a point. Taking care of Jake and Frannie on top of everything else she had going on would be a challenge.

She would manage, though. Gretchen had asked her to help. No way would she let Auntie G down.

"I'm here and I'm willing," she said. "The kids need me and they know me." She raced on before he could start objecting again. "Honestly, I have a plan and it's a good one. This house has seven bedrooms and only four people live here now—including the twins."

After his parents died, Daniel and Lillie had raised his seven surviving siblings right there in the Bravo family home. All the Bravo siblings had moved out now, though. Except for Grace. A junior at Reed College in Portland, Grace still came home for school breaks and between semesters. She had the only downstairs bedroom, an add-on off the kitchen.

Keely forged on. "I can take one empty upstairs room for a bedroom and one for my temporary studio—specifically, the two rooms directly across the hall from the twins' playroom and bedroom. It's perfect. And most nights, once you're here to take over, I'll probably just go home." She had a cute little cottage two blocks from the beach, not far from her gallery. "But if you need me,

I can stay over. With a studio set up here, I can work on my own projects whenever I get a spare moment or two. I have good people working at Sand & Sea, trustworthy people who will pick up the slack for me."

He leaned back against the counter, crossed his big arms over his soft flannel shirt and considered. "I don't know. I should talk to my sisters first, see how much they can pitch in."

Besides Grace, who would be leaving for Portland day-after-tomorrow, there were Aislinn, Harper and Hailey. Aislinn worked for a lawyer in town. She couldn't just take off indefinitely to watch her niece and nephew. As for Harper and Hailey, who'd been born just ten months apart, they were both seniors at U of O down in Eugene and wouldn't be back home until after their graduation at the end of the semester.

And what was it with men? Why did they automatically turn to their sisters and mothers-in-law in a childcare emergency? Daniel had three brothers living nearby. Keely *almost* hit the snark button and asked him why he didn't mention asking Matthias, Connor or Liam if they could pitch in, too?

But she had a goal here. Antagonizing Daniel would not aid her cause. "Well, of course everyone will help out, fill in when they can. But why make your sisters scramble when I'm willing to take on the main part of the job?"

"It just seems like a lot to ask."

"But, see, that's just it. You're not asking. I'm offering."

"More like insisting," he muttered.

"Oh, yes, I am." She put on a big smile, just to show him that he couldn't annoy her no matter how hard he tried. "And I'm prepared to start taking care of Frannie and Jake right away. I'll move my stuff in tomorrow, and I'll take over with the kids on Sunday when Grace leaves to go back to school."

He scowled down at his thick wool socks with the red reinforced heels and toes. Daniel always left his work boots at the door. "There's still Gretchen to think about. If you're busy with the kids, who's going to be looking after her until she can get around without crutches again?" Keely's uncle, Cletus Snow, had died five years ago. Auntie G lived alone now.

"She's managing all right, and I will be checking in on her. And that's not all. She's called my mom."

One burnished eyebrow lifted toward his thick dark gold hair as Daniel slanted her a skeptical glance. "What's Ingrid got to do with anything?"

It was an excellent question. Ingrid Ostergard and Gretchen Snow were as different as two women could be and still share the same genes. Round and rosy Gretchen loved home, children and family. Ingrid, slim and sharp as a blade at fifty, was a rock musician who'd lived just about all her adult life out of her famous purple tour bus. Ingrid had never married. She claimed she had no idea who Keely's father was. Twenty years younger than Gretchen, Keely's mother was hardly the type to run to her big sister's rescue.

Keely said, "Mom's decided to change things up in her life. She's coming home to stay and moving in with Aunt Gretchen."

Daniel stared at her in sheer disbelief. "What about the band?"

Pomegranate Dream had had one big hit back in the nineties. Since then, all the original members except Ingrid had dropped out and been replaced, most of them two or three times over. "My mother pretty much *is* the band. And she says she's done with touring. She's talking about opening a bar here in town, with live music on the weekends."

He just shook his head. "Your mother and Gretchen living together? How long do you think that's going to last?"

"There have been odder odd couples."

"Keely, come on. Those two never got along."

She picked up the bottle of scotch and poured them each another drink. "How 'bout we think positive?" She raised her glass. "To my new job taking care of your adorable children—and to my mom and your mother-in-law making it work."

He grabbed his glass. "I would insist on paying you the going rate." He looked as grim and grouchy as ever, but at least he'd essentially accepted her offer.

"Daniel, we're family. You don't have to—"

"Stop arguing." He narrowed those silvery eyes at her. "It's only fair."

Was it? Didn't really matter. If he had to put her on salary in order to agree to accept her help, so be it. "Go ahead then. Pay me the big bucks."

"I will." He named a figure.

"Done."

He tapped his glass to hers. "Here's to you, Keely. Thank you." He really did look relieved. "You're a life-saver." And then something truly rare happened. Daniel Bravo almost smiled.

Well, it was more of a twitch on the left side of his mouth, really. That twitch caused a warm little tug in the center of her chest. The man needed to learn how to smile again, he really did. Yes, he'd caused Lillie pain and Keely resented him for it.

But Lillie, diagnosed with lupus back in her teens, had craved the one thing that was most dangerous for her. She'd paid for her children with her life and left her husband on his own to raise the sweet babies she just had to have.

Life wasn't fair, Keely thought. At least there should be smiles in it. There should be joy wherever a person could find it. Jake and Frannie needed a dad who could smile now and then.

"What are you looking at?" Daniel demanded, all traces of that tiny twitch of a smile long gone.

Keely realized she'd been staring at Daniel's mouth for way too long. She blinked and gave an embarrassed little cough into her hand. "Just, um, thinking that you ought to smile more often."

He made a growly sound, something midway between a scoff and a snort. "Don't start on me, Keely. You'll give me a bad feeling about this deal we just made."

It was right on the tip of her tongue to come back with something snippy. *Do not get into it with him*, she reminded herself yet again. They would be living in the same house at least some of the time, and they needed to get along. Instead of a sharp retort, she gave him a crisp nod. "Fair enough."

Claws clicking gently across the floor, Lillie's sweet basset hound, Maisey Fae, waddled in from the family room. The dog stopped at Keely's feet and gazed up at her longingly through mournful brown eyes.

"Aww. How you doin', Maisey?" She knelt to give the dog a nice scratch under her jowly chin. "Where's my sugar?" She pursed her lips, and Maisey swiped at her face with that long, pink tongue.

When Keely rose again, Daniel was holding out a house key. "I'll give you a check tomorrow to cover the first week."

"Thanks. I'll be here nice and early with my car full of clothes, equipment and art supplies."

"I can't wait," he said with zero inflection as she headed for the front door. "What time?"

"Eight," she said over her shoulder.

"I'll come over and help."

"No need." She waved without turning. "I've got this."

The next morning, as Keely was hauling her prized Bernina 1015 sewing machine out to her Subaru in the drizzling rain, Daniel pulled up at the end of her front walk in his Supercrew long-bed pickup.

He emerged from behind the wheel, his dark gold hair kind of scrambled looking, his face rough with beard scruff, wearing a heavy waffle-weave Henley, old jeans and the usual big boots.

"I told you I can handle this," she reminded him as he took the sewing machine from her.

"You're welcome. Happy to help," he said, and for a split second she imagined a spark of wry humor in those ice-blue eyes.

She remembered her manners. "Thank you—and be careful with that," she warned. "Those aren't easy to find anymore, and they cost a fortune." She swiped at the mist of raindrops on her forehead, then stood with her hands on her hips watching his every move as he set the machine carefully in the back seat of his truck. When he shut the door again, she asked, "So Grace has the kids?"

"Yeah, they're with Grace. Let's get the rest." He headed up the walk, his long strides carrying him to the front porch of her shingled cottage in just a few steps.

She hustled to catch up. "You want some coffee? I can make some."

"I had two cups with breakfast. Let's get this done."

Half an hour later, all her equipment, including her spare Bernina—a 1008 model—a raft of art and sketching supplies and the giant pegboard loaded with industrial-sized spools of thread in just about every color known to man, was either in the rear seat of his crew cab or tucked in the long bed beneath the camper shell. He'd loaded up her two collapsible worktables, too, and the smaller table she liked to keep beside her easel. That left only her suitcase to go in the Subaru. She'd figured it would take three trips to get everything up to the Bravo house. Thanks to Daniel, they would get it done in one.

"See you back at the house." He climbed in his truck.

"Thank you. I mean that sincerely."

With a quick wave, he started the engine and drove off.

She locked up and followed him, leaving the mist-shrouded streets of town to head up Rhinehart Hill into the tall trees and then along the winding driveway that led to the beautiful old Bravo house, with its deep front porch flanked by stone pillars.

Keely stopped behind Daniel's truck in the turn-around in front of the house. She grabbed her biggest suitcase and hauled it inside and up the curving stair-case to the room she planned to use for sleeping when-ever she stayed over.

He emerged from the other room to meet her as she

headed back down. "I'm putting your sewing stuff in the white room." He shot a thumb back over his shoulder. "You're using it for work, right?"

"How'd you guess?"

"It has better light than the other one. You want me to get the bed and dressers out of there?"

"I can use the dressers for storage, if that's all right. Are they empty?"

"I think they've got a bunch of old clothes nobody wants in them. Just clear out the drawers, and I'll take everything away."

"Thanks." *Note to self: be nicer to Daniel.* He really was a handy guy to have around when a girl needed to get stuff done. "And as for the bed, yes, please. I would like it gone."

"I'll have it out of there before dinnertime." And off he went down the stairs to bring up the next load of her stuff.

She peeked into the kids' bedroom and also the play-room before following him. Nobody there. Grace must have them downstairs somewhere.

Working together, they hauled everything up to her two rooms, bringing the big thread pegboard up last.

"You want this board mounted on the wall?" he asked.

"That would be terrific."

"I'll get to that tonight. Once we get the bed out, we can set things up pretty much like the room you were using at your place."

It was exactly what she'd hoped to do, and she got a minor case of the warm fuzzies that he'd not only pitched in to help move her things, he'd also given real thought to making her as comfortable as possible in his house. "Totally works for me. Thanks."

With the barest nod of acknowledgment, he pulled a folded scrap of paper from his pocket—a check. "First week's pay." She took it. "I need to go on up to Warrenton," he said. Valentine Logging operated a log sorting and storage yard, deep water and barge cargo docks, and a log barking and chipping facility in nearby Warrenton at the mouth of the Columbia River. The company offices were there, too. "You planning to look in at the gallery today?"

"I am, yes. But I'll be back in the afternoon, ready to take over with the kids."

"No rush. Grace is here until tomorrow. She'll watch them today and tonight so you can get settled in."

That didn't seem fair. Grace had spent her whole week helping with the kids. "I'm fine on my own with them."

His regular frown got deeper. "Grace'll be here. In case you need her."

She considered the wisdom of arguing the point further. But his mouth was set and his eyes unwavering. Maybe not. "See you later then."

With a grunt, he turned and went down the stairs.

From the docks in Warrenton, Daniel called a handyman he trusted to haul the bed from the white room down into the basement. He'd been feeling pretty desperate yesterday when Keely showed up to save his bacon on the childcare front.

True, her offer had seemed like a bad idea at first. He'd been afraid they wouldn't get along. In the last years of Lillie's life, as his marriage unraveled, Keely had never said a mean word to him directly. But he got the message in her disapproving glances and careful silences whenever he happened to be in the same room with her. She'd been firmly Team Lillie, no doubt about it. Still, for the twins' sake, she'd stepped up to provide the care they needed.

It was important to do everything he could to make her happy in his house. He planned to be home for dinner and then to help her get everything just the way she wanted it.

But the day came and went. By late afternoon, he still needed to go through the stack of paperwork he hadn't managed to get to during the week. After a short break to grab some takeout, he headed for the office, ending up by himself at his desk until after seven.

When he finally pulled his truck into the garage, he caught Grace, in tight jeans and full makeup, as she was coming down the stairs from the inside door. She flashed him a smile and tried to ease past him on the way to her car.

"Hold on."

"Daniel." She made his name into a serious complaint. "I have to go. I'm meeting Erin at—"

He caught her arm. "We need to talk."

"But—"

"Come on."

She let out a groan, but at least she followed him back into the house. "What? Can you please make it quick?"

"Let's talk in my study." She trudged along behind him to his home office off the foyer. Once they were both inside, he shut the door. "The kids and Keely?"

There was an eye roll. "Jake and Frannie are already in bed. Keely's upstairs, putting her stuff away, fixing up her room and her workroom. She said it was fine for me to go."

A hot spark of anger ignited in his gut. But when he

got mad, Grace just got madder. He reminded himself to keep his cool. "The agreement was that you would give Keely a hand tonight, help her get comfortable, pitch in with the kids." He kept his voice level. Reasonable.

Still, Grace's eyes flashed blue fire. "The kids are in *bed*. Got it? And what agreement? You told me what to do as you were going out the door."

"Grace, I—"

"No. Uh-uh. I talked to Keely. I *asked* her if she needed me. She said go, have fun."

"Of course she would say that."

Grace looked up at the ceiling and blew out a furious breath. "You know, some people go to Cancún for their spring break. Me, though? I come home and help your mother-in-law look after your kids. And then when she trips over Jake, it's just me. Until Keely stepped up— which I totally appreciate. Keely's about the best there is. But me, I've got one night. One night of my spring break to myself. A few hours with my friends, and then I'm on my way back to school."

When she said it like that, he felt like an ogre. A litany of swear words scrolled through his brain. Playing stand-in dad to his own sisters and brothers should be more rewarding, shouldn't it? How come so much of the job just plain sucked?

She's the last one at home, he reminded himself. He was pretty much done with raising his siblings.

Too bad he still had a couple of decades ahead with his own kids.

"Come on, Grace. Don't exaggerate. You've spent time with your friends this week."

"Not much, I haven't."

"You went out last night, remember?"

Another giant sigh. More ceiling staring. "For like two hours."

"I want you to stick around tonight in case she needs you."

"But I promised Erin—"

He put up a hand. "You're needed here. And that's all I have to say about it."

If looks could kill, he'd be seared to a cinder. He waited for the yelling to start, dreaded the angry words about to erupt from her mouth—*I hate you, Daniel* and *Who died and made you king?* and the worst one of all, *You are not my father.*

As if he didn't know that. As if he'd *asked* for the thankless job of seeing that his brothers and sisters made it all the way to fully functioning adulthood without somehow crashing and burning in the process.

But this time, Grace surprised him. "Fine," she said way too quietly. And then, shoulders back and head high, she marched to the door, yanked it wide and went out.

He winced as she slammed it behind her. And then, even with the door shut, he could hear her boots pound the floor with each step as she tramped through the downstairs to her room off the kitchen—and slammed that door, too.

Chapter Two

Daniel scrubbed both hands down his face. And then he stood stock-still, listening for cries from upstairs— Jake or Frannie, startled awake by Grace's slamming and stomping. He didn't breathe again for several seconds.

Finally, when he heard nothing but sweet silence, he stuck his head out the door and listened some more.

Still nothing.

By some minor miracle, Grace had failed to wake up the kids.

Daniel retreated into the study and quietly shut the door. He really ought to go straight upstairs to see how Keely was managing.

But Grace might still have angry words to hurl at him. He would check his email now, hide out for a few minutes. If Grace came flying back out of her room again loaded for bear, he didn't want to be anywhere in her path.

* * *

Keely was in her bedroom, putting her clothes in the dresser when she heard a door slam downstairs, followed by the loud tapping of boots across hardwood floors.

Grace. Had to be. Keely tucked a stack of bras into the top drawer, quietly slid it shut—and winced as another downstairs door slammed.

Apparently Daniel had come in before Grace could escape.

Keely felt a stab of guilt. Daniel had made it abundantly clear he intended for his sister to stay home tonight. If Keely had only asked Grace to stick around, the confrontation that had so obviously just occurred downstairs could have been avoided.

But come on. Grace had a right to a little fun with her friends now and then. And Keely really didn't need her tonight.

The question now: Should she leave bad enough alone and stay out of it?

Yeah, probably.

But what had just happened was partly her fault. At the very least, she could offer Grace a shoulder to cry on.

Still not sure she ought to be sticking her nose in, she tiptoed out into the hall, down the stairs, past the shut door to Daniel's study and onward to the back of the house, into the hall off the kitchen. She tapped on Grace's door.

After a minute, a teary voice called, "Go away, Daniel!"

Keely tapped again. "Grace, it's me."

Silence. Keely steeled herself to be told to get lost.

But then she heard footsteps in there. Grace opened the door with red-rimmed eyes and a nose to match.

Keely held out a tissue. "I come in peace."

Grace took the tissue and wiped her nose. "Where is he?"

"Still in his study, I think."

"Jake and Frannie?"

"Not a peep."

Grace sniffed again. "Come in." She stepped back. Keely entered and followed her to the bed where they sat down side by side.

Keely made her apology. "He told me this morning that he expected you to stay in. I should have warned you that he seemed kind of dug in about it."

"He's kind of dug in about everything." Grace stuck out her chin. "You know it's true." Keely didn't argue. Why should she? She agreed with Grace on that. "He treats me like I'm a borderline delinquent. I'm twenty-one years old, getting decent grades in school, doing a perfectly fine job of adulting, thank you so very much. I could just get up, get in my car and go."

"But you won't. Because you are sweet and helpful. You love your brother, and you want to get along with him. You know he's got way too much on his plate, and so you try your best to be patient with him."

Grace let out a reluctant snort of laughter. "Yeah, right."

"I want to make a little speech now. It will probably annoy you, but I hope you'll listen anyway."

"Go for it."

"When he was your age, he was married, working, fitting in college classes as best he could and raising you and your brothers and sisters—and probably getting zero nights out with his friends."

Into the silence that followed, Grace shot her a surprised glance. "That's it. That's the speech?"

"That's all."

Grace seemed to consider. "I know you're right. He hasn't had it easy. But he still drives me crazy. I mean, does he *have* to be such a hard-ass *all* the time?"

Keely put her hand over Grace's and gave it a pat. "I'll go talk to him."

Grace scoffed, "Like there aren't a thousand ways that could go horribly wrong."

"Trust me."

"I do. It's *him* that I'm worried about."

Daniel was still holed up in his study, reluctant to venture out and possibly have to deal with his sister again when the tap came on the door.

Grace? Doubtful. Probably Keely. He didn't really want to listen to whatever she had to say right at the moment either. Chances were she'd only come to give him a bad time about Grace.

There was another knock.

He gave in and called out, "It's open."

Keely pushed the door wide and then hesitated on the threshold. She wore what she'd had on that morning— jeans rolled at the ankles, a black-and-white-striped shirt half-tucked-in and hanging off one shoulder, with high-tops on her feet. Her hair was naturally reddish blond, but she liked to change it up. Today, it fell in fog-frizzed brown waves to her shoulders. Her big, wide-set green eyes assessed him.

He leaned back in his swivel chair and cracked his neck to dispel some of the tension. "Go ahead. I'm listening."

She braced a shoulder in the doorway, stuck her hands in her pockets and crossed one high-top in front of the other. "I really did tell Grace I didn't need her, and I urged her to go out and have a little fun."

Women. They always knew how to gang up on a man. "All right."

She pushed off the door and straightened her shoulders. "All right, she can go—or all right, you heard what I said and I should get lost?"

He stared at his dead wife's cousin and reminded himself all over again that he was really grateful she'd come to look after his children, even if she did consider him to blame for all that had gone wrong between him and Lillie.

And maybe he *was* to blame.

When his parents had died suddenly on a second honeymoon in Thailand, he was eighteen. The most important thing then was to keep what was left of his family together. He'd stepped up to take care of his three surviving brothers and four sisters. Lillie, a year behind him in school, stepped right up with him. He and Lillie had been together—inseparable, really—for two years by then. They'd agreed to get married as soon as Lillie graduated high school.

A born nurturer just like her mother, Lillie was only too happy to take over as a second mom to his big brood of siblings. She always claimed that choosing a life with him and his ready-made family was the perfect solution for her. She could have the kids she longed for and not risk her health.

But as the years passed and his brothers and sisters grew up and moved out, her yearning for babies of their own only got stronger. He didn't share that yearning. No way. An empty nest. That was what he'd looked forward to. He'd thought they might travel a little, get to know each other all over again…

"Daniel? You all right?" Keely was waiting for him to answer her last question.

He shook himself and put his regrets aside. "Sorry." *Grace.* He needed to smooth things over with Grace. "You're sure you don't need her?"

"Positive."

He got up. "I'll go talk to her."

Grace opened the door at his knock. "What now?"

"Grace, I'm sorry we got into it."

"It's all right," she said flatly. He got the message. It was not all right. It was anything but.

"Listen, go ahead. Go meet Erin. Enjoy your last night home."

She almost smiled. But she was still too pissed at him for that. "Thanks."

Don't stay out too late. He closed his mouth over the words. She was an adult after all. He had trouble sometimes remembering that. She'd been a sweet little six-year-old in pigtails with two missing front teeth when George and Marie Bravo decided they needed a romantic getaway in Thailand. They got there just in time for the tsunami that killed them. And Grace had had to grow up without them.

No, he wasn't his baby sister's father, but sometimes he felt like it. He liked it when she stayed home—and not only because she helped out with the kids. He wanted her safe, damn it, wanted all of them safe. Life was too dangerous. Anything could happen. He knew that from hard experience.

"Have a good time." He pushed the words out of his unwilling mouth.

"I will," she said obediently and then lifted her arms in a limp offer of a hug.

He gathered her close, but only for a moment. She pulled free quickly, and he left her to go offer Keely some help setting up the white room for her studio.

By a little after eleven, they had the thread pegboard hung and covered with giant spools. He'd put up some shelves for her, ones he'd found down in the basement. The shelves used to be in his brother Matthias's room way back before Matt moved out. She had two work-tables set up, one for sketching and one for her sewing machine. There was an easel in the corner and another, smaller table next to it piled with paint and brushes.

"This is looking good, Daniel. Thank you."

"What else needs doing?"

"That's it." She hid a yawn behind her hand. "We are finished."

"You sure?"

She pushed in the chair at her sewing table. "Yep."

He felt the oddest reluctance to head for his own room. After Grace left for her night out, it had been pretty much a no-pressure evening. He'd felt useful, helping Keely get the room the way she wanted it. And besides that, it was kind of good just to hang with her. Kind of companionable.

He hadn't had much of that, of companionship. Not for a long time. Not for a couple of years at least. Not since he'd found out that Lillie was pregnant.

And really, since before that, even. More like five

years, since about the time Lillie started really pushing him to try for a baby of their own.

"Okay, what'd I say?" Keely asked.

"Huh? Nothing. Why?"

"You looked… I don't know. Faraway. Unhappy."

He tried for a laugh. It came out as more of a grunt. "I always look unhappy. Ask anyone who knows me."

"Now, see. I want to say that's not true. But, Daniel, it kind of is."

He had the absolutely unacceptable urge to start talking about Lillie, about how angry he still was at her after all this time, for betting on her life. And losing.

What was the matter with him? To even consider spilling his guts about Lillie to Keely, of all people? That would be a bad idea of spectacular proportions.

Wouldn't it? Why did he have this powerful feeling that Keely would understand?

Didn't matter. He just wasn't going there. No way.

And he needed to get out of there. Now.

He rubbed the back of his neck. "What can I say? Except, yeah, I'm a gloomy guy. And since you're good to go here, I'll see you in the morning."

She didn't reply for several seconds, just looked at him, kind of thoughtful and sad, both at once. A soft sigh escaped her. "All right then. Night."

"Night—come on, Maisey. Let's go." The dog, stretched out by the window, got up and followed him from the room.

With Maisey trotting along behind, he went down the stairs to let her out before bed. He walked fast, too, just in case Keely got it in her head to try to stop him, to start asking questions he saw no win in answering.

* * *

Daniel got in bed around midnight. He had trouble sleeping until a little after two, when he heard Grace come in. Relieved that she was home safe, he finally drifted off.

He woke to the sound of one of the kids crying. Maisey was already out of her dog bed and sniffing at the door. She gave a worried little whine, urging him to hurry as he yanked on track pants and a frayed Go Beavers T-shirt. When he opened the door, she pushed out ahead of him, leading the way along the hallway to the twins' bedroom.

The door stood open, dim light spilling out. Maisey went in first.

Keely was already there, Frannie in her arms. She was pacing the floor in the muted light from the little lamp on the green dresser. She turned when he entered, her hand on the back of Frannie's head, stroking gently as Frannie sobbed against her shoulder.

He felt that familiar ache his chest, the one he got when one of his own was hurting. A quick glance at Jake's crib showed him his boy was still asleep. That miracle wouldn't last long. "Let me take her," he whispered.

Keely kissed Frannie's temple. "Here's your daddy," she murmured, keeping it low, probably hoping Jake wouldn't wake up.

Yeah. Good luck with that.

Daniel held out his arms. With a sad little cry, Frannie twisted in Keely's hold and fell toward him. "Da-Da!" she wailed. He caught her and gathered her in. She dropped her head against his chest. "Ow. Ow, ow, ow."

Keely moved in close, the soft sleeve of her flannel pajama top brushing his arm. He got a faint whiff of sweetness—her shampoo? Her perfume? "Ear infection?" she whispered.

He felt the back of Frannie's neck as she sobbed against his chest. "She seems kind of hot."

"I thought so, too."

"We should take her temperature."

"I'll get the thermometer."

"It's the one that says *rectal* on the case," he advised over Frannie's unhappy cries. *Rectal.* Story of his life. Rectal thermometers and never enough sleep—and did Keely know where to look? "Cabinet in the big bathroom," he added. "On the left, second shelf. Just to be sure it's sterile, clean it with alcohol and a little soap and water."

"You got it." She disappeared into the hallway. Really, she was a champ, that Keely.

About then, Jake woke up with a startled cry. "Da?"

"It's okay, big guy."

"Fa-Fa?" It was Jake's name for his sister.

"She's not feeling so good."

Jake stood up in his crib. "Fa-Fa?" he called again.

Frannie answered, "Day!" She couldn't make the *j* sound yet, and she tended to drop hard sounds at the ends of words, so the *k* got lost, too, and she called her twin Day. "Ow, ow, ow!"

"Shh." Daniel soothed her. "It's okay..." Gently, he laid his wailing daughter on the changing table. As she wiggled and whined, he took off her one-piece pajamas and her diaper. Meanwhile, Jake jumped up and down in his crib, calling out "Fa-Fa, Fa-Fa!" in frantic sympathy, followed by a bunch of nonsense words to which Frannie replied with nonsense of her own—well, maybe not nonsense to the two of them. They had their own language that only they understood.

Keely came back with the thermometer in one hand, a bottle of liquid Tylenol and a dosing syringe in the other. "We'll probably need it," she said, meaning the Tylenol. Chances were way too good she was right.

He held out his hand as Frannie continued to cry and squirm. Keely passed him the thermometer—and Jake let out a wail from his crib.

"I'll get him," she said. "Tylenol's right here." She set it on the shelf above the changing table and went to reassure Jake.

The thermometer registered 102 degrees. He put a fresh diaper on Frannie and dosed her with the Tylenol as Keely sat in the corner rocker, soothing the worried Jake.

Once he had Frannie back in her pajamas, he walked the floor with her until the Tylenol seemed to kick in. She went to sleep against his shoulder.

He kissed the top of her sweaty little head and glanced over to find Keely watching him.

She mouthed, *Sleeping?* At his nod, she nodded back, pointing at Jake, who was curled up against her, sound asleep, too.

It was only a few steps to Frannie's crib. He carried her over there and slowly, gently, laid her down. She didn't stir as he tucked the blanket in around her.

Across the room in the other crib, Keely was tucking Jake in, too. She turned off the lamp, and they tiptoed from the now-quiet room together.

"Psst. Maisey," he whispered. The dog lurched to her feet and waddled out after them. Daniel closed the door. "Whew."

Keely leaned back against the wall next to her bedroom and said hopefully, "Maybe they'll sleep the rest of the night and Frannie will be all better in the morning."

"Dreamer. And what rest of the night? It's already morning, in case you didn't notice."

"Don't go overboard looking on the bright side there, Daniel." She glanced through the open door to her room and blew out her cheeks with a weary breath. "Sadly enough, though, you're right. The clock by my bed says it's almost five. Tonight is officially over."

"Let's hope we get lucky and they both sleep till, say, eight."

"As if." She laughed, a sort of whisper-laugh to go with their low, careful whisper of a conversation. The low light from the wall sconces struck red glints in her brown hair, and she looked sweet as a farm girl, barefoot in those flannel pajamas that were printed with ladybugs.

He thought of Grace suddenly, knew a stab of annoyance that kind of soured the companionable moment between him and Keely—and there it was again, that word: *companionable*. He'd felt companionable with his dead wife's cousin twice in one night, and he didn't know whether to feel good about that or not.

"What?" Keely asked. "Just say it."

He went ahead and admitted what was bugging him. "Grace. She's got one of the baby monitors in her room, so she had to hear what was happening. But she didn't even come check to see if we needed her."

"Yeah, she did. She came in the kids' room before you. I knew she'd been out late and could use a little sleep, so I said I could handle it and sent her back to bed."

He hung his head. "Go ahead. Say it. I'm a crap brother."

Maisey chose that moment to get comfortable. She

yawned hugely, stretched out on the floor and lowered her head to her paws with a soft doggy sigh.

Keely said, "You love Grace. She loves you. Ten years from now, you'll wonder what you used to fight about."

"Uh-uh. I'll remember."

"Maybe. But you'll be totally over it." Would he? He hoped so. She said, "When I was little, living with the band on my mother's purple bus, I used to dream of a real house like this one, dream of having sisters and brothers. Family is hard, Daniel. But it's worth it. And I think you know that it is."

"Yeah," he admitted. "You're right."

Family was everything. But that didn't stop him from fantasizing about totally non-family-related things. Partying till dawn, maybe. A game of poker that went on till all hours, with a keg on tap and all the guys smoking stinky cigars, telling politically incorrect jokes. A one-night stand with a gorgeous woman he'd never met before and would never see again, a woman who only wanted to use him for hot sex.

Now there was a big *as if.* He'd been with one woman in his life and was perfectly happy about that—until the past few years anyway. He just wasn't the kind of guy who went to bed with women he hardly knew. The one time he'd tried that, six months ago, he'd realized at the last possible moment that sex with a stranger just wasn't for him. His sudden change of heart had not endeared him to the lady in question.

And Keely was watching him again, a hint of a smile on her full mouth.

"I'm going to work on thinking positive," he promised her, because she did have a point about his negative attitude.

She gave a whisper-chuckle. "Anything is possible."

He clicked his tongue at Maisey and she dragged herself up on her stubby legs again. "Night, Keely." He turned for his room at the end of the hall.

"Night, Daniel," she whispered after him.

When Keely woke up it was ten after eight Sunday morning and no one was crying. She put on her vintage chenille robe over her pajamas and looked across the hall.

Both cribs were empty.

Downstairs in the kitchen, she found two smiling cherubs eating cut-up pancakes off their high chair trays and both Daniel and Grace at the breakfast table, neither one scowling.

Yes. Life was good on this beautiful, foggy-as-usual Sunday morning in Valentine Bay. She poured herself coffee.

Grace said, "I'm here till two, Keely, so if you need to run errands, go for it."

"Keewee!" crowed Jake, pounding on his tray.

Keely stepped over and kissed his gooey cheek.

"Kiss, kiss, Keewee!" Frannie pounded her tray, too, and smacked her rosebud lips.

Keely kissed her as well, and then returned to the stove where a stack of pancakes waited. She put a couple of them on a plate. "Thanks, Grace. I'll run by Sand & Sea and stop in to check on Aunt Gretchen."

The gallery opened daily at eleven. Keely arrived at nine thirty. Her top clerk, Amanda, promoted temporarily to manager, joined her five minutes later. They went through the books and discussed the schedule. Sand & Sea was 3500 square feet of exhibit space on Manzanita

Avenue, in the heart of Valentine Bay's downtown historic district. With a focus on Oregon artists, Keely offered contemporary work in just about every form imaginable, from painting to printmaking, sculpture to woodworking. She displayed and sold artisan jewelry, furniture, textiles and photography.

Sand & Sea also hosted receptions and special events. Every month or so, she featured an individual artist or a group of artists in a themed joint show. The first Friday in April, she would hold an opening for a new group show with several top Pacific Northwest artists working in various mediums on the theme of the ever-changing sea. Everything was on schedule for that one so far. Amanda was knowledgeable, organized and more than competent, and they had almost three weeks until the opening. Keely needed to find help with Frannie and Jake for the opening-night reception party and the few days before it. But that should be doable, one way or another.

Feeling confident that Sand & Sea wouldn't suffer while she focused on Daniel's twins, she left the gallery at eleven thirty to check in on her aunt.

Gretchen still lived in the house she'd shared with her husband, the house where she'd raised her precious only child, Lillie. Keely considered the four-bedroom craftsman-style bungalow her childhood home, too.

Yes, she'd spent most of her growing-up years living on the tour bus. But now and then, Ingrid's career would get a boost and the tour schedule would get crazy. Those were the times that Ingrid took Keely to Valentine Bay to live temporarily with Aunt Gretchen and Uncle Cletus. Keely loved when that happened. She was constantly begging her mother to let her live with the Snows full-time.

When Keely was fifteen, Ingrid finally gave in. Keely moved in with her cousin. At last, she got the settled-down life she'd always dreamed of in the seaside town she considered her true home.

Keely knocked on the green front door, but only to be considerate. She had a key and she used it, sticking her head in the door, calling, "It's just me! Don't get up!"

"I'm in the kitchen!" Gretchen called back.

Something smelled wonderful. Keely followed her nose to the back of the house. She found her aunt balanced on her good foot, one hand braced on the counter, as she pulled a tray of cookies from the oven.

Keely waited until Gretchen had set the tray on top of the stove and shut the oven door to scold, "You're not supposed to be on that foot."

"Sweetheart!" Gretchen turned and hopped toward her.

"You are impossible." Keely caught her and hugged her, breathing in the familiar, beloved scents of vanilla and melted butter. Her aunt not only always smelled delicious, she was still pretty in a comfortable, homey sort of way, with smooth, pale skin and carefully styled hair she still had professionally colored to the exact Nordic blond it used to be when she was young.

Gretchen laughed. "You know you need cookies."

Keely grabbed a chair from the table and spun it around. "Here. Sit."

"Oh, don't fuss." Gretchen held on to Keely for balance as she lowered herself into the chair.

Keely tried to look stern. "You will stay in that chair. I mean it."

Gretchen swept out a plump arm in the direction of the big mixing bowl on the counter. "I have two more cookie sheets to fill."

"Stay where you are. I'll do it." She grabbed another chair and positioned it so that Gretchen could put her foot up. "There. Want coffee?"

"Please—and where are my babies?"

"At Daniel's." Keely filled a cup and set it on the table next to Gretchen. "Grace isn't going back to Portland until this afternoon, so she's watching them."

"I miss them already."

"I'll bring them by during the week."

"You're a good girl. The best."

Keely got to work dropping spoonfuls of dough onto a cookie sheet. "Looking after Frannie and Jake is no hardship. You know how I always wanted babies." She'd been married once. A hot and charming driftwood artist, Roy Varner had come to town six years ago, before Keely opened Sand & Sea. Another local gallery had given him a show. Keely went to his opening. The attraction was instant and mutual. Roy swept her clean off her feet. They'd married within weeks of that first meeting. Roy traveled a lot to various art shows all over the west. Slowly Keely figured out that all the traveling wasn't only about selling art. When he traveled, Roy behaved like a free man in every way. Including sleeping with other women. Keely had divorced him four years ago.

"Don't you worry," said Gretchen. "You've still got plenty of time. A good man and babies will be yours."

Keely sent her aunt a fond glance over her shoulder. "Love you, Auntie G."

"Love you more."

"Heard from Mom?"

"Not since the other day."

"So we still don't know exactly when she's coming?"

"Keely, I am managing just fine—and what about you? All settled in at Daniel's?"

She considered mentioning Frannie's earache. But the little girl had seemed fully recovered this morning, so why worry Gretchen? "It's going great. And I'm all set up. I've got a bedroom across from the twins, and I'm using the room beside it as a work area—and you know, I've been thinking that we could get you some live-in help. Or you could move to Daniel's temporarily."

"I like my own house."

"But—"

"Don't start. I mean it. I've hired the boy next door to handle the yard. His sister will come in and clean when I need her. I'm having my groceries delivered. I'm used to doing things for myself, and I like my independence. Plus, in the Bravo house, all the bedrooms except Grace's are upstairs. That's not going to work with this foot."

Keely scooped up another spoonful of dough. "I'll call Mom, pin her down on when she'll be here."

"Don't you dare. I will handle this. You've got enough to do, and you know it."

"Auntie G, it's just a phone call," she said into the bowl of dough.

"Put down that spoon and look at me."

Keely dropped the spoon back in the bowl and turned to face her aunt. "Yeah?"

"Your mother *is* coming, but she'll be doing that in her own good time. That's how she rolls and don't we all know it."

Keely stifled a laugh. "How she *rolls*?"

Gretchen's blue eyes twinkled. "You know it's true.

Ingrid makes her own rules and sets her own schedule. Trying to change her at this late date? Never going to happen."

Keely picked up a cooling cookie, took a bite and groaned in appreciation. "You shouldn't be up making cookies. But these are *so* good."

"I made lunch, too. It's in the fridge. Don't ruin your appetite."

"No chance of that. Not when it's your cooking—and were you on your feet to make the lunch?"

"Don't nag, sweetheart. Nagging is not attractive."

"What am I going to do with you?"

"Finish your cookie, get the rest of them in the oven— and then serve us both the amazing crab salad and crusty rolls I threw together."

Keely got back to the Bravo house at a quarter of two, and Grace left for Portland a few minutes later. As usual, Daniel had stuff to do at the office. He promised to be back by dinnertime.

She stood on the porch, one twin on either side of her, waving as Daniel headed off down the driveway. The sun had made an afternoon appearance, so for a while she took the kids out back, where there was a big wooden playset that had been there for as long as she could remember. They played in the sandbox, slid down the slide and she swung them on the toddler-friendly swings.

Back inside, she gave them a snack and took them upstairs for diaper changes and nap time. They went down like little angels, reaching for kisses, settling right in and closing their eyes.

She got a full hour in her new studio, bent over her

precious Bernina before Frannie started crying. When Keely went to check on her, she had a fever again.

That night, poor little Frannie didn't sleep much. Neither did Keely or Daniel. Or Jake, for that matter. Frannie's ear hurt, and nothing seemed to make it feel better.

The next day, one of the ladies from Gretchen's church came by to watch Jake so that Keely could take Frannie to the pediatrician. Diagnosis: ear infection. Keely picked up the antibiotic and eardrop prescriptions on the way home.

Frannie had another bad night. All day Tuesday, she fussed and cried. Tuesday night, though, she only woke up crying twice.

"I think she's better," Keely whispered to Daniel when they tiptoed from the kids' room for the second time that night.

"I hope so." He had dark circles under his eyes. "We could all use a good night's sleep."

Wednesday morning, Frannie woke up smiling.

When Keely said, "I think you feel better, honey," the little angel replied, "I fine, Keewee. I goo."

And she really did seem fully recovered. After breakfast, Keely took both kids to see Gretchen, who still had no idea when Keely's mom would be showing up. But Auntie G was all smiles to get to spend an afternoon with her beloved babies. She held them on her lap and sang the nursery songs she used to sing to Keely when she was little and staying with the Snows.

On Thursday, Jake got sick.

It was some weird flu bug. There was vomiting and a lot of mucus. Keely called the pediatrician, who suggested a humidifier, cool baths, cough medicine and

Tylenol for fever. No need to bring Jake in, the doctor had said, unless his fever hit 104 or he wasn't better within a week.

The next three nights were hell. Jake woke up crying and that woke Frannie. Keely and Daniel took turns looking in on them. The weekend went by somehow, not that Keely even cared what day it was. Making art with her sewing machine? Not even happening. And as for the original plan that she might go back and forth between the Bravo house and her cottage?

She never once made it home. In fact, she had to call a neighbor to water her plants.

She was exhausted, run ragged—and she found herself beginning to seriously admire Daniel. He worked all day and then stayed up with her all night to help with the kids. So what if he wasn't the happiest dad on the planet? The man was dedicated to the well-being of his children. He mopped up vomit and changed diapers with the best of them.

By late Sunday, Jake had weathered the worst of it. He coughed less frequently and the mucus factory seemed to be shutting down. The sweet little guy was definitely on the mend. Sunday night, Keely actually slept straight through. The kids didn't wake once, from bedtime until six the next morning.

Monday, Daniel woke her with a tap on her door.

"Ugh?" She blinked and yawned. "It's open."

He peeked in the door, looking almost rested for once. "Sorry to wake you."

She yawned again. "It was bound to happen sometime. What's up?"

"I'll get them up and downstairs if you'll start the breakfast."

"Deal."

She was at the stove when he came down with the little ones. She glanced over her shoulder to see him wiping Frannie's streaming nose. They stared at each other across the gorgeous expanse of the soapstone island. "Oh, no," she whispered, as though if she didn't say it too loudly, Frannie wouldn't be getting the bug Jake had just recovered from.

"No fever," Daniel said. He didn't add *yet*, but it seemed to her the unspoken word hung in the air between them.

By that afternoon, Frannie's nose ran nonstop. By dinnertime, she'd thrown up twice and a persistent cough seemed to rattle her little bones. By then, she also had a fever. It hovered at around 101.

Keely and Daniel spent another night taking turns waking up to soothe a sick baby. Really, they were getting the nighttime nursing care down to a science, as though they had radar for whose turn it was. Keely barely stirred when it was his turn, and the master bedroom door remained shut when it was hers.

Once that night, she woke when it was his turn.

"This one's mine," he mumbled when she stuck her head out into the hall.

"Unh," she replied and went back to bed.

On Wednesday, a week and a half into the endless string of illnesses the twins had been suffering, Daniel had a timber owner he had to go meet with. It was a small grove of Douglas firs ready to harvest, and Daniel would walk the grove with the landowner, explaining how Valentine Logging would maximize each tree to its full potential. The landowner wanted to meet at eight in the morning and Daniel wanted the contract, so at a quarter after seven he staggered out of the house, bleary-eyed, armed with a giant travel mug of coffee.

Keely spent the morning alone trying to keep her eye on Jake while doing what she could to ease poor Frannie's misery. She dosed the little girl with over-the-counter meds, kept the humidifier running and gave Frannie cold-water sponge baths at regular intervals.

The day never seemed to end.

Finally, at around two in the afternoon, she got both kids down for a nap. To the soft hissing of the humidifier, she tiptoed from their room with Maisey at her heels. Across the hall, both of her doors were open. She cast a despairing glance toward her studio room. *As if.*

Right now, her beloved Bernina was the last thing she wanted to cuddle up with. The bed in the other room, though...

Nothing had ever looked so beautiful.

She dragged her tired body in there and fell gratefully across the mattress as Maisey flopped down on the rug right beside her. Blessed sleep settled over her.

She dreamed of walking the foggy beach not far from her back door—with Daniel of all people. They didn't talk, just strolled along the wet sand, side by side but not touching, the waves sliding in, foaming around their bare feet.

"Keewee! Da-Da!"

"Wha—huh?" Keely shuddered, instantly wide-awake.

"Da-Da!" Frannie cried from the other room, followed by a long wail of sheer misery.

Keely shoved herself backward off the bed, raked her hair out of her eyes and hustled for the other room. Frannie was standing up in her crib, sobbing and coughing, snot running down her flushed little face.

"Oh, honey…"

"Keewee! Ow!"

Keely ran over and lifted the poor sweetheart into her arms. "Frannie. Oh, now. It's okay…" She settled her on her shoulder.

At which point, Frannie threw up. It went down Keely's back. That caused Frannie to wail all the louder.

"It's okay. It's all right," Keely promised, though clearly it was anything but. Gently, she peeled the little girl off her shoulder. "Shh. Shh. Let me…"

It was as far as she got. Frannie hurled again, this time down Keely's front. "Oh, bad!" Frannie wailed.

"No, no," Keely promised her. "It's not bad, honey. It's okay."

That was when Frannie threw up again, all over herself. She wailed even louder, "Keewee, I sowwy. I sowwy, sowwy, sowwy."

From his crib, Jake cried, "Fa-Fa? Fa-Fa, oh, no!"

"She's okay," Keely promised and wished it were true. "Jakey, she's going to be fine."

Maisey appeared in the doorway to the hall. She moaned in sympathetic doggy distress.

Keely carried Frannie to the changing table and quickly got her out of her soiled clothes. "Jakey, we'll be right back," she promised the increasingly agitated little boy as she grabbed the little girl and a clean diaper. Holding both out and away from her vomit-soaked body, she stepped over Maisey and carried baby and diaper across the hall to her room, moving straight through to her bathroom, which had a traditional tub-and-shower combination.

Shoving the shower curtain aside, Keely lowered the little girl into the tub. "Here. We'll get you all cleaned up."

"'Kay." Frannie sniffed.

Keely turned on the water. Once she had it lukewarm, she grabbed a washcloth and rinsed Frannie off.

Frannie was quiet, sniffling a little, watching her through wide eyes, as Keely dried her off and carried her—held out and dangling—to her own bed, where she put on the diaper.

"You feel better now, honey?"

Frannie solemnly nodded, eyes wide and wet. Keely scooped her up again and put her in the playpen she kept set up in the corner for any time she needed to corral the kids in her room.

"Fa-Fa? Keewee?" Jake cried from the other room.

"Coming, Jakey. Just a minute!" Keely called back.

A plush pink squeaky kitten lay waiting in the playpen. Keely squeezed it and it meowed. Frannie took it and hugged it close.

"I'm just going to go into the bathroom to clean up. I'll be right back. Okay, honey?"

For that, she got another somber nod from Frannie. Though still flushed, her eyes red and her nose running, Frannie did seem much calmer at least.

Thank God, the vomiting bout seemed to be through.

Jake called again, "Keewee?"

"Just another minute, Jakey. I'll be there. I promise!" Peeling off her smelly shirt as she went, Keely darted for the bathroom. Standing on the bathroom rug by the tub, she wiggled free of her bra, kicked out of her shoes and shoved down both her jeans and panties at once.

"Keewee!" Jake shouted.

"Jakey, I'm right here! Just a minute!" she called, as she hopped around in a ridiculous circle, whipping off one sock and then the other. Flipping on the taps, switching the flow to the showerhead, she got in under the still-cold spray and yanked the curtain closed.

Three minutes, tops, she was in there. Jake called her name repeatedly. Once or twice, Frannie did, too. Keely got the mess off, rinsed in record time, flipped off the tap and shoved the shower curtain wide.

She'd stepped, dripping wet to the bath mat, and reached for her towel before she happened to glance through the open bathroom door to the bedroom.

Jake in his arms and Maisey at his feet, Daniel stood by the playpen staring at her with his mouth hanging open.

Chapter Three

Keely grabbed her towel, whipped it around her, stepped to the bathroom door and shoved it shut.

Only then did she sink to the toilet seat and hit her forehead with the heel of her hand. Never in her life had she been so embarrassed. Not even the day she wore white jeans on the tour bus and got her first period. Except for her and her mom, everyone on that bus was a guy. Keely just knew all those rockers had seen her shame—and okay, on second thought, that might have been worse.

But this was plenty bad.

The look on his face. Like someone had just dropped a safe on his head.

God. Daniel had seen her naked. That was so wrong. In all the ways that really counted, she was Lillie's sister and a man ought never to see his wife's sister naked.

Seriously. Would it have killed her to shut the damn bathroom door?

But she'd thought they were alone—just her, the kids and Maisey. She'd wanted to be able to hear them while she cleaned up, just in case...

Just in case, *what*? Come to think of it, she had no idea.

It's not the end of the world, Keely. No one will die from this. Get over yourself.

Daniel tapped on the door. "Keely? You okay?"

"Fine! Really!" Her voice had the tinkling brightness of breaking glass. "We, uh, had a little accident."

"But...you're okay?"

Oh, hell, no. "Yes. I'll be out in a few minutes."

He made a nervous throat-clearing sound. "I'll just take the kids into the other room."

"Great! Be there in a few."

"Uh. Take your time."

She started to call out something frantic and cheerful. "Righto!" or "Absolutely!" But she shut her mouth hard and folded her lips between her teeth so that not one more ludicrous word could escape.

Fifteen minutes later, she found Daniel and the kids in the bedroom across the hall. He sat in the rocker, holding Frannie, who looked like a slightly flushed angel, all curled up in his arms, sucking peacefully on a baby bottle half-full of water. He'd dressed her in a cozy pair of pink pajamas.

Jake lay on the floor nearby, gumming a plastic teething pretzel, one plump arm thrown out across Maisey, who lay at his side. He took the pretzel from his mouth and gave her his most dazzling smile. "Keewee. Hi there."

"Hey, honey."

"Da-Da home."

"Oh, yes, he is."

Jake stuck the pretzel back in his mouth and chewed some more. Maisey nuzzled him, and he gave a lazy little giggle around the toy in his mouth.

The puddle of vomit on the rug was only a damp spot now, and the room smelled of the all-natural cleaner they used around the kids, a citrusy scent.

She made herself raise her gaze and look at Daniel. Those sea-glass eyes were waiting. She made herself speak. "You're home early."

"I was worried about Frannie and thought maybe you could use a break or at least another pair of hands."

She forced a smile. "Thank you. I see you cleaned up the mess already."

"Seemed like the least I could do." Gently, he stroked Frannie's fine gold hair, his rough hand big enough to cradle the whole of her little head. He pressed a kiss to her temple. "She's cooler. I think the fever might have broken."

"Wonderful."

He rocked slowly, back and forth. In his arms, Frannie looked so peaceful. Safe. Content. "I am sorry." His fine mouth twisted, and a hot flush swept up his thick neck. "For barging in on you. I should have knocked. But Jake was calling for you and for Frannie. I picked him up and he pointed at your room…"

Did they really need to talk it over?

Maybe. After all, it could be good, right? To be frank and open about it? They could clear the air, so to speak.

"I left both doors open. It's not your fault. Of course you came right in." How red was her face? As red as his? *Oh, God.* "It's not a big deal, Daniel."

"You're right," he said and swallowed hard. "Not a big deal at all."

And it wasn't.

Oh, but it *was*.

For Daniel anyway.

Nothing had changed. But for every minute of the rest of that day, Lillie's cousin was suddenly very much on his mind.

Not to mention wreaking havoc lower down.

His longtime sexual abstinence had never felt so painful. Could he *be* more inappropriate? All of a sudden, he was a man obsessed. Who did that? Who *thought* like that?

He needed to stop. Stop thinking of her, fantasizing about her, imagining what it might be like if they...

No. Uh-uh. That wasn't going to happen. Ever. And it *shouldn't* happen.

She was family. She was great with the kids. He no longer felt that she judged him for the troubles between him and Lillie during the last years of her life.

They were, well, *friends* now. Weren't they? He counted on Keely, enjoyed talking to her. Liked having her around.

No way would he mess with that.

He wasn't even considering messing with that.

Uh-uh.

He needed to focus on the positive and forget the smooth white curves of her shoulders shining wet from her shower, not think about those full, tempting breasts, her dusky pink nipples puckered and tight. He needed to block out the memory of that tiny, shining rivulet of water sliding down the center of her, filling her navel, spilling over and dribbling lower, into the water-beaded landing strip of red-brown hair that did nothing to cover the ripe swell of her mound.

Yeah.

Right.

All that. He needed to damn well forget about all that. To focus on what mattered.

Family. The kids. Not rocking the fragile boat of their lives, a boat that had finally steadied after almost capsizing with the loss of Lillie.

By that evening, Frannie seemed fully recovered. She ate a big dinner and kept it down. Both children slept straight through that night and the next night and the night after that, too.

Daniel could go to the office or out on a job in the morning and concentrate on both his bottom line and the potentially dangerous work that needed doing. His kids were safe and well with Keely. He needed her, and he was grateful to her.

And he was not going to jeopardize all the good she brought to his family by doing something stupid like putting a move on her.

That Sunday, he picked up Gretchen and brought her over for dinner. She'd baked a chocolate cake for their dessert, and though she was still using a walker to get around, she claimed she felt better every day.

She praised Keely's pot roast and fussed over the kids. "I do miss taking care of them."

"Now that they're both recovered after the mystery

bug from hell, I'll bring them to your house this week," Keely promised.

"What day?" Gretchen demanded.

"Tuesday, for lunch—my treat. That means I'm bringing the food along with the children," Keely lectured. "Don't you dare fix a thing." Daniel watched her plump lips moving, admired the shine to those wide green eyes, wondered what it would feel like to press his mouth to the smooth white skin of her throat, to stick out his tongue and learn the taste of her skin.

"Right, Daniel?"

He blinked and stared at his mother-in-law. "Er, what was that?"

Gretchen chuckled. "I swear, you are a thousand miles away. I hope you're not letting work run you ragged."

"Uh, no. I was just, you know, thinking…" *About Keely. Naked.* "But anyway, what was the question?"

"Well, I only said that it wouldn't be right, not to at least have some cookies ready Tuesday when Keely brings the twins over. The babies love my cookies." She aimed a chiding glance at Keely. "*Keely* loves my cookies. I'll send some home for all of you to share."

"Cookies!" Jake pounded his high chair tray and then shoved a hunk of potato into his mouth.

"She needs to stay off that foot," Keely grumbled. "Auntie G, that cake you brought looks fabulous, but cake and cookies are not necessities. For you to take care of yourself, that's what matters."

Gretchen pursed her lips. "I've worked out a way I can sit down to do most of the work."

"Oh, please. Like I believe that one."

"It's true. I'm very careful of my injured foot, and it's healing quite nicely, thank you very much. And part of taking care of myself is doing what makes me happy. Baking makes me happy, and one way or another, I am bound to bake."

"Bound to bake." Keely pressed her lips together. In the two weeks she'd been living in his house, Daniel had already learned to read her expressions. Right now, she was trying to stay stern, trying *not* to burst out laughing. She glanced toward the ceiling as though calling on a higher power. "What am I going to do with you?"

"Not a thing." Gretchen drew her plump shoulders back. "Just be my sweet girl and stop trying to tell me how to live my life."

Keely glared, but then she gave it up. "All right. Fine. Bake your heart out."

"I intend to."

Keely focused on her dinner. Daniel recognized the move for the ploy that it was. She pretended to let the argument go, but she was only regrouping before trying again. After carefully chewing and swallowing a bite of pot roast, she set down her knife and fork. "I have to ask. What about Mom?"

"What about her?" Gretchen replied way too sweetly.

"She's supposed to be with you, helping you as you recover. Have you heard from her? Have you called her? Do you know when she's coming?"

Daniel considered interrupting, suggesting that Keely leave it alone. Really, Gretchen seemed to be managing pretty well on her own. But then again, siding with his mother-in-law against the woman he needed to take care of his kids... Well, that wouldn't be very smart, now, would it?

If he was going to mess things up with Keely, he

might as well just make a pass and take a chance she might say yes—not that he would do that.

Never.

Uh-uh.

Not going to happen.

"Ingrid will come when she comes," declared Gretchen.

"That does it." Keely's eyes had gone flinty. "I'm calling her tonight."

While Daniel drove Gretchen home, Keely straightened up the kitchen and then took the kids upstairs. She watched them in the playroom for a while and then hustled them to the hall bathroom and knelt by the tub to supervise as they splashed and giggled and even allowed her to swipe at them with a washcloth now and then.

"Clean children. My favorite kind," said Daniel from behind her in the doorway. Keely glanced at him over her shoulder. Their eyes met and a hot little shiver slid through her.

Hot little shivers? She'd been having those a lot lately, ever since the day she left the doors open and he saw way more than he should have seen.

It was so crazy, this growing awareness she had of him now, as a man. Like a secret between them, that was how it felt. A secret that created a forbidden intimacy, an intimacy that, really, was only in her mind. She *imagined* he felt it, too.

But she had no real proof of that.

None. Zero. Zip.

As a matter of hard fact, she kept telling herself, this supposed secret intimacy between them didn't even exist. It wasn't real.

So why did it only seem to get stronger, day by day?

"Da-Da!" Jake crowed and waved his favorite rubber duck.

Daniel came and stood over her where she knelt by the tub.

She looked up, over his long, strong legs in dark blue denim, past the part of him she really needed *not* to focus on, to his broad, deep chest, his thick tanned neck, his sculpted jaw. All the way to those eyes staring down into hers.

A weakness swept through her, delicious and hot. She wanted to reach up her arms to him, have him pull her to her feet and tight against his chest. She wanted his mouth on her mouth, hard and deep.

Seriously, what was the matter with her?

Why couldn't she stop imagining what it might be like—if he touched her in a man-woman way. If he kissed her. If he took off all her clothes and took his off, too.

It had to stop.

Nothing was going to happen between them.

She really needed to let this crazy new yen she had for him go.

"Go ahead and call your mother." He dropped to the bath mat beside her. "I'll finish up here."

"Great. Thanks." Did she sound breathless? If she did, she didn't think he noticed. She pushed herself to her feet and turned for the door.

As she went out, Frannie demanded, "Kiss, Da-Da. Kiss," followed by Frannie's usual lip-smacking sound.

Keely stifled a jealous groan. Oh, to be Frannie, to demand kisses of Daniel and have them instantly bestowed.

Not that she would be satisfied with the innocent kisses he gave his daughter. She would want deep kisses, wet and slow and long.

The kind of kisses she was never going to share with him, the kind of kisses she was not going to think about anymore.

Starting now.

She marched to her bedroom and grabbed her phone, punching up the contact for her mother and hitting the call icon.

It went straight to voice mail. She was leaving a quick, angry message asking Ingrid to call her back the minute she got this when the phone rang in her hand.

After Daniel put the kids to bed, he went looking for Keely.

He didn't have to go far. He found her sitting at her sewing machine in her workroom and tapped on the door frame to get her attention. She turned and gave him a strange little smile.

"You busy?" he asked.

She looked at the length of fabric in her hand as though wondering how it got there. And then she smiled at him—God, that smile of hers. It lit up her face. "Let's get a drink and sit out on the back steps," she said.

Warmth filled him. Even if he wasn't ever having sex with her, it was damn good to have her here in his house with him, someone smart and interesting and pretty to talk to after the kids went to bed. "Deal."

At the wet bar in the family room, he poured himself a scotch and she asked for cranberry juice with ice and a splash of vodka.

Outside, the air was damp and cool, mist creeping in

around the thick branches of the evergreens, shimmery and soft-looking in the golden glow of the in-ground lights dotted here and there around the yard. They sat on the deck, with their feet on the steps. Maisey, who'd come out with them, flopped down a few feet away.

Keely shivered, and he almost forgot himself and wrapped an arm around her.

Almost.

But not quite.

Instead, he grabbed a faded afghan off one of the deck chairs and draped it across her shoulders.

"Thanks," she said as he dropped down beside her again. She gathered the afghan close and sipped her drink. "Much better."

He stared off past the playset, along the bluestone path that wound through the clumps of landscaping out to the woodshed and the tree fort his father had built for him and his second and third brothers, Matthias and Connor, back before any of his sisters were born, when he wasn't much older than Frannie and Jake. "Did you talk to your mother?"

"Yeah." She said it on a sigh.

"Is she really coming?"

Keely nodded. "A week from Wednesday, she said. She got hold of a real estate agent, some friend of hers from way back, and bought the Sea Breeze." The landmark pub on Beach Street had been closed for several months now.

"She bought it sight unseen?"

"Yeah. She says the price was right and that it's been her dream for the last decade or so to come home someday and open her own place, that when she pictured that place it was always the Sea Breeze. She's going to settle in with Auntie G and fix up the bar, get it ready for business. She's aiming for a grand opening over the Fourth of July."

"Your mother is something else."

She nudged him with her shoulder. "And you mean that in the best possible sort of way, am I right?"

He was still kind of marveling. "Just like that, she buys a bar."

"She always knew what she wanted and how to get it—not to mention how to manage her money. No, she never got rich, but she's a good businesswoman. She paid for more than half of my college education. And I wouldn't have Sand & Sea or my cottage if she hadn't written me big fat checks when I needed them the most."

"All because of that band of hers?"

"Because of *her*, Daniel." Ingrid not only sang and played lead guitar. She was the owner and manager of Pomegranate Dream.

"I know. But still…"

"When members of the band dropped out, she replaced them and went on. When Pomegranate Dream stopped drawing big crowds, she booked them into county fairs, casinos and smaller clubs. She got her commercial driver's license and started driving the bus herself. She runs everything out of the bus. That keeps the overhead low."

"I thought you hated being raised on that bus."

"It wasn't all bad. Yeah, I always dreamed of a more settled kind of life than my mother ever gave me and sometimes she gets on my last nerve, but she's a dynamo and I admire her." Keely held up her glass and he tapped his against it.

He offered the toast. "Here's to Gretchen and Ingrid making it work."

She laughed. The sweet sound played along his nerve endings, stirring up all that yearning and hunger he kept trying to quell. When she put her glass to her lips, he drank, too.

And then he stood. Maisey got up, as well.

Keely tipped her head back and looked at him. "Going in?" He stared into those moss green eyes that he'd been seeing in his dreams lately.

"A few things I need to catch up on." Actually, those things could wait. But the temptation to touch her would only get stronger the longer he sat there. "I'll be in my study if you need me."

How about if I need you right now? Keely thought but didn't say. "Fair enough." She gave him a nod, then turned back to the fog-shrouded yard again. A moment later, she heard the back door open and the tapping of Maisey's claws on the floor. The door clicked shut.

The week went flying by. Keely had that opening at the gallery on Friday night. Daniel called the nanny service and got a woman to watch the kids all day Thursday and Friday, so that Keely could be at the gallery, making sure the group show was ready to go. And he came home from work early Friday to take over kid care from the temporary nanny. Keely was able to work straight through, grabbing a break at six in the evening to run home to her own little house by the beach and change into her favorite vintage teal blue cocktail dress and kitten heels.

By eight that evening, the gallery was packed with artists and their friends, supporters and family. Plenty of paying customers came by, too. The show did brisk business. Keely sipped a nice Oregon Pinot Noir, nibbled great finger foods provided by her favorite local caterer and enjoyed the party.

Aislinn Bravo, one of Daniel's sisters and Keely's longtime BFF, dropped by. Keely was older than Aislinn by four years, but she'd got to know all the Bravos back when Lillie married Daniel. From the first time they met, Keely and Aislinn had hit it off. The age difference hadn't mattered, even way back then. They'd always liked to hang out together. Then when Keely opened Sand & Sea, Aislinn had worked in the gallery for a while and the two of them had grown even closer.

Aislinn had a house not far from the beach. She raised Angora rabbits and made jewelry in her spare time, beautiful pieces that Keely was proud to showcase at Sand & Sea. But jewelry making was only a hobby for Aislinn. She liked variety in her work. She'd done everything, worked on local ranches and at the used-car lot on the south end of town. She'd even worked for Daniel at Valentine Logging, running the office for a while. Now she was essentially a legal secretary.

"So how's the law business?" Keely asked her.

Aislinn wrinkled her nose. "Boring. I think I need a job outside next. Maybe fishing, something on a salmon troller."

"Oh, I can just picture that."

"Hey. I'm a fast learner, and I'm not afraid to get my hands dirty—and how's it going playing nanny for my niece and nephew?"

"I adore them. They have me wrapped around their tiny pinkie fingers."

"Consider this my offer to babysit any weekend day or night that you need me."

"Thanks. I might take you up on that one of these days. So far, though, we're making it work."

"Daniel treating you right?"

"He's been great." *And lately he's driving me wild with unsatisfied lust.*

Aislinn laughed. And then she leaned closer. "You have a funny look on your face. What's going on?"

"Funny how?"

"Evasive much?"

Should she tell Aislinn? Ordinarily, Keely never held back with her best friend. But Daniel *was* Aislinn's brother and, well, it felt somehow awkward. Maybe even wrong.

Because really, wasn't it just a little bit strange for her to suddenly get a wild, burning yen for Daniel Bravo? Not only had he belonged to her beloved Lillie, he was not her type, all stalwart and solid. She went for the artsy guys, the charmers, the fast-talkers, guys like her ex-husband, Roy.

Aislinn watched her, narrow eyed. "That does it. You're hiding something. We need to talk. Lunch, I think. A *long* lunch. Next week's no good. They're running me ragged at the office with a couple of big cases. But the week after that…?"

Why not? By then, she might be totally over this bizarre fixation on Daniel. At the very least, she'd have plenty of time to decide how much to say. "Sure. I can get a sitter from the nanny service. Let's say tentatively Wednesday after next?"

"You're on."

Keely got back to Daniel's at a little after midnight that night. Slipping off her shoes as soon as she got inside, she locked up and turned to find him standing in the open doorway to his study, wearing his usual jeans and a flannel shirt with the sleeves rolled to the elbows, his shoulders a mile wide, muscled arms crossed over his chest, his eyes cast into shadow by the chandelier high above.

Like if Paul Bunyan was a sex god.

Nope. Not her type, no way.

Not her type, but…

More.

So. Much. More.

"How'd it go?" he asked.

"Really well. Good sales. A great crowd. Everyone talking and laughing at once. The kids?"

"We played a lot of peekaboo. I'm worn-out."

She laughed. She'd come to love his dry sense of humor, which she'd never even noticed he had until she'd come to live with him and the twins. "And then, after the peekaboo, the bath that never ends."

"All that splashing." He pretended to grumble.

"Exactly. And then you have to read to them."

"And they just *have* to turn the pages for you."

Maisey's claws tapped the floor behind him. She appeared at his side, plunking down on her haunches right there in the doorway.

Keely wanted to ask him to maybe go out back with her, sit on the deck. It was a clear night. They could count the stars, pick out a few constellations.

She might make a move on him.

Oh, God. She just might.

And where would that take them?

Somewhere wonderful—or straight to disaster?

"Good night, Keely," he said. Did she hear regret in his voice?

Or was that only in her coward's heart?

"Night, Daniel." She flipped her shoes back over her shoulder and headed for the stairs.

Ingrid arrived that Wednesday.

Keely took the kids over to Gretchen's to help out while Ingrid got moved in. Her mom had streaked her graying auburn hair with pink and blue. She looked good, Keely thought, slim and straight and strong as ever, in a giant purple Pomegranate Dream T-shirt with the arms ripped off over a sports bra and tropical print leggings, all that pink-and-blue-striped auburn hair piled in a sloppy updo, red Converses on her feet.

Gretchen started right in, ragging on her about her hair and her clothes. "Honestly, Ingrid. You're fifty years old. Your rock and roller days are over and that outfit is simply not age appropriate."

Keely's mom took her big sister by the shoulders and planted a kiss on her plump cheek. "My rock and roller days will never be over. And don't cramp my style. You know that never goes well—Keely, leave the kids in that playpen and help me carry a few things in from the bus…"

For the next few hours, Keely fetched and carried while Gretchen fed Frannie and Jake too many of the cookies that she never should have been on her feet baking in the first place.

Actually, it wasn't that bad. The kids didn't seem to mind sitting in the playpen while Gretchen fed them and fussed over them. And Ingrid sang as she worked, all the great old songs she and the band used to cover when they toured—"Wanted Dead or Alive" and "Crazy on You" and "Purple Rain." More than once, Keely found herself singing along.

As they made the bed in Ingrid's new bedroom with sky blue sheets and a fuchsia duvet scattered with gold stars, Keely's mom said, "How's it working out, the whole pinch-hit-nanny thing?"

"Really well." *Except for this insane burning lust I've developed for Daniel.*

"The gallery?"

"Runs like clockwork, no problems. I have a great manager, Amanda. And I get by there to check in and help out with whatever needs doing almost every day. I like it. I'm keeping busy."

"You always had a lot of energy."

Keely gazed across the brightly made bed at her mom. "I get that from you."

"As long as you're happy."

"I am."

"But you do seem a little on edge."

No way she was touching that. Keely plumped the hot-pink pillows and grinned like she didn't have a care in the world.

Ingrid let it go. "Well, all right. I'm here whenever you want to talk."

Uh-uh. Not happening.

She followed her mother back out to the bus to haul in more stuff and tried not to think about Daniel and this feeling she had for him that kept getting stronger. Denial wasn't working. Her body seemed to hum with yearning—to touch him. To get close enough to breathe in the scent of his skin.

Every morning she woke up freshly resolved to stop

this silliness. It was all just in her mind, and she'd had enough of it.

But then she'd go downstairs and there he would be at the breakfast table, spooning scrambled eggs onto the kids' high chair trays, answering, "Yeah, Jake," and "Okay, Frannie," at every new imperiously delivered toddler demand. Somehow, the guy who wasn't her type had slowly become the most desirable man in the world.

And her resolution to stop this idiocy?

Out the kitchen window every time.

That night, at eight thirty with the babies tucked in bed, Keely and Daniel sat in the kitchen, drinking coffee that would probably keep them awake way too late. It was raining out. Keely watched the raindrops hit the kitchen window and slide down like tears.

They'd been talking about mundane things—the lumber business, how she would need to have the part-time nanny back a few times this week. She'd got a couple of commissions to make wall hangings. One for a customer's living room and one for a bank in town that liked to support local artists.

And then they were quiet, both staring toward the dark, rainy window.

He said, "Lillie always loved the rain."

Keely nodded. "She said it made her feel cozy and safe, to be inside looking out at the rain coming down."

Another silence. She thought of the wedding portrait that hung in the upstairs hall—Lillie gorgeous in white lace and Daniel so handsome and young in a tux. Two people full of love and hope, with no idea of the ways they would hurt each other.

Keely realized she was holding her breath. With slow care, she let that breath go.

Daniel broke the quiet. "I would have said yes, to the kids, to Lillie getting pregnant. It wasn't…what I wanted. But I did want her to be happy."

Keely sucked in another breath and had to remind herself again to breathe out. It was one thing to talk about Lillie lightly, to remember her fondly—the things she loved, her habits, her quirks.

But what Daniel had just said? Not a light thing. Apparently he'd decided to stumble toward something deeper.

That should feel dangerous, shouldn't it? Or maybe just wrong.

But it didn't.

It felt…honest. Real.

Now Keely longed to reach across the table, to lay her hand over his. "She was *born* to be a mom. I mean, I've always wanted children, but if I never have them, I'll be okay. There's so much to life. I love my gallery, the work I do. My family. Friends. There are a lot of babies to love in the world, even if they aren't my own. But for Lillie, it was an imperative. A yearning in the blood."

"I know."

"Daniel, it was just so wrong that the one thing she wanted above anything was the thing she couldn't have."

A muscle twitched in his square jaw. "Sometimes in life you just don't get what you want. And given that having a child could kill her, I wasn't budging. No kids. We'd already lost my parents and one brother."

The lost brother's name was Finn. He was the fifth born, after Aislinn. He'd vanished on one of those trips that Daniel's parents were always taking. In Siberia, of

all places. The family still had investigators searching
for him. But a lot of years had gone by, so it didn't look
all that likely that Finn would ever be coming home.

Daniel said, "I couldn't do it, couldn't stand to chance
losing Lillie, too." He looked across at her, ice-blue eyes
piercing. "I've always wondered…" Keely knew what
he was about to ask. And then he did ask, "How much
did she tell you?"

She couldn't lie about it. Not now. "A lot."

He fisted those big hands on the table between them.
"I thought so. I…felt it. In the way you looked at me
sometimes. Like you thought I was a real rat bastard,
but I was family, so you were going to have to put up
with me after all."

She shouldn't have chuckled. But she did. "I was mad
at her, too. That she couldn't just accept that her body
wouldn't do what her heart wanted so much."

His eyes. They saw inside her. They knew too much
and they demanded to know more. "Keely. Tell me what
she told you."

"That you were going to have a vasectomy, but she
talked you out of it—and looking back, I don't know
why that made me mad at you. Except that she also said
you didn't want children. It really pissed me off that
you didn't want what she wanted more than anything."

He shut his eyes and swore low, with feeling. "'You
never know how things will turn out,' she said to me.
'Someday I might not be here.' I said I didn't care. I'd *had*
my kids. I'd raised my brothers and sisters as my own.
It was enough. I'd done my bit playing dad. I was done.
But she kept after me not to do it. It seemed so important
to her that I still be able to change my mind in some far,
distant future, if something happened to her. So I let it

go. I never got around to actually having the procedure."
He stared at his own dark reflection in the rainy window.
"I should have known what she was up to."

Keely's hands kept trying to reach for him—and then
she just gave in. She reached.

And so did he.

They held hands across the table. His were big and
rough and warm, and she wanted to feel them, touching
her, running over her skin, learning the secrets of her
body—and later, afterward, when they were both satisfied, she wanted his arms around her, holding her close.

He said in a low rumble, "I'm still so damn mad at
her."

"I know." It came out in a whisper because her throat
had clutched.

"I need to forgive her, but I can't forgive her. When we
first got married, we used condoms and she used a dia-
phragm, too. We were so careful. But then her rheuma-
tologist approved her for the low-dose estrogen pill. She
was on it for years. I thought it was safe not to use anything else. She didn't tell me she'd stopped taking it until
she was already pregnant. I thought the pill had failed
and I was furious. I was going to go after her doctor, to
sue the guy. That was when she admitted she'd stopped
taking the pill. She tricked me. And it killed her."

Keely wanted to hold on to him forever. But if she kept
holding on, well, how would she ever make herself let go?

Carefully, she eased her hands away. She wrapped
them around her almost-cold coffee and sipped the bitter dregs. "There's no win in not forgiving her. You get
that, right?"

"Win? What's any of this got to do with winning?"

"Daniel, what I'm saying is…" Okay, really. What *was*

she saying? She tried again. "I mean, you know about forgiveness, right?"

"What about it?" he demanded, gruff. Impatient.

"It's not for the forgiven. It's for the one who forgives. Until you forgive, you're a prisoner of your anger and resentment, at the wrong that's been done to you. But when you forgive, you don't have to be eaten up with anger anymore. When you forgive, you are set free."

"Who told you that?" He sounded almost angry.

She held his gaze. "My mother."

"The crazy rock chick who dragged you all over the country when all you wanted was to come home to Valentine Bay?"

"Ouch."

His expression softened. "Sorry. That was harsh."

"But also true. My mom does what she wants to do, and people get fed up with her. But she really does know stuff. She tells the truth as she sees it. And about forgiveness, well, I think she's got forgiveness right."

He pushed back his chair and carried his empty cup to the sink. "I'm going to bed."

Let me come with you...

Ha. Like that would ever happen. *She* might give in, definitely. But Daniel? Even if he really did want her as much as she wanted him, he would see all the ways things could go wrong. He wasn't the kind of man to take dangerous chances.

She gave him a soft good-night and sat alone for a while, thinking of Lillie, who loved the rain.

Lillie, who had betrayed her husband's trust to get what she wanted more than her life.

Chapter Four

Friday, Keely had the temporary nanny, Jeanine, watch the kids for the whole day. Keely worked all morning on the art-quilt hanging for the bank and gave Jeanine a break for lunch. When the nanny returned to take over with the kids, Keely went to the gallery for a couple of hours.

She stopped by Gretchen's before returning to Daniel's house. Ingrid was at the Sea Breeze, getting a start on the renovations she had planned.

Auntie G brought out the cookies, poured Keely coffee and complained about her housemate. "At least she's finally moved the bus to the bar parking lot. This is a *neighborhood*, Keely. People don't want giant purple vehicles cluttering up the street where they live—especially not when they have half-naked, pot-smoking women painted on the side."

Actually, the half-naked woman was Ingrid herself. More than twenty years ago, she'd talked the famous cartoonist R Crumb into drawing her—in ratty cutoffs and a low-cut tank top, clearly braless underneath, playing her Telecaster and smoking what looked like a big fat cigar, but according to Ingrid was a giant doobie. She'd had the image blown up bigger than life-size and used it to decorate her tour bus.

"I love your mother," added Auntie G, "but she can be so thoughtless sometimes. She plays her guitar at *night*. That's not right. I had to ask her this morning to please just go to that bar she bought when she has to… bang out a riff, or whatever it is she calls it when she beats on that old acoustic guitar of hers and wails at the top of her lungs."

Keely asked gingerly, "What are you telling me?"

Gretchen raised both hands out to the side and glanced toward heaven. "Sweetheart, what do you think I'm telling you? Your mother makes me insane."

"Are you worrying it won't work out, with her living here?"

Her aunt blinked in obvious surprise. "Whatever makes you think that?"

"Well, you do sound pretty annoyed with her."

"Of course I'm annoyed with her. She's very annoying, and she always has been. I knew that when we decided she would be coming home to live. It doesn't mean I don't want her here. She's my sister and I love her and she's going nowhere. We are going to learn to get along and support each other in our waning years."

Keely winced. "'Waning years'? I hope you don't use that term around Mom."

A sly smile curved Gretchen's pale lips. "Oh, but I

do and she hates it, too. She claims it makes her want to scream—"

"Wait." Keely put up a hand. "Let me guess. Because she's *only* fifty and about as far from 'waning' as a vital, brilliant woman can get?"

"Sweetheart." Auntie G's sly smile now had a smug edge. "I do believe that you know your mother almost as well as I do."

"So…no plans to kick her out then?"

"None. Don't you dare tell her I said so, but life is so much more interesting when your mother's around."

Sunday morning, Keely's mom called while she and Daniel and the twins were having breakfast. Keely barely got out a "Hi, Mom," before Ingrid was off and running.

"Gretch has got some potluck thing at her church this afternoon. She asked me to go."

"Well, that sounds—"

"Boring? Stifling? Mind-numbing? Tedious? All of the above?"

"So, then. Let me guess. You're not going?"

"You bet your sweet ass I'm not. I told her that you invited me to dinner up there at Daniel's. And then after I told her that, I realized it was a great idea. So what time are we eating?"

"Hold on." Keely muted the call and turned to Daniel, who was wearing a blue-and-black-plaid button-down, the blue of which made his eyes look like oceans— oceans she could happily drown in.

"What?" he asked.

She shook herself. "My mother wants to come to dinner tonight."

"Sure. Gretchen, too?"

"No, she's got something at church." Keely unmuted the call and said to her mother, "We like to eat with the kids, so it will be early."

"I knew when I decided to move home that nothing in my life would ever be civilized again."

"I'm rubbing my fingers together," Keely teased. It was an old joke between them. As a child, whenever Keely would whine about this or that, Ingrid would rub her thumb and middle finger together to signify the smallest violin in the world playing "My Heart Bleeds for You."

Ingrid released an audible sigh. "I raised you to be wild and free and sophisticated in a boho sort of way, to drink deep from life's bounteous cup. Instead, you live in the same small town where I was born, and you spend your days taking care of your cousin's toddlers."

"Hey. I own an art gallery and my work has been written up in *Oregon Art Monthly*. That's kind of sophisticated."

"I rest my case. What time?"

"Come at four, earlier if you want to. We'll eat at five."

"I'm driving Gretch to the potluck, dropping her off and then picking her up. The church gig is from four to six thirty, so the timing is perfect. I'll bring wine. Two bottles. Red or white?"

"You choose. We're having chicken."

"White then. See you about four."

Ingrid came early, armed with the promised bottles of Oregon Sauvignon Blanc. She joined Keely and the twins in the kitchen.

"It's pouring rain out there." She set the wine on the counter and then smoothed little tendrils of damp pink-

and-blue-streaked hair back from her forehead. "I'll just put these in the fridge, keep them cold for dinner." She grabbed up the two bottles again. "Where's Daniel?"

"He had to run out to the office." Keely slid a beautiful, plump roaster chicken into the oven. "Some minor detail he needed to deal with on a job that starts tomorrow. He'll be back in time for dinner."

Ingrid leaned over the playpen to give kisses to the twins.

Jake held up his arms to her. "Out. Pwease."

And she asked, "Is it okay if I release them from prison?"

Keely opened the cupboard to grab the rice. "As long as you watch them."

Ingrid took the kids out of the playpen and sat on the floor with them while Keely cooked. When they lost interest in the toys Keely had brought downstairs for them, Ingrid turned for the cupboards. She soon had a wide array of pots and pans, lids and utensils out on the floor and she was tapping spoons on the pans and banging pot lids together.

Keely watched her fondly, remembering her own little-girlhood, when Ingrid would use any object she could get her hands on to make music. Keely used to love that, banging things together to make loud sounds.

So did Frannie and Jake. They pounded and banged, laughing and shouting, while Maisey sat in the doorway to the family room, watching through those droopy eyes of hers and occasionally even throwing her head back to howl along with them.

Daniel came in at four thirty. He took over with the kids, and Keely's mom set the breakfast-nook table.

Everything was going so well, her mom chatting easily

with Daniel about how his various brothers and sisters were doing. He asked about the bar, and she filled him in on her plans to put a roll-up door in the wall that faced the beach so she could fully open the place up to the outdoors in good weather. Daniel uncorked the wine, and Keely put the kids in their chairs and tied their bibs around their necks. She gave them rice and cut-up chicken and cooked carrots in bowls along with spoons, because sometimes they actually managed to scoop food onto a spoon and get it into their mouths. She handed them their sippy cups of milk.

The adults sat down. Wine was poured and bowls were passed. The kids were focused on their food and acting like little angels. The conversation flowed easily—for a while anyway.

At what point did Ingrid start darting looks back and forth between Keely and Daniel?

Keely wasn't sure.

But when her mother asked, "What *is* this?" tipping her head to the side, eyes narrowed, like she had the scent of something she hadn't quite named yet, Keely got that sinking feeling.

Whatever her mom was thinking, Keely dearly wished that Ingrid might keep it to herself. Her mother often had intuitions and when she had them, they were usually right—and also mostly about the things no one really wanted to talk about.

"Chicken, Mom," she said, going for the obvious, hoping against hope that Ingrid really was only wondering about the food. "It's chicken and mushroom rice. I added a teaspoon of curry to the rice, to change it up a little."

"I don't mean the dinner, which is delicious." Ingrid gestured grandly at the meal before them and sipped her wine. "But no. This is not about the food." She lifted her glass in a silent toast, first to Daniel and then at Keely. "This is about the two of you…"

"Who two?" Keely demanded, though of course she already knew.

Ingrid sweetly smiled. "Oh, yeah. I'm getting a very strong vibe that you two are having some hot sexy times."

Daniel made a distinct choking sound. Keely sent a frantic glance his way as he coughed into his napkin. "Sorry," he croaked out, looking nothing short of stricken.

Keely longed to jump up and run out into the driving rain, run and run and never come back. Sadly, escape wasn't any kind of option. Besides, she'd done nothing wrong and had nothing to be ashamed of. Her mother was the one who was out of line. She yanked her shoulders back and took a valiant stab at outright denial. "Mom. Come on. Where do you get these crazy ideas?"

"Crazy? I think not. You should see your face. You look like a landed trout…" Ingrid widened her eyes and let her mouth fall open, an apparent imitation of Keely's expression. Then she actually had the nerve to laugh. "And now you are blushing. Oh, yeah. I'm right. I know I am." She reached across and patted Keely's hand. "Baby, come on. Lighten up. I'm on your side. I think this is simply wonderful, really! Daniel deserves a little pleasure in his life, and so do you."

Keely stuck with denial. "You're wrong, so wrong. And you're being ridiculous. Not to mention, you are embarrassing me."

Ingrid sipped more wine and refused to stop smiling. At least she was quiet. For the moment.

Too quiet. The faint sound of the rain coming down outside seemed to swell to fill the silence. Even the kids just sat there, little fists full of chicken and carrots, staring from one adult face to the other, not sure what was going on, let alone how to react to it.

Daniel spoke up then. "Oh, come on, Ingrid." His eyes still had that freaked-out look, but his voice? Wonderfully calm and assured. "Your imagination is running away with you. Keely's been amazing, taking over with the kids, doing a terrific job with them. We get along great, she and I. But that's it. That's all that's going on here."

Ingrid gave a lazy little one-shoulder shrug. "Well, if you're not having lots of fabulous sex together, you should be."

"Mother," Keely muttered. "Shut. Up."

But Ingrid just went blithely on. "Make hay while the sun shines, I always say. And I mean, whoa!" She pointed at Daniel and then at Keely and then back to Daniel again. Before Keely could remind her how rude pointing was, she let out a loud hissing sound. "Sssssmokin'. You two could burn the house down with the heat you're generating."

Jake chose that moment to crow in delight. He grabbed his spoon, pounded it on his high chair tray and imitated his great-aunt. "*Sssssss!* Moke!"

Frannie took her cue from her twin. "*Sssssss!*" she hissed, then burst into giggles and pounded her hands on her tray. Rice and pieces of chicken went flying.

Ingrid laughed. "See? Even the kids know."

"You are out of your ever-lovin' mind."

"Oh, baby." Ingrid had the sheer gall to cluck her tongue. "Don't be ashamed."

"Ashamed? I'm not—"

"Sex is natural and right, and far too many of our

social norms are nothing more than ways to sap all the joy from life. You know that. I taught you that."

"Can you just drop it? Please?"

But Ingrid was on a roll. Keely purposely refused to even glance at poor Daniel as her mother replied, "No. No, I will not drop it. Not until I remind you both that life is too short *not* to do what comes naturally, and that it's nobody's business but your own if you find a little pleasure along the way—and wait."

Jake clapped his hands. "Wait!" he crowed, and Frannie clapped too.

"Is it Gretchen?" demanded Ingrid. "You're worried about Gretch?"

"Gwet," repeated Frannie experimentally and let out tiny cackle.

Ingrid huffed out a breath. "You think she's going to judge you for somehow 'betraying' Lillie?"

"Ingrid." In a careful, level tone, Daniel tried again to call a halt to this insanity. "Come on. The kids don't need to hear this."

"Oh, please. No harm is being done here. They're too young to understand anyway. As long as we keep the language clean and our attitudes civil, this conversation is totally kid-friendly—and where was I? Right. Gretch. If she's going to judge you for finding what joy you can in this life, well, that is just wrong and she will need to get over it. Lillie was a lovely woman and the world is emptier without her in it. But frankly, she's dead. Gretchen needs to accept that—not that I would ever say a word to my sister about any of this. What you two do in private is none of Gretchen's business anyway. It is nobody's business but your own—and did I already say that? Well. If I did, it bears repeating."

Silence.

Again.

At last.

Keely longed to throw in a snide remark to the effect that if it was their private business, what the hell was Ingrid doing butting in about it? But Keely knew her mother much too well. To challenge her would only set her off again. Thus, Keely settled on a soft-spoken "Tell us you're done, Mom. Please. Just tell us you're done."

Something wonderful happened then. Ingrid nodded. "Yes. I have said what I needed to say. The rest is up to you. Now, lighten up and pass the wine."

Ingrid kept her word. She didn't bring up the subject of Keely and Daniel and their "smokin'" attraction again.

She stayed for dessert, helped clear the table and played with the kids for a few minutes after that. And then it was time to go pick up Gretchen from church. Ingrid kissed the kids, hugged Keely, bade a fond goodbye to Daniel and breezed out the door.

Keely was thinking they would put the kids to bed and then maybe they could talk about her mother's cringe-worthy behavior. She would advise him not to take her mom too seriously, reassure him that it really wasn't a big deal. They could clear the air about the whole thing.

But the minute Ingrid walked out the door, Daniel suddenly remembered he needed to go to the office again—at six twenty on Sunday night.

"Sorry," he said, his gaze skittering away from hers. "I know it's not right to leave you here to deal with the kids alone on Sunday night. You deserve a little time to yourself, but this is something I really should get handled before—"

"The kids are no problem, honestly. I'll put them to bed."

"I just forgot a couple of important things, and I really ought to get back over there and make sure that—"

"Daniel." She put up a hand. "It's okay. Just go."

And he went—practically at a run. It would have been funny if it wasn't so awkward and depressing.

No, Keely didn't really blame him for fleeing the scene. Of course, he would want to get away after the Sunday dinner from hell that her mother had just put him through. Really, he'd been a prince not to just get up, grab the kids and get out the moment her mother started in on them.

Maybe they would talk about it later. Or maybe they wouldn't. In any case, Ingrid had essentially promised not to bring the subject up again. She'd damn well better keep her word about that.

The kids sat on the kitchen floor gazing up at her expectantly.

"Bath time," she said.

"Baf!" Frannie sang out, and Jake let out a happy cry.

Keely took them upstairs, gave them a long bath and then let them loose in the playroom for a while, getting down on the floor with them, joining in as they played with their toys. As bedtime approached, she led them into her room and cuddled up with them on the bed to read them a few of their favorite stories.

By eight thirty, they were both asleep, one on either side of her. She took Jake across the hall first and tucked him into his crib, then went right back and got Frannie. Neither of them made so much as a peep as she crept from their room and silently shut the door behind her.

Without the kids to keep her busy, the house seemed

way too quiet. She stood there in the hall, listening to the distant roar of the rain outside, like a whispered secret in the quiet of the night.

What now?

Thoughts of Daniel came rushing in—the sadness in his eyes the other night when they spoke of Lillie. The freaked-out expression on his face tonight when her mother wouldn't shut up about the hot sex he and Keely ought to be having. The way he wouldn't even look her in the eye before he left tonight.

When would he be home? When he did come back, should she try to talk to him?

Or just let it be?

Until tonight, she'd pretty much convinced herself that he didn't need to know about this crazy crush she had on him, that she could take care of his babies and be his friend for as long as he needed her.

Really, she'd been thinking that this yearning she had for him would eventually fade. Sooner rather than later, she hoped.

Well, it wasn't fading. And tonight had been like that day he saw her naked all over again. She felt stripped in the worst kind of way. Revealed.

And she really didn't know how *he* felt. Sometimes, the way he looked at her, she was absolutely certain he had it bad for her, too.

But that could so easily be wishful thinking. He'd never even hinted that he wanted more than her help with the kids and maybe someone he could talk to. In fact, tonight at the dinner table, he'd laid it right out there. He'd told her mother that he appreciated her stepping up with the twins, that he enjoyed her companionship…

And nothing more.

She needed to stop obsessing about this.

Maybe she should work.

She wandered into her studio room and sat down at her sewing machine where her current project waited. With her index finger, she traced the shapes of flowers and starbursts she'd sewn into the fabric, flattening her palm on the material, feeling the metallic thread scratch at her skin.

How long had she been the twins' nanny? About a month. So quickly, she'd settled into a life here at Daniel's.

And her original plan to go home most nights? She'd given that up right away when the babies got sick—and then, after they got well, it had just seemed so much easier and more convenient to continue living here.

Convenience wasn't all of it, though. Not by a long shot. She loved it here in the big Bravo house among the tall trees on Rhinehart Hill. She loved taking care of Jake and Frannie, hanging out with Daniel for an hour or two every night, waking up in the morning to find him downstairs fixing breakfast, the twins already in their high chairs, waving their fat little fists full of Cheerios at her, demanding morning kisses.

With a wry smile, she rose and wandered to the window. Through the pouring rain, she stared out at the backyard, lit in smudges of gold by the lights dotted here and there amid the bushes, along the paths—one leading to the side gate and another that wound its way farther back, toward the rear fence. Way back there, a light glowed by the door to the woodshed.

Keely shut her eyes and leaned her forehead against the cool glass. Time to face the truth. The twins were not her children. And Daniel was not her man.

She didn't need to talk with him about the silly things her mom had said. She just needed to tell him he would have to start looking for someone else to watch the kids full-time.

As for working tonight?

Not happening. Her work required a steady hand and concentration. Right now, her mind was a hot stew of yearning and regret, and she felt shaky with emotions she had no business feeling.

No working. No waiting up to talk to Daniel. She'd have a nice long bath and take a good book to bed with her.

And tomorrow, she would tell him it was time for her to go.

With a soft cry, Keely sat up in bed.

The juicy hardcover romance she'd been reading flopped to the mattress and shut with a snap. She'd left the lamp on. She shoved her hair back off her forehead and glared at the clock.

Ten past midnight—and she'd heard something, hadn't she?

A strange sound had jolted her from sleep.

The kids?

She sat completely still, willing her racing heart to slow a little, not even daring to breathe, as she listened.

No sound from across the hall—let alone from the baby monitor right there at her bedside by the clock.

Not the kids then.

Thump-thump.

There. That. It was coming from the backyard.

Another thump, followed by a clatter.

Distant. Rhythmic.

Thud-thud. And then that faint clattering noise, like bowling pins toppling in on each other.

The thudding and clattering continued as she pushed back the covers and went to the window she'd left open a crack to let in the moist night air and the soothing, constant whisper of the falling rain.

She gazed out on essentially the same view she'd had from her workroom—the dark backyard, the bright smears of garden lights through the veil of the rain.

Thunk-thunk. Clatter...

Her gaze tracked the path through the trees, seeking the source of the sound.

She saw him then. Daniel. There. Revealed in the light by the woodshed door, shirtless and wielding a splitting maul in the pouring rain.

Thud. Thud. Clatter. The log sheared down the center and the two pieces tumbled from the chopping block into the mounds of split wood on either side.

Daniel...

No, she couldn't see him all that clearly, but she knew him by his height, by the breadth of his shoulders, the proud shape of his head.

And who else would be chopping wood in the backyard in the middle of the night?

Those poor logs. He attacked them without pause or mercy.

A tiny stab of guilt pierced her. She shouldn't be watching this. She should leave the man alone, let him work out his obvious frustration in his own way, undisturbed.

But, well, what else could be driving him but her mother's utter tactlessness at dinner?

Maybe something at work?

Yeah. That was more likely. Ingrid's big mouth might have embarrassed him, but shouldn't he be past that by now?

Whatever it was, she just couldn't stand to see him punish himself this way. And maybe, if she went to him, they could actually talk it over, get it out in the open, whatever it was.

Because however he felt or didn't feel about her as a woman, and whatever happened tomorrow when she told him she was leaving, he *had* called her a friend and she truly believed that he'd meant it. What kind of a friend was she if she just left him all alone out at the woodshed in the middle of the night? The least she could do was go to him, ask if he needed someone to talk to and then listen if he said yes.

Decision made, she whirled from the window, yanked an old green zip-up hoodie from the dresser and pulled it on over her pajama top. Barefoot, she opened her door to find Maisey right there, looking up at her expectantly.

"What? You want to go out?" She got a hopeful whine for an answer. "All right," Keely whispered. "Let's check the kids."

She tiptoed into their darkened room and leaned over one crib and then the other. Both slept like little angels— angels who were unlikely to wake up anytime soon. And she would be back within minutes, hopefully dragging the dripping, shirtless Daniel along behind her.

Off she flew, along the upper hall, down the stairs, to the kitchen and the mudroom beyond, Maisey trotting along behind her. Her red rain boots with the white polka dots were right there by the door. She shoved her feet into them, pulled the green hood up over her head and ran out across the back deck. Maisey trailed her down the wide stairs but stopped to sniff the bushes by the walk.

Keely went on alone, racing down the lighted path to the back fence.

Her boots made splashing sounds, but Daniel didn't seem to hear her coming. He just kept raising and lowering that maul. He was like a machine, turning to grab a log, plunking it on the block with a thud, cleaving it with a single perfect stroke—and turning for the next one as the pieces fell. Never once did he look up.

Dear sweet Lord, he was a gorgeous man, the beautiful, water-slick muscles of his shoulders and arms shifting and bunching beneath his skin as he set and attacked each log.

She stopped not ten feet away from him, her hoodie already soaked through, her pj's clinging wet. Still, he didn't look up.

"Daniel!" she shouted as he turned and bent to grab the next log.

He froze in midreach. And then, slowly, he rose to his height and faced her. Those ice-blue eyes found her, pinned her where she stood.

"Keely." His voice was a low, rough rumble, dredged up from the deepest part of him.

That did it. As he gazed at her, unblinking through the pouring rain, she knew the truth at last.

It was more than just her own wishful thinking and vivid imagination.

She wasn't alone in her need and her yearning.

Daniel wanted her, too.

Chapter Five

Daniel stood in the rain and stared at the soaking wet woman who'd made his house a home again, the woman he wanted now. Beyond all reason.

Of all the crazy things that could happen in life.

He wanted Keely, Lillie's little cousin, with the wide-set eyes and the soft mouth and the smattering of pale freckles across her pretty nose. He wanted Keely, wanted her so bad he'd cut and run after dinner because of the scary, true things that her mother had said.

Run off like a candy-ass to the office, where he sat for more than three hours, alternately staring at the far wall and playing "Space Invaders" on his phone.

Wanted her so much he'd come straight to the wood-pile when he got home, hoping to chop that want away.

It hadn't worked. Not even a little bit.

And now she stood there in her soggy pj's, drooping

hoodie and shiny polka-dot rubber boots, her eyes locked to his—and he wanted her even more now than he had when he ran away from her after dinner.

It was a whole conversation they shared, with not a word spoken, in the space of a few seconds, standing in the pouring rain.

She wanted him, too.

If he'd had any doubts on that score, the look in those big eyes when he glanced up and saw her standing there blew them clean away.

She wanted him. He wanted her.

And now, well, what the hell? Ingrid was right.

Nothing stood in their way. Why shouldn't they have each other?

The maul was heavy in his hand now. He almost dropped it where he stood. But the habits of a lifetime took precedence. A man looked after his tools. Afraid if he broke the hold of her gaze, she might just vanish—disappear like a dream, melt away in the rain—he backed to the woodshed, elbowed the door open a crack and set the maul inside, out of the wet. He pulled the door shut then, until he heard the latch click.

The rain beat down on her, but she didn't move. She had her head tipped up, watching him from under the soggy green hood, but she hadn't spoken except for that one word—his name.

Well, okay. Words were unnecessary at this point, anyway. She'd told him all he needed to know by the simple act of coming for him, of standing right there on the path back to the house, calling his name.

And he was tired. So damn tired of resisting, of coming up with reasons why having her wasn't right.

His shirt was around here somewhere. Where had he thrown it? He had no idea and really didn't care.

Keely. *She* was what mattered. He took a step toward her. She blinked but held her ground.

The rain beat down on him and he welcomed it. His body burned and each cool drop felt so good.

Another step. She swallowed, but she stayed where she was, watching him, unmoving, as though mesmerized by the energy that zapped back and forth between them.

Two more steps and he was there with her, staring down into those wide green eyes of hers. Slowly, in order not to spook her, he lifted his hand.

"Daniel." She said his name for the second time, in a whisper, giving it only her breath, but no real sound.

"Keely." And he touched her, touched the high, wet curve of her cheek. "Like velvet," he said. "I knew it would be."

"I, um, don't know if—"

"Shh." He pressed his finger to that mouth of hers, that mouth he was going to kiss all night long. "You do know."

"Oh, Daniel…" Her breath around his finger, sweet and warm. He wanted his tongue in there, in the heat and the wet. When he kissed her, he would coax her mouth to open for him, take that warm, sweet breath of hers into himself. "I don't know—"

"Yeah, you do. Come on, your mother knew it. We both know and we have known. Since that day you pushed back the shower curtain and stepped out of the tub without a stitch on."

"I shouldn't have left that door open."

"I shouldn't have barged right in. But so what, at this point? We did what we did."

"I was thinking, earlier, that maybe it's time I—"

"No."

"No?" She looked adorably bewildered.

"Forget about earlier." He eased his fingers under the soaked hoodie, along the silky curve of her neck, around to her nape, which he cradled in the palm of his hand.

"Forget?"

He nodded. "Let's just think about right now."

"Um. Okay." A soft, surrendering moan escaped those beautiful lips as she tipped her mouth up for him. "Okay," she repeated as his mouth closed over hers.

It was perfect, that first touch of his mouth to hers, the softness of her cold lips, the warmth inside, slick and welcoming, so good.

She smelled of some faint, tempting perfume and she tasted so damn sweet. Her nose was cold and her hair dry at her nape under the hoodie, like silk against the back of his hand, short little wisps of it curling under his fingertips.

Glad. He was so damn glad.

Glad in the way he hadn't been for years and years. Years of doing what needed doing. The right thing. The careful thing. Looking after everyone else, putting his own selfish desires aside.

Not tonight. Tonight, he would be selfish. He would take what wanted, and he wouldn't feel bad about it.

Because she wanted it, too.

The rain beat down on them, trickling out of his hair and into his face, his mouth. And hers. He could stand here just kissing her forever.

But really, a dry, warm room. A cozy bed.

That would be better.

Reluctantly, he broke the kiss. Pressing his forehead to hers, he asked her, "Come inside? With me, to my room, into my bed?" He thought his heart might explode as he waited for her answer.

"Yes," she said, and he could breathe again. "Yes, Daniel. Please. Take me inside."

"Done." He put a hand at her back and one under her knees and scooped her right up off the ground.

She let out a little screech of surprise, grabbing for him, wrapping her arms around his neck. And off they went along the winding path and up onto the deck, where Maisey waited under the deck cover, out of the rain. She bumped in ahead of them when he pushed open the mudroom door.

Once inside, he let Keely down so they could both toe off their boots. He took off his socks, too, and she draped her sopping hoodie on a free peg.

When she turned to him, he grabbed her hand and pulled her after him, through the kitchen, along the short hall to the living room, into the front entry and on up the stairs. They paused at the kids' room, just long enough to glance in and see that both of them were sleeping soundly. Maisey had a bed in there. She headed for it.

"Come on," he whispered and pulled Keely along to the big room at the end of the hall, tugging her in there, closing the door and then pressing her up against it to steal another kiss.

She moaned into his mouth, a needy little sound. Everything about her thrilled him, her soft, curvy body, her wet hair, the sweet, sexy sounds she made, the scent of her skin. He kissed his way down over her chin and licked the rain off her throat as she clutched at him, sighing, whispering, "Yes. Oh, yes…"

"I want to see you." He scraped his teeth down her neck, licked the tight, sweet flesh over her the points of her collarbone. "You taste so good. I can't believe this is happening." He fumbled with the pink buttons on her soggy pajama top. "I really need to get you out of these wet pj's…"

"Let me help you." But instead of getting to work on her own buttons, she went for his belt buckle.

He froze and looked down in total wonder at her soft, pretty fingers as they undid his belt and whipped it away, dropping it to the floor at their feet. When she glanced up, he would have kissed her again.

But then she asked, "Is your monitor on?" They had three receivers—one in her room, one in his and a third downstairs somewhere.

He commanded, "Do not move from this spot."

She laughed and gave him a playful shove. "Go. Do it."

He was back in a flash. "The damn thing is on. Now, about all these buttons…"

"What, these?" She went to work on the row of pink buttons down her front. Quick work it was, too. A moment later, he was sliding the soggy pajama top off her shoulders, revealing more gorgeous expanses of beautiful, smooth skin.

He said, "Beautiful." And he bent his head and took one dusky nipple into his mouth.

"Oh!" She wrapped her arms around him and pulled him close as he drew on the tightened bud, using his teeth just a little, flicking at her with his tongue.

But then she interrupted him, taking his head between her hands and pulling him up so they were face-to-face.

"What?" he complained.

"I forgot." She bit her lower lip and he wanted to take that mouth again, to kiss her right there where her teeth sank into the plump, tempting flesh. "We need condoms."

"I have some—and don't look so surprised."

"You're just so…"

He tried to glare at her but didn't succeed all that well. "Say it. I'm so what?"

"Upright?" she suggested. "Stalwart? Not a guy who has condoms handy, that's for sure."

He groaned, "You're killin' me here. And if you have to know, several months ago, I tried Tinder."

"No. Really?"

"Yeah."

"Daniel." She spoke in a hushed little whisper, like they were sharing a secret too delicious for anyone else ever to know about. "You hooked up with someone?"

"I made a date. As it turned out, the hooking up didn't happen, but I did get the condoms."

She giggled. He loved when she did that. Her whole face lit up. "You have to tell me all about it."

"Later," he growled at her. "Right now, I'm kind of busy." And he swooped down and covered those sweet lips with his.

That kiss went on forever. Her hands stroked his shoulders, gliding upward to wrap around his neck. She threaded those soft fingers into his hair.

And he? He got to go on touching her, first framing her wonderful face in his hands for a long kiss. But he didn't stop there. He needed to touch her. He needed to get intimately acquainted with every perfect, womanly inch of her skin.

He ran his eager hands along her neck, over the damp velvet flesh of her shoulders, down her arms and back up again. He palmed her waist. And when he pulled her in close and wrapped his arms around her, he got to feel those beautiful breasts against his chest as he traced the delicate bumps of her spine.

Her wet pajama bottoms were in his way. He shoved at them, impatient to be rid of them. The elastic waistband couldn't hold out against him. Down they went.

She was shivering as she stepped out of them.

He lifted his mouth from hers. "Cold?"

"Um," she replied, which could have meant anything. And then she surged up on tiptoe to capture his lips again.

"You're cold," he accused in the middle of that kiss. He clasped her waist and lifted her. Her bare legs went around him. He groaned at the feel of that, her thighs spread wide against his fly, his aching hardness pressing into the heat and wet of her, so close to where he couldn't wait to be.

Were they really doing this?

If this was a dream, please, please let him never wake up.

He kissed her as he carried her to his bathroom, set her down on the rug and groped for a towel.

She allowed him to dry her off, standing there without a stitch on, smiling at him, her eyes moss green and glowing as he used the towel on her hair first and then the rest of her, pausing now and then in order to scatter quick kisses across her skin.

He knelt to dry her thighs, to rub the towel a little

longer than necessary along the backs of her knees and down to her slender feet with their purple-painted toes.

When she stopped shivering, he tossed the towel aside. Sinking back on his bent knees, he looked up her body as she gazed down at him.

How could he resist a long, thorough touch? He trailed a slow hand up her shin, over her knee, along the firm skin of her thigh to the soft white pillow of flesh where her thighs joined. She was just so pretty. With that neat strip of hair, that tempting pink cleft.

He eased a finger into the wet heat of her. She sighed and a low moan escaped her. "More, please," she said, sweet and soft and oh, so tender.

Daniel gave her more, slipping another finger in, using his other hand to grasp her waist, to hold her in place while he touched her at will. And then, wanting even more, he leaned into her and used his mouth, too.

She signaled her approval with a hungry little cry as she widened her stance for him. He took full advantage, kissing her, touching her deeply, moving his fingers within her, trying to pick up every cue her body gave him, trying to show her how much he wanted her through sheer attentiveness to her needs.

It was amazing. It had been such a long time for him, years, since sex had been like this—a glow that got brighter, a hot shiver that kept getting stronger, burning wetter, quivering harder, a feeling of wonder, a pleasure so deep.

His body ached to have her, his hardness painful against the prison of his fly. But he wanted to make it last, take his time with her, to caress every inch of her, drink every drop.

Life could be so cruel sometimes. He might never get this chance again.

She came on his tongue. It was straight-on amazing, her smooth thighs wide, fingers fisted in his hair, her head thrown back, her slim neck straining as she moaned and begged him, "Please, yes. That. Like that…"

He stayed with her, drinking her, until the pulsing within her settled to a faint throb.

And then he commanded her, "Again."

She gasped. "Daniel. I can't."

"Yeah, you can," he insisted. "You are so beautiful, Keely. Like some miracle I never thought to find. And tonight, here you are. And I want to see you. All of you. How you are. What you do. Come for me. Again."

A wild laugh escaped her, followed a few seconds later by a plaintive little cry.

And then she was rising a second time as he played her, as he caught the rhythm she liked with his fingers. Shameless, he used everything he had—his lips and tongue and even his teeth to get her there, to make her go over, lose herself completely to his touch and the wet press of his hungry mouth.

That time, as the pulsing faded, he swept upward, catching her as she started to crumple. He gathered her into his arms and carried her to his bed, setting her on her unsteady feet just long enough to throw back the covers, then scooping her up again and laying her down.

She stared up at him, her damp hair spread out on his white pillow, her mouth soft and vulnerable, eyes full of stars.

Reaching into the bedside drawer, he found the strip of condoms he'd been absolutely certain would be out-of-date before he ever had a chance to use them. He tore one off and set it in easy reach. Then, with a grateful sigh, he ripped his fly wide and pushed down his boxer briefs along with his jeans, letting out a relieved sigh as his erection sprang free.

Stepping out of the tangle of soggy pants collapsed around his ankles, he went down to the bed with her.

"Daniel." She reached for him.

He stretched out beside her and pulled her close. "Kiss me, Keely."

And she did, a perfect kiss. The slow kind, nipping and teasing to start, then going deep and wet.

She touched him, running her hands over him, showing him that she felt as he did, that she couldn't get enough of touching his body. Perfection. There was no other word for this, just lying here with her, touching her as she touched him.

Talk about a dream come true.

Her fingers strayed over his hips and around to his butt. She grabbed on and squeezed so hard. Chuckling, he buried his nose in the velvety curve of her neck.

And then he bit her, right there where her neck met her shoulder. She was so ripe and tender, he needed a taste.

"Ouch!" She slapped him sharply on the shoulder.

"Sorry. I can't control myself. I just want to eat you right up."

"You already did."

They laughed together.

And then she took him by the shoulders and pushed him away enough to meet his eyes. "Daniel. I don't think I've ever heard you laugh before. At least, I haven't for a very long time."

What was he supposed to say to that? He had no idea.

So he said nothing, just cradled her head in his two hands to hold her in place for another kiss.

She wrapped her fingers around his aching length and she stroked him, slow strokes, her grip nice and tight. But he wasn't going to last long if she kept that up.

"Too good," he groaned at her and gently peeled her hand away.

She was the one who reached for the condom. He let her deal with it. She seemed to know what she was doing. Holding him in place, she rolled it down over him.

"Eyes on me," he whispered, taking her shoulders. Pushing her down to the pillows, he rose up over her and settled between her thighs.

This. Now. It was a moment to remember. Those green eyes holding steady on his, shining with heat and pleasure as he came into her.

She felt so good. Tight, giving way to him slowly, so he had to take his time. But slow was fine with him. Slow was just right—no, better than right. Pure perfection, the pleasure rolling over him, through him, threatening to take him down way before he was ready.

He guided a damp curl of hair away from her cheek. "You're so beautiful, Keely."

"Daniel. Is this real?"

He nodded at her slowly, holding her gaze. "I want to make it last forever. But I don't think that's going to happen."

She lifted her hips to him, drawing him deeper.

He groaned at the pleasure as it shimmered all through him, a pleasure that somehow skimmed the sharp, delicious edge of pain.

"Wait," he whispered. "Just for a moment. Just for a

little while, I want to be with you. Just for a little while, don't even move."

She licked those sweet lips of hers. And when she did that, well, he had to kiss her. He lowered his head and plundered her beautiful mouth.

And the stillness?

It just couldn't last. As he kissed her, she was shifting restlessly under him, raising her legs and wrapping them around him, pushing herself up him as he pushed into her.

They rolled, and she had the top position. He captured her face in his hands, holding her still so that at least she had to look at him, *know* him in this intimate way, feel him in her and with her as she rocked against him slow and deep, her folded legs pressed tight along his sides now, her breath all tangled, eyelids drooping.

"Keely. Look at me."

And she did. She looked right at him.

His finish barreled at him much too fast. "I don't think I can wait for you."

And then she gasped. Her eyes went wide. "Daniel!" He felt her climax throb around him.

That did it. With a strangled groan, he joined her, pushing up into her, hard and tight, as his release arrowed down his backbone, undeniable now.

What could he do but give himself up to it?

With a guttural shout, he surrendered, let his finish roll through him, let her sweet, pulsing heat take him down.

Chapter Six

Keely loved the tender way Daniel pulled the covers up and settled them around her, as though she was infinitely precious to him.

He made her feel special. Treasured, somehow.

Daniel, of all people.

She'd just...never known.

He kissed the tip of her nose. "I know I'm being selfish, but I want you in this bed with me. I want you to stay here with me. I want to wake up beside you in the morning. And the next morning. And the morning after that. I don't want you to get up and go."

"I don't want to go either." But they were in uncharted territory here. Yes, they were both single and had every right to find comfort and pleasure together. Still. He'd belonged to Lillie for so many years. Keely just didn't know how the family would react. Lillie had died more than a year and a half ago, but for Gretchen, the pain of losing her only child lingered—and always would. How would she take it to see Daniel moving on? And with Keely, of all people? How would his brothers and sisters see it? She really couldn't predict what their reactions would be. With families, well, you just never could tell.

"So you'll stay?" He looked so hopeful. And very sexy, with his bedhead and his beard scruff and that mouth she wanted to kiss again and again.

"I'll stay," she said. "But I really think, at least for the time being, that as for telling the family that we're spending our nights together…" She sought the right words.

He found the words for her. "They don't need to know." And he laughed. For the second time that night. "You should see your face. I've surprised you?"

"Well, yeah. I mean, that was exactly what I was about to say. But I guess I was kind of afraid you would take it wrong."

"No. Uh-uh. This is between us." Now he sounded a little bit grim and a whole lot stalwart, very much the nonsmiling, laughter-averse Daniel she knew best.

She admitted, "It's only, well, I could do without another rant on the wonders of sex from my mother. And I have no idea how Aunt Gretchen will react, but at the moment, I'm not ready to find out. I can't see why we even need to deal with the family about it. Not right now at least. Not while it's all so new."

He smoothed a few errant strands of hair behind her ear. "It's just better…"

"If we keep it between the two of us."

"Da? Da-Da? Da-Da, Da…" It was Jake's voice in a lazy singsong coming from the baby monitor, luring Keely from sleep.

"Da-Da! Keewee!" Frannie joined in more insistently. "Up!"

Keely opened her eyes to find a sleepy Daniel watching her from the other pillow. He reached out, brushed the hair from her eyes and traced the curve of her ear with a lazy finger.

She gave him a slow smile. Wonder of wonders, he smiled back.

And to think, last night she'd been about to tell him it was time for her to go.

Well, forget that. As of this morning, she was going nowhere.

Everything had changed with that first kiss in the rain.

Now she knew that he wanted her, too. Hadn't he proved it in the most spectacular way?

She wasn't giving him up. Not until…

When? She had no idea. And she refused to get all tied in knots about how things would end up.

Right now, it was only beginning and it was glorious.

"What?" he asked gruffly.

"I was thinking that you and I have a thing now. A secret thing, just between the two of us. It's exciting. Also, kind of crazy."

He wrapped his big hot fingers around the back of her neck. "Just as long as you're not trying to tell me you've changed your mind."

A lovely shiver quivered through her. "No way. I'm in."

"Da-Da, now!"

"Coming!" he called, loud enough the kids could probably hear him even through the solid-core bedroom door. And then he spoke low again, just for her.

"I would love to lie around in bed with you for the rest of the day…"

"Me, too. But the kids are hungry and Valentine Logging isn't going to run itself."

That evening after they put the twins to bed, Daniel led her to his room again.

The night before had been spectacular. Keely hardly thought it possible that it could get any better.

But oh, my. It did.

Daniel was the very best kind of lover—attentive and patient. Kind of bossy, too. He could be tender, and he could be just a little bit rough. She loved the way he touched her, the way he said her name as he caressed her and when he was inside her.

As though she was everything.

As though there could never be anyone but her.

He kissed her as though he could never get enough of the taste of her mouth. And he smelled so good, clean and manly, like cedar branches, like the forest right after the rain.

Later, when they settled in with the light off, she stroked her hand down the beautiful muscles of his arm and asked about the woman he'd met on Tinder.

"What can I say, Keely? We both swiped right."

"But you said it didn't happen…" Her hand strayed downward, to his wrist, over the back of his big hand.

He spread his fingers, and she slipped hers between them. "You're sure you want to hear this?"

"Yes, please."

He made a low sound in his throat. "It's not all that interesting."

"Tell me," she demanded.

He muttered a bad word, but he did give in enough to mutter, "So we got on chat together."

She coaxed him. "And then?"

"She seemed nice. I bought condoms, and we met for a drink at the Hotel Elliott in Astoria." A port city near the mouth of the Columbia River, Astoria was about fifteen miles northeast of Valentine Bay. "I liked her," he went on. "She said she liked me, too, and she'd already taken a room. We went upstairs." He buried his face against her neck. "Never mind," he muttered, his breath so warm, his mouth brushing her skin in a way that made her want him desperately all over again. "I'm not telling the rest."

She pushed him away enough to look at him, to hold his gaze. "It can't be that bad."

He rolled onto his back and pulled her down on top of him, guiding her head to rest on the powerful bulge of his shoulder. She felt his lips against her hair. "I went into her room with her and she started to undress and I knew it wasn't happening. I put up both hands. 'Whoa,' I said. 'Hold on a minute.' She stared at me like maybe I'd lost my mind. And I said I was sorry, but this was a bad idea and I had to go."

"And…that's it? You left?"

"Yeah. She called me a few ugly names as I was ducking out the door…"

"Oh, Daniel." She pressed a kiss to his shoulder, and she felt his big hand on her head, gently stroking her hair.

"I should have known better. Because I couldn't, that's all. With a stranger, like that? That's just not me. I've been with Lillie. And now you. I need a woman I can talk to, a woman I can trust. I'm thinking that makes me kind of a dweeb."

She kissed his shoulder again. "Naw."

"Yeah."

Stacking her hands on his chest, she rested her chin on them. "Daniel, no dweeb looks like you."

"I'm a dweeb *inside*, where it counts." He petted her, running his hand down her hair some more, catching a random curl and wrapping it around two of his fingers. "God. You are beautiful."

"You're blinded by lust."

He wrapped her hair around his whole hand and then guided her up so her mouth was an inch from his. "You're beautiful. Don't argue with me."

"You are so bossy."

"And I think you like that."

"It is just possible that I might."

He kissed her. For a man who'd been with only two women, he sure knew what he was doing with that mouth of his.

The kiss led to yet more spectacular lovemaking. They didn't get to sleep until almost two.

"You look tired, honey." Gretchen slid the plate of snickerdoodles closer to Keely's elbow.

Keely took one. "You're a cookie pusher, Auntie G. You know that, right?"

"Enjoy, sweetheart." Gretchen had Frannie on her lap. Jake lay sprawled on the floor, hugging his favorite stuffed rabbit, staring dreamily up at the ceiling. "Your mother said she had a great time at dinner Sunday night."

Keely ate a bite of cookie and tried to judge how much Ingrid might have told her aunt—not a thing, she decided. First, because Ingrid knew nothing. And second, because Ingrid had clearly stated that whatever was or wasn't going on between Keely and Daniel, it was none of Gretchen's business.

"Mom seems happy," she said, "about how things are going with her plans for the bar and about living here with you."

Frannie dropped the rubber frog she'd been chewing on. Gretchen caught it and gave it back to her. Frannie stuck it in her mouth again, leaned back in her grandmother's arms and closed her eyes. "All in all, your mother and I are doing just fine. How about you, honey? You've been juggling kids and work and the gallery for five weeks now."

"It's going really well. I don't get home to my place much, but I've got my workshop set up at Daniel's and we found a dependable woman who fills in for me when I need her. I get in to the gallery several hours a week."

"Are you sure you don't need a break?"

"Absolutely."

"Because I'm getting around without the walker now, and I would be happy to start watching the kids again."

Keely hardly knew what to think. Here she and Daniel had this secret thing going on—and all of a sudden, Gretchen wanted to take over with the kids again? "Just give your foot the full eight weeks to heal," she said gently but firmly. "Then we'll talk."

Frannie was fading off to sleep. She dropped the rubber frog again.

Gretchen caught it and set it on the table. "I have to confess that I'm beginning to feel guilty. I'm afraid we're taking unfair advantage of you."

Keely asked cautiously, "We?"

"Daniel and me. Daniel, because you watch his children. And me, because I'm the one who roped you into this."

"I wasn't 'roped' into anything. You asked me to step in and I was happy to. I'm *still* happy to. I love watching the kids. Daniel pays me well. Honestly, I see no reason to fix what isn't broken."

Gretchen was frowning. "Sweetheart, you've always wanted a family of your own. How are you going to find the right guy if you're living at Daniel's, running yourself ragged taking care of my grandchildren?"

Keely tried not to scowl at the woman who was truly a second mother to her. Seriously, did Gretchen somehow *know* what was going on with her and Daniel?

But that made no sense. If Gretchen knew, she would say so. Wouldn't she?

"How many ways do I have to say it?" Keely pasted on a smile and put real effort into keeping her tone even and low. "I love taking care of your grandchildren. I'm not feeling overworked in the least. And what's this all about anyway?"

Gretchen's blue eyes seemed guileless. "This?"

"Aren't you the one who's always telling me I have plenty of time for marriage and a family?"

"Well, of course you do. It's only, as I said, I'm beginning to feel guilty, that's all."

"Don't. I mean it. There is absolutely nothing for you to feel guilty about."

"But you have your own life, and how can you live it if you're up there at Daniel's all the time? It's not right."

"Auntie G, I'm perfectly happy. I have everything I need up at Daniel's. If things get to be too much for me, I will tell you. I promise."

"Has something got you upset?"

"What? No, of course not." *Except I'm having a totally*

torrid, amazing love affair with your son-in-law, and I don't know how you'll take it if you find out.

Gretchen had said she felt guilty. Well, Keely did, too. And there was absolutely no logical reason for her to feel that way.

Her aunt looked at her sideways. "You're sure you're all right?"

"I am. Truly."

"Daniel can be…difficult, I know. He's such a self-contained sort of fellow, so hard to get to know."

"He and I get along great. I mean that." *In more ways than you need to know.*

Careful not to jiggle the sleeping toddler, Gretchen reached across the table and laid a soothing hand on Keely's arm. "You know you can always talk to me about anything that's bothering you."

"Thanks," Keely said, trying really hard to mean it. "I love you, Auntie G, but there's nothing to tell."

The next day, Jeanine came to watch Jake and Frannie from eight to three.

Keely headed straight for her doctor to get a prescription for the pill. From there, she went to her hairdresser for a cut and a color change to strawberry blond. Then at noon, she met Aislinn for lunch at Fisherman's Korner, a cozy diner on Ocean Road.

They both had the fish and chips—the absolute best anywhere—and tall iced teas.

Keely had just swallowed her first incomparable bite of beer-battered Albacore tuna when Aislinn started in on her.

"I love your hair that color. It really sets off your

eyes—and, Keel, why do I have a feeling you've met someone?"

Keely tried her best to look totally unconcerned. "I have no idea what you're talking about."

"You've got one of those faces."

Keely ate a french fry. "One of *what* faces?"

"An honest face. An open face. A face that currently has a definite I-am-getting-it-good sort of glow."

Keely let out a groan. "'Getting it good'? Ew."

"Well, you do. Now. Tell me everything."

Keely had to press her lips together to keep from doing just that. No, she did not want Gretchen to know, but she *did* want to confide in Aislinn. She'd had three true, forever friends in her life so far, the kind of friends to whom she could bare her soul: Lillie, lost to her now. Meg Cartwell, who'd recently moved to Colorado and married the love of her life. And Aislinn.

But Aislinn was not only her BFF, she also happened to be Daniel's sister. Keely had promised Daniel she wouldn't say anything to anyone in the family.

But maybe if she just didn't say *who* the guy was...

Aislinn shook malt vinegar onto her fish. "Come on. You know you're dying to tell me." She set down the vinegar and sipped her tea. "And I'm not leaving this booth until you come clean."

"Okay, fine." Keely leaned closer across the Formica tabletop and confessed gleefully, "There's someone— and that's all I can say."

"Ha! Yes! I knew it. Who?"

Keely picked up another crunchy-crusted, perfect piece of fish. "What did I just say? I can't tell you."

"Omigod!" Aislinn burst out. "No!"

Keely flinched back. "What?"

"I just had a horrible thought."

Keely groaned, "Aislinn. What thought?"

"Is he married? Is that it?"

Keely was still clutching the uneaten piece of fish. Now she dropped it back in the basket without taking a bite and grabbed a napkin from the dispenser at the end of the table. "Married?" She wiped the grease from her fingers. "Please. After what Roy did to me, do you actually think I would turn around and do that to another woman? You know me better than that."

Aislinn slumped against the red pleather seat. "I'm sorry. You're right. Forget I asked. That question was more to do with me than you." A few years back, Aislinn had fallen for a married man. Nothing had happened between them, but she'd been totally nuts for the guy and miserable over it. "Of course, you would never get involved with a married guy."

"Damn right I wouldn't—and you didn't either, so stop beating yourself up about it." Keely picked up the piece of fish again. They ate in silence for a few minutes.

But Aislinn hadn't given up. "Come on. Tell me. Who *is* this guy you're seeing?"

"I *can't* tell you. Not right now."

"Why?"

"It's all new, you know? We just want to be private. That's all. For now." Did that sound lame? Yeah. Maybe. A little.

And Aislinn wasn't buying it. "Okay, I get that you don't want to wander down the street talking about the guy to complete strangers. But you can tell *me*."

"Aislinn, come on. What I will say is that I'm crazy about him and he's terrific. He's steady and good. And totally hot."

"Steady?"

"Well, yeah."

"But you never go for the steady ones."

"Hey. Give me some credit. I'm thirty years old. About time I grew up and fell for a responsible, trust-worthy human being for once."

Aislinn's eyebrows had scrunched together. "I know him, right? If I didn't know him, why not just tell me who he is?"

"Ais, stop. I told you I can't say—"

"Wait." Aislinn picked up a french fry, studied it as though for clues and then bit it in half. "Really, with the kids and the commissions and the gallery, you don't have *time* for a man." Now she was sounding way too much like Gretchen.

Keely tried to look stern. "I can see I shouldn't have told you anything."

"Get outta town." Aislinn plunked her half-eaten french fry back in the basket, leaned forward and peered hard at Keely as though she couldn't believe what she saw. "No." She sat back again.

"No, what?"

"No, it can't be."

"What are you babbling about? Will you chill?"

Aislinn stared at her piercingly and accused, "It's Daniel, isn't it?"

Keely barely escaped choking on the bite of fish. She swallowed hard and washed it down with a big gulp of cold tea before launching into a stammered denial. "No. Uh-uh. I don't, um… No. Not Daniel. Absolutely not."

Aislinn so wasn't buying it. "Uh-huh. Daniel. Has to be. Makes total sense. You're around each other all the time. You *live* together. And I can see how you two would be good for each other. You can help him lighten up a little. And for once, you've found a guy with both feet on the ground, a guy you can actually count on. I mean, it was probably bound to happen, if you think about it."

"What? No. Wrong—I mean, not necessarily."

Aislinn laughed. "You are blushing. It's so cute. Cop to it. It has to be Daniel. You're all alone in that big house together every night after the twins are in bed. And you told me at the gallery a week and a half ago how *great* he is." Keely opened her mouth to spout more denials, but Aislinn just shook her head. "Don't lie to me, Keel. It will only hurt my feelings, and I won't believe you anyway."

Keely let her shoulders slump. "I don't *want* to lie to you."

"Hey." Aislinn reached across the table. Keely stared at her outstretched hand. "C'mon." Aislinn wiggled her fingers. "Gimme." With a giant sigh, Keely reached back. They laced their fingers together, palms touching. As they stared at each other, Keely felt acceptance settle over her, that her best friend had figured it out, that it wasn't a *bad* thing, that Aislinn knew her so well—far from it. Keely was grateful to have such a good friend. After a long moment of mutual silence, Aislinn asked softly, "You really like my big brother?"

"I do. I really do."

"Well, all right then." One corner of Aislinn's mouth kicked up in a half smile. "Let's finish our fish." They focused on the food until Aislinn glanced up again. "He *is* a good guy."

Keely nodded. "The best."

"Too bad he's got that poker up his butt."

"Stop!" Keely slapped at her friend with her napkin.

"Hey. It's only the truth. Maybe with you, he can relax, enjoy life a little."

"It's all really new, Ais. We're kind of feeling our way along as we go."

"I just want you to be happy. Both of you."

"Thank you—and I really don't want anyone else to know."

"Keely, I promise you. Nobody's going to hear a thing about it from me."

As soon as the kids were in bed that night, Daniel did what he'd been waiting all day to do. He took Keely's hand and led her down the hall. In his room, he shoved the door shut with his foot and reached for her.

Her happy laughter filled his head as she kissed him. He walked her backward toward the bed. But before they got there, she pushed him into the bedside chair.

He caught her hand. "There is no escaping me." With a tug, he pulled her down across his lap. She laughed again and wrapped her arms around his neck. He couldn't get over how right it felt—the two of them, together. After too many years of just doing what he had to do, he had something really good to come home to at night. He had Keely.

And that was pretty damned amazing.

He nuzzled her neck and breathed in the perfect scent of her skin. She was wearing way too many clothes, though. And she didn't need that big clip holding her hair off her neck. He undid it and set it on the bedside table. Her hair drifted down in soft waves to her shoulders.

"I like this new color," he whispered, combing his fingers through the red-gold strands.

"It's pretty close to my natural color."

"I know. And it suits you." He caught her chin on his finger and guided her closer for a kiss, claiming that mouth he couldn't seem to get enough of. She tasted as good as she smelled.

When the kiss ended, she rested her head on his shoulder. "I had lunch with Aislinn today."

Something off in her tone alerted him. "She okay?"

"She's fine. But she, um, knows about you and me."

Aislinn knows.

It wasn't anger he felt, exactly. More like frustration. He wanted this thing with Keely to be just theirs, for the two of them alone and no one else. The family owned him. It was all about them and had been ever since he was eighteen years old.

With Keely, for the first time in forever, he felt free. He didn't want the family butting into that, bringing demands, making judgments, feeling cheated or disapproving that he was crazy for Lillie's little cousin and wanted to spend every moment he could with her.

He just wanted to come in this room with her and have the world disappear. At least for a while, he wanted her all to himself, wanted everyone to leave them the hell alone.

She pressed two soft fingers to the space between his eyebrows. "You're scowling at me."

He took care to keep his voice level when he answered her. "I thought we agreed that, for now, we won't tell the family."

She hunched her shoulders, put her hands between her knees and chewed her lower lip a little. "I didn't tell her. She figured it out." He wasn't sure what to say to that, so he didn't say anything. Keely chided, "Aislinn's not only your sister—she's my best friend, Daniel. She knew there was someone, and she guessed it had to be you. And I just couldn't outright lie to her. So I didn't. She promised to keep our confidence. I believe her."

He really couldn't blame her for breaking their agreement. He *didn't* blame her. She and Aislinn were tight. "Okay, then."

"What does that mean?"

"It means I see your point." He traced the line of her hair where it fell along her cheek. "You can't go telling lies to your best friend. Aislinn *is* someone who keeps her word, so she's not going to say anything. And I'm being completely selfish anyway. I want you all to myself."

She looked at him then, that mouth he couldn't get enough of kissing soft and pliant, eyes so bright. "I kind of feel the same. Like this should be *our* time, just you and me. Most people get a little space to get to know each other when they start something together. The families don't enter into it until things get serious."

Serious.

To him, this *was* serious. He didn't really know how to be any other way.

"There's something else," she said.

"You're frowning." He pulled her closer, kissed her cheek, nuzzled the tender corner of her delicious mouth. "Whatever it is, it can't be all that bad."

"It's not. Not really. But I didn't tell you yesterday, and it's been bothering me. I took the kids to see Gretchen."

"You mentioned that."

"Yeah, but what I didn't say was that she got after me to let her take over again with Jake and Frannie. She even said she felt guilty, that she was taking advantage of me."

He had to order his arms not to lock tight around her.

No one was taking her away from him, not Gretchen. Not anybody.

But she *had* been taking care of his children for weeks now. It had to be getting old. So really, Gretchen had a point. He made himself ask, "Maybe it's getting to be too much for you?"

That got him an eye roll. "Of course not. I love it here. I love the kids. I'm getting everything done that needs doing, with my work and at the gallery. It's all going great for me."

Suddenly, he could breathe again. But was he being unfair to her? "You're sure?"

She turned a little, caught his face between her hands and kissed him quick and hard. "Yes, I am sure."

"Well, all right then." He caught her hand, opened her fingers and pressed his mouth to the soft center of her palm.

But when he looked up, a frown still crinkled her forehead. "There's more. It wasn't only that Gretchen said she worried about taking advantage of me. She also started talking about how she knew I wanted my own family. She asked how I thought I was going to accomplish that while taking care of your kids and living in your house. I don't know. I couldn't help wondering if she suspects that we're together and she doesn't like it."

"She's pretty outspoken. If she knew, I think she would say so."

"You're right. It was just odd, that's all. Think about it. You and I get together. We decide to keep what we have to ourselves, to have a little time just for us—and suddenly Gretchen, who asked me to take care of the kids in the first place, thinks I should be moving on."

He hated what he knew he had to say next. "Okay.

Maybe we're handling this all wrong. Maybe we're just going to have to be up-front about what's going on between us after all. Let anyone who's going to get weird about it go ahead and have at it. Then we can move on from there."

Her gorgeous smile bloomed wide. "I love that you said that. But you know what? I just don't want to do that. Not yet. Do you?"

"Hell, no," he replied with feeling.

"Well, then. It's decided. We'll go on as planned—for a while, at least. And we'll reevaluate as necessary." She snuggled close again.

"Deal." He rested his cheek against her hair and felt way too relieved they weren't immediately inviting the family into the middle of their business.

She fiddled with the top button of his shirt, her head tucked nice and close, over his heart. "This weekend should be interesting…"

It was Easter weekend. Grace would be home Friday. And Sunday, they were planning the kids' first egg hunt, with a big family dinner in the afternoon.

Keely tipped her head back to meet his eyes. "I'm assuming you don't want to tell Grace about us yet?"

"Please no," he answered fervently. "If we tell her, she's way too likely to blab to everyone. Or get mad at me."

"Why would she get mad at you?"

"As if she needs a reason. One way or another, Grace always ends up pissed off at me."

Her soft mouth twitched. A definite tell. She wanted to lecture him but didn't know how it would go over. "Grace is young and she wants to be free, and to her it seems like you're the one holding her back."

"I *am* holding her back. She doesn't need to be free until she's at least forty—preferably fifty."

Keely gaped. And then she giggled. "Daniel. You actually do have a sense of humor."

He put a finger to his lips. "Do not tell a soul. I have a certain image to uphold."

"You mean the one where they all think you're crabby and uncompromising?"

"And narrow-minded and controlling—oh, and did I mention I never crack a smile?"

That had her grinning. "What in the world do I see in you?"

"I'm handy around the house, good with babies and amazing in bed."

Her cheeks got pinker. He loved to watch her blush. "True." She nodded. "On all counts. And we're agreed that we're not telling Grace yet?"

"We are agreed, yes."

She slipped his top shirt button from its hole. Finally. "You know that means I won't be staying all night with you while she's here? We'll have to be careful or she'll find out, whether we're ready for that or not." She undid the second button.

"That does it." He took her hand and guided it down to button number three. "I changed my mind. We're telling Grace."

"No, we're not." Button number three gave way, and four and five, as well. "We deserve our privacy for as long as we want to keep what we have just between us. And it's only for Friday and Saturday. She goes back to Portland Sunday." She undid the last button. "At which time we can go back to being secret lovers in a full-time kind of way." She sat up enough to work the shirt off his shoulders.

"I don't know. Waking up without you…" He took her red knit top by the hem and pulled it up. "I don't think I can do that." She raised her arms so he could pull it off over her head. Underneath, she wore a pretty pink bra. He made short work of that, undoing the hooks at the back and tossing it aside. Her breasts were so beautiful. He cradled them, felt her hard little nipples pressing into his palms. She moaned—and jumped off his lap. "Get back here," he commanded.

"So bossy…" But she did come back, swinging one slim thigh across him, straddling him, so his growing hardness pressed right where he most wanted to be— well, except that her jeans and his jeans and two sets of underwear barred the way. He cradled her breasts again. "Oh, Daniel…" She was suddenly breathless. He loved that about her, when she got breathless and wanting, when she looked at him through heavy-lidded eyes the way she was doing now. He rolled those pretty nipples between his thumbs and forefingers, and she let her head drop back, all that glorious red-gold hair tumbling down behind her. "Daniel…"

"Yeah?"

"Um. What were we talking about?"

"Not a clue," he said rough and low, sliding his hands to her waist, lifting her as he stood and setting her on her feet long enough to get rid of her jeans and her panties, her shoes and socks.

He *had* to kiss her. As much of her as possible. Gathering her close again, he pressed his lips in the center of the five freckles on her left shoulder that seemed to him to make the points of a star. He scraped his teeth along her collarbone, licked his way up the center of her throat, over her strong little chin until he reached that plump mouth of hers. She opened for him on a happy sigh.

But only for one too-brief moment. And then she was dropping away from him, folding to her knees in front of him.

She had his jeans undone and down around his ankles in seconds. The woman amazed him. How could he have thought he knew her for all these years and years?

He'd known so little.

And she was so much more.

He put his hands in her shining hair, holding on for dear life as she took him inside that warm, wet mouth of hers. All the way in, right down her smooth throat. How did she do that?

Not that he cared how. What mattered was that she was here, in his room, with him. What mattered was that touching him, kissing him, taking him inside herself, driving him crazy with want and need, seemed to please her every bit as much as it pleased him.

It was too much in a very good way, what she did to him. He didn't last very long. His mind shattered along with his body, into a thousand happy, smiling pieces.

He forgot about everything—all the bits of his life and his family's lives that he was responsible for. He let it all fade away, the million and one little things he had to keep a constant eye on so that no new disaster could strike those he loved.

With her, he could just let go. With her, at last, he knew what it felt like to be free.

Chapter Seven

Grace arrived on Friday at ten in the morning.

She burst into the kitchen where Keely had the kids in their high chairs for a morning snack.

"Munchkins, I am home!" Cheeks pink and white-blond hair windblown, Grace dropped her giant shoulder bag and overstuffed pack to the floor.

The twins beat on their tray tables in glee at the sight of her. "Gwace! Gwace! Kiss, kiss!"

She went to them for hugs and sticky kisses. Then she turned to Keely. "Oh, look! It's my favorite nanny." She whipped Keely's sketchbook and colored pencil right out of her hands and plunked them on the table.

"Hey!" Keely laughed in protest. But Grace only pulled her out of her chair and waltzed her once around the kitchen, not letting her go until they were back at Keely's chair again.

"God. I'm starved," Grace announced as she knelt to give Maisey a good scratch and a hug.

Keely picked up her sketchbook and pencil and reclaimed her seat at the table. "You want breakfast?"

"Had that, thanks."

"There's tuna salad in the fridge."

"Dave's Killer Bread?"

"Got that, too."

"I love you, Keely. You have all the right answers to the most important questions." Grace got busy gathering what she needed for a fat tuna sandwich, including Tillamook cheddar slices, tomatoes, lettuce and dill pickles. "Old Stone Face at work?"

"Yep."

"How you holding up watching the little darlings day after day?"

"So far, spectacular."

Grace popped a hunk of pickle into her mouth. "I can't believe you're still here, that you've yet to run screaming into the night."

Keely chuckled as she added shading to the mountains in the background of the wide, green field she was sketching, the artist in her hard at work planning how she might create a similar, but more striking effect with fabric and thread. "What can I tell you? I have zero complaints—how's school?"

Grace launched into a monologue about the co-op she lived in, how much she loved studying Shakespeare's relevance to the modern world and how the guy she'd met last Saturday might be driving up to party with her and her friends this weekend.

By the time she finished her sandwich, scooped up her stuff and disappeared into her room, the kids were getting restless in their high chairs. Keely wiped their gooey hands and faces, and took them and Maisey outside for a while.

When she came back in, Grace had emerged from her room. She offered to watch the kids. Keely took her up on it. Promising to return by two, she grabbed her purse and headed out to check in with Amanda at Sand & Sea.

She left the gallery at one and swung by Gretchen's. Keely's aunt was baking like a madwoman in preparation for the family get-together Sunday. Ingrid was nowhere in sight.

Gretchen waved a flour-dusted hand. "She's off at that bar. Have you been by there?"

"No. I keep meaning to stop in."

"Well, go anytime. Your mother will be there. Not that I'm complaining. We get along best, your mom and me, if we're not around each other too much—and have you given any more thought to what we talked about the other day?"

"If you mean my finding someone else to watch the twins—"

"That is exactly what I mean—have a cookie, sweetheart."

Keely took one. They were chocolate with chocolate chips. "Amazing. I think I gained ten pounds just from this first bite."

"You look great. You can afford a cookie or two—and I do still want you to think about letting me fill in with them at least some of the time."

"What did we already decide? You get the go-ahead from your doctor, then yes. I would love a few hours off every once in a while."

Gretchen released a long, drawn-out sigh. "I do worry about you, honey. You deserve a break now and then."

"I have plenty of time to myself."

"Not enough. I'm going to have to talk to Daniel about it."

That did it. Keely knew she had to speak up. "Auntie G, don't you dare."

Gretchen sent her a wounded look, her pink mouth drawn down. "You don't have to snap at me. I have your best interests at heart."

Keely took her aunt by the shoulders and turned her around so she could look her squarely in the eye. "You and I both know how Daniel is."

Gretchen wiped her hands on her apron. "What do you mean?"

"He takes on everybody else's burdens. And that means he has plenty to deal with. He doesn't need you whispering in his ear about how I want him to find someone else for the kids. It isn't true, and it will only worry him. That's just not right."

"I would hardly be whispering," Gretchen muttered. Then she sniffed and lifted her round chin. "I only want what's best for you."

Keely's heart seemed to expand in her chest. It was an ache, but a good kind of ache. "Auntie G…" She wrapped her arms around Gretchen. "I know you do."

Gretchen sniffed again. "You're going to get flour all over that pretty sweater of yours."

"I don't care." She pulled back enough to give her aunt a smile. "And you have to let it be. *I'm* the one who gets to decide what's best for me. And I mean it when I say that I'm enjoying myself with Frannie and Jake. I will have no problem telling you and Daniel when and if I've had enough."

"But...you're happy? You mean that?"

"Yes. I'm very happy with the way things are right now, and I have no plans to make a change."

They made it halfway through dinner that night before Daniel and Grace got into it.

It was the same thing they always fought over. Grace wanted to go out with her friends, and Daniel wanted her to stay in.

"Gracie," he said, and Keely tried to take heart that at least he spoke in a mild tone. "You just got here. We've missed you. It's not going to kill you to stay home to-night."

Grace let out an exaggerated groan. "God. You drive me insane. I've *been* home all day, and I haven't seen Erin or Carrie in weeks. Plus, there's this guy I met in Portland. He and a couple of his friends are driving up, meeting us at Beach Street Brews." The brewpub on Beach Street served local craft beers.

"What guy?" Daniel's voice had gone distinctly growly.

Grace blew out an angry breath through her nose. "His name is Jared Riley. He goes to Reed. I like him, all right? Daniel, come on. He's a great guy and he's driving all the way up here and I'm looking forward to seeing him. And Erin. And Carrie. Okay?"

"I just think—"

"Don't." Grace leaped to her feet. The twins startled in unison at her sudden move. "Just don't. I do not want to hear it." And with that, she shoved back her chair, whirled on her heel and ran across the kitchen, straight to her room, slamming the door good and hard when she got there.

The slammed door scared Frannie. She burst into tears. Jake saw his twin crying and let out a yowl.

Keely and Daniel rose as one. She took Jake. Daniel took Frannie. They both delivered soothing reassurances and comforting hugs until the kids stopped fussing and were ready to go back into their high chairs.

Daniel returned to his seat. Keely stayed right where she was. He didn't notice she'd remained on her feet until he'd picked up his fork again.

"Okay." His fork clattered back to his plate. "What?"

"I've got to say something." She took extra care to make her voice even and drama-free. "You need to give this up, Daniel."

"Give what up?"

As if he didn't know. "This…overprotectiveness with Grace."

"I'm not—"

"Could you just not go straight to denial, please?" Keely waited to make sure he was listening. After he'd glared at her for a solid ten seconds, she continued, "Yes, you *are* overprotective. I get that it's for all the right reasons and you love her and you want her safe. I get that she's the last of your brothers and sisters to strike out on her own and that even if you can't wait for that to happen, you're still going to miss her when she goes."

"I—"

"Uh-uh. Not finished."

He took a long drink of water. "Right. Wrap it up."

"Thank you," she said and tried to mean it. "I get that you want to protect her, that you feel it's your job to keep her safe. But then again, she *is* twenty-one. She sets her own hours and takes care of business just fine while she's in Portland. The first thing she did when she arrived today was offer to watch the kids so I could run errands. It's not right that you still treat her like a child when she comes home."

"I don't…" That time he caught himself in middenial. He drank more water as Jake let out a string of nonsense syllables. Daniel set down his glass—and surrendered in a growl. "All right. I'll talk to her after dinner."

"Wonderful." Keely sank to her chair. As she smoothed her napkin on her lap, she heard a door open. Grace appeared, unsmiling but composed. She returned to the table and sat down again.

"I'm sorry I lost my temper, Daniel," she said. "I promised myself I would stop doing that."

"Ahem," Daniel said stiffly. "I came on pretty strong. Apology accepted."

"Thanks." Grace sat up straighter. "And I *am* going out after dinner."

Daniel scowled. Keely braced for him to start barking orders again. Instead, slowly and carefully, he cut a bite of pork roast. "Just be safe," he muttered, adding with great effort, "and…have a good time."

Grace left at a little after eight. By eight thirty the kids were in bed, and Keely enjoyed a glorious few hours in Daniel's bed.

He caught her arm when she tried to get up to go at a quarter of midnight. "Stay. I don't like it here without you. Grace probably won't come in until after two, and there's no reason she'll come up here when she does."

"Uh-uh. Either we tell her or we don't. Setting ourselves up to get caught is just beyond tacky. She doesn't need that and neither do we."

"Sometimes you're too damn reasonable," he grumbled.

She chuckled and cuddled in close, just for a minute more, nuzzling his broad chest with its perfect light dusting of gold hair and that wonderful happy trail she wished she could stick around and follow to her favorite destination. Again.

He tipped up her chin and kissed her. She savored the moment. And then, with a playful shove, she rolled away from him and out from under the covers.

He braced up an elbow and watched her pull on her jeans and shirt. His eyes, silvery in the lamplight, sent shivers down the backs of her knees.

"Don't look at me like that," she chided.

"Like what?"

"Like you're thinking about all the naughty things you're going to do to my body."

"But I *am* thinking of all the things I want to do to your body. Come on back here. Let me show you."

Somehow, she made her bare feet carry her to the door. "Night," she whispered as she slipped from the room.

Her bed felt huge and empty with just her in it. It took her a long while to get sleep. She wondered if she and Daniel were doing the right thing to make a secret of what they had together. And she marveled that everything about what she had with him felt so good and real and right. As though they were perfectly suited, each to the other. As though this was a love affair that would never wear itself out.

Saturday night Grace went out again. Keely and

Daniel stole some precious time alone. She left him at midnight for her too-empty bed, where she lay awake again, missing him, though he was just down the hall—missing him and hoping that this thing between them would never have to end.

Was she being ridiculous? They'd only been lovers for a week.

Didn't matter.

She knew her own heart, knew she was falling. Falling hard.

And scary-deep.

Easter morning, Gretchen and Ingrid arrived at ten thirty with a big basket full of old-school dyed eggs, a cake and a few dozen cookies, plus an array of side dishes to go with the prime rib roast Keely would serve for the main course.

Keely and Daniel helped the sisters bring everything in from the car as Keely tried not to let nerves get the better of her. She dreaded that her mother might start in about the "smokin' hot" chemistry between her and Daniel.

But Ingrid never uttered a single embarrassing word or cast Keely so much as a meaningful smirk. She must have actually meant what she'd said last Sunday night—that what went on between Keely and Daniel was nobody's business but their own.

Gretchen kept the kids entertained while Ingrid, Daniel and Keely hid the eggs out in the foggy backyard.

Aislinn arrived with a salad at eleven, about the same time Grace emerged, sleepy-eyed in pajamas and a giant floppy sweater. Outside, the fog had thinned a little.

Grace poured herself a mug of coffee and followed the rest of them out back.

At first, Frannie and Jake seemed unsure of the whole egg-hunting concept. Ingrid and Gretchen led them around pointing out the bright eggs, many of them in plain sight. And the twins would look up at their grandma and great-aunt, their faces simultaneously curious and confused.

But eventually, they seemed to catch on, laughing and holding up their prizes as they found them. The hunt went on for over an hour, mostly because the twins tended to get distracted. They would plunk down on the grass and put their fingers in their mouths until Gretchen or Ingrid got them up and moving again. By noon, they'd started fussing. Keely took them inside for a little lunch and a nap, leaving Aislinn and Grace to gather the rest of the eggs.

More Bravos arrived. Harper and Hailey, who shared Aislinn's rambling beach cottage with her when they were home, hadn't made the three-hour-drive back to Valentine Bay for the holiday, but Daniel's brothers, Matthias, Connor and Liam, appeared. There was also a great-aunt and uncle, the eccentric brother-and-sister duo, Daffodil and Percy Valentine. The two were the last of the Valentines, the founding family for which Valentine Bay had been named. Neither Aunt Daffy nor Uncle Percy had ever married, and they both still lived in the house where they'd been born. A slightly crumbly Italianate Queen-Anne Victorian, Valentine House sat on a prime piece of real estate at the edge of Valentine City Park. Aunt Daffy kept a beautiful garden, and Uncle Percy considered himself a genealogist as well as something of an amateur detective.

At two, when they all sat down at the long table in the dining room, Keely felt wonderfully relaxed and happy. All her life, she'd dreamed of a big family around her. This, now, today? It felt a lot like her dream come true.

Gretchen said grace. When the soft *amens* echoed around the table, Keely couldn't help but look to Daniel first. He gave her the most beautiful, private, tender smile. She glanced away quickly, so no one would see.

That evening, Grace returned to Portland and Keely slept again in Daniel's bed.

By Wednesday, Keely had been on the pill for a full week. After they put the kids to bed that night, she and Daniel had the contraceptive talk. He'd only been with Lillie and Keely. And she'd been tested after she broke up with her last boyfriend two years ago. They agreed it would be safe to go without condoms.

But then Daniel shook his head. "I would just feel better if we used both." He looked kind of sad when he said it.

And she understood. After Lillie's betrayal, Daniel was unlikely to trust his partner to take responsibility for contraception. They continued to use condoms, which was totally fine with her.

The next week, at the very end of April, Daniel left for Southern Oregon to meet with timber owners near the California border and to look in on several jobs in progress along the way. It started out as a two-day trip, but there were issues at one of the mills and with a few employees in key positions on two current jobs. Two days stretched to three and then four.

Gretchen insisted she was well enough to help out with the kids, and she did seem to be walking just fine without even a cane. She came every day and stayed for three or four hours, giving Keely a break to work in her studio or stop in at Sand & Sea. On the fourth day, Ingrid pitched in, too, so that Keely could concentrate on getting everything ready for a new show opening at the gallery on Friday.

With her aunt and mom helping out, Keely had no trouble keeping on track workwise. The nights were lonely, though. She missed the delicious, perfect pleasure of Daniel's big hands on her body, not to mention the addictive wonder of his kiss and the feel of his muscled body, so warm and solid, right there beside her as she slept.

And yes, she spent her solitary nights in his bed. Somehow, it wasn't quite as lonely in his room as in hers down the hall.

Thursday night he called to say he wouldn't be home until Saturday. They talked for two hours—about his work and hers, about Frannie and Jake, about how well it was going for her because she had Gretchen and Ingrid taking up the slack.

"I want to take you out," he said. "Find out what night Jeanine's available, and then I'll make dinner reservations. There's this great place in Astoria…"

Astoria. Because as long as they were keeping their true relationship from the family, they'd be safer to take date night somewhere out of town. Same as he had with the woman he'd met on Tinder—and yes, she knew that what she had with him was so much more than a hookup.

They really needed to talk about coming out to the family. The secrecy was starting to wear on her nerves.

"Miss you," he said gruffly as they were ending the call.

I love you. The three little words filled up her mind and created a sensation of radiating warmth in the center of her chest. But she didn't say them out loud. A first *I love you* should not be said on the phone.

"Miss you, too," she replied. "See you Saturday..."

She felt the absence on the line as he hung up and she wanted to cry, of all the self-indulgent reactions. He would be home in two days. It was nothing to cry over. She grabbed his pillow from his side of the bed and pressed her face into it. It still smelled faintly of him, kind of piney and fresh.

With a groan, she tipped her head toward the ceiling. "Get ahold of yourself," she commanded out loud, tucking the pillow behind her head and dropping onto her back, feeling mopey and bereft and achy all over.

Hormones? Not likely. She was on the pill now. Her periods on the pill tended to be regular and pretty much mood-swing, bloat- and pain-free.

And it wasn't her placebo week anyway. There were two more weeks to go until her mild, pill-controlled period was even due.

She ordered herself to stop being a big baby and put all thoughts of weird hormone swings from her mind.

Friday, she ran around like a madwoman, handling the hundred and one final details before the new gallery show. It was all worth it, though. The opening went off beautifully.

Saturday, Daniel came home while she and Gretchen were out in the backyard with the twins. Gretchen hung around until dinnertime and then stayed to eat.

Which meant that at seven thirty that night, when Gretchen finally left, Keely still hadn't felt Daniel's big arms around her or enjoyed the taste of his mouth on hers.

They all—Daniel, Keely and the twins—stood at the front door, waving as Gretchen drove away.

The twins loved to wave goodbye. It was, "Bye-bye, Gwamma! Wove you!" from Frannie.

And "Bye-bye, bye-bye!" from Jake.

As Gretchen's enormous silver Escalade sailed off down the driveway, Daniel shut the door. "For a while there I was scared to death she planned to stay the night." Every inch of Keely's skin seemed to spark and flare at the way he looked at her—like she was everything, like he couldn't wait to get her alone and take off all her clothes.

"Baf!" demanded Frannie.

"Baf now!" Jake concurred.

Which was great. Wonderful. The sooner the twins had their baths, the sooner they could all go to bed— Jake and Frannie, to sleep.

Daniel and Keely, to make up for lost time.

They all went upstairs together and straight to the big bathroom. The kids were out of their clothes and into the tub in record time.

"I can't stand it," Daniel muttered.

"What?" Keely sent him a worried glance as he rose from the side of the tub, grabbing Keely's arm and pulling her up with him. "Not having you in my arms."

He hauled her close and kissed her forever, melting her heart and incinerating her lady parts, while Frannie and Jake laughed and splashed and demanded kisses of their own.

A great moment, Keely thought, one that almost made up for not being free to run to his arms that afternoon, when he'd first stepped out on the back deck to tell them he was home.

With obvious reluctance, he let her go. The kids finished in the tub. Daniel and Keely dried them, diapered them and put on their pj's.

The twins were pros at the pulling of heartstrings. As soon as they had their pajamas on, they wiggled and squirmed, demanding, "Dow! Now!"

Once on their feet, they ran to the bookcase, each returning with a stack of favorite kids' stories.

Daniel sat in the rocker, one child on either arm, and read them four stories.

Finally, by the end of *Goodnight, Goodnight, Construction Site*, the twins could hold out no longer. They slept in that endearing way little kids do, heads hanging like wilting flowers on a stem, lower lips sticking out, drooling just a little down their pajama fronts.

"We have to go ahead and tell them, tell the family," Keely said breathlessly ten minutes later.

They were in Daniel's room by then, with the door shut at last. He'd already whipped her shirt up over her head and taken away her bra and was in the process of pushing her denim skirt to the floor, her panties along with it. She kicked off her shoes and she was naked.

"God, I missed you." He grabbed her close.

She wanted to get closer. He helped by picking her right up off the floor so that she could wrap her legs around him. He braced her against the door and kissed her until she feared her lips might fall off. And oh, she could feel him, so hard and ready, pressed against her so intimately, but with his pants and boxer briefs in the way.

She wanted him naked, too.

But she *needed* him to listen to her first. She really did have a point, and she was going to make it.

Fisting her hands in his hair, she yanked that amazing mouth of his away from her. "Listen." She tried to glare at him in a purposeful manner, but she knew her cheeks were flushed and her eyes low and lazy. Even her breathing betrayed her. It came in ragged, hungry little gulps. "I mean it."

"You're so beautiful. I need to kiss you. Kiss you all over. Come back here…"

Somehow, she managed *not* to give in to him. She kept that tight grip on his hair and turned her lips away so he couldn't take them. "When are you going to be ready to tell the family about us?"

"Soon," he said, and a strangled groan escaped him. And well, how could she resist that, when he groaned that way, as though it would kill him stone-dead not to have his hands and mouth all over her?

"Daniel," she moaned. And that did it. He claimed her lips again. And oh, she had missed him, and they had a lot of lovemaking they needed to catch up on. Days' worth, seriously.

She was practically love starved. They needed to get busy making up for lost time.

With another moan, she pressed her mouth to his.

Incendiary, that kiss, a hot tangle of breath and seeking tongues. It went on forever as she unbuttoned his shirt and pushed it off his shoulders. He had a white T-shirt on underneath, darn it. She wanted him closer, needed skin on skin.

Grabbing a fistful of T-shirt on either side of him, she scraped it upward. He let her down to the floor again so she could drag the shirt off over his head.

"There now. Better." She sighed as she pressed her hands to his broad, hot chest, gliding them upward to clasp behind his neck. She dragged that mouth of his down to hers again.

They kissed some more—endlessly, gloriously—as she went to work on his belt and his pants.

Finally they were naked—except for his socks. Luckily, socks had no bearing on what she was after.

He lifted her again. Neither of them could wait. He slid right into her, right there against the door.

Heaven. Paradise. Her arms around him, holding him tight, joined with him at last.

He groaned, broke their never-ending kiss and pressed his forehead to hers. "Forgot…"

She remembered, too, then. "The condom."

"I shouldn't have…" He let that thought trail off. Another low groan escaped him. "Keely. You feel so good." He kissed her chin, the side of her throat. "It should be okay." He kissed the words onto her skin. "Right?"

She was on the pill. Of course, it should be fine.

"Okay?" he asked again—well, more like pleaded, really.

She took him by his square jaw. "Yes." And she kissed him, kissed him so deep as he moved within her. "Missed you," she whispered against his mouth.

"Keely. Me, too. I missed you so much…"

And then all actual words were lost to them. They rocked together, with her wrapped tight around him. They rocked and swayed in perfect rhythm.

Nothing else mattered then. Except that he was holding her, so close, so perfectly.

Her climax came spinning at her, rolling like a river

of heat and wonder, down her spine to the core of her where she held him, rocked him, home with her at last.

Alone together, Keely and Daniel.

Right where they belonged.

Chapter Eight

The days went by.

Full days. Happy ones.

Friday night Jeanine came to babysit, and Daniel took Keely to dinner in Astoria. The meal was lovely. He ordered a nice Oregon Pinot Noir. Her stomach had been acting up on and off for the past few days, so she didn't have more than a sip or two. Daniel teased her about being a lightweight and she shrugged and agreed with him.

After dinner, they strolled the Riverwalk, holding hands like lovers do, watching the big boats out on the majestic Columbia, even wandering out onto the East Mooring Basin boat ramp to get a look at the lazy sea lions that had taken over the docks there. It was wonderful.

They didn't get home until after midnight. They

thanked Jeanine and sent her on her way, then went upstairs hand in hand, to check on the kids, who slept like little angels, feathery eyelashes fanned across their plump cheeks.

An hour later, tucked up nice and cozy together in his big bed in the dark, Keely said, "I want to tell the family that we're a couple. I know it will probably be awkward. But, Daniel, we really need to do it."

Daniel agreed with her. "We *will* do it. Soon." He went on, "Sometimes it feels like all my life, I've never had anything that was just mine. Everything's about the family, and it has been since I was eighteen. You and me, here, now, in this room with the door closed? It's just us, Keely. You and me and no one else. I'm jealous of that. Protective of that."

She captured his hand under the covers and wove her fingers with his. "It's only that I'm getting tired of lying, you know?"

"We're not lying. We're just…not sharing."

She laughed at that and then she warned, "Before you know it, Grace will be home for the summer and living in this house with us. If we're not telling her, we'll have to start sneaking around again. No more waking up together every morning."

He kissed the tip of her nose. "We've got two weeks till then. Don't rush me, woman." With a low growl, he pulled her closer and bit her lightly on the chin. "Give me a kiss."

She laughed again and kissed him and that led where kissing him usually went—to more kisses and endless caresses and a satisfying ending for both of them.

Later, as she held him close and listened to his breathing even out into sleep, she decided that she would stop pushing him to tell the family about the two of them. He wasn't ready yet, and she needed to give him time. She would leave the subject alone until he brought it up.

She grinned to herself in the darkness. He just needed the proper motivation. Once Grace got home and he got a taste of sleeping alone again, she had a feeling he'd see telling the family in a whole new light.

The following Saturday, they went out again. Jeanine wasn't available that night. But they got someone else from the nanny service instead. Daniel took her to a great seafood place in Cannon Beach. She watched his beloved face across the table from her as they waited for their food. He looked relaxed. Happy.

She was happy, too—except she was in her placebo week on the pill now and her period hadn't come. It didn't mean anything. It would probably come tomorrow or the next day. She felt kind of puffy and crampy and that was a good sign that everything was on schedule.

Except that she'd never got preperiod cramping when on the pill in the past.

She just wanted to tell him about her silly worries. Just open her mouth and say it. *My period's a couple of days late and I'm a little concerned about that...*

He probably wouldn't look all that happy then.

No. Uh-uh. Not doing that.

She would wait. Her period would come. If it didn't come, she would buy a test and take it before she brought it up to him. Then she could joke about it. *Guess what? I had a pregnancy scare! Isn't that hysterical?*

She had a feeling he wouldn't find even a scare all that humorous. He loved his kids, but they hadn't been his idea. Not by a long shot. He'd wanted a little freedom at last now his brothers and sisters were grown. But Lillie had got pregnant anyway—and then lost her life for it. The poor guy had some serious baggage around having babies.

That she might have to tell him they had another baby on the way?

Uh-uh. That fell squarely into the category of things she very much did not want to do.

And why was she fixating on this? She wasn't pregnant. She was a few days late, that was all.

Thursday, her period still hadn't put in an appearance.

At eleven, her mom came over to watch the twins for her.

Ingrid took one look at her and demanded, "Okay. What's wrong?"

"Wrong?" There was nothing wrong. Okay, yeah, she was maybe obsessing over the possibility that she might be pregnant. Just a little. But how in the world could her mother sense that? She stared at Ingrid's high green ponytail and deep purple bangs. "I'm fine. A little tired, I guess."

"You're lying. I can tell. I always could."

"No, I am not lying," she lied.

"Yeah, you are. But you don't want to talk, I get that. When you do, I'm ready to listen. You know that, right?"

"I do, Mom. And I'm grateful."

Ingrid fiddled with her bangs. "You like the purple and green?"

"I do. Purple and green works for you."

"Gretch hates it." Ingrid chuckled.

"And that means you love it even more, right?"

"No, I love it because it looks super bad in a very

good way. Gretch hating it is just a little extra bonus that makes me smile."

"I do not understand your relationship with Auntie G."

"And there's absolutely no reason you have to understand, so don't worry about it." Jake toddled over and held up his ragged stuffed bunny. Ingrid scooped him into her arms. "You are the handsomest little man, Jakey."

"Kiss my wabbit." Ingrid kissed the ugly stuffed toy on its matted face.

Keely bent to pet Maisey, who was always following her around. "Okay, I'm outta here." She picked up Frannie, planted a kiss on her cheek and set her back down. "Bye, Frannie-Annie."

"Bye, Keewee. Wove you."

"Back by three," Keely promised.

"No rush," said her mother as she bent to let Jake down.

Keely ran errands, including a quick trip to Safeway, where she bought three pregnancy tests.

No, she did not think she might be pregnant. But if her period didn't come by the weekend, she would take the tests just to prove to herself there was nothing to worry about. She bought three because it never hurt to triple-check, and if the first test came up positive, triple-checking was exactly what she planned to do.

So what if false positives were extremely rare? Negative or positive, she would test and test again, just to be sure.

At lunchtime, Keely sat across from Aislinn at Fisherman's Korner and longed to tell her best friend everything.

But she just couldn't, not about this.

Daniel was Ais's brother after all. Once he knew—*if* it turned out there was anything *to* know—then she could confide in Aislinn. Until then, laying her crazy worries about possibly, *maybe* being pregnant on Daniel's sister felt beyond unacceptable.

Keely had been kind of afraid that Aislinn, like Ingrid, would know she had something on her mind.

But Ais seemed distracted. And Keely was the one who ended up asking, "What's wrong?"

"It's that weird old Martin Durand. Remember, I told you about him?"

"I remember." Durand owned a horse ranch, the Wild River Ranch, inland on the Youngs River. Aislinn had worked there as a stable hand one summer, back when she was still in college.

"He called me—Martin Durand did—this morning, at Deever and Gray." That was the law firm she worked for. "I had no idea the old guy even knew I had a job there. I mean, I've seen him like twice since that summer I worked for Jaxon at the ranch." According to Aislinn, Jaxon Winter, the nephew of Durand's deceased wife, had been responsible for the actual running of the ranch for years. Jaxon also just happened to be the married man Aislinn had fallen so hard for once.

"What did Durand want?"

"He said, 'Hello, Aislinn. This is Martin Durand. Jaxon's divorce is final, in case somehow you didn't know.'"

"Jaxon Winter got divorced?"

"Yeah. Over a year ago."

"You already knew?"

"So?"

"Well, I just thought—"

"Keel. I told you. There was nothing between us. It was all in my mind—now, is it okay with you if I tell you the rest?"

"You don't have to get mad at me."

Aislinn huffed out a breath. "You're right. I'm sorry. I'm just freaked about that call and overreacting is all."

Keely reached across the table of their booth to clasp Aislinn's arm in reassurance. "It's okay. What else did he say?"

"He laughed. Like Jaxon's marriage not working out is funny, somehow. And he said, 'It's been final for a year, Aislinn Bravo. Just in case you might not have heard.' He put this weird emphasis on *Bravo*. 'Aislinn *Bravo*,' he says, like I'm living under an assumed name or something. I mean, that's creepy, right?"

"So Martin Durand knew that you had a thing for Jaxon Winter?"

Ais flinched. "I guess so, but I don't have a clue how he knew. Keely. I swear to you. I mean, it was five years ago. Jax was *married*. Nothing happened."

"Of course it didn't."

"I worked for him for eight weeks one summer. That's it. Once the job was over, Jax never called me. And I never called him. Yeah, I really, um, liked him. I got the feeling maybe he liked me, too, but I think I just wanted to think that, because of how I felt. When I heard he got divorced, it just seemed better to leave it alone—and what business is it of Martin Durand's anyway?"

"It's not his business, not in the least." Keely wiped her greasy fingers on her napkin.

"I hardly knew that old man, never exchanged more than a few words with him. But he always used to look at me funny—kind of like he was keeping an eye on me, you know, waiting for me to sneak in the house and steal the silverware or something? And I swear, he let poor Jax do all the work. Old Mr. Durand would get up at noon and sit on the front porch of the main house in his bathrobe. One of the other hands told me that Jax is his heir because Durand and his wife never had kids of their own and the ranch belonged to Mrs. Durand in the first place and Jax was *her* nephew, so at least Jax gets something eventually."

"I'm happy to hear that. And you know, maybe the old guy was just trying to help out."

"Help out how?" Aislinn demanded, scowling.

"Whoa." Keely patted the air between them. "Back it up. I mean, maybe he was kind of playing cupid a little."

"When he called today, you mean? Ew."

"Hey. I'm just trying to look on the bright side here."

"There is no bright side. That old man is scary." Ais set down her tea glass harder than she needed to. "And I do not feel *helped* by him, let me tell you."

Keely said gently, "You're acting like a guilty person, and you know there is nothing at all for you to feel guilty about."

Aislinn had hold of her straw now. She poked the ice chunks in her glass. "I do feel guilty."

They'd been speaking quietly, but now Keely lowered her voice even more. "I know you didn't do anything, Ais. Stop beating yourself up."

"He was *married*. My heart just didn't care. I felt… I don't know, like he was meant to be mine. And so I really, really *wanted* to do something."

"But you didn't. That's what counts. And is that—

your guilt, I mean—why you've never followed up with him now that he's free?"

"Excuse me, but he's never followed up with me either. And there's no reason that he would. There really was nothing between us. It was all in my mind."

"You do get that you're trying way too hard to convince yourself of that?"

"Look. Like I said, it's just better this way."

"But, Ais, you're not acting like it's better."

Aislinn opened her mouth as if to speak—and then drank more tea instead.

Keely dared to suggest, "Just call him."

"I'll think about it—and can we change the subject? Please?"

They talked about Keely's next show at the gallery, which opened in mid-June. They discussed how Aislinn was really getting tired of Deever and Gray, news that was no surprise to Keely. It always went that way with Aislinn and a new job. She loved it at first, when it was all new and she had lots to learn. Once she'd mastered the work, though, she got bored and started wanting a change.

Aislinn said how happy she was that Keely and Daniel were together and when would that stop being a secret?

"Soon, I hope," said Keely.

"He's holding off, right? He wants you all to himself."

It was pretty much what Daniel had said. "How did you know that?"

"He's my brother and you're my best friend. You think I can't see that you're wild for each other? You're the best thing that's ever happened to him, and he doesn't want anyone else butting in."

Keely didn't know how to feel. There was the unlikely pregnancy she couldn't stop obsessing over. And all the family members Daniel didn't want to tell. But still, Aislinn's joy in what Keely had with Daniel was a definite spirit lifter. "We're that obvious? No one else seems to have figured out what we're up to."

"It's only obvious to me. I mean, I did finally get you to admit he's the one. So when I see you together, I already know what's going on. And it looks to me like what's going on is very, very good."

Keely thought of Lillie, of how much Lillie and Daniel had loved each other once. And now Lillie was gone forever...

Suddenly Keely's spirits weren't so lifted anymore.

"What?" demanded Aislinn. "And on second thought, you don't have to say it. I get it. Lillie, right?"

"How did you know that?"

Aislinn shrugged, as if to say "How could I not?" "He did love her. A lot. But they were so young to have so much piled on their shoulders. They were sort of married by necessity. It's not the same as you and Daniel. You're older now, both of you. You've each been married already, and you can choose each other with your eyes wide-open."

"Are you saying you think Lillie was the wrong choice for him?"

"No. Absolutely not. I'm saying that what you have with him takes nothing away from what he once had with her. It's two different things. You have to see that, Keel. Accept it. Let yourself be happy with the man that you love."

Keely felt her face go hot. She pressed her hands to her cheeks in a failed attempt to cool them. "I never said the word *love*. You know I didn't."

"Doesn't matter what you said or didn't say. You *are* in love with my brother, and he's in love with you. I think that's terrific, so I do not get why you're all tied in knots about it."

Again, Keely couldn't help longing to tell Aislinn about the might-be baby. But no. Not yet. "You just... never know how things will work out, that's all."

Aislinn scoffed at her. "Is that supposed to be news? Stop worrying about what could just possibly, *maybe* go wrong and enjoy everything that is clearly going so right."

"I'll do that."

"Ha!"

Keely pointed her last french fry at her friend. "As for you, Ms. Bravo. Pick up the phone and give Jaxon Winter a call."

Aislinn glanced away. "I'll think about it."

Keely knew she wouldn't, and that made her sad all over again.

Back at Daniel's an hour later, Keely left the three pregnancy tests in the car until after her mother had gone.

Then she dithered for a while about where to put them. She ended up sticking them in the empty suitcase under the bed in the room where she never slept, ready in case she needed them.

Which, of course, she would not.

Her period did not show up that day, or the next.

On the day after that, Saturday, Grace arrived home for the summer. She put her things away in her room, helped with the twins and pitched in to fix dinner.

When they all sat down to eat, Grace said, "I'm leaving at seven. Carrie's picking both Erin and me up. I can't wait to see them."

Keely caught Daniel's eye and gave him a minuscule shake of her head before he could even think about objecting. He did take the hint about Grace going out—but he just had to ask, "Any luck on the job front yet?"

Grace pushed a string bean around on her plate. "I'm working on it."

"I can put you to work at the front desk, answering the phones—and we can use a clerk in Payables and Receivables."

Grace left the string bean alone and went to work poking at a bite of oven-browned potato. "Thanks, Daniel. I have something I'm working on, though, a job I think would really be fun and interesting."

"What job is that?"

"I'm going to need a few days to see if it pans out, okay?"

"Some reason you don't want to tell me about it?"

"Daniel." Grace set down her fork. "I want to work it out for myself. And *then* I'll tell you about it."

"Summer doesn't last forever," he warned in a ridiculously dire tone. He was close enough that Keely could have given him a good, sharp kick under the table. But she'd interfered enough. He and Grace needed to figure out ways to get along without Keely constantly stepping in to referee.

"Just give me till Monday." Grace ate the bite of potato she'd been torturing.

"Till Monday. And then what?"

"If I can't make it happen by Monday, Valentine Logging, here I come."

* * *

Daniel made a point not to say anything critical to Grace through the rest of the meal.

He knew Keely had it right, that he was being overbearing and too protective, and he needed to give his baby sister her freedom as an adult. He had to let her make her own choices. Still, it got him all itchy and pissed off that he couldn't just make the right decisions for her.

The end of her school year had kind of crept up on him. He wasn't ready for it, for Grace to be home all the time. And not only because he worried she would end up wasting her summer sitting around the house and hanging out with her friends.

There was also what he had with Keely. With Grace living in the house, they either needed to tell her that they were together or sneak around.

Sneaking around wasn't something he approved of. It showed a certain lack of integrity. Sneaking around had seemed excusable back at Easter, when he and Keely had just found each other and Grace was only home for three days.

But now?

No. Now, sneaking around was cheap. Unacceptable.

He and Keely hadn't said the words yet. But he meant to say them, and soon. She was *his* in the deepest way. He wanted what they had to continue. Forever, if possible.

And to get forever with her, he was going to have to get honest, not only with Grace, but with the rest of the family, too. Keely was more than ready for that. She'd pushed him repeatedly to come out with the family—though she seemed to have given up on that lately.

He didn't know if he liked that, her giving up. Yeah,

he'd felt pressured when she kept after him about it. But her pushing meant she saw them as a couple, as two people with a future together. Her giving up could mean any number of things, some of them not good.

No, he didn't want the family in their business. But the family *was* their business.

So there wasn't a choice in the matter, not really. Telling the family had to be done.

He waited until Grace left and they'd put the kids to bed.

Then he took Keely to his room, shut the door and backed her up against it for a long, sweet kiss. When they came up for air, he caught her hand and led her to the bed. "Okay, I've been thinking." He pulled her down beside him.

She gave him the side-eye. "This sounds ominous."

He might as well just come out with it. "We need to tell the family about us."

"Finally." She laughed. He loved her laugh. It was an open laugh, musical and free. However, he wasn't all that sure he cared for it right at that particular moment.

He turned her hand over, smoothed her fingers open, then curled them shut again. "You do still want to tell them then?"

"You thought I didn't?"

"Well, you stopped pushing for it."

"Daniel." She turned her body toward him so she was fully facing him. "Pushing wasn't exactly getting me anywhere."

"Hey." He wrapped his arm around her, pulled her close and pressed his lips to the smooth, cool skin of her forehead. "I'm an ass."

She glanced up at him, that mouth he never tired of

kissing curling in a hint of a smile. "On occasion, you are most definitely an ass." Before he could act insulted that she'd agreed with him, she went on, "But you're still the best man I know—and you're mine." She whispered that last part, and his heart beat a faster, triumphant rhythm.

"Yeah. As you are mine." It felt so good to say it. He wanted to say more. *I love you, Keely.* The words sounded damn fine in his head. But was it too soon for that?

He lost his chance to go big when she added, "So yeah. We need to get honest with them. It's Gretchen and Grace I'm most concerned about."

"I agree. Aislinn already knows. Your mother made her position on the subject very clear that first Sunday she came to dinner. My brothers and Harper and Hailey have their own lives."

"Exactly." She rested her head on his shoulder. "I think they'll all just be happy for us. And really, Grace should be fine, too, as long as we're up-front with her."

He stroked her hair, rubbed his hand down her arm. Touching her soothed him. Plus, he was reluctant to put it right out there about his mother-in-law. It had to be said, though. "So, it's Gretchen we're talking about really. She's the one who might not be happy to learn we're together."

She nodded against his shoulder. "It's hard to say how she's going to react. Yeah, Lillie's gone forever and you're single now. But you and me together…"

"There are just too many ways Gretchen could see that as a disloyalty to Lillie's memory," he finished for her. "Too many ways it could stir up all the loss and the grief for her all over again."

Daniel hadn't forgotten how bad it had been for

Gretchen when they lost Lillie. His mother-in-law had tried to put on a brave face, but for almost a year, she'd rarely smiled. And she didn't bake a single cookie for thirteen months. That had freaked him out the most. For Gretchen, baking was an act of joy and love. He'd never felt so relieved as the day she showed up at the house to watch the twins with a smile on her face and a big plastic container full of butter pecan sandies.

"We have to tell her, Daniel. We should tell her first of all, privately, just Auntie G and you and me. Then Grace. And then the rest of them, which shouldn't be a big deal. I'll tell my mom, and however you want to tell your other brothers and sisters, that's fine with me."

"Agreed." Still, he dreaded it. He would miss having her all to himself. He knew he was being an idiot. She'd just called him *hers*. No way she was going anywhere. But he felt anxious and jumpy nonetheless. "So, as for telling Gretchen. When?"

"As soon as possible."

"Tomorrow then?"

"No. Tomorrow she'll have all kinds of church stuff going on. Monday night is bingo night at the senior center and Tuesday she plays bridge. How 'bout this? I'll call her, ask her to watch the kids Wednesday, in the afternoon. Then I'll suggest that she can just stay for dinner. We'll tell her then."

"But what about Grace? Chances are, she'll be here for dinner on Wednesday, too."

"We'll work it out, wing it, you know? Get Grace to take the kids upstairs after we eat and tell Gretchen then, maybe. Then once Auntie G knows, we can just tell Grace that night."

He swore under his breath. "Isn't this getting way too complicated?"

"Maybe. But I really think we need to tell Auntie G first. No matter how she reacts, she'll at least know we came to her specifically, that we love and respect her as Lillie's mom and your mother-in-law and the woman who has always treated me as a daughter."

"Okay. Wednesday. We'll try for that."

"In the meantime, we have to be careful. I really don't want Grace to find out by accident, to see me sneaking out of your room or to knock on the door when I'm in here in bed with you. It could upset her, not only because we didn't trust her enough to tell her what's going on, but also because of the problems between the two of you. You're the classic overprotective big brother, and yet you're fooling around with the nanny behind everyone's back."

Okay, that was kind of insulting—to both of them. "I'm not fooling around with the nanny, I'm fooling around with *you*."

She dimpled. How could she be so damned adorable while simultaneously pissing him off? "I think you just made my point for me."

He was getting a headache. "Keely. You can't control everything."

"Says the man who won't let his grown-up baby sister go out on Saturday night."

"I did let her go. I'm working on that. And why would Grace come wandering up here at night out of the blue? We're taking care of the twins, the two of us. She doesn't have the baby monitor in her room anymore. There's no reason for her to come upstairs."

Keely leveled those green eyes on him and chided,

"She lives here, Daniel. There's no reason for her *not* to be upstairs whenever she feels like it. I just think it's better if we don't sneak around, period."

Okay, he truly did not like where this was going. "You mean, we're not sleeping together until after we tell Gretchen and Grace that we *are* together?"

Now her eyes widened, kind of pleading with him. But her soft mouth was set. "I really think it's the best thing to do, the *right* thing to do."

He didn't. He thought it was crap. "I get that you won't spend the night with me until all this is settled. But for a few hours after the kids are in bed, we could at least—"

She cut him off with a shake of her shining red-blond head. "It's only until Wednesday. It's not like we'll die from four nights apart."

"Four nights?" He scowled at her. "You mean tonight, too? Come on. Grace won't be home till late. We have hours yet."

She pressed her cool, smooth hand to the side of his face. "I just want to do this the best way, the *right* way..."

"I don't like it." The nights with her were everything. He didn't want to lose a single one. Fate was a real bitch sometimes. You never knew what might happen. A man needed to grab what he wanted and hold on good and tight.

"Oh, Daniel." She kissed him then, a lingering kiss that only served to remind him of all the reasons he needed her here with him—tonight, and every night.

"Don't go."

Gently, she pushed him away. "I think we're doing the right thing."

"But—"

She stopped him with a finger to his lips. "Good night, Daniel." And then she was up and out the door before he could convince her how much he needed her to stay.

Silently, Keely shut the door to the master suite and tiptoed along the upstairs hall to her own room.

Four nights without his big arms around her. She could do that. She'd already done it while he was traveling at the end of last month. *Only* four nights. And then she wouldn't have to leave Daniel in the middle of the night again—not that she *had* to leave him, she reminded herself. She was choosing to leave him in order that Grace would have less chance of finding out they were together until they were ready for her to know.

And really. Did Daniel have it right? Was she making this whole thing way too complicated?

Uh-uh. No. This was the right way to handle it. For everyone—especially Gretchen, who'd already suffered way more than enough. Telling Gretchen first was the right thing to do. And until they told Gretchen, nobody else should know, not even by accident.

In her room, Keely took a long bath to relax. It didn't help much. She ended up lying there alone in the dark, trying not to think about what waited for her in the suitcase under the bed.

The last couple of days, her breasts had felt swollen and sensitive. Her stomach continued to be just a little bit queasy.

The signs were there and her placebo week was over without a period to show for it. But really, she just wasn't ready to know for sure.

And no way was she ready to tell Daniel. She would

get through telling Auntie G that she and Daniel were together. After that, she would need to stop being a big fat chicken and pull that suitcase out from under the bed.

Chapter Nine

In the morning, Keely came downstairs to find Daniel at the breakfast table and the kids in their high chairs.

"Sleep well?" he asked, and she felt the knot of tension in her belly unwind. He didn't seem mad or even annoyed at the way she'd left him last night.

"Grace?" she asked, with a glance toward the short hall that led to his sister's room.

"Still sleeping is my guess."

Keely couldn't resist. She needed the contact. She stepped close and bent down to him. They shared a quick kiss. "Missed you," she whispered.

The tender look he gave her made everything right.

She poured herself a scant cup of coffee. For the past week, she'd been allowing herself one small cup a day just on the off chance that she might actually be pregnant. Setting her coffee on the table, she grabbed her phone and autodialed her aunt.

Gretchen answered on the first ring. "Sweetheart. I'm just on my way out the door to catch the early service."

"I won't keep you, but I was hoping maybe you could come over Wednesday around two and watch the kids for a couple of hours."

"Happy to."

"You're a lifesaver. And how about staying for dinner, as long as you're here?"

"I would love it."

They chatted for a couple of minutes more and then said goodbye.

"We're set," Keely said to Daniel as she hung up the phone.

"Good." He caught her hand and pressed his wonderful lips to the back of it as Jake let out a string of nonsense words and Frannie shoved a fistful of Cheerios into her mouth.

Keely bent close to give him one more quick kiss. She'd barely brushed her lips against his when Grace emerged from her bedroom in sleep shorts and a giant Reed College T-shirt.

Her heart lurching into overdrive and her stomach performing a scary pitch and roll, Keely pulled out the nearest empty chair and dropped into it.

Had they just been busted?

Grace went straight to the coffeepot and poured herself a cup. When she turned, she sipped her coffee and announced, "Brace yourselves. It's happened." Her slight grin turned to a full-on smile. "I've found my summer job."

Keely's heart slowed to a more sedate rhythm, and she breathed a careful sigh. Grace hadn't seen a thing.

"Good news," said Daniel, and he even put on one of his low-key Daniel-style smiles. "Where are you working?"

"At the Sea Breeze." She beamed at Keely. "I had an interview with your mom set for tomorrow, but she was out at Beach Street Brews last night, sitting in with the band they had playing. We started talking between sets, and she said of course I had a job with her if I wanted it. I start tomorrow. Nine to five, Monday through Friday until she opens for business."

"Terrific." Keely got up again and gave her a congratulatory hug.

Grace laughed. "I think it's going be fun. Your mom's the best."

Daniel asked, "What *is* the job, exactly?"

Grace picked up her coffee again. "A little bit of everything. Light construction, helping plan and set up for the grand opening, and playing general all-around gofer for now. Then I'll be a waitress when the place opens in July."

Daniel had that stern look he got when he was about to tell someone something they probably didn't want to hear. Grace's smile fell. But at the last possible second, he must have remembered that he was supposed to be letting her run her own life. All he said was "Sounds good."

Grace's face lit up again. "I think so. Ingrid's paying me twelve an hour to start." She tipped her chin higher, as though still anticipating some sort of criticism. When Daniel only nodded, she went on, "I'll make more when we open. I'll work nights then. Tips should be good."

"Gwace!" Jake made a bid for his favorite aunt's attention. "Hey there!"

"Hey there, Jakey." She went to him and kissed him on his puckered little mouth. "How's my favorite boy?"

"I goo." He offered her a Cheerio.

She took it and popped it in her mouth. "Delicious. Thank you."

Jake jabbered out something that was probably meant to be "You're welcome."

Keely watched the interaction with a giant grin on her face. She wanted to jump up and kiss Daniel for working so hard to let his sister go. Right now, though, she needed to keep a serious lid on the PDAs. She settled for sending him a quick secret glance of love and approval, feeling a little glow inside herself that Grace had a job she wanted for the summer and Daniel had let her go about finding it in her own way.

Daniel felt good about things with Grace—at least he did for the rest of the day.

But their hard-won peace didn't last. After dinner, Keely took the kids upstairs, and he and Grace cleaned up after the meal. Once that was done, his sister vanished into her room. He went to his study off the front hall to check email on his desktop before heading upstairs to help with the baths and the bedtime stories.

He'd left the study door open or he wouldn't have caught Grace on her way out the front door.

Okay, he should have just let her go. Keely would want him to let Grace have her freedom, and Keely was probably right.

But he was out of his chair and calling, "Grace!"

before he could remind himself that he had to let his little sister make her own mistakes.

"What now?" She let go of the door handle and turned on him. In a skimpy metallic top, tight jeans and red high-heeled sandals, she had to be headed for another party night. "Erin's waiting out in front for me."

He felt he had to say something. "Doesn't your job start tomorrow?"

Grace flipped her hair back over her shoulder and braced her hands on her hips. "Rhetorical question much? Yes, Daniel. My job starts tomorrow."

"Well, it seems to me that it would be smarter for you to stay home tonight and get a good night's sleep, that's all." He put a lot of effort into sounding more helpful than critical.

Too bad Grace did not seem the least grateful for his wise advice. "I told you. Erin's waiting."

"Don't you want to be rested for your first day of work?"

"God. Listen to yourself. You're like some old mother hen."

"Grace. Come on. I'm just trying to—"

"Stop." She showed him the hand. "I'm going. Please don't worry. I won't stay out late, and I'll be on time for work tomorrow."

"I think this is unwise."

"I know you do. I'm going. Good night, Daniel." She pulled open the door and went through it before he could muster another objection.

Once she was gone, he stood rooted to the spot, listening to the sound of voices out in front, of a car door opening and shutting, and then the engine revving as Erin drove away. He scrubbed his hands down his face, rubbed the tension knots at the back of his neck and re-turned to his study long enough to shut down his desktop and turn off the light.

Upstairs, Keely had the kids in the tub.

He leaned in the doorway and watched her with them as they splashed her and giggled and played with their tub toys. She was something amazing, all right. With her bright smiles and her easy ways, juggling the kids, her gallery, her mom, her aunt and those quilt things she made. And somehow finding time to fill his nights with magic, too. With her, it was all worth it again, to get up in the morning and go to work every day. To come home to the demands of a whole new family. He could do that, even enjoy that.

As long as she was there, too.

And they were young yet, really, he and Keely. The kids were almost two. Another sixteen years or so and they would head off to college. He and Keely would have the whole house to themselves. They could go where they wanted when they wanted without having to consider who would watch the kids. It was a long time off, but it wasn't forever.

And in the meantime, well, he didn't mind things just as they were—or as they would be, come Wednesday night.

Until then, he'd be miserable sleeping without her. It was his own damn fault, though, and he owned that. He'd been the one who put off telling the family about them.

But as of last night, when she left him to sleep alone, he damn well couldn't wait to break the big news to Gretchen. However that went off, at least once it was over, nobody and nothing could keep him and Keely apart.

"Da-Da!" cried Frannie, holding up a red rubber monkey. She gave it a squeeze and it squeaked at him.

He entered the room, skirted Maisey, who was stretched out on the floor a few feet from the tub, and knelt beside Keely.

She leaned his way and butted him with her shoulder. "Did I hear you and Grace downstairs just now?"

"Yeah," he confessed.

"Are you trying to avoid admitting that once again, you failed to keep your mouth shut?"

"We got into it. She went out with Erin anyway."

"Da-Da!" Now Jake had the monkey. He squeaked it several times in succession. Daniel stuck out a hand and tickled his round little belly. Crowing in delight, Jake splashed wildly, flinging water at Daniel, getting Keely wet, too.

Keely laughed. "Look at it this way. You made your point with her, right?"

"I spoke my mind, yeah."

"Perfect. You made your point, and she did what she wanted to do. It's a win all the way around."

Screw keeping his hands off her. Nobody here but the four of them anyway—five, counting Maisey. He yanked her close and kissed her while the twins screeched, "Kiss! Da-Da! Keewee!" and splashed water everywhere.

Later, after they'd tucked the kids in, Daniel managed to steal a few more kisses.

But when he tried to coax her into his room, she balked and shook her head. "Tonight and two more nights. Then I am yours—but right now, I'm going to get a little work done in my studio."

Reluctantly, he left her to it.

He went to bed alone and couldn't sleep, missing

Keely beside him, hoping Grace was exercising good judgment while staying out way too late.

At 2:46 a.m., he heard her come in. Relieved in spite of his aggravation with her, he turned over and shut his eyes.

In the morning, Grace joined them in the kitchen at a little before eight. She had dark circles under her eyes and a scowl on her pretty face.

He knew that he needed to keep his damn mouth shut. The words got out anyway. "Looking kind of ragged there, sunshine."

She pointed a finger at him. "Just don't start. I'm not in the mood."

Keely said unnecessarily, "Coffee's ready."

With one last dirty look in his direction, Grace headed for the coffeepot.

He had to know. "You still going to work?"

Grace took her time filling her cup. She turned to him slowly, enjoying a long sip before grumbling at him, "Of course I'm going to work. I'm looking forward to this job and I take my responsibilities seriously."

When he left for the office, Grace was still taking her sweet time getting ready in the downstairs bathroom. With his sister occupied behind a shut door, Keely allowed him a quick kiss as he was leaving.

He said, "Call me if she decides to stay home."

For that, she gave his shoulder a playful slap. "Not on your life."

"Nobody does what I tell them to around here."

Keely only smiled sweetly and pushed him out the door.

Keely felt relief when Grace emerged from the bathroom dressed in old jeans, a chambray shirt and a worn pair of black Converse, her hair pinned up out of the way. "Your mom said to wear comfortable clothes, that there might be painting to do today. You think this is all right?"

"As long as you don't mind getting paint on anything, it's perfect."

Grace leaned close. "Has the ogre left the building?"

"Your brother is gone for the day, yes."

"He's such a—"

"Uh-uh." Keely put up a hand. "Don't go there." She pressed her hand to Grace's smooth cheek. "Have a great first day of work." Grace had the strangest look on her face. "What? You okay?"

She seemed to shake herself. "Yeah, sure. I'll take overtime if Ingrid offers it, so don't count on me for dinner."

"No problem. There will be plenty of leftovers to heat up if you have to work late."

"You're the best." Grace gave her a quick hug and headed for the inside door to the garage.

She'd been gone about half a minute when Frannie, on the floor with Jake a few feet away, let out a wail.

Jake had grabbed a stuffed giraffe from her. Keely moderated the dispute, reminding Jake to share and offering him his favorite ratty rabbit in exchange for Frannie's toy. A few minutes later, they were playing as happily as ever together.

Daniel called at ten. Keely reported that, yes, Grace had gone to work on time, and then she said goodbye quickly, annoyed with him for promising to back off his sister and then calling Keely to check up on her.

At eleven, she fed the twins. At one, she put them in their cribs for a nap.

And then, before she could invent more pathetic excuses not to face the truth, she marched into her bedroom and pulled the suitcase out from under the bed.

She took two of the three tests. They both told her what she already knew.

As for when to tell Daniel, she was finished stalling. Tonight, as soon as the kids were in bed, she would break the news that they were having a baby.

She was dropping the second test wand into her bathroom wastebasket when the doorbell rang downstairs.

Quickly, in hopes that whoever it was wouldn't have time to ring again and increase the likelihood of waking the twins, she rushed out into the upper hall and ran down the stairs. Through the etched glass on the top of the door, she could see who it was.

Gretchen. Keely recognized her by the set of her plump shoulders and the halo of carefully arranged blond hair around her head.

But she couldn't see her aunt's expression until she pulled the door wide-open. "Keely. Hello." She looked… irritated, maybe? Her eyebrows were pinched together, her mouth all pursed up.

"Gretchen? Are you all ri—"

Her aunt cut her off. "May I come in?"

"Of course." Keely stepped back. "Come on to the kitchen." She gestured toward the arch that led to the back of the house.

"The babies?"

"Napping at the moment—and it's warm out. How about something cold to drink?"

"No, it's fine. Daniel's at work?"

"Yes."

"It's just us?"

"That's right."

"Good. We need to talk." Gretchen turned and headed for the kitchen. Keely just stood there and stared after her, wondering what in the world was going on. Her aunt paused just past the arch to the living room and aimed an impatient glance over her shoulder. "Well? Are you coming?"

"Sure." Keely hurried to catch up. In the kitchen, she gestured at the table. "Have a seat. I can make some—"

"No. Nothing. Really." Gretchen went and stood by the island. Not sure what to do next, Keely followed her over there. Her aunt stared at her for a long, very uncomfortable string of seconds before announcing, "I just feel I have to say something. It's about Grace."

"Grace?" Keely's stomach lurched. "Is she all right?"

Gretchen wrung her hands, blinked and looked down at them. Shaking her head, she smoothed the ruffles on the front of her shirt and tugged on the side seams of her A-line skirt. "She's making things up. That's what she's doing. Hurtful lies."

Dread crept over Keely, like a cold fog on a dark night. "What lies?"

"Well, I just dropped in at the Sea Breeze to see how things were going. And there was Grace, painting the wood trim on the door to the restroom hallway. She said Ingrid had run out for more paint but would be back soon. I decided to wait and we started chatting, Grace and I. And then, out of nowhere, she asks me if I know about you and Daniel."

Keely blinked. There was a sudden buzzing sound in her ears. She put her hand on her stomach and prayed that everything in there wasn't on the verge of coming up. "What about me and Daniel?"

As if she didn't know.

Dear, sweet Lord, this was the exact wrong way for Gretchen to find out that she and Daniel were a couple. It was supposed to be done on Wednesday, done kindly, with love and respect.

We never should have kept the secret in the first place, said an accusatory voice in the back of her head.

But they had. And now came the part where they got to live with their bad choices.

"Grace said she saw you and Daniel kissing, right here in this kitchen, yesterday morning." Her aunt touched her then. She reached out and gently squeezed her shoulder. All Keely could do was stare. "Sweetheart. Don't look so crushed."

"I'm not, I—"

"Because of course, I don't believe a word of it. I just really felt that you should know that Grace is, well, she's spreading tales about you. It's a problem, a big one. She has all these…issues with Daniel, though the good Lord knows why. He's been a saint, we all know that. With Grace, with *all* of his brothers and sisters. He and my Lillie, what they did to keep that family together…"

"Auntie G—"

"No. Wait. I haven't finished. I ask you, where would Grace be if not for Lillie and Daniel? She could have ended up in foster care. Anything might have happened. I just don't understand what has got into her, to speak so disrespectfully about Daniel. About *you*. It's an outrage and—"

"Auntie G." Keely took her arm. "Come on. Please. Sit down." Gretchen allowed Keely to lead her to the table, pull out a chair for her and ease her down into it. "Now, how about some ice water?"

"I—yes. All right. Ice water. Good."

By rote, Keely went through the motions of getting down a glass, adding crushed ice from the dispenser, filling it the rest of the way with water, all the while knowing the moment for exactly what it was.

The moment of truth. All her careful plans to break the news to Gretchen just so, after a nice dinner, in a gentle, reasonable way?

Right out the kitchen window.

It was happening now, like it or not. With Auntie G already upset and saying cruel things about poor Grace. It was happening without Daniel here, with no time to prepare.

"Here you go," she said to her aunt.

"Thank you, honey." Gretchen took the glass and had a long drink. "It's only… I suppose I'm overreacting. But that girl has no right to speak of you and Daniel that way."

Keely pulled out the next chair over and lowered herself into it. Where to start?

The answer was painfully simple.

Start with the truth. Nothing would make the news go down easy for Gretchen. And looking at her aunt's red face, Keely doubted that it would have gone much better on Wednesday night.

Better to just say it straight-out. "Auntie G, I'm sorry if this upsets you. But Grace wasn't lying. She did see me kissing Daniel yesterday morning."

Gretchen set down her glass. "What are you…?" She forced out a tight little laugh. "Oh. I understand. An innocent, friendly kiss that Grace has blown all out of proportion then?"

Keely's heart seemed to bounce off the walls of her

chest. It was beating so hard. "No. Grace saw what she said she saw. I kissed Daniel. It was a real kiss."

"A real...?" Gretchen scoffed. "Sweetheart, you can't be serious."

"Yes. Yes, I am. Daniel and I have...feelings for each other. We're in a relationship, Auntie G."

Gretchen's flushed face went white. "No."

"Yes. We should have told you sooner. I'm so sorry that you had to find out in this way."

"Sorry." Gretchen spit the word.

"Yes. We...we didn't know how things would work out at first, so we kept our feelings to ourselves. But then, well, we do want to be together. So we were going to tell you Wednesday."

"Sorry," Gretchen repeated, as if she hadn't heard a word of what Keely had just said. "You're *sorry*." She slapped the table hard enough that her glass bounced. "How could you, Keely? After everything, after all the years, all that I've done for you. All *Lillie* did. We *loved* you. Like a daughter. Like a sister. We took you in, gave you a real home, provided the stability my sister never gave you, the settled family life you always longed for."

Keely's heart no longer felt like it would burst out of her chest with its frantic beating. Now it felt heavy as lead, aching. And out of that ache, she felt fury rising, adrenaline spurting. Hurtful words to match Gretchen's rose to her lips. It took all the will she had to swallow those words down, to try to speak reasonably. "Auntie G—"

"No."

"Please don't—"

"I don't want to hear your ridiculous, unacceptable excuses. I will not accept your apology. You are supposed to be *helping* here, not taking advantage of poor

Daniel's loneliness, sneaking around behind everyone's backs. I tried, you know I did, to talk you into letting me take over again. I tried weeks ago, at Easter. But no. You were too *happy* here. You just wouldn't go. And now I know why, don't I? Now I know what you have been up to. It's unacceptable, Keely. Unforgiveable and so cruel."

Keely's carefully banked fury tried to spike again. "You really should hear yourself. You're telling me you *plotted* to keep Daniel and me apart."

Gretchen blinked several times in rapid succession. "Plotted? There was no plotting. How could I plot? I had no idea what you were up to. I was only trying to take the pressure off you—and you wouldn't let me because you were having a secret affair with my son-in-law." Gretchen's eyes had glazed over with tears. "How dare you?" she demanded. "How *could* you?"

Keely said nothing. She let the last of her own defensive fury sputter and die. Now she felt only sadness as she waited to be sure her aunt had finally run out of steam.

"Well?" Gretchen swiped away tears, hitched up her chin and glared.

Keely asked, just to be certain, "Are you finished?"

"I... What? What in the world can you possibly have to say for yourself?"

"Well, first of all, you're wrong."

"Wrong? No. No, I have it right and you know that I do."

"No, you do not. I'm sorry this hurts you, but most of what you just said? All wrong. You say 'secret affair' as though Daniel and I are cheating on Lillie somehow. You haven't accepted yet that Daniel is a single man now. You need to do that. You need to accept in your heart that Lillie is truly gone from this world. We loved her. We lost her. And our lives have to move on."

"Excuses," insisted Gretchen, looking down at the table, shaking her head. "These are flimsy, cowardly excuses you are giving me."

"No. That's not true. Daniel loved Lillie very much and would never have betrayed her. Neither would I. You know me, Auntie G. And you know very well I never would have done such a thing. But Lillie really is dead, and Daniel and I are both single adults with every right to find a little comfort in each other."

"Comfort," Gretchen uttered the word as though it disgusted her. "That's not what I would call it." She shoved back her chair, her face starting to crumple all over again. "And I...I cannot stay here one minute longer. I can't... I just... I really do have to go." And with that, she was turning, striding out of the kitchen toward the front of the house.

Keely just sat there, staring at Gretchen's half-finished glass of water until she heard the sound of the front door closing hard.

That did it.

Her stomach went beyond merely roiling. It completely rebelled.

Leaping up, she ran for the downstairs half bath, making it just in time to drop to her knees and throw back the toilet seat before everything came up.

Chapter Ten

Once the vomiting had finally stopped, Keely wandered upstairs to brush her teeth and check on the twins. Maisey, who'd been napping in Keely's studio room, wanted to go outside. Keely took her down and let her out into the backyard. Then she went upstairs again and stretched out on her bed. Maybe a nap would help.

But within five minutes, she knew she would only lie there and stew over the absolutely rotten things Gretchen had said. She got up again, went back downstairs and let Maisey in. The dog stretched out on the kitchen floor as Keely put some crackers on a plate and poured herself a ginger ale.

As she was resolutely chewing a saltine, Grace came running in from the garage all spattered in paint, with red-rimmed eyes. "Keely! Are you…okay?"

Maisey looked up with a worried whine. Keely only shrugged and finished her saltine.

Grace darted over and stood at the table, clutching the back of a chair. "She was here, wasn't she—Gretchen?"

"Yeah." Keely took a careful sip of her ginger ale. "She was here."

"Oh, God." Grace burst into tears.

Keely couldn't bear to see her so miserable. "Hey. Come on…" She got up, went around the table and gathered Grace close.

"Oh, Keely…" Grace hugged her hard—for a moment. And then she pulled away. Her nose was red and tears streamed down her face. "Gretchen said she was coming straight over here. I should have stopped her. I should've kept my damn mouth shut."

"Hold on." Keely went to the island, grabbed the tissue box she kept there and brought it back to Grace, who blew her nose and swiped at her eyes. "I'm so sorry. Oh, Keely. I hate myself. I…" She let out a moan. "I should have talked to you or Daniel—well, not Daniel. Every time I talk to Daniel, I just want to scream. But I *can* talk to you. And I *didn't* talk to you…"

"So you did see me kiss him yesterday morning?"

Grace yanked out the chair, collapsed into it and whipped another tissue from the box. "I did. And I pretended I didn't because… Well, I don't really know why. And before that, I kind of figured there might be something going on between you two. It was nothing specific. Just, you know, the way you look at each other. And then there's Daniel. Other than treating me like I'm still in diapers, he's been…different lately. Happier. I know that's because of you. And now, look what I've done. I've ruined *everything*." That brought on a fresh spurt of tears. Keely, still right there beside her, clasped her shoulder and waited for the tears to play themselves out. Finally, Grace grabbed yet more tissues and dabbed at her eyes. "You should probably hate me—yeah. No doubt about it. I deserve your disgust."

Keely moved squarely behind her so she could put both hands on Grace, one on either shoulder. "No way."

Grace let her head drop back. They shared a long look. Then Keely gave Grace's shoulders one more good squeeze and returned to her chair. She ate another cracker and sipped her ginger ale.

Grace drew herself up and said, "I knew what I was doing when I told Gretchen. I was *trying* to cause trouble. I knew it, and I did it anyway. I went straight to the one person who was likely to have issues with Daniel moving on. What is the *matter* with me?"

"Nothing is the matter with you. You're frustrated with your brother, so you did something mean. Now you're doing what you can to make amends."

Grace sniffed. "I told your mom everything."

"Good."

"She sent me here to explain what I did, to tell you I'm so sorry—which I am—and to make sure you're okay."

"I am. I'm okay." Keely almost believed it as she said it. "And yes, it would have been much better if you'd come to me or Daniel about it when you saw us kissing. But, Grace, it's really not the end of the world. You're not the only one who could have behaved better. Gretchen is no saint in this. And Daniel and I shouldn't have kept our relationship a secret from the family. It was one of those things, you know? You start out keeping a secret and then the longer you keep it, the harder it gets to tell the truth."

"But it was awful with Gretchen, wasn't it?" Grace burst out. "Just admit it!"

Keely hated to see Grace so miserable. But she didn't want to lie either. "It was pretty bad."

"I knew it!" Grace wailed. "I'm a complete bitch, and everything's all my fault."

"Gracie, come on," Keely soothed. "Quit beating yourself up. It's all going to work out." Would it? Really? Keely had no idea. But Grace was hurting and Keely couldn't bear to add to her suffering.

Maybe another hug was in order. Keely got up again. With a cry, Grace rose, too. They met midway between their two chairs and wrapped their arms around each other.

Grace grabbed on tight and whispered, "I love you, Keely."

"And I love you."

"Daniel doesn't deserve you." Grace sniffed.

Keely pulled back enough to cradle Gracie's pretty face and smooth her pale hair away from her eyes. "Don't say mean things about your brother."

"Not even if they're true?"

Keely laughed. And then Grace laughed, too, right through her tears.

"Keewee?" called a small, sweet voice from the baby monitor Keely had left on the sideboard by the door to the dining room. That was Frannie.

Jake joined in. "Up, Keewee! Up!"

Keely let go of Grace as the twins babbled to each other over the monitor in the special language only they understood. "Nap time is over, I'm afraid."

Grace nodded. "I need to get back to work anyway."

"Do me a favor?"

"Anything."

"Come home from work right at five?"

"Absolutely."

"If you would watch the kids so that Daniel and I can talk about what to do next...?"

"Of course—he's going to kill me, isn't he?" Grace face-palmed with a drawn-out groan.

"No, he is not." Once Keely told him about the baby, getting mad at Grace would be the last thing on his mind.

A half hour later, Ingrid called. By then, Keely had got the kids up, changed their diapers and turned them loose with their toys in the upstairs playroom.

"Just checking on you," said her mother.

"I'm okay."

Ingrid gave a snort of laughter. "Oh, please. I do know what's going on. And I also know you're about as far from okay as a girl can get."

"Yeah. Well." Keely reached down to Maisey, who lay at her side. She gave the dog a quick rub on the top of her head, followed by a couple of long strokes down her back. At a time like this, having Maisey to pet really did help. "It's been one of those days." Jake wandered over with his ratty rabbit. He held it out. Keely bent and kissed it. The smile he gave her melted her heart to a puddle of mush. She stared after him as he toddled away again.

"I'm so sorry that Gretch has made a damn fool of herself," Ingrid said. "The woman has a dark side. I suppose I should have warned you, but I kind of hoped you'd never have to see it. You always adored her, and now she's let you down. Do you need me to slap her silly?"

"No, Mom. But I appreciate the offer."

"How 'bout some motherly support? I can be there

in ten minutes. I'll make you peanut butter and jelly on white bread with the crust cut off."

Keely smiled at that. When she was little and living on the purple tour bus, crust-free PB&J was her go-to comfort food. "Sit tight. Have the peanut butter ready. I'll keep you posted after I talk to Daniel."

"What? You think he's going to get all up in your case about it for some reason? Well, he'd better not or he will be dealing with me."

"Back it down, Super Suzie." "Super Suzie" was a Pomegranate Dream song about a reluctant superheroine named Suzie, who took on all the small-minded bullies in her hometown.

"I'm here," said her mother. "You just need to know that."

Keely shut her eyes and swallowed the sudden lump in her throat. "Love you, Mom."

"Call me."

"You know I will."

Grace got home as promised, at ten past five. Keely had dinner all ready.

She spoke to Grace about how things would go. "If possible, I would like to put off talking about what happened today until after dinner. If you would take the kids upstairs as soon as we're through eating, I'll talk to Daniel privately in his office."

"Works for me. Then if he wants to yell at me, you take over with the kids and he and I can go a few rounds somewhere they can't hear us fighting."

Keely chided, "Don't go planning for trouble."

"I don't need to plan. Trouble between me and Daniel happens naturally, no matter what we do."

Daniel came in at five thirty. Keely had worried that Gretchen would track him down and confront him, too—that she might have called Valentine Logging or shown up at the office unannounced. But if she had, Daniel gave no sign of it. Which was great. Perfect. Keely didn't want to get into it with him until Grace took the kids upstairs.

Grace put the twins in their high chairs while Daniel filled the water glasses and Keely brought the food to the table.

Neither Keely nor Grace felt much like conversation, but the twins kept up a steady chatter, partly in English, partly in twinspeak. Their bright voices filled up what might have been uncomfortable silence.

Daniel asked Grace how she liked working for Ingrid.

Grace put on a bright voice and talked about the job itself. "Already I love working there. Lots of variety. I painted woodwork, ran errands and helped Ingrid rearrange her office in back. We experimented with a couple of possible signature cocktails, and she taught me the POS system she's going to be using."

"I'm glad it's working out." Daniel sounded sincere.

"Yeah," said Grace, both awkward and strangely hopeful at once. "Me, too."

The meal ground on, with Frannie waxing poetic over her love of peas. "Peas! Yummy, yum, yummy, in my tummy!" And Jake chortled maniacally at intervals, beating his spoon on his chair tray, sending food flying.

When it was finally over, Grace wiped up the kids and swept them off upstairs. Daniel cleared the table as Keely loaded the dishwasher.

She'd just set the cycle and pushed the dishwasher door shut, when Daniel said, "Okay. What's going on?"

Her heart kind of stuttered in her chest and then became a warm little ache, that he *had* noticed something was off. That she loved him so and she really had no idea how he would take all that had gone down that day—with Grace, with Gretchen and with two of the tests from under the bed.

"Keely." He moved in closer, smelling of cedar and soap and everything good. Tipping up her chin, he brushed the sweetest, softest kiss across her mouth. "Tell me."

"Let's go into your study?"

He ran a slow finger down her cheek to her chin, stirring up sweet sensations, causing the ache in her heart to deepen. "Sure." His finger trailed along the side of her throat, out to her shoulder and down her arm. He took her hand.

In his study, she eased free of his grip and shut the door.

He went to the sofa against the inside wall, folded his powerful frame down onto the cushions and patted the space beside him. "Come on. Whatever it is, tell me everything."

She approached with caution, hardly knowing where to begin. He reached up a hand to her. She took it but stiffened her knees to stay on her feet when he tried to pull her down next to him.

"Damn, Keely. What?" He searched her face.

She opened her mouth, and the words kind of tumbled out all over each other. "Gretchen, Grace and my mom all know about us. Grace and Mom are fine with it. Gretchen is furious. She came over here today and she—"

"Hold it." He squeezed her hand—and then let go.

Keely wrapped her arms around herself and stepped back. "What?"

"How did they find out?"

She kept her shoulders square and looked down at him steadily. "Yesterday, in the kitchen at breakfast…?"

He knew then. His pale blue eyes went icy. "Grace did see us kissing."

"That's right."

He unfolded to his full height. "I knew it. Grace." He started for the door.

"Daniel," she said forcefully. At least he stopped walking and turned back to her. Good. She wasn't about to let him go after Grace. Not until he'd heard all she had to say. "I'm not finished yet."

A muscle twitched in his jaw. "I'll be back. I want to hear it from Grace, though, okay?"

She clutched her arms tighter around her middle. "No, Daniel. It's not okay. I want you to hear me out, please. Then you and Grace can talk."

"But—"

"No *buts*. I have things to say, and I intend to say them. Grace isn't going anywhere. She'll be here when I'm finished."

A stare down ensued. She didn't feel much relief when he gave in. "Fine, then. Go ahead."

Now it was a face-off between them. She stood by the couch, clutching her middle for dear life. He loomed a few feet from the door. Not the way she'd wanted to begin this difficult discussion.

But no way was she backing out now. "The way it happened, Gretchen stopped by Mom's bar. Mom was out. Grace and Gretchen started talking. Grace told Gretchen that she'd seen us kissing. Gretchen didn't believe her and came running over here to tell me how awful and unappreciative Grace is of all you've done for her. I set Gretchen straight, after which she accused me of betraying Lillie's memory and seducing you in your loneliness and a whole lot of other crappy things that I think I've already blocked from my memory. Then she stormed out."

"I'm sorry," he said. And then he went to his desk, crossed behind it, pulled out his big leather chair and dropped into it. "What a mess."

She stared at his bent head and went on, "Grace came home next. She'd already confessed to my mom what she did. Mom had sent her to me. Grace knows she did wrong, and she feels terrible about it. Your jumping all over her on top of her own disappointment in herself isn't going to help the situation in the least."

His head came up. He cracked his powerful neck, raked his thick hair off his forehead, the beautiful muscles of his arm flexing and bulging as he moved. "Nobody's talked to Gretchen since then?"

"Why should we? I may never talk to her again."

"Keely." His voice was velvety soft, coaxing. He pushed to his feet, but this time he came around the desk to her and reached for her. With a grateful sigh, she let herself sway against him. "You don't mean that." He kissed the words into her hair.

She rested her head on his giant rock of a shoulder. "Right at this moment? Oh, yes, I do."

"Well. We'll work it out." He clasped her arms. When she looked up at him, he bent for a kiss, a slow one. Not deep, but so comforting—and then he ruined it by setting her away from him and announcing, "In the meantime, I'm going to go talk to Grace."

Like hell he was. "I'm still not finished yet."

A frown formed between his thick eyebrows. Apparently he'd noticed she wasn't all that happy with him and his bullheaded insistence on making this disaster all about Grace. "You're kidding." At least he tried to lighten up a little. He made a real effort to speak teasingly. "There's more?"

Oh, is there ever. "Listen. I get that you're worried about Auntie G. I am, too. Even though I want to wring her neck right now, I know she's suffering, that she's still not over losing Lillie. I mean, really, who is? Lillie's death isn't something any of us who loved her are ever going to get over. But we do need to learn to go on, to make the most of a world without her in it. So Gretchen's reaction didn't really surprise me. And I do hope she'll get past this. But she *was* in the wrong, Daniel. This is more about her than it is about Grace."

He backed up enough to hitch a leg up on the corner of his desk. "I don't think so. Grace was purposely stirring up trouble and that's what I want to talk to her about."

"She *knows* that. You don't have to tell her. Why don't you try surprising her for once and being a little bit understanding?"

That muscle in his jaw was back, twitching away. He asked in a flat voice, "What else did you want to tell me?"

Her body kind of went crazy on her—throat-clutching, breath-catching, stomach-churning crazy. She worried she would have a choking fit or maybe throw up on him. "I, um…"

"Just say it." He reached for her hand again.

She flinched. She knew if he touched her, she would lose it completely.

"Keely, what in the—"

"I'm pregnant." The words burst from her mouth like a volcanic eruption.

His eyes seemed to tilt back in his head. "What? I don't—"

"It's for sure. I've been feeling strange and bloated and kind of crampy for a while now. My period should have come last week. It didn't. And in the past several days, I've been having… I don't know. All the signs? Breast sensitivity, feeling sick to my stomach. I finally took a test this morning."

"A test," he echoed, as though the word made no sense to him.

She nodded frantically, her head bouncing up and down like a bobblehead doll's. "Two tests, actually. They were both positive. So it's real. It's happening. I'm having a baby."

He'd frozen there, like a statue, one leg on the desk, one arm bent on his thigh. "But we always used condoms except the past few times. You're on the pill."

"It was probably that first time we were together or one of the times right after that. Before I started on the pill or before it started working. Back when we were using just condoms. One of them must have been faulty. Torn, maybe. Or broken." He was still in statue mode, staring straight ahead at her. But also right through her. She threw up both hands. "Daniel. Could you just not look at me like that? We've always used birth control, and I don't know how it happened. I did not plan this, and if you're thinking that I did because of what happened with…" She caught herself. This wasn't about Lillie, and she refused to bring her lost cousin into this. She tried again. "If you're thinking I tricked you somehow, well, I don't know what to say. I would never do that. But I *am* pregnant. It did happen. We're having a baby."

He kept looking right through her.

Something was going wrong with her heart. It seemed to be breaking. A roaring sound filled her ears. Maybe she was drowning.

Drowning in heartbreak.

What kind of silly idiot was she anyway? There was no way to explain herself, no way to get through to him. Not about this. Not when the last thing he'd ever wanted was another child.

"Daniel. I'm sorry, I am. I did not mean for this to happen. But I do want this baby. And I am keeping it. That doesn't mean I expect anything from you. I am fully self-supporting and completely capable of raising a child on my own. And I will, if that's how you want it. You can, you know, think it over. There's plenty of time for you to decide how involved you want to be. My mother raised me on her own, and it worked out just fine." Her throat locked up again, and she swallowed convulsively. "Ahem. So…okay, then. You think about it. Take your time. You don't have to decide anything today."

Daniel watched Keely's mouth move. She looked too pale. The freckles stood out on her adorable nose and twin spots of bright red stained her cheeks.

She thought he was blaming her.

He wasn't, not one bit. He was only struck speechless. It was way too damn much to take in.

Straighten up, you idiot. Pull yourself together, yelled a frantic voice in the back of his mind. He needed to snap out of it, say the comforting, supportive words she had every right to hear from him.

But…

Another baby.

More years to add on before he got his empty nest, before he finally knew what it felt like to be free. How many more years? Three, maybe? Four?

"Daniel," she whispered on a bare husk of breath. "You are breaking my heart. I really am sorry, but this is just bad. All wrong, you know? You take the time you need. I'm…well, I'm just as stunned by this thing as you are. I need some time to think, too. I'm guessing Jeanine will fill in where you need her until you can find some-body permanent. If she can't, you'll just have to work it out, because, really, I've gotta go."

"Go?" He blinked, shook his head, brought himself back into the moment. "What are you saying to me?"

"Daniel. I'm saying I'm going to pack a few things and go."

"No."

She stood up straighter. "Yeah."

"You're leaving?"

"Yes, I am."

"Just like that? You can't leave." He got up from the desk. "We have to work this out, damn it. We have to decide what to do next." He reached for her.

But she only jerked back another step. "No, we do not. We don't have to decide a thing right now. For me, this has been one never-ending train wreck of a day, and I'm in no condition to decide anything. Right now, I need a break. I need to get away."

"Get away?" he echoed numbly.

"Yeah." Now her chin hitched up. She'd set her mouth in defiance.

"Get away where?"

"I haven't decided yet. I'll…call you. Let you know."

Could this actually be real? "This isn't happening."

"Yes, Daniel. It is. I don't like it. I'm not happy." She darted around him and went to the door. "But right now, I just need to go."

What could he say to make her reconsider? "If you walk out that door, I'm not going to follow you."

"Terrific. Please don't." She pulled the door open, went through and shut it behind her.

Keely called her mother as she paced back and forth, grabbing stuff she thought she might need and tossing it into her suitcase.

Ingrid skipped the hellos and went straight to "Are you okay?"

"I need a break, Mom."

"And I'm just the one to make sure you get it."

"Meet me at my house?"

"I'm on my way."

Keely ended the call, stuck the phone in a pocket and finished packing. She zipped the suitcase, grabbed her big shoulder bag and headed for the door. From down the hall, she could hear Grace in the bathroom with Frannie and Jake. Grace said something, and Jake laughed.

Frannie giggled. "Mine!" she announced.

Keely's heart just seized up at those sounds.

Maybe they weren't her babies, but her silly heart had somehow claimed them. She left her purse and suitcase in her room and went down the hall and through the open bathroom door.

Jakey called, "Keewee!" and splashed with both hands.

Grace turned from the tub. She knew instantly that

something had gone very wrong. "Bad?" was all she asked.

Keely nodded. "I'm taking off for a while. Sorry to leave you on the hook, but I can't stay here right now."

"It's okay." Grace levered back on her heels and came for her, grabbing her, pulling her close.

Keely hugged her back, hard. "If he makes you too crazy, come stay at my house. And if I'm not there, I'll text you where I put the key."

"Oh, Keely. What do you mean, if you're not there? Where are you going?"

"Hell if I know."

"Keewee!" called Frannie.

Grace released her and she went to them. She knelt to kiss their wet cheeks and whisper, "Bye-bye. Love you."

"Wove you!"

"Bye-bye!"

Their beautiful, wet faces almost changed her mind, made her stay.

But then she thought of Daniel, of the words he didn't say and the bleak, distant look in those cold blue eyes. She pulled herself to her feet.

With a last nod at Grace, she marched back to her room, grabbed her suitcase and her purse and dragged them down the curving staircase and out the front door.

Chapter Eleven

Ingrid was already there, as promised, sitting on Keely's porch, her hair a red never seen in nature—candy apple, fire-engine red. It perfectly matched the paint on Keely's front door.

Keely pulled into the pebbled driveway, jumped out and ran to her mother's waiting arms. Grabbing on tight, she sobbed, "I love your hair," as she burst into tears.

"Come on. It's all right." Ingrid held her tighter. She smelled of sandalwood and a hint of weed. The silver bangles on her wrists jingled against each other as her hands moved, soothing and stroking, over Keely's shoulders and down her arms. "Let's go inside." She didn't wait for Keely's answer, just turned her gently and guided her to the red door.

In the kitchen, Keely sat at the table as her mother made tea. Outside, dark was falling, fog creeping in.

When she sat very still, she could hear the sigh of the ocean, down the hill and across the rolling dunes from her back porch. She'd always loved that sound, like the great Pacific shared a secret just with her. It was the main reason she'd chosen the cottage, snared on a short sale for a ridiculously low price. Ingrid put the steaming cup in front of her, and Keely sipped it slowly.

Her mother took the chair across from her. "Tell me."

And Keely did, starting with the pregnancy tests she'd taken that afternoon, moving on to all the bad stuff Auntie G had said and ending with the awfulness that had happened in Daniel's study. When she was finished, her mom poured them more tea.

Keely stared into the steaming cup. "I don't believe how Daniel reacted. When I told him about Auntie G, he blamed Grace. And then, when I said there would be a baby, he looked at me like I'd hauled off and punched him in the face."

"He's a good man. He'll recover. You'll work things out."

Would they? She just wasn't sure. She wrapped her arms around her middle and the new life growing there. "I left most of my stuff up there at the house, my Berninas included. I dread going back for everything."

"Stop. Your sewing machines will be there when you need them. Don't get ahead of yourself."

"Oh, Mom. I still don't really believe it, you know? A baby…"

"It's fabulous," declared Ingrid. "You're going to be an amazing mom. And babies bring good luck. You're living proof of that. Best thing I ever did, having you."

Keely answered her mom's broad smile with a wobbly

one of her own. But then she thought, *Daniel*, and that brought the misery crowding in on her again.

Ingrid said, "Have you told him you're in love with him?"

How did her mother know these things? "It seemed too early, you know? Too soon."

"Forget that. You're having a baby. You two will get nowhere until you face how much you mean to each other."

"Until today, I kind of thought we *had* faced it. No, we hadn't said the words. But I *believed* in us, that we were really together, you know? That we had what I've been looking for all my life. Now, though, I'm not so sure."

"Give it till tomorrow. You'll feel better. You'll be ready to talk to him again."

Keely let her head drop back and groaned at the ceiling. "Mom. I don't want to think about tomorrow, about what will happen next. And right now, I'd just as soon never talk to Daniel again."

"You don't mean that."

"I just want to get away, okay? I want to take off, like we used to when I was little, get on the road in the Pomegranate Dream bus. I want to drive up to Seattle, see Dweezle." Dweezle Nitweiler had been the band's first bass player—or maybe the second? Keely wasn't absolutely sure. "And then we could maybe head on to Boise, see what Wiley Ray and Sammy are up to." Wiley Ray was a drummer. His wife, Sammy, had sung backup and played the marimba. Last Keely had heard, Wiley Ray and Sammy had five kids. She sent Ingrid a sharp glance. "Don't you dare say I'm running away."

"Wouldn't dream of it."

"So...?"

"You want to go, baby girl? We are outta here."

Her spirits didn't lift exactly. But the awful pressure in her chest seemed to ease just a little. "You mean it? Really?"

"I'll call Grace, put her in charge at the bar while we're gone."

"That's a lot to ask of her. She just started today."

"I'm my own boss. If nothing gets done until we get back, I'll reschedule the opening. Not a big deal, but you'll need to get in touch with Amanda about the gallery."

"And Aislinn. I'll call her, too. She'll help out wherever she can." Keely leaned across the table and held her mother's gaze. "I mean it, Mom. I don't want to dither around about this. We're leaving tomorrow."

"You got it." Ingrid pulled her phone from her pocket. "We'd better start making calls."

Twenty minutes later, Amanda had said she could handle the gallery no problem. Aislinn, Keely learned, had just quit Deever and Gray. She would be picking up the slack wherever Amanda needed her.

Grace had instantly agreed to take over at the bar. She said that, yes, she could meet Ingrid there in half an hour to get emergency instructions on being the boss.

When Keely took the phone to see how she was holding up, Grace reported that the kids were in bed and Daniel had been surprisingly civil. "I'd just put the kids in their cribs, about half an hour ago. He came upstairs as I was going down, just said good-night and went on up to his room."

The ache in Keely's chest intensified as she pictured him, alone in the room that had become both of theirs.

To reclaim her resolve, she closed her eyes, sucked in a slow breath and focused on the goal, which was to get out of town. "Mom has a key to my house. She'll give it to you, just in case you need a place to get away."

"Thanks, Keely. Be safe."

They said goodbye. Keely handed her mom back her phone, and Ingrid left to meet Grace and stop in at Gretchen's to pack a bag for the trip.

"Don't even talk to her," Keely advised with a sneer as Ingrid was leaving. "She'll only say rotten things you don't need to hear."

Her mom just chuckled. "Sweetie, don't worry. I've been dealing with your aunt a lot longer than you have."

It was after ten, and Keely had just finished repacking her suitcase for their open-ended tour of the Great Northwest and beyond, when Ingrid returned.

Keely ran out to the living room when she heard the front door open. "How'd it go?"

Ingrid rolled her Frida Kahlo Skull Art spinner suitcase in the door and then shut it behind her. "Grace is up to speed. As for Gretchen, I told her everything."

Keely felt slightly breathless suddenly. "What do you mean, everything?"

"That you and Daniel had words and you need a getaway, so we're going on the road, you and me, up to Seattle, probably over to Boise and after that, wherever the wanderlust takes us. She was outraged, she said, that I could even think about taking you on the road at a difficult time like this."

"That sounds just like her."

"My sister is remarkably consistent in her opinion of a nice road trip. So I said that a time like this is exactly the right time to go on the road, after which I asked her what was *wrong* with her to begrudge you and Daniel a chance at happiness?"

"What did she say to that?"

"I didn't give her time to say anything to that. I just told her where she could stuff her self-righteous attitude, after which I broke the big news that you and Daniel are having a baby."

"Omigod, Mother." Strangely, Keely felt nothing but relief that Gretchen knew about the baby. "What did she say?"

"Not a word. I have to admit I found her silence supremely satisfying."

Keely sank to the couch. "All of a sudden, I'm hoping she's okay. I mean, I wanted to strangle her this afternoon, but I do love her and I don't want her to be suffering or worrying about us."

Ingrid came and sat beside her. "It's all going to work out."

"You keep saying that."

She hooked an arm around Keely and pulled her close. "I'm your mother. That's what mothers say."

Keely surrendered to her mom's embrace. She let her head rest on Ingrid's shoulder. "I'm so tired, Mom."

Ingrid stroked a hand down her hair. "We don't *have* to go anywhere, you know."

A weakness stole through her, to give in to her own misery, to go to her room and cry for a while. And then maybe tomorrow, to head up Rhinehart Hill to try to work things out with Daniel…

But then her belly knotted, and she ground her teeth at just the thought.

No way.

She wasn't working anything out with him if he

couldn't accept the baby. She hadn't meant to get pregnant, but now that she was, well, she *wanted* her baby. If he didn't, that was his loss. She couldn't be with a man who refused to love and welcome his own child. "I need this trip and I am going. Don't you dare back out on me now."

"Baby doll, I'm in if you're in."

"Good."

Rising, Ingrid took Keely's hand and pulled her to her feet. "Come on then. Let's get some sleep. I want to get an early start in the morning."

Daniel went to bed at a little before eleven, an exercise in futility if ever there was one. He spent the night staring into the darkness, afraid he'd lost Keely forever.

No, he argued with himself. That could never happen. The words had not been said, but they lived inside him.

He loved her.

And he knew she loved him—or at least, she had until she'd witnessed his reaction when she told him about the baby. Was it actually possible that he'd killed her love stone-dead?

He didn't know what to do, how to make it up to her. Somehow, he had to figure out what to say to her, how to tell her, how to prove to her that she was everything while also convincing her that he was happy about the baby...

The baby.

Every time he thought about the baby, he went numb. He needed to cope with that, with the reality of that. If he didn't, he had a sneaking suspicion he would only blow it all over again when he tried to make it up with her.

* * *

The kids woke up at six thirty as usual. The monitor by the bed came to life as they called to him. "Da-Da, Da-Da!"

"Keewee!"

"Up! Now."

As Daniel dragged himself out of bed and reached for his jeans, Jake's said, "Gwace! Up."

And Grace answered, "Hey, sweet monkeys. Good morning to you." She must have taken a monitor to her room last night so she could go to them if they needed her—and so she could give him a break this morning.

Daniel sank to the side of the bed, his chest gone tight, his jeans still in his hands.

Grace. Keely had it right about her. Grace was a good kid. She helped a lot. And she deserved to be treated as an adult.

He'd been way too hard on her. That had to change. He pulled on his pants along with yesterday's wrinkled shirt and headed for the playroom.

"Grace," he said, when he stood in the doorway to the playroom.

"Morning." She handed him Jake and picked up Frannie. "Let's get some breakfast."

"B'eafus. Yum!" Jake decalred and stuck his fingers in Daniel's mouth.

Daniel pretended to chew on them, which made Jake chortle in glee.

Downstairs, Grace poured kibble and fresh water for Maisey and got the kids their fruit and dry cereal. Daniel scrambled eggs and fixed toast for all four of them.

When they sat down to eat, Grace revealed that Keely

and Ingrid had gone on a road trip. "I'm temporarily promoted to manager of everything that needs doing at the bar, which unfortunately means there's no way I can watch the kids today."

Where did they go and when will they be back? he longed to demand. Instead, he said, "Congratulations on the promotion. As for the kids, you've been a lifesaver, always helping out with them. Don't worry about today, I'll figure something out." Aislinn probably had to work. Harper and Hailey were still at U of O until the second week of June. He would try the nanny service. If they couldn't help him, he would take a damn day off from the office. Gretchen would most likely come running if he asked her to watch them, but over the past sleepless night he'd realized he was seriously pissed off at his mother-in-law. He wouldn't be reaching out to her until his anger had cooled a little.

Grace set down her fork with a bite of scrambled egg still on it. "Did you just say I'm a lifesaver?"

"I did. And you are. And I'm going to do my best to respect your, er, adulting skills and be a better big brother to you."

She just looked at him for several seconds, her blue eyes suspiciously moist. "Thanks," she said in a husky little whisper. At his nod, she added, "They went to Seattle first. And she does have a phone, you know. You need to just call her."

"Yeah," he said with a half shrug.

Grace shook her head at him. "You're not going to call her, are you?"

He didn't answer her. She made one of those my-brother-is-an-idiot faces and let it go at that.

* * *

Aislinn had to work at Keely's gallery that day. The nanny service had no one to send on the spur of the moment, so Daniel stayed home.

The sun came out early. He took the kids for a walk, letting them lurch along beside him until they got cranky and then tucking them both into the double stroller to push them back home. He took them up to the playroom, changed their diapers and then stretched out on the playroom floor to keep an eye on them as they played with their toys.

The twins alternated between using Maisey as a pillow and decorating Daniel with various toys, placing them on his chest and stomach, then grabbing them up and wandering away, only to return with some other toy to set on him.

Frannie bent over him and asked, "Keewee?" causing his heart to pound like it wanted to burst from his chest and go searching for the woman he didn't want to live without.

He replied, "She went on a little trip."

"Back soo'?" demanded Frannie.

He didn't know how to answer that and settled for the painful truth. "I don't know."

With a snort and a sigh, Frannie dropped to her butt beside him. She reached out and patted his shoulder with her fat little hand. He stared at her, loving her, as Jake plunked down on his other side.

"Da-Da," Jake said and lay down next to him.

They weren't close enough. He gathered Frannie in with one arm and Jake with the other. They settled, tucked right where he needed them, on either side of his heart.

For a minute, maybe two, he knew the sweetest sort of peace.

He thought of Lillie, and for the first time, the anger didn't come. He felt only gratitude and tenderness, that if she had to go, she hadn't left him alone. She'd given him these two little ones, not as an eighteen-year sentence to struggle through.

But as a gift. The greatest gift.

What was freedom, really? He'd never had much of it, and he'd believed that he hungered for it.

But freedom was nothing. Not compared to his children, not stacked up against Frannie and Jake.

And the new baby, his and Keely's baby?

What a jackass he'd been.

He wanted the new baby, too. He truly did.

That guy who wanted freedom? He, Daniel Bravo, wasn't that guy and he would never be. He was a dad and a damned good one. He wanted his woman back, so he could be a husband, too. He wanted it all with her— the two of them together openly, with the family around them, raising Jake and Frannie and the new baby, as well.

Downstairs, he heard the front door open.

Keely?

His heart raced with hope. Maisey perked up her floppy ears as the kids wriggled free of his hold and sat up. Footsteps mounted the stairs.

Gretchen appeared in the open doorway to the upstairs hall.

"Gwamma!" Frannie got up and went for her.

Gretchen scooped the little girl into her arms, kissed her once on her forehead, then propped her on her hip. "My sister and Keely have gone to Seattle."

"I know. Grace told me."

"What is the matter with you, Daniel? I can't believe you let Keely go." She scowled down at him.

"What are you doing here?" Toys dropping off him and clattering to the rug, he rose. "I thought you were furious with her—and with me."

"I was." Frannie squirmed, so she let her down. Both kids headed for the toy box as Gretchen continued, "And I was wrong—don't look at me like that, Daniel Bravo. I'm capable of admitting when I'm in the wrong. I love you. And I love her. She's the only daughter I have left. And she took off with Ingrid in that embarrassing purple bus, took off to Seattle to visit someone named Dweezle. I know it's your fault, Daniel. I behaved very badly, and I realize that now. But she wouldn't leave just because of me. What did you do to her? What did you say?"

Shame rolled through him. He confessed, "All the wrong things."

"I knew it." Gretchen sagged in the doorway. But then she seemed to catch herself. She drew herself up. "I've been trying to call them. Both of them. My calls go straight to voice mail."

"Maybe they don't want to talk to you."

She made one of those faces women were always making at men, as though they can't help wondering how one-half of the species could be so thoroughly aggravating and hopelessly dense. "No kidding. Have *you* tried calling them?" When he didn't answer, her expression turned smug. "Coward."

He couldn't let that remark stand—even if it did happen to be true. He grabbed his phone from where he'd left it on the kids' dresser and autodialed Keely.

And got voice mail.

As he waited through her recorded greeting, he tried to decide what the hell to say.

He had nothing. Whatever he managed to sputter out would be hopelessly inadequate.

And what good would leaving her a message do anyway? He needed to be there. He needed to see her beautiful face when he told her all the ways he'd been a thickheaded jerk and begged her to please, please forgive him.

When he ended the call without leaving a message, Gretchen rattled off Ingrid's number. He tried that, too.

"Voice mail," he admitted, as he hung up.

"We need to stop wasting time and go get them," Gretchen cried. "We have to apologize and mean it and beg them to come home."

He completely agreed with her—in theory anyway. "Go get them how, exactly?"

"I know what route they took."

"How do you know that?"

"Ingrid told me. The Coast Highway to I-5."

"Why would she tell you that?"

"Why does my crazy sister do anything?" A determined gleam lit her eyes. "You think we can catch up with them?"

We? "How 'bout this. If you'll stay here and look after Frannie and Jake, I'll—"

"You can stop right there," she cut in before he could finish. "I have apologies to make, too, you know. I'm going with you. And I'll thank you not to argue with me. Arguing will only waste valuable time."

They took Lillie's minivan. It had plenty of room. Gretchen sat in the first row of back seats between the kids' car seats, armed with snacks and toys to keep them happy through the drive. Maisey went, too. She claimed the front passenger seat. Daniel rolled down her window so she could let her ears flop in the wind.

"I know we're going to find them," Gretchen kept saying as the miles rolled by. Daniel didn't share her certainty. They crossed the bridge at Astoria and entered Washington State, heading north along the coast, at first with the mouth of the mighty Columbia on one side of them and then, as they aimed true north, other, smaller rivers and then Willapa Bay. Once past the bay, they headed slightly inland again, where the trees grew thick and the banks at roadside were covered in moss and sword ferns, sometimes with green meadows stretching toward the mountains to the east.

The longer they rode, the more certain he became that Gretchen was kidding herself. That damn purple bus with the giant cartoon of Ingrid playing her Telecaster emblazoned on each side was probably miles and miles ahead of them. Depending on when the two women had set out, they could have reached Seattle by now—or changed their route or got off the highway for a bathroom break just long enough for the minivan to roll right on past.

They were approaching South Bend, and he was about to tell Gretchen they needed to give it up and go home when they rounded the next curve of the highway and he saw it—the butt end of the giant metallic-purple vehicle rolling along at a majestic pace about a hundred yards ahead.

Gretchen made a low noise in her throat, a sound both self-satisfied and triumphant. "What'd I tell you? There they are."

* * *

Ingrid was up to something. Keely had no doubt about that.

So far, they'd pulled over to the side of the road a total of six times since they left home. It had not escaped Keely's notice that her mother only thought she had engine trouble when there was enough of a shoulder that to stop wouldn't be illegal or dangerous. Only then would she start complaining that the engine was knocking or maybe it was one of the tires going flat as she eased the giant vehicle to the generous space at the side of the road.

Then she would get out and check the tires and go around to the back of the bus to look in on the engine. Each time, she took forever about it. When she came back, she would shake her head and say how everything seemed okay after all. She would start the bus up again, and they would get back on the road.

After the most recent of her pointless inspections, she'd insisted that before they moved on, they might as well have some of the tea and muffins she'd brought along.

Keely didn't want tea or muffins. She sat on the bench seat next to the door, holding her phone, hoping Daniel would call.

And he did call. Once, at a little after ten, causing her pulse to race, her whole body to catch on fire and her tummy to heave alarmingly. She almost answered that call. But she let it go to voice mail. Better to just hear what he had to say before she decided whether to talk to him or not.

He hung up without bothering to leave her a message.

And they drove on. And stopped. And drove on. And stopped.

After four hours on the road, they were just now approaching South Bend, Washington. The shoulder was wide and clear on one side. Any minute, her mother would start in about the engine knocking and when she did, Keely was going to throw back her head and scream.

Behind them on the road, someone honked. People did that all the time. The bus was big and purple, after all. And there was also the famous R Crumb cartoon of her mother playing guitar and smoking suggestively plastered on both sides. Keely craned her head to check the road behind them in the giant side mirror just as whoever it was honked again.

"A white minivan," she murmured to herself. Her heart started racing again. "That's Lillie's van! Mom, it must be Daniel."

"About freaking time," muttered her mother, as she smoothly turned the big wheel and eased the bus to side of the road.

"You planned this, didn't you?" Keely accused.

The hydraulic brakes hissed as they stopped. "Let's just say I planted the seeds. I told your aunt what route we were taking. Gretch did the rest—and she took her own sweet time about it, too."

"I'll go first," proclaimed Gretchen as Daniel pulled in and stopped behind the bus. "You stay here with the babies. Once I've made my apologies, it will be your turn. I'll bring Ingrid back here, and we'll watch the babies while you and Keely have some time alone in the bus."

He wanted to argue with her. Unfortunately, her plan made a scary kind of sense.

"Wish me luck," she said briskly and eased out between

the two car seats with surprising flexibility. She slid the door shut and walked quickly to the door on the right front side of the bus. Her gait was even and steady, without a trace of a limp left over from the injury that had broken four bones in her right foot and given him the chance to get to know Keely. To learn to love everything about her, to find what he hadn't realized he needed most: the right woman to stand beside him, the truest kind of freedom, the kind he found in her arms.

He had both front windows down and heard the bus door open. Gretchen disappeared inside.

Keely watched in the side mirror as her aunt got out of the minivan.

From behind the wheel, her mother was watching, too. "Gretchen's coming this way."

"I know. I can see her."

"She looks determined."

"Oh, yes, she does."

"Shall I let her in?"

"Yes." Keely rose and went through to the galley area. She couldn't make herself sit down for this, so she just stood by the table. "I'll talk to her in here."

The door opened with a wheezing sound. Keely heard her aunt's footsteps on the stairs.

"I would like to speak with Keely," Gretchen said stiffly.

"Through there," her mother replied.

And then Gretchen came and hovered in the doorway, her head high and her plump shoulders back. "I'm sorry," she said. It came out in a whisper as her shoulders drooped and her blue eyes filled with tears. "I had it all wrong. I said terrible things, and I have no excuse for them. I really thought I had made my peace with losing Lillie, but now I see I still have a ways to go on that. But I didn't want to let you leave without saying that I love you so much, sweetheart. And I am sorry for the rotten things I said to you. They were born of my own pain, untrue and completely unfair to you, to Grace and to Daniel, too. You and Daniel have every right to find happiness with each other. I hope that you do. I hope you can get past all the trouble I've caused and somehow find your way back to each other. I...well, I..." A tear escaped and trickled down her cheek. She sniffed, swiped the tear away and held her head high again. "I guess that's all. I'm sorry. I love you. Someday, I hope, you'll find a way to forgive me."

Keely's heart ached so bad. But it felt a little lighter, too. And there was only one thing to do now. "Of course I forgive you. I love you, Auntie G." She held out her arms.

With a soft cry, Gretchen came to her and grabbed her close.

In the back seat, as Daniel waited, the twins babbled to each other, amazingly content even after more than two hours in the car. Maisey, beside him, gave a little whine. He got out, went around to her side, let her out to do her business and then gave her a boost back in.

He'd just settled in behind the wheel again when Gretchen emerged from the bus. Ingrid, her hair a blinding cherry red, stepped out right behind her. They marched toward him.

Ingrid went to the driver's door, Gretchen to the passenger side. The sisters leaned in the windows.

Ingrid said, "You're up. Make it good."

His heart went wild inside his chest. But somehow he spoke calmly. "I'll give it my best shot." He turned to his mother-in-law. She'd clearly been crying. Her eyes and nose were red. "Did she accept your apology?"

Gretchen gave him a brave little smile. "She did. And I'm grateful."

"I'm glad for that," he said.

She nodded. "I do love that girl."

The next move was his. He got out. Ingrid took the seat behind the wheel. Gretchen put Maisey in the back and then came and sat next to her sister.

"This may take a while," he warned.

"Not a problem," replied Ingrid.

"We've got water and snacks and toys for the babies," said Gretchen. "Take as long as you need to show her how much you love her. We'll be waiting right here."

Ingrid had left the bus door open.

His heart in his throat and his pulse roaring in his ears, Daniel mounted the steps and went inside.

"Keely?"

"In here."

He found her sitting in the galley, on the long seat across from the table, wearing a little white T-shirt, faded bib overalls and white Keds. She rose as he went to her.

Tired. She looked tired, those green eyes sad, her bright hair gathered in a messy bun on the top of her head. His arms ached to hold her. He kept them tight at his sides.

"I did everything wrong," he said.

"No." Her lush mouth curved in the saddest little smile. "You did so much right. Almost everything. But, Daniel, I can't be with you."

"Because of the baby?" When she bit her lip and nodded, he clarified, "You think I don't want our baby."

For that, he got another nod, a tiny one, the barest dip of her pretty chin, as her face flushed deep red and her eyes shone with tears. It gutted him to see those tears, to know he was the cause of them.

"Keely. Don't you cry." His hands lifted of their own accord—but he lowered them when she fell back a step. He went on with his confession, "I found out today that I'm not who I thought I was." She frowned, like he'd spouted some nonsensical riddle. He said, "I've been bitter. I've believed that my freedom had been stolen from me."

"You *believed*?" She seemed to ponder the word. "Are you saying it isn't true?"

"That's right. I had it all wrong, what I want. What I need. And what you saw when you told me we were having a baby—that was the man I *thought* I was coming up against who I really am. In my bitterness, I'd convinced myself that what I wanted, what I *needed*, was freedom. I couldn't wait for Frannie and Jake to be grown, to get my so-called freedom at last. It took your leaving me to make me see that I'm not that guy. I'm a family man and I will always be. Everything I really need, I already have. Or I did, until yesterday, when I chased you away."

She searched his face. "Are you telling me, then, that you're okay with the baby?"

"More than okay. I've been stupid and blind. But the truth is I *want* our baby. I love you, Keely. I want us to be a family—all of us—you, me, Frannie, Jake, the little one that's coming—and more babies, if that happens, if you want them. I want to marry you. With you, I have everything. The family I need and the right person to talk to, the one I want beside me when things are good *and* when times get tough, the one who makes me free in all the ways that matter."

She stared up at him—hopeful and yet cautious, too. Proud and beautiful and true. "Daniel, I do love you, so very much."

She loves me. His heart beat at the wall of his chest, urging him closer. "Keely…" Again, he would have reached for her.

But she put her hand up between them. "You really mean this? I need to know. I need the brutal truth from you. If your heart isn't open, if you still have doubts about taking on another child, I need you to tell me."

He captured her raised hand, brought it to his chest and pressed it close, at the spot where his heart beat so hard for her. "No doubts. No regrets, not a one. Not anymore. I hate that you left, Keely. But I understand why. You were right to leave. It put the fear of God in me, let me tell you. It showed me the hard truth, that I've been a complete ass in a whole bunch of ways. It showed me that I could actually lose you.

"I couldn't stand that," he said. "I want you and I want our baby. I want us all to be together. I love you, and I want to spend the rest of my life with you." He lifted her hand higher, bringing it to his lips so he could kiss the tips of her fingers, one by one. "Just think about it, okay? Go ahead with your mom, up to Seattle and wherever else you need to go. Just, while you're away from me, know that I will be waiting, hoping that when you come back, you'll be coming home to me, that someday you'll say yes and be my wife."

She lifted her other hand and pressed it to his cheek. So cool and soft, that hand, soothing him, easing the

painful pounding of his heart, a balm to the ache of longing in his soul. "Daniel." She said his name in a breath
as she lifted her sweet mouth to him.

A kiss, so slow and tender, growing wet and deep. It
ended far too soon.

She sank back to her heels again. "I love you, Daniel.
And yes, I will marry you. As for the road trip, I don't
need it anymore. I'm ready to go home."

Eight weeks later, on the last Saturday in July, Keely
married Daniel in the backyard of their house on Rhinehart Hill. The whole family attended, all the Bravo brothers
and sisters, Great-aunt Daffy and Great-uncle Percy, and
Ingrid and Gretchen, of course. There were a lot of family
friends as well, including several of the musicians who used
to play with Pomegranate Dream—Dweezle, Sammy and
Wiley Ray among them. Meg Cartwell McKenna, Keely
and Aislinn's mutual BFF, came too. She and her husband,
Ryan, had driven in from Colorado.

Keely wore a vintage fifties' white lace dress that
came to midcalf with a short veil. She was already showing, her stomach noticeably rounded, as she walked the
petal-strewed grass between the rows of white folding
chairs, her eyes on the man waiting in front of an arbor
covered in roses.

When Daniel smoothed back her veil and took her
hands in his, Jakey shouted from the front row, "Da-Da!
Keewee!" and everybody laughed.

Keely said her vows, strong and proud. Daniel's voice
was rougher, lower, the words meant for her ears alone.

And when he took her in his arms for the kiss that
sealed their bond, each to the other, she knew she had
found the love and trust that mattered most between a

man and a woman. She felt such joy and gratitude, that he would be hers and she would belong only to him.

From this day forward.

They held the reception right there in the backyard, including dinner and champagne toasts and, later, a four-tier cake. Ingrid and her former bandmates played music on the grass.

And after dark, when Keely stood on the upper deck outside the master bedroom to throw her bouquet in the glow of endless strands of party lights, she took careful aim before she flung the lush bunch of sunflowers, orange dahlias, baby's breath and daisies into the waiting crowd below.

The flowers sailed out, bright and hopeful, full of the promise of love-to-be. They landed right where she wanted them.

In Aislinn's outstretched hands.

* * * * *

LET'S TALK
Romance

For exclusive extracts, competitions
and special offers, find us online:

f facebook.com/millsandboon

◎ @millsandboonuk

𝕏 @millsandboon

Or get in touch on 0844 844 1351*

For all the latest titles coming soon, visit
millsandboon.co.uk/nextmonth

Want even more
ROMANCE?

Join our bookclub today!

'Mills & Boon books, the perfect way to escape for an hour or so.'

Miss W. Dyer

'Excellent service, promptly delivered and very good subscription choices.'

Miss A. Pearson

'You get fantastic special offers and the chance to get books before they hit the shops'

Mrs V. Hall

**Visit millsandbook.co.uk/Bookclub
and save on brand new books.**

MILLS & BOON